TH

S. E. Lund

Dedication

Dedicated to Suzanne, my first editor and the first other writer to consider my writing seriously and offer an honest constructive critique. Without your critical eye and supportive words, I would never have seen both the potential in my work and where it needed improvement. You gave me the courage to continue writing despite difficulties in the early years. You will be missed.

R. I. P.

Acknowledgements

Thanks to my family and friends who supported me during the long hours when I would lock myself into my office with my computer jammed in my face, writing. Without your tolerance, my books would never have been written or finished, but my house would have been a lot cleaner! Many thanks to my editor Michelle Saunders for all her hard work – any remaining mistakes are all mine!

CHAPTER ONE

Agreeing to wear the shoes was a mistake.

Although I worked as a cocktail waitress during my undergrad and wore heels for years, once I started my Masters degree and worked as a teaching assistant instead, I'd been dressing casual and was out of practice.

My best friend Dawn ignored my protests, insisting on choosing my outfit for the fundraiser my father was hosting for Doctors Without Borders, his favorite charity. I went to her apartment before the event so she could style me. After she did my makeup, she selected a dress from her collection instead of my own sorry closet, choosing a little black wrap dress that only made my already-slightly-too-ample chest more obvious. I even wore real nylons with a seam up the back and her garter belt instead of pantyhose because the only pair I had ripped as I pulled them on, a fingernail snagging them along the calf and all she had were nurse's white stockings.

"Use these," she said, pulling them out of a drawer. "They're Brenda's."

"I can't wear those," I said, making a face. Brenda was Dawn's sister, who moved out to get married a few months earlier, leaving Dawn with the clothes she no longer wanted.

"Why not? It's all women used to wear. I think they're pretty."

"What if I had to go to the ER and the nurses and doctors saw them?"

She laughed. "They'd think you were a sexy little thing. Listen," she said, handing them to me. "In the middle of a trauma, the last thing the ER doctors and nurses are thinking of is your clothes except how to cut them off as quickly as possible."

I sighed and put them on. They did look nice. I felt a bit like Greta Garbo as I turned back and forth in the mirror. Then, she fixed my hair, straightening it with a flatiron so that it hung long and straight down my back. But it was the shoes that did it.

Super high and sexy.

With four-inch stiletto heels and black leather straps, they were a tiny bit too big and I wobbled when I walked.

"I don't know about these," I said in meek protest as I walked across her hardwood floors, feeling like I was walking a tightrope. I looked at myself in the full-length mirror, adjusting the neckline. "I haven't worn high heels since I quit waitressing at O'Hanlan's."

"Doc Martens and lumberjack shirts won't get you and Nigel donations, Kate. Those shoes and that dress will."

I pulled down the hem of the dress, feeling like it could spring up at any moment and reveal my garters. "I'm not so sure I'm appropriately dressed for a charity fundraiser."

"Nonsense," she said and gave me the once-over, her head tilted to one side. "You look marvelous. I feel like Professor Higgins in *My Fair Lady*. The stuffed suits will want to donate money just to get next to you so it's all for a great cause."

I sighed, giving myself over to her as she did her best to transform me from an ordinary twenty-four year old woman into someone who belonged at a Manhattan fundraiser.

Going to a local pub before the fundraiser was another mistake. Located in the Upper East Side, it was a few blocks from NY Presbyterian and a lot of staff went after their shifts for a drink. Not too far from my father's brownstone on Park

Avenue where the fundraiser was being held, it would be a quick cab ride once I was ready. I needed a drink or two before seeing my father. We'd been at odds because I changed focus for my Master's thesis from politics to pop-culture. We didn't argue openly but he had a way of letting his displeasure be known.

Since I'd changed my focus, I'd kept under his radar, being a good girl, not making waves. When he specifically invited me to the fundraiser, I couldn't say no. Going was my chance to mend fences. Dawn agreed to come to the pub with me and help me loosen up. Then, I'd face him and his crowd of philanthropic doctors and Wall Street money managers.

So add two strawberry daiquiris to overly-high-heels and you have a train wreck in the making.

On our second round of drinks, we scoped out the men in the pub, rating them, deciding which ones we'd hook up with, given the chance. Except of course, that we were both total geeks and didn't do that kind of thing. I had *The Hangin' Judge* as a dad and she was a mostly-good Catholic and had just spent six months in Calcutta volunteering for Mother Theresa's charity. But it was fun and a way to let off a bit of steam. With deadlines looming on several papers I was working on, and Dawn with nursing clinical exams coming up, we both needed some fun.

"He's trouble." Dawn leaned down to whisper in my ear, her frizzy blonde curls poking my face. "Stay away from *him*."

"Oh, oh," I said, glancing over at the bar. "You know those are the wrong words to say to me." I checked out the man she pointed to. "Why is *he* trouble?"

"The OR nurses call him either Dr. Delish or Dr. Dangerous, depending on who you talk to. *Look* at him." Her brown eyes twinkled. She waved her cocktail towards him. "He's gorgeous with those blue eyes and dark hair. And that jaw..." She smacked her lips. "Definitely dangerous." She glanced at me and shot the rest of her drink down in one gulp. "He," she said and pointed her finger. "He's a lady killer and a bona fide bad boy."

"Who *is* he? How do you know him?"

"Some surgeon at NY Presbyterian. I saw him during orientation when I volunteered there. He was playing 60s Brit Invasion music in his O.R. during surgery. Can you believe it? The Yardbirds, *Heart Full of Soul* or something. The nurses say he's a bit of a controlling bastard."

I glanced at him. He *was* gorgeous. Dr. Gorgeous-but-Dangerous leaned against the bar facing the room, one arm outstretched as if he owned the place, a martini in his hand. Dressed in a very expensive suit, his tie loosened, his top button undone, he looked like an executive out for a drink during happy hour. Next to him, a man leaned forward against the bar, his back to us. He moved in close, speaking to Dr. Delish as if whatever he said was confidential.

Dr. Delish surveyed the bar crowd, nodding at what his drinking partner said.

"He's a doctor. How could he be dangerous?"

"I don't mean dangerous in the *slit your throat in your sleep* way, silly." Dawn rolled her eyes. "You read too many crime novels. I mean dangerous in the *steal your heart and never give it back* variety."

"Oh," I said, somewhat disappointed. "That's too bad. You know me. I love a good thriller."

"You are confirmed nuts. Didn't flyboy convince you to lay off the bad boys?"

I thought he had. Kurt was a former Marine pilot who my father dubbed 'flyboy'. He only made me want a bad boy even more. Despite his desire for kink – or maybe because of it – he was exciting. Looking back on our disastrous relationship, I realized he actually made me feel something for a change – the first time I felt anything after my trip to Africa. Until Kurt, I'd been numb.

"I'm so over Kurt."

"You cried like a baby when you two broke up."

"Really over him," I said, as much to myself as to Dawn. "No more bad boys for me." Of course, I was so full of it, considering that I just got off the phone a few hours earlier with "Mistress Lara" – a Domme in Manhattan's BDSM community – about my upcoming meeting with a *real* Dominant. I told myself it was no big deal – just research for an investigative article I was thinking of writing for a journalism class but I couldn't lie to myself. I was so damn curious. I couldn't tell Dawn anything about it and it was killing me. Unlike me, she hated 'those books' and thought they were practically the product of the Devil's spawn. I knew she'd only freak and try to stop me from going through with the interview so I neglected to tell her on purpose.

That was another mistake.

I *should* have confessed everything so Dawn could keep me on the straight and narrow. She would have talked me out of doing the interview. Instead, I swallowed my urge to tell her and kept my mouth shut.

"I'll believe you're over him when you hook up with someone new. It's been almost a year, Kate, since Greg. You're allowed to date again. Give up Big and find someone real."

Greg was Dawn's antidote to Kurt. Mr. Master of Fine Arts in English Lit, Greg couldn't say *fuck* even when he was doing it. He was nice, but I had to make all the moves, and that made me so... *insecure.*

Big, as we called it, was the gag gift we all got at a friend's bachelorette party a year earlier. A dildo ten inches long and six inches in girth, Big was a monster. All of us joked about Big as if he were our collective boyfriend.

How's Big doing? Got any action from Big lately? Want to come out for a drink or are you busy with Big tonight?

"He *is* handsome, though," I said of Dr. Delish, trying to change the subject.

"You told me to warn you off the next time you even *thought* about someone who wouldn't be good for you. So here's me, warning you off. Stick with Big. *That* man is trouble. Just *look* at him." She leaned over to me. "He's examining the women in the bar as if we're all his to take and he's just deciding which one he wants. I think he's found his next target, by the way he's staring so intently at her."

I watched him from over the top of my glass as I took a sip. He surveyed the bar crowd as if judging, but his eyes continually returned to someone he watched very closely. I craned my neck to see which woman he'd chosen.

The television – a weather report on the Nor'easter brewing off in the Atlantic.

"He's watching the weather channel, you *nut*."

Dawn glanced back to the television in the corner.

"Oh," she said, only somewhat chastised. "Well, he *looks* dangerous."

"For all we know, he might be the sweetest man." I examined Mr. Not-So-Dangerous-After-All. Suddenly, he wasn't quite as titillating as he had been only moments before when I thought he was really looking for his next victim. "I'd still go out with him," I said.

"You and practically every woman who lays eyes on him. Just think of the power. He has to be a dick because of it."

"That's prejudiced," I said, frowning.

"But probably true. Take my word for it."

I put down my drink and picked up my bag, needing to visit the restroom. "I'll be right back. Gotta hit the head, as my father calls it."

Dawn nodded and turned her focus back to her own drink.

As I made my way through the cluster of tables to the back where the restrooms were located, I thought of my father. A former Marine who fought in Vietnam during the last two years of the war, he still wore his gray hair in whitewalls, almost shaved on the sides of his head, brush cut on top. At fifty-nine, he was a current Justice of the Supreme Court of New York. Defense lawyers referred to him as 'The Hangin' Judge' even though we didn't have a death penalty in the state. After the war ended and he returned Stateside, he finished his law degree and began his career, following a long line of lawyers in our family stretching back to the 19th Century.

Now, he was seriously considering a run at the House seat coming vacant due to the incumbent's illness. Growing up, my brother and I called him *The Drill Sergeant* in secret, *Father* in public. I still called him Daddy when I was in his good books, which I wasn't currently.

After washing up, I pushed the door open and knocked into Dr. Delish himself as he was walking past to the men's room.

When I bumped into him, my ankles almost turned in completely like a kid on ice skates for the first time. I fought to stand up, grasping onto him to prevent myself from falling.

"*Whoa*," he said, catching me by the arms, pulling me close. "*Steady*..."

"Oh, so sorry," I said as I grabbed onto his shoulders and glanced up into his eyes.

Oh. My. *God*.

He was gorgeous. He smelled like heaven.

His glanced at my feet and the ridiculously high heels on which I tottered like a child learning to walk.

"I'm not really used to these."

"Trying to defy the laws of physics?" he said and smiled as he helped steady me, his gaze moving slowly down my body to my feet again. "Nice shoes though. *Love* the leather straps..."

"Thank you," I said, my cheeks heating. I straightened up with his help and smiled, then I turned back to the tables, my heart racing just a bit.

When I got back, I took a huge sip of my drink.

"I just bumped into Dr. Delish."

Dawn raised her eyebrows. "What's he like?"

"He smells as good as he looks."

I watched Dr. Delish return to his place at the bar. He spoke to his drinking partner for a moment, finished his martini and then checked his cell. After he buttoned his top shirt button and tightened his tie, he threaded his way through the tables. When he left, he glanced my way, catching my eye briefly, a quick smile on his face when he recognized me. What a smile it was. I felt a little thrill go through me and smiled back.

"There goes trouble," I said, wistfully. "Maybe you're right after all. My spidey-senses *are* tingling."

"And *that*," Dawn said, leaning in closer, "is why you're stuck with Big. You, my dear BFF, are a *bona fide* dork. *Spidey-senses...*"

I grinned at that. "Well then, we're nerd central." We smiled at each other. While Dawn didn't like bad boys, I couldn't help but wish I was the natural companion to Doctor Dangerous instead of the techies at Columbia's IT department.

After finishing my drink, I checked my cell. There was a message from Nigel, wondering where I was.

> *Get your sweet little self over here. I couldn't bring Brian tonight, given the company your father keeps, so don't leave me all alone with these stuffed suits!*

"Guess it's time for me to go to my father's," I said and finished the last of my drink. "Nigel's texting me. Will you be ok until Jill gets here?"

"She just texted me. She'll be here any minute. Have fun!"

"Have fun? Have you ever been to one of these fundraisers? It's all fake smiles and shaking hands. Besides, my *father* will be there."

"Nigel too," she said, reminding me.

Nigel – *Sir* Nigel Benson, recently knighted by Her Majesty for his humanitarian service. Host of *Travel with Nigel*, his popular TV show on PBS. He was active in Doctors Without Borders and spent time with me in Africa when I was there doing volunteer work, writing an investigative piece for my Honors project in Journalism at Columbia. He quickly became part big brother, favorite uncle and best friend to me. We'd been through so much together in Africa, and he'd seen me at my absolute worst but still stood by me. I felt as if he knew me almost better than I knew myself.

"Thank God for Nigel."

I pulled on my coat and left the bar, hailing a cab to take me to my father's apartment on Park Avenue. I decided to enter through the rear door to the building. I did *not* want to go into the front door where I knew everyone would be standing around with drinks in their hand, and all eyes would turn to me. My fourth mistake was thinking I could maneuver the back alley in the dark in those heels with two drinks in me. I was no match for the terrible cement with its cracks and loose gravel...

I fell just outside the door to the building, my ankle twisting, me going down on one side, my ankle, knees and the palms of my hands bearing the brunt of the fall. The only saving grace was that I was alone so no one witnessed my awkward tumble. My knees were cut by rough stones, my palms scuffed, and my ankle was killing me. My pride hurt almost as much as my other wounds.

By the looks of the cuts, I'd have a few more scars to add to the others I'd received over the years from trying to do things I shouldn't. As a young tomboy fighting to keep up with my brother, who was older by four years, I'd received a fair number of scars. My knees had first been christened when I tried to pogo stick after he did and fell ingloriously. Then, there were the stilts... My bottom lip still bore a faint scar where my teeth went through it.

After I removed my shoes, one of the heels having broken when my ankle went over, I had to struggle up to my feet. I limped in stocking feet into the rear of the building, gasping each time I put pressure on my injured foot, using the pass code to get inside. I took the service elevator up to the top floor to my father's apartment. I entered what was once-upon-a-time the servant's entrance, hoping to sneak into the bathroom and tend my wounds, find a pair of my stepmother's shoes before facing the financial elite and asking for handouts for Nigel's charity.

I hopped down the hall to the bathroom only to find that Dr. Delish himself was there, on his way out. Dr. Dangerous is at my father's fundraiser? Doctors Without Borders – made sense but I did *not* want someone that good looking to be witness to my ineptitude.

He spied me before I could turn and hop away, my nylons torn, palms, ankle and knees bloody.

"You're *hurt*," he said and frowned, coming right to my side, glancing at the heels I held in one hand. "Those shoes again?"

"Yes." Of all people to see me, he had to be the one... "I fell outside in the alley. The heel of my shoe broke."

Up close, he was devastatingly handsome, and when our eyes met, I swear heat rose in my face like mercury in a thermometer. I had this instant response that my conscious mind had no control over, as if my body was screaming *Mate with this one. He's got the goods.*

My response was purely animalistic.

Absolutely *gorgeous,* he was tall but not too tall, about six feet compared to my five foot three. Up close and in good lighting instead of that in the pub, his hair was almost black, his brows and eyelashes as well, and his eyes were that blue which reminded me of the Aegean off the coast of Corfu. Fair skin. A thin layer of whiskers covered his chin and jaw. A face of such symmetry, it was geometric, all planes and angles but his mouth – his mouth was soft, his lips full. I could imagine that mouth on mine, or moving over my skin...

All of this registered in the merest of seconds while he adjusted his slate grey silk suit jacket, which was open to reveal a crisp white linen shirt and grey tie, the fabrics all the best quality. He had good taste in clothes, and the money to feed it.

"Here," he said and put his arm under mine and then he actually picked me up.

"*Whoa*," I said, trying to resist, hating to be carried by anyone. "You don't have to pick me up."

"Don't worry. You're light as a feather. You've probably sprained your ankle."

My hands went around his neck and I was two inches from his face, my own face hot with embarrassment. He found my parent's bedroom at the rear of the apartment and placed me on the bed, sitting across from me. My dress had hiked up, the tops of my sheer black nylons and black lace garters on display for him to see.

He raised his eyebrows, his eyes widening. I quickly drew down my dress to cover them.

"Oh, I'm sorry..."

"Don't worry," he said, smiling just a bit. He placed my injured foot on his lap so he could examine it. "I'm a doctor."

I took off my coat, warm from it and his gaze. "Still, you shouldn't have to see that."

"Oh, I don't mind." He grinned without meeting my eye as he moved my ankle back and forth. "I don't mind at *all*."

"Ouch!" I said when he moved my ankle a bit too far in one direction.

He glanced up at my face. "That hurts?"

I nodded.

"What about this way?" He twisted it the other way, gently this time.

"Not as much."

He felt around, prodding my foot, my ankle and the bone above it in my calf.

"Don't think it's broken. You might as well take off those nylons. I'll have to treat those lacerations."

"Oh, yeah," I said, and hesitated. I waited, and he watched me expectantly.

"*Oh.*" He glanced away, smiling a bit sheepishly.

I quickly unhooked the garter clasps to one leg and rolled down the nylon. Then, the bastard peeked while I was busy undoing the garters to the other leg.

I cleared my throat. "Excuse me?"

"Sorry," he said and turned his head away again, grinning widely. "Just don't get to see real garters very often."

"My best friend made me wear them. Now she'll be pissed that I ruined her nylons."

"It's a shame they were destroyed," he said softly, a hint of humor in his voice. "I especially like the ones with the seam up the back. Really retro."

Once my nylons were off and I readjusted everything, he started to examine my calves, running his hand up my leg on the injured side, checking the bone. I had to spread my thighs a bit so he could examine my knees, and blushed profusely when I had to jam my dress between them to cover my crotch.

"Calves and knees look *great*," he said, a faint smile on his face.

He left me on the bed and went to the en-suite bathroom. I heard him opening and closing cabinet doors and drawers. Finally, he emerged with a bottle of peroxide and some cotton balls, some gauze and bandages. He also had a wet washcloth.

He then tended my wounds, wiping the dirt off my knees and ankle.

"What kind of doctor are you?"

"Neurosurgeon."

"So you cut up brains?"

"Something like that," he said, a half-smile on his lips. "I don't cut them up as much as fix them. Robotically-assisted electrophysiology is my specialty. Using electrodes to treat disorders like Parkinson's and epilepsy. You're thinking pathologist. But don't worry," he said as he washed the dirt off my knees. "We also learned to look after superficial wounds. And I have a truckload of insurance, just in case you're wondering..."

He daubed the cuts and scrapes with the peroxide-soaked cotton balls. It stung a bit, but not too badly. All the while he was tending my injuries, I got the chance to see him up close. Man, was he beautiful. His black hair was a bit longish and wild as if he was just caught in the wind. Dark arched brows. Blue *blue* eyes fringed with thick black lashes. A bit of scruff on his face, and a jaw that screamed perfection.

He was perhaps the hottest man I'd ever seen.

"You'll be fine. Don't need stitches. Just a bit of antibiotic ointment and a few bandages. But you should rest your ankle. Are you going to stay or do you need a ride home?"

"I better stay. Do you know who Elaine is? Can you ask her to come and speak to me?"

He nodded. "Sure. If that ankle doesn't get markedly better in a couple of days, you might want to get an x-ray. Can't do anything for a broken bone in your foot but rest it. You could probably use some crutches."

He smiled at me and left me on the bed.

I'd just met Doctor Delish. It took me a few moments to recover.

CHAPTER TWO

In a moment, Elaine came rushing in and sat on the bed, hugging me.

"Oh, Kate it's *you*! You poor dear," she said, examining my cuts and ankle. "Drake told me this guest had fallen and wanted to talk to me. I had no idea it was you!"

Drake? Dr. Delish finally had a name.

"Yeah, we didn't introduce ourselves. Can I borrow something safe in the shoe department? I fell outside because I wore *those*," I said and pointed to the high heels on the floor.

"Of course," she said and went right to her huge walk-in closet with racks of shoes, sorting through her collection. She pulled out a pair of black ballet slippers and held them out. "Will these do?"

"Yes, thank *God* you have some. I should have been wearing those in the first place."

I put them on and limped out using Elaine as a crutch.

"Leave your coat here," Elaine said. "I'll have one of the staff hang it up."

We stood just inside the entry to the living room, and I was so reluctant to be there. The suite itself was huge, two full stories with cathedral ceilings in some of the rooms and floor to ceiling windows. Everything was cream and gold with rich dark wood on the furniture, floors and all the trim.

Almost two dozen people were there, most of them rich businessmen in several-thousand dollar suits, a couple of women there as arm candy, tall leggy bottle blondes who were managing quite fine in their own stiletto heels. I was a dwarf compared to the rest of the women in attendance.

Now, I'd have to explain to everyone why I was bandaged up and limping. I searched for Nigel. Immediately, he called out to me.

"There you are my girl," he boomed, pushing through the people standing around him to get to me. My cheeks burned as everyone in the room turned at the sound of his voice.

I smiled when I saw him and he opened his arms wide. Close to three hundred pounds and six foot six, while I was all of five foot three, and one hundred and fifteen, we made a comedic pair. He picked me up and hugged me like a bear.

"Hey, hey!" I said when he held me up. "Watch it – I fell and hurt my ankle."

He placed me gingerly back down on the ground, kissing both my cheeks in that Continental manner, a huge arm around my shoulder, helping me limp into the room. Immediately, a group of men surrounded us and Nigel introduced me to them all.

A few minutes later, Peter, my father's chief of staff for his campaign, came by.

"Kate what happened?"

"I fell in the back alley."

"Are you all right?"

"I'm fine."

"Your father's in a conference call. Can I introduce you to a few people?"

Nigel let go of me and now Peter escorted me around the room, letting me lean on his shoulder for support.

It was then I saw 'Dr. Delish' – *Drake* – standing with a man I met two years earlier before I went to Mangaize with Nigel.

Dave Mills was an MBA type who worked in fundraising. He also happened to hit on me, blatant about wanting to take me home at the end of a long booze-filled party. I refused him and his advances.

"I'm Justice McDermott's daughter," I'd said, hoping that would scare him off.

"You need lovin', too," was his reply.

He was attractive with blond hair and brown eyes, well-dressed and erudite. He was a catch. But he was far too glib for my tastes. He'd hit on me each time we met after that. I could almost predict what he'd say and it bothered me, as if he couldn't see me as anything other than fuck material.

He placed his beer down on the table and stood up straight, adjusting his jacket when Peter led me towards them, me limping along beside him.

"Drake, Dave, may I introduce—"

Before Peter could introduce me, Dave stepped forward. "Ahh, the lovely Miss *Bennet*," he said in an affected British accent. "Um, I mean the lovely *Kate* needs no introduction."

"It is a truth universally acknowledged that a man in possession of a good fortune must write out a check and make a donation to the cause," I said in an equally affected British accent, not wanting to miss the opportunity to tease him and also continue with the *Pride and Prejudice* reference.

Dave laughed. "Well played, Ms. McDermott, well played."

At that, Drake made a face of surprise. "You're *Katherine*..."

"Oh, this is Kate McDermott," Dave said, gesturing to me. "Kate, this is Dr. Drake Morgan, brain surgeon, bass player, philanthropist. I assumed you already knew each other."

"I met, but didn't really formally *meet*, Ms. McDermott," Drake said, his voice soft. "I've known you by reputation for years. My apologies for not introducing myself."

"By reputation?"

"Your father told me about you, and I read your articles on Mangaize."

I smiled briefly, surprised that he knew who I was.

Dave turned to me. "Dr. Morgan's father Liam fought with your father in Vietnam. Drake volunteers with Doctors Without Borders," he said, sounding mock officious. "I run his foundation, which donates surgical equipment. Drake goes to war zones where civilians have experienced brain trauma and fixes them up."

It was then I realized who Drake was and I turned to him, totally surprised. "My father's spoken of you before." I smiled. "It was Dr. Morgan this, Dr. Morgan that. He thinks you're practically a saint."

Drake gave me this warm *I'm smiling just-for-you* smile. I felt a little flip in my gut in response to him.

"Sorry, I didn't introduce myself earlier," I said, my cheeks hot. "I was in *kind of injured* mode."

"Nice to finally meet Ethan's beloved daughter." He extended his hand. "Your father told me so much about you. I should have known it was you by your eyes, but I was in *slightly caddish doctor with bad bedside manner* mode and not my *charming and gracious guest* mode."

Our eyes met again as he kissed my knuckles and I felt a jolt of adrenaline surge through me at his kiss.

"I'll leave her with you then," Peter said and left the three of us. Then, Dave stepped forward as if trying to get in between us.

"So, Ms. Bennet, how have you been since our last meeting?"

"Mr. Mills," I said and turned to him when Drake let go of my hand. "I wouldn't have taken you for a fan of Miss Austen's work."

"Ah, but I studied Victorian Lit in college," Dave said. He extended his hand. "I've brains behind this beauty, in case you failed to notice."

"Oh, I noticed." I took his hand to shake.

"It didn't help my case." Dave kept my hand in his. "So tell me, Ms. McDermott, what *would* help my case?"

I succeeded in extracting my hand from Dave's.

"My father warned me about men like you, Mr. Mills," I said, thinking of Drake. "Suave. Charming. Devastatingly handsome..."

"Oh, that's *riiight*. Your father *The Hangin' Judge*... Does he keep a shotgun under his bed to keep away your suitors? I take it you only go for the nerds? The dorks? The ones who don't have a clue what to say or how to treat a woman? Some of us do know."

"I don't know why I'd be of much interest to you," I said, trying to change the subject. "I'm looking for donations. Care to donate to Nigel's foundation?"

Dave smiled at me and we locked eyes for a moment as if in battle.

"Kate was with Nigel in West Africa during the famine," Dave said to Drake.

"I'm well aware of her work in Africa," Drake said to Dave, not taking his eyes off me. "The Judge talks about you a lot."

"He does?" I frowned, surprised that my father spoke of me at all, especially since my trip to Africa. It was usually Heath my father paraded around, his little clone.

"It was always, Katherine this and Katherine that. He's very proud but he's kept you pretty well hidden."

"I've been really busy with school and work..."

Drake nodded, watching me, his expression hard to categorize. Interested, surprised? I couldn't tell which.

"Your father told me you got a job with *Geist*. What are you writing about now?" Drake said, his hands in his pockets.

Geist was an indie paper run by Columbia Journalism students. Another black mark against me. My father wanted me to use his connections with *The New York Post* instead but it just wasn't my kind of paper.

"Philanthropy in the age of social media."

Dave turned back to me. "Drake's foundation funds a number of hospital projects in West Africa if you're interested in philanthropy. I'm his manager of fundraising."

"Yes, that's what my father told me." I smiled again at Dave, unable to keep looking in Drake's oh-so-blue eyes. The idea he was a doctor just *did* something to me. Doctors knew their way around bodies... "I'm doing an article for *Geist*," I said, trying to divert my mind from Drake. "Maybe I could do an interview?"

Dave stepped closer to me, leaning in.

"I'd be only too happy to do an interview, Ms. McDermott. Your place or mine?"

I laughed uncomfortably at Dave's balls.

"I think she meant she wanted to interview *me*," Drake said.

Dave wouldn't let up, waving him off.

"You're *far* too busy with all your important breakthroughs in robotic brain surgery, your band and humanitarian projects, Drake. I'd be *more* than happy to oblige, take Ms. McDermott off your hands."

"Either one of you would do fine," I said and smiled. Just then, Peter came back and put a hand on my shoulder, scooping me up and away from them. Dave made a telephone sign with his hand and mouthed *call me*.

"Nice to meet you Dr. Morgan."

"Please, call me Drake, considering," he said, pointing to my knees.

I gave him a quick smile and left them, limping off with Peter to the next group of wealthy suits.

For the next half hour, Peter introduced me around to everyone who mattered in the room. I was still recovering from meeting Doctor Delish, Drake Morgan, brain surgeon, bass player, philanthropist... Someone my father thought walked on water.

The conversation got going again, this time about new regulations governing tax shelters but my mind was occupied thinking of Drake. My father told me before of this brilliant young surgeon who ran his father's charitable foundation, using the wealth he earned from the robotic surgical implement business his father founded to fund charity projects in Africa. My father thought he was a stellar example of manhood. I didn't believe I'd ever seen a more beautiful man in my life. But if my father liked him, I could strike him off my list of men I would go out with. A Republican with social conservative religious roots, my father's kind of man was definitely not mine.

Despite being off-limits, Drake Morgan was imprinted on my brain. Later, I knew I would fantasize about him when I was alone in my chaste little bed back in my apartment in Harlem.

"Tell me more about Drake Morgan," I said to Nigel while we circulated, trying to keep my voice nonchalant.

"Why?" he asked, raising his eyebrows. "Are you interested?"

"*No*," I said a little too quickly. Then I shrugged. "My father's talked a lot about him, but I never really listened."

Nigel pursed his lips for a moment as if debating whether to say anything. "I know he's a very big supporter of your father's candidacy for the House seat and absolutely loaded with cash from his father's business. He's a Republican. I also know he's divorced and quite the lady's man."

"He is?" I frowned. Not my type, in other words.

"Quite. But he's rich and a big supporter of Africa, so I make sure to butter him up when I can, get us some of his excess money. It wouldn't hurt if you did, too."

"I don't like buttering people up, Nigel. I hate hypocrisy."

"I know, my dear." Nigel patted my cheek. "But we need their money. Can you smile sweetly and stroke a few egos if it means we can fund more campaigns?"

I took in a deep breath. "I can be as fake as the next person if necessary."

"Good girl. Go out and rake in the donations. I knew you could do it."

We were talking about West Africa when I saw Drake Morgan standing on the edge of the group, watching me. I had almost finished my first glass of champagne, and my tongue was even looser and my inhibitions a bit muted. I tried my hand at buttering him up.

"People with influence have to step up to the plate and use their power to do good." I turned to Drake and looked at him directly. "Like Dr. Morgan, using his father's foundation to provide hospital equipment to Africa. Those who have the means should use them."

He seemed pleasantly surprised that I referred to him and bowed his head, touching his chest.

"My father was committed to Africa," Morgan said. "I'm just trying to fill his big shoes using whatever influence I have."

As that conversation ended, Nigel pulled me away and I noticed that Drake followed me with his eyes as I left to meet someone else. Dr. Drake Morgan was a rich doctor with family money. He was probably a lady's man like Nigel said, a jet-setting lothario. Self-absorbed, self-important. Dr. Dangerous. Republican.

My father's kind of man.

Not *my* kind of man.

I decided I would do the interview with Dave Mills instead of Drake. I didn't think I'd be able to stand interviewing someone that gorgeous. I'd send Dave a text later and see when we could meet for the interview.

My father didn't show up for his own fundraiser until a few minutes before it was scheduled to end. A teleconference with several powerful types in the Party advising him about his run for the Congressional seat went longer than anticipated.

When he finally did arrive, I was just getting ready to leave, saying goodbye to Elaine and Nigel. Nigel and I were able to garner a pretty impressive amount for his pet project in West Africa, started after we returned two years earlier. My father breezed in and was greeted by Peter and others, who surrounded him, wanting to shake his hand and hear the latest on the campaign.

He saw me from the doorway and came right over.

"There you are," he said, kissing my cheek, his characteristically gravelly voice ebullient. "Have you met everyone? There was someone I wanted you to meet in particular." After he glanced around, he took my arm and I limped behind him to the door where Drake and Dave stood.

"Drake, did you get a chance to meet my daughter, Katherine? I don't believe the two of you have met."

Drake stopped and turned, his face brightening as he saw my father. He held out his hand and the two men shook and it was quite the contrast. My dad was on the shorter stout side, with a growing pot belly and a grey brush cut. His several thousand dollar suit was on par with Drake's, but it was rumpled, his eyes a bit weary.

"Judge McDermott," Drake said, shaking my dad's hand vigorously. "Glad to see you. Yes, I did meet Katherine. *Finally*. You've kept her pretty well-hidden."

I turned to my father. "Dr. Morgan used his medical skills on me, father. I fell in the alley and he patched me up." I pointed to my knees and my dad made a face but then smiled.

"Well, that's just great," he said and shook Drake's hand once more. "I knew you'd come in handy one day." Drake shook my father's hand again, an amused expression on his face. "Thank you for looking after my very tomboyish daughter, Drake. She has a tendency to take a bigger bite out of life than she can always chew." My father winked at me, and I saw a hint of affection in that moment instead of criticism. *For a change.* "Can't call her timid, at least. Maybe foolishly brave."

I frowned at that and turned to him. "How am I foolishly brave, Daddy?"

"All your life, you've been trying to keep up with the older kids, like your brother. Going to Africa with Nigel and staying in one of the camps is a perfect example. How many of your friends can say that?"

I shrugged. "Lots of us volunteer, Dad. We have to in order to stand out on college applications and for scholarships. Dawn went to India."

He nodded. "Still, you have to admit it was pretty brave." A thrill went through me when he put his arm around my shoulder and squeezed. He rarely had anything nice to say about me, so it felt great. "Thanks for looking after my baby girl," he said to Drake.

"No, my pleasure," Drake said, his voice soft. "Thank you for inviting me. I was pleased to finally meet the mysterious Katherine you've spoken so much about." Drake smiled at me.

"Not hidden," my father said. "Katherine's been very busy with school and the student paper, haven't you, sweetheart?"

I smiled, feeling a little overwhelmed by the attention.

"Of course," Drake said.

Then, Peter came by and dragged my father off to speak with some high roller and I was left with Drake and Dave by the front closet where our coats were hung. I took mine out and was just about to put it on when Drake stopped me.

"Here," Drake said. "Let me get that."

Drake took my coat out of my hands, holding it out for me to slip on.

"I can do that," I said, not wanting anyone to fuss over me.

"Please, allow me."

I slid one of my arms in the coat and he helped me on with the other arm, and for a moment, he stood behind me, adjusting the shoulders while I pulled my hair out from under the neck, and I swore he bent forward and smelled me – my hair. I heard him inhale as he stood with his hands adjusting the collar.

I turned around and smiled at him, feeling a bit awkward, not certain if I was right.

"Thank you," I said. He nodded and just watched me as I gathered up my things and limped to my dad, who was standing a few feet away, now engaged in a conversation with Nigel. When my dad saw me coming, he leaned to me and offered his cheek.

I kissed him the way I always used to when I was a girl and still lived with him.

"Good night Daddy," I said, pleased that he seemed so nice.

"Good night, sweetheart." I saw him glance over at the door where Drake and Dave were standing. Then Drake came over and said his own goodbyes to my father. After another round of handshaking and back slapping, my father turned to me.

"Do you need to use the limo service?"

I shook my head. "I'll catch a cab."

Drake made a face at that. "Nonsense," he said. "Let me drop you off. Where do you live?"

My father rolled his eyes. "In a hovel of a rent-controlled apartment building in Harlem," my dad said as if it was an affront to him. Drake pursed his lips at that.

"Don't ask," my father said. "She could live somewhere nice, but that's my Kate. Independent to a fault."

"*Daddy*," I said, frowning. A nice moment between us was ruined. "I have a perfectly fine apartment." I turned to Drake. "I'm sure it's out of your way. I can catch a cab. But thank you."

"I insist," Drake said. "I won't take no for an answer."

I sighed and my father kissed me this time and we were off. Drake opened the door and he and Dave escorted me into the elevator. Dave offered me his arm as did Drake. I didn't want to encourage Dave, but I also didn't want to pick Drake. Instead, I took both their shoulders and limped inside.

"So, Katherine," Drake said, as we went down to the garage. "You should watch those cuts, make sure they don't become infected. If they do, you can go to a clinic to have them cleaned."

"Thank you," I said. "My best friend is a nurse, so I'll get her to check."

"Where does she work?"

"Harlem," I replied. "She's doing her Master's right now and only works part-time."

He nodded. When the elevator opened, he very purposely took my arm to help me walk. I initially resisted, but finally gave in when he kept hold of me. As we walked through the garage, I held onto his shoulder to take the weight off my ankle. When we arrived at his car, a shiny black Mercedes, I thought it seemed perfect for him, sleek and expensive. Drake held the door for me and I got inside.

"Where do you live?"

I gave him directions and we drove through the streets north and west to Harlem. Dave turned and glanced back at me from the front seat.

"So Kate, do you feel like going out for a drink? I'm still up for some fun tonight."

"I don't think so..."

"Come on, live a little. I've been trying to get you to go out with me for a long time. Why not tonight? *Muse* is just around the corner from your place. We could have a drink and something to eat."

I shook my head and caught Drake's eye in the rearview mirror. He was frowning a bit.

"I don't think so," I said. "I have class tomorrow early..."

"Kate, you are just such a mean woman," Dave said, laughing. He turned to Drake. "See what I mean? Turned down again!"

"Maybe you should take a strong *hint*," Drake said, his voice low, sounding a bit impatient.

Dave made a face and turned back to me. "No offense meant, Kate."

I shook my head, my cheeks heating. "No offense taken." I forced a smile but saw Drake watching me in the rearview.

Still, Dave didn't give up. "One of these days, you *will* have to go out with me, Kate. Live a little. Nigel told me you've been practically a hermit for the last two years."

"Final year of classes before I write my thesis," I said. "I've been working hard trying to keep my grades up."

We drove up to my apartment and I was never so glad to be able to get out of a car, feeling like Dave was totally ignoring Drake's not so subtle warning to leave me be. Dave hopped out when the car stopped and opened my door.

Drake got out of his door and watched as Dave walked me up the stairs to the front entrance.

"Good night, Kate," Dave said when we reached the door. "Call me about that interview."

"I will," I said, regretting that I agreed to it. No doubt he'd take the opportunity to hit on me once more. I turned back to the car where Drake stood watching us. I smiled at him. "Thank you for the ride. Nice to meet you."

"Nice to finally meet *you*," he said and smiled back. "Take care of those knees. If you have any problems, feel free to call me."

I turned and went inside.

Once I was in my apartment and had my coat off, I called Dawn.

"You won't believe what happened."

"What?" she said, her voice excited.

"I broke a heel on your shoes and fell in the alley on the way to the fundraiser."

"Oh, *God*, Kate," she said. "Are you OK?"

"I'm fine, but your shoes are ruined."

"Don't worry about the shoes. I got them from my sister, and you know her. The queen of cheap shoes. She'll never even notice they're missing."

"You won't believe who I met at the fundraiser," I said, my thoughts turning to Drake.

"Who? Tell me!"

"Doctor Dangerous himself."

"Oh, *oh*," Dawn said, her voice sounding hesitant. "I can smell trouble over the Ether. Don't tell me you have a date with him or I'll have to come over there and knock you upside the head."

"No, but he did have his hands all over my bare legs."

"*What?*"

I told her the story of my fall and Drake's doctoring. "Thing is, he's a big friend of my father's. His father and my father were both Marines in Vietnam. Real buddy-buddy. My father thinks Drake is a saint."

"You better not be getting any ideas. The nurses I spoke to at NYP thought he was a dick."

"Of course not. I'm meeting with his business manager to do an interview on his father's charitable foundation for my article for *Geist*, but speaking of dicks, I don't know if I really want to now. I couldn't do an interview with Doctor Delish, Dawn. He's far too gorgeous."

"Keep away from him. Someone that good looking and rich has to be a total asshole. Plus he's a surgeon. Balls of steel. I'm warning you. *Huge* balls. Ego galore. Control freak. It's just impossible for him to be anything but a jerk on some level."

"That's awfully judgmental," I said, feeling a need to defend him for some reason, having faced my own share of criticism from my friends on the left because I was born into a wealthy family. "Don't blame him for being born good-looking and wealthy."

"This is just for safety's sake, Kate," she said, a warning tone in her voice. "*Your* safety. He can probably have anyone he wants whenever he wants and knows it. Stay away."

"I doubt you have anything to worry about."

I felt somewhat saddened. Part of me wished I *could* go out with him. He was so gorgeous, like Dawn said, that he probably would barely even notice someone like me. On the short side, mousy brown hair, non-descript green eyes and tits a bit too big for the rest of me which I usually took pains to keep hidden under layers of clothes, I blended in with the background most of the time. Except when I wore a revealing dress and had bloody knees and a sprained ankle.

I went to bed later that night, desperately trying not to think of Dr. Drake Morgan. Dr. Delish. But of course, each time I closed my eyes, I remembered his mouth, his jaw, his eyes, which I could barely stand to look into.

I tossed and turned for several hours, fighting with my urges, not wanting to resort to Big. I did *not* want someone like Drake – someone who was friends with my father – someone who was the opposite to everything I wanted in a man – to invade my private sexual fantasies. He was a Republican. Comfortable around my father's 'people'. Suave. Filthy rich. Powerful.

Yes, he was the best looking man I'd ever seen, but he was just so wrong for someone like me.

Finally, I got up and made a cup of chamomile tea and read *Anna Karenina* until I fell asleep, the book in my hand, Big still in a tangle of socks at the back of my dresser drawer.

Three days later, I sat in a café across from NY Presbyterian so I could interview Dave. I had on my Doc Marten shoes, with an elastic bandage on my ankle the only sign I'd been injured, my cuts and scrapes mostly healed over. I had the sheet of paper that contained my questions and my iPhone so I could record his answers. I'd called Dave earlier to confirm our interview. I suggested we meet at a café near the Foundation's offices and he suggested one. He called a few moments after I arrived.

"I'm on my way over. Dr. Morgan hoped to be able to do the interview, but he's unable so I'll be doing it after all. He has a busy day in the O.R."

Good. Despite disliking Dave, I didn't want to have to interview Drake. He was just so attractive that I knew I'd feel all tongue-tied around him. As I waited for Dave to arrive, I wondered if he would be his usual self and hit on me. He really was a lothario, although very friendly about it. When Dave arrived and saw me, he made a beeline for me. I remained seated, glad he didn't bother trying to kiss my hand again.

"Kate, so glad you could come meet me," he said, friendly but more formal. "I've been looking forward to this since the fundraiser."

"Nice to see you again," I said, not meaning it for a moment.

He took a seat across from me and ordered a coffee when the waitress came to our table. After she left, he turned to me and folded his hands on the tabletop.

I conducted the interview, turning on my iPhone's recorder. I asked questions about how the foundation started, where it had its main projects, how it choose hospitals to fund, the usual questions I needed to write my article. I asked him what he thought were the most successful projects and he responded, articulate, informed, and helpful. For once, he talked to me as a person, not a Don Juan, and I wondered why. Had Drake said something to him?

"I just checked out our projects, and we have twenty currently open."

"Wow," I said. "That's quite a lot going on."

"We're very busy. When I'm not fundraising, I spend most of my time coordinating shipments of surgical implements and supplies. Dr. Morgan donates a lot of his own money as well as raising funds from other donors. He keeps me busy."

"Well, I guess that's it," I said and turned off my iPhone voice recorder. "Thank you so much for this. I really appreciate it."

Before I could rise to leave, Drake Morgan entered the café from the street. Still dressed in his scrubs and white lab coat, he stopped at the front and glanced around the café before spying us in the rear. When his eyes met mine, I felt my cheeks heat. I quickly gathered up my things. I did *not* want to have to talk to him.

He was just too good looking and powerful.

"Thank you for coming down, Kate," Dave said, extending his hand. I had to shake, but he didn't lean down and kiss my hand. I just smiled back, anxious to see if Drake came to our table and if I could escape before he did.

I couldn't. He walked over and before I could leave, he came up behind Dave and laid a hand on his shoulder, a smile on his face.

"There you *are*," he said. "I was wondering if I'd make it down in time."

"We just finished," I said and shrugged, smiling in relief.

He nodded, his lips pressed a bit thin. "I *told* Mr. Mills that I'd be right over and he was *supposed* to wait and let me do the interview." He made a face at Dave and then turned to me and caught my eye. "Perhaps you could stay behind for a moment so we can speak alone."

I glanced at Dave, who smiled sheepishly. "I didn't want you to waste your time in case Drake wasn't able to get away from the hospital. Sometimes his surgeries take longer than planned. Nice talking to you again, Kate. Good interview."

I watched as he left the café, closing the door behind him.

I turned back to Drake. He didn't sit in Dave's vacated chair across from me but the one next to mine, his arm on the back of my chair. He looked at me directly.

"Well," I said after a moment when he did nothing and said nothing, just sat there looking at me. "I'm here. What did you want to talk about?" I forced a smile.

"How's your ankle? Your knees?" He peered down at my legs, which were covered by tights under my short jean skirt.

"Almost all better."

"Good."

We smiled at each other and I finally sighed. "So? You wanted to speak with me?"

"I just wanted to offer you the chance to ask me anything now that I'm here," he said, his voice low, soft.

"I think I got everything I need from Mr. Mills."

"You don't want to hear my side of things? Considering it's my father's foundation..."

I sighed. I really *should* ask him some of the more personal questions I skipped because I was interviewing Dave instead of him.

"I do have a few questions, more about motivation." I took out my iPhone and started the recording. I took in a deep breath. "Can you tell me why he started this foundation?"

He moved his chair a bit closer, and leaned in as if he wanted to say something personal. He was a bit *too* close for my comfort.

"He was a socialist, committed to eradicating poverty. He didn't expect to become rich and so when he did, he poured almost every extra cent into helping hospitals in third world countries, especially Africa. He said something about unequal development and capitalist exploitation – you'd know more about that than me."

I frowned, not certain I knew what he meant, but not wanting to push him.

"The Foundation continues his work today. Everything we do in the Foundation," he said, "is to try to fulfill my father's vision, even if only in a small way. He was so committed to his causes. He made a lot of money, and his company is still making a lot of money. I know he'd want it to be put to good use. He hated being rich and gave most of his money away. We lived in the same apartment all my life, once my mother left. He lived off his salary as a trauma surgeon, which while high, was nothing compared to what his company made."

I watched as he spoke, keeping my eyes on his mouth instead of his eyes. So bright blue and piercing, I found it hard to look at them directly.

There was silence for a moment and I realized he wasn't speaking any longer. He smiled indulgently.

"I'm *sorry.*" I grimaced in embarrassment, although something he said about his mother stuck in my mind. "Can you tell me what project you're most proud of?"

He spoke about a pediatric neurosurgery program that brought patients to the US for the most delicate surgeries that couldn't be done as safely in local hospitals. I nodded and listened, my eyes focusing on everything but his eyes.

"Your father died while in Africa several years ago," I said, remembering the story.

"Yes. He died just after you came back from Africa."

"What happened?"

Drake blinked a few times, his eyes becoming distant. He fiddled with the cutlery.

"He was flying into a small base camp where he was going to do some work with a local charity." He glanced down at his hands when he spoke, as if it still hurt. "Even though we were political opposites and didn't always see eye to eye, when he died, it was as if the ground was ripped out from under me." He glanced back up and met my eyes. "Nothing has been able to fill the hole. *Nothing.* I took over the helm of his foundation because I thought doing his work might heal me in some way. That's how your father and I became friends. He came to the funeral and it was like he adopted me."

I shook my head. "I guess I just never saw my father as someone who would do that."

"What? Act fatherly?"

I nodded. "I mean, he's an authoritarian type – head of the family and all. But not to, you know, step in and act as a father substitute."

"He did. I relied on him to get through it." He looked back up at me and his expression was so earnest. Seeing his raw emotion, hearing it in his voice, something in the way he said it brought out emotions that were just under the surface and I couldn't help myself. My throat choked up a bit.

"I know what it means to lose a parent."

He smiled softly. "Your mother died of cancer a few years ago. The year before you went to Africa. Your father told me."

I nodded and a silence passed between us.

"Well, that's all I have," I said a little reluctantly, suddenly wishing I had more to ask. "I guess I should go. Don't want to keep you from the OR."

We both stood and he extended his hand. I took it and instead of shaking, he lifted my hand to his mouth, his lips soft against my knuckles.

"People have spoken so highly of you," he said, keeping my hand in his. "So has your father. In the past few days, I've read up a bit about you, reread your articles on Mangaize. Still so impressive. I don't know who I was expecting when I thought about meeting you. Someone older. Different. I was so surprised to actually meet you."

I pulled my hand away. "What do you mean?"

"Your writing – it's so visceral. Insightful for someone so young." I didn't know what to say about that and glanced away, stuffing my iPhone into my bag.

"I'm glad we could meet and talk," he said. "I'd like to interview *you* sometime, talk about Africa."

"I don't really like to talk about Africa."

"Why?"

"It was upsetting."

He nodded as if in understanding. "Your father told me you had problems after you came back. You were there at the height of the famine. It had to be very hard."

Problems... I didn't say more for my throat choked up at the thought. I nodded, glancing away.

For my Honors Degree, I wrote an investigative series on the politics of famine in West Africa. I had the opportunity to go there and volunteer, then report from the scene because of my father's connections in philanthropic and political circles. I was so ambitious back then – so certain of my own mental strength. So determined to succeed and become a foreign correspondent and please my father. In the end, it was too soon after my mother's death. I was still grieving but saw the trip as a chance to move forward.

My project had gravitas. Because of it, I won the Honors prize for my BA in Journalism at Columbia.

I also had a nervous breakdown.

Five weeks surrounded by the death and chaos that was the Mangaize refugee camp in Niger was enough to change my focus from politics to popular culture. From grave to glib.

"I'd really like to just take you out for coffee or a drink," he said. "I feel like I've known you forever from everything your father's told me about you. But I probably shouldn't."

"Probably," I said, although I didn't know why I agreed or what he meant. I stopped and turned to face him, our eyes meeting. "Can I ask why?" My face heated, but I was curious now why he thought he shouldn't ask me out.

He shook his head quickly. "You're *The Hangin' Judge's* daughter," he said, his face dark, his brow furrowed. "I'm not the kind of man Judge McDermott's daughter should get involved with."

I frowned. "He thinks very highly of you."

He cracked a strange grin, that didn't reach his eyes. "He doesn't really know me."

I said nothing more. *What does he mean by that?*

We walked to the door to the café, his hand very soft on the small of my back, and he opened the door for me.

"Thank you for doing an interview," I said once again as I stepped outside into the cool air, still a bit taken back by what he said.

He smiled, a crooked grin. "Goodbye, lovely Katherine."

That sent a jolt of pleasant surprise through me that only added to my confusion. Then the door closed and he walked one way, while I walked the other, the image of his face, his smile, in my mind's eye as I made my way down the street to the subway.

Before the door to my apartment was even closed, I was on the phone with Dawn, telling her about my meeting with Dave and Dr. Morgan.

"So I think you were right about him being a bad boy," I said, remembering his words at the café.

"Why? What did he say?"

"He told me he wanted to ask me out on a date, but that he wasn't the kind of man someone like me should get involved with."

"*What?*"

"I know," I said, frowning. "Strange, right? He said my father didn't really *know* him."

"Holy *crap*," Dawn said. "That's cryptic. And ominous. Like I said, stay away from him, Kate. He's trouble."

I spent the rest of the week interviewing other people on my father's list of philanthropic giants for my article on charity for *Geist*. I had to turn it in before the weekend and so I spent my spare time working on it, polishing it before I had to send it to my editor.

I wished I could see Drake again, despite his warning for there was just something so... *enticing* and slightly dangerous about him. It wasn't just that he was drop-dead beautiful. It wasn't just that he was a surgeon and skilled. He was powerful. Self-assured. But there was something else.

It was something in his bearing that made you believe he could sweep you off your feet, like one of those bare-chested heroes in the bodice-ripping romance novels my girlfriends and I consumed like candy when we were teens. His dark arched brows and deep voice made you think he was out for plunder, like a pirate searching for treasure or some rich Lord of a great estate surveying the pretty daughters of his indentured serfs for his next trifle.

I had to admit I resorted to Big a few times in the ensuing days...

CHAPTER THREE

Later that week, I sat at a tiny table in the corner of the patio at a small café in the upper West Side of Manhattan. I was waiting to meet Mistress Lara to talk about meeting the Dominant she'd promised I could interview for my research project. Although late October, the weather was perfect. I didn't want to miss the chance to sit outside one last time before winter set in. There were few patrons outside despite the warm weather and so we could talk in relative privacy.

The sunshine and the nice weather did nothing to calm the butterflies in my stomach.

I could have chosen a safe topic for my paper – something uncomplicated and straight-forward, familiar ground for me. Like the war in the Congo or rendition to Guantanamo Bay. I could have met with someone from the military – a veteran with combat experience or a military strategist – and used them as an informant. But I'd changed focus from politics to pop-culture, no longer able to handle the darkness of my previous areas.

Instead, I decided to write about sexual politics and the world of BDSM, which had become quite a topical subject since those books were published a few years earlier. I created a profile at FetLife.com and spent some time reviewing profiles and reading message boards, fending off a few Doms who expressed an interest in spanking me.

One of the Dommes on the board took me under her wing, offering to help me. I set up a meeting with Mistress Lara, as she called herself, a Domme who happened to be a lawyer in real life. She contacted me after I indicated I was a student interested in learning about the lifestyle for a paper I was writing. She was hesitant to meet with me in person, interrogating me about why I needed to be anonymous. I had to confess my identity to her, and when she heard my last name, she made the connection and agreed to meet with me.

"Just invite me to one of your father's fundraisers," she said over the phone. "When you're a defense lawyer, it never hurts career-wise to have friends in high places, especially judges."

While I waited for her, I read over the excerpt she sent me of a Dom's letter to his sub. She said if I wanted to read more, she'd give me the password to the website where it was posted.

I glanced down at my iPhone and read the excerpt for the fifteenth time.

A letter to my sub.

You trust me completely to know what you need.

And I <u>do</u> know what you need. I know what to whisper in your ear to make you need me even more. I know how to touch, where to touch, when to touch.

I know <u>you</u>.

I've known every part of you – every naked inch, inside and out.

You can relax completely with me. You can feel everything possible with me. You can respond with total abandon with me.

It is what I most desire.

*I can't wait to bind you with my soft leather restraints
and make you cry out my name as you come, again and
again. Then I will kiss you, smothering your moans
with my mouth...*

When Lara walked up to my table, I tore my attention away
from the email. She looked so normal compared to her profile
photo on FetLife, dressed in a sober blue pinstripe suit fitting
to her occupation as a defense lawyer, her blonde hair pulled
back into a tight bun, makeup impeccable, her lawyer's
briefcase on rollers towed behind her. I didn't know what to
expect, but in my mind's eye, I pictured her wearing a mask and
black leather dress with impossibly high-heeled-thigh-high
leather boots.

"Kate?"

I put my phone away and smiled.

"You must be Lara."

"The very one."

She ordered an espresso from the waitress, and then sat
down. After she adjusted her suit and removed her sunglasses,
she turned her focus on me.

"You look so different from what I expected," I said, my
cheeks heating.

"We're ordinary people, Kate. Just like you." She looked me
up and down. "You're a pretty little thing. Petite. Sweet
looking. I love those huge green eyes. I won't have any
problems finding you a proper Dom, if that's what you really
want."

"I need someone to *interview*," I said, my cheeks hot. "I'm
not here to find a Dom for myself."

"Of *course*." She smiled, her eyes narrowing. "So, tell me why
you *really* want to write about the lifestyle, of all things." The
waitress brought her espresso, and she sipped it, eyeing me over
the rim. "It's quite a stretch from the article you wrote on

famine in West Africa. Aren't you more of a political writer? This is sub-culture."

I took in a deep breath and went over my rehearsed response, having expected this question. I practiced my answer in my mind all morning, wondering exactly how to phrase my reasons so she would agree to be my contact in this quasi-secret world.

"This is topical, given the popularity of recent books and films. I made the switch from politics to popular culture after my trip to Mangaize."

"There has to be more than that. Something personal."

There was, but I didn't really want to admit it. It wasn't a particularly stellar moment in my personal life. I sighed and decided to be honest. If I wanted her to be, I figured I should be as well.

"To be honest, my last real boyfriend and I parted company over his interest in kink and my fear of it. Ever since we split, I've been thinking about how I responded. It scared me, but the truth is," I said, stirring sugar into my cappuccino, "I regret my over-reaction."

She smiled knowingly. "And now you're curious. Did you read the excerpt from the letters I sent you?"

"Yes."

"And?"

I shrugged, not wanting to admit how much it aroused me. "He's a good writer."

"That's it? Nothing else?" She leaned forward. "It didn't make you want someone like him?"

"Well..." I said, embarrassed that I responded so strongly to it. "It was... *thought* provoking."

"I bet you can't stop thinking about him."

My face grew hot, and it wasn't the warmth of the sun. "Yes, but because of *who* I am, who my *father* is, I can't risk doing anything that might get me in trouble. I might get away with writing an investigative piece, but to really explore it as a woman?" I shook my head. "Can't go there."

"That's a shame," she said and eyed me from under a frown. "People like you can't ever really be satisfied without doing it for real. I read your profile on FetLife."

"What do you mean, people like me?"

"You're a sub."

I frowned. "What was in my profile that made you think that?"

"Things." She smiled. "Besides, if you weren't a sub at heart, if submission didn't appeal to at least some part of you, you wouldn't have gone beyond reading a few books, fantasizing a bit. To actually contact someone in the lifestyle?" She shook her head. "That's the next step and that means this is really *you*, somewhere deep inside underneath all that self-judgment. You're pretty vanilla but there were a few hints in your list of fetishes that suggest you could be a secret sub."

I frowned at that. "Like what?"

"Bondage, bare handed spanking, hair pulling, leather corsets, kneeling..."

"I just put those in so I didn't appear like a poser."

She just grinned. "*Sure.*"

"So you don't think I can just be interested as a student writing a paper?"

"It must appeal to you on a human level, sexual level, or else you'd write about something else. Either you're totally against it and want to criticize it or you're totally fascinated and can't stop thinking about it. I can help you. In fact, I enjoy teaching. But here's my warning to you. I won't go along with any kind of *shocking exposé*," she said, making air quotes, "so if that's what you thought you'd do, forget it. I *will* help you understand how things work and introduce you to some people I know. No names, though. As you can imagine, we're quite..." She paused and shrugged a shoulder. "*Protective* of our lifestyle. Puritans and moralists would love to try to discredit us. If people found out who *really* frequents our dungeons and fetish parties." She grinned at that. "Even people like your father."

"Not my *father?*"

"Not that I know of, but people of his status. All kinds of men and women enjoy kink, Kate. The public has the wrong idea. Some of us just get off on a bit of bondage, a bit of power exchange. Enhanced sensual experience."

"You mean pain. I'm not into pain."

"The pain and pleasure responses in the brain are very similar. It's all sensation."

"My boyfriend wanted to spank me," I said, remembering our very brief and upsetting foray into kinky sex. "He wanted to do mock rape scenes, and it was too much. I was afraid I was with some kind of serial killer in the making."

"He sounds like he had no idea what he was doing. Don't use him as an example of what most Doms are like."

"Since I did some reading," I said and took in a deep breath. "I can't stop thinking about this. Not S&M, but bondage and dominance. Some of the descriptions by the Dominants – the way they talk about their subs. The way the Dom spoke to his sub in the letter you sent me." I shook my head. "It did something to me and I realized that I've always had this secret fantasy..."

"But you always denied it, right? Because it was upsetting."

I nodded. "I'm a feminist."

"So am I." Lara smiled quickly. "You're attracted to a strong man who wants to take control over you in the bedroom, but that conflicts with your feminist sensibilities outside of it. It's a very common fantasy, Kate. Probably one of the most common fantasies for women. It's harmless as long as you're safe and it's all done consensually." She looked out over the street and then her gaze returned to me. "That's our motto – safe, sane, consensual. Sex is sex. Pleasure is pleasure. Don't judge yourself

– I always add unless it's illegal, of course. No animals or children."

I sighed. "Of course. But it's hard as a modern woman to admit that I even *consider* it. My mother was a big feminist. How can I want this?" I shook my head. "I'm embarrassed by it."

"You shouldn't be. Human relations are all about power exchange, finding some kind of balance that benefits those who interact together. Sexual relations are about pleasure and sensation, but power exchange still plays a role even in sex. Some people need equality in sex. Some people love to give up power to their partner during sex, some like to hold it. Some people prefer vanilla ice cream, some like Rocky Road with chocolate, marshmallow and nuts. That's all, sweetie." She raised her eyebrows. "Nothing moral about it."

I took another sip of my cappuccino and studied her over the rim. "You make it sound so... normal. Logical. You teach?"

She nodded. "I teach Dominants how to do D/s and S&M, how to be safe when using toys and restraints. I can tell you about my experiences as a Domme with male subs, but if you want a male Dominant's perspective, you need a man."

"And you have someone for me?

She nodded. "A friend. An actual professor. He's a great teacher and totally discrete."

"He'll have to be really trustworthy. He'll have to show complete discretion and he'll have to agree that I remain anonymous."

"I understand. I'm meeting with him later this week. In the meantime, I have this." She reached into her huge briefcase filled with files. "It's a template I use to get subs thinking about what they want. Fill in the blanks, cross things out, as if you were really interested and get it back to me. I'll give it to him and he can think about how he'd train you if you really *were* his new sub, and then you can meet and discuss it."

"He knows this is all just theoretical."

"Of *course*, sweetie," she said, but there was this tone in her voice that said otherwise.

I took the contract and flipped through it. The first paragraph said it all:

SUBMISSION CONTRACT BETWEEN
_____ hereinafter referred to as
"Master", AND _____,
hereinafter referred to as "slave" in this Submission
Contract. Said Contract refers to total dominance and
control of Master in his relationship with said slave.

A total novice to this world, I had only my very upsetting experience with Kurt. Sure, I read a few novels and non-fiction books since we broke up, spent some time on the website reading, but I was still new to this. Lara knew the ropes. She'd done this dozens of times and had connections.

"What's this Dom like?"

"He's a *god*, Kate. He's absolutely gorgeous. Experienced. Buff. *Hung*," she said and wagged her eyebrows.

"How do *you* know?"

"I trained him myself. He's healthy. Safe. Smart. Wealthy. He's everything a submissive like you could want."

"I'm *not* a submissive."

"Not experienced, no. But I suspect there's one buried deep inside of you."

I shrugged, not wanting to argue with her. "He's not into pain, is he?"

"He isn't a sadist, if that's what you mean, although he would probably spank you for punishment. He's just a plain old sexual dominant, into a bit of bondage, especially leather, but mostly D/s and mindfucks."

"*Mindfucks?*"

"You know, getting right into your mind, knowing exactly how to get you off so you experience the most pleasure. He's studied psychology. Wanted to be a psychoanalyst. He's not into pain."

"How old is he?"

"Mid-thirties."

"He isn't married?"

"Divorced."

"What does he do? You said he's a professor. What does he teach?"

"Uh, *uh*," she said and shook her head. "I've given you as much as I can at this point. Just know that he's a friend and a real professional. Top in his field. Seriously, if you needed his services, you'd want him. Just hope you never need his services."

"That's cryptic. Is he an undertaker or something?"

She grinned. "No. Far from it. No more, Kate. You want anonymity. So does he. Maybe one day, you'll sign that for real." She pointed to the contract, "Then you two can know each other, but now? No. He needs anonymity as much as you."

"All right." I read over a few more pages. "I'm just so curious." I thought of the excerpt she sent. "Who wrote that piece you emailed me?"

"Not telling." She shook her head. "That's just something that some of us use to explain to new subs how Doms see sexual domination."

I felt a bit saddened to think I wasn't meeting the writer and I wondered what he was like, this man who liked to control a woman's sexual pleasure. After reading that excerpt, I couldn't get the idea of sexual submission out of my mind. I told myself this was just to gather research for an investigative reporting piece for *Geist*. But I was really just so damn *titillated*...

"Look, you know my situation," I said, anxious that I remain completely anonymous. "Can you imagine if it ever got out that *the* Ethan McDermott's daughter is interested in this, even if it's only academic?"

"*Academic...*" She rolled her eyes at me. Then, she waved her hand. "Don't worry. Your Dom is pretty well known in his own profession, so there's *no way* he wants this public either. The two of you will be fine. He can tell you things from his side, maybe introduce you to some of his former submissives, if they're interested in being interviewed, take you to a few functions."

I was apprehensive but still, a thrill went through me at the thought of meeting a real-life Dominant. The truth was that I couldn't stop thinking about this world. I wanted to understand why so many women were attracted to this lifestyle and why I was as well. What did it say about women and the feminist movement that so many women wanted to be sexually dominated?

But as the daughter of a prominent judge with aspirations for the House, this was *just* research. It had to stay that way. I was just a student looking for material for a paper, not a curious might-be-submissive looking for a Dominant. This was just research.

"What have you told him about me? Did you tell him I'm just a researcher like I asked?"

"I did, but Kate, be honest with yourself," Lara said, shaking her head. "You're really interested. Seriously. He'll see right through you. He's really *really* smart. Besides, if you like him and if he likes you, things could work out..."

"No way," I replied. "Tell him I'm seriously freaked about him knowing who I am. Tell him," I said and held up my cup, "that I'm just doing research."

"*Just* you wait and see." She winked at me. "You'll be signing a contract for real in no time."

I made a face. "Lara," I said, defensive. "No contracts. This is just an agreement so I can do research. I don't want him getting any ideas."

Lara smiled again. "It's *you* who will probably get ideas. This is quite a stretch from the article you sent me, but whatever you say. Oh, and if you want the password to that website? It's *leather4you*."

Leather4you. I wouldn't forget it.

Lara packed up her files and shot back the remnants of her espresso.

"Just as long as this is all anonymous, Lara." I read over the contract one more time. "Scandal is the last thing my father needs."

"This man is a professional. I know him personally, and I trained him. He has to keep his two lives separate. Just like you." Then, Lara walked away, her lawyer-sized briefcase on wheels pulled behind her.

Later that night, I used the password Lara gave me to the website where the Dom's letters to his sub were archived. I eagerly entered and opened the first letter.

A letter to my sub.

I come to you, my little one, where you sit naked in wait for me in the darkness, a blindfold covering your pretty wide eyes. You've been waiting for almost half an hour as I commanded, and your senses are all primed. The noises of your apartment that you never noticed before are so much clearer now that you're vision has been blocked – the hum of the refrigerator in your tiny kitchen, the sweet strains of classical music on the music system in the apartment above you, street noises outside your building, cars starting, a horn blaring in the distance. Even the sounds of your own body are clearer now that your eyes are covered. The rush of blood through your veins, the pounding of your heart in your chest, the air flowing in and out through your open mouth – all these sounds are enhanced.

The scents around you are more intense – the vanilla of the candles on your bedside table, the floral of your own perfume on your pillows, the ozone from rush hour traffic filtering in from under your open window, your own arousal from the warmth between your legs.

Your naked skin is sensitive now, exposed to the ambient temperature change. The silk of your pillow is cool against your calves as you sit waiting. A cool breeze wafts in from your open window, and your nipples pucker. You think of my mouth on them, my tongue wet and warm, and a stab of lust flows through you.

My key clicks in the lock, the door creaking open, my footsteps loud on the hardwood floor, the thunk thunk as I remove my boots.

I open the refrigerator and remove the bottle of vodka you keep just for me, pour the liquid in a shot glass, and then my lips smack in satisfaction. It's my favorite Russian vodka infused with anise, called Anisovaya. I have only one shot, for I must keep my mind clear so I am in total control of everything – you, the scene, and most of all, myself.

Then, the zhrrr of a zipper and the swish of fabric sounds so loud. Your body tenses for a moment as you anticipate my next move.

I stand in the doorway and watch you. You picture me there, my eyes on you, my body naked, my thick cock already hard. You're breathless, your body ready for me. Your heart is beating so fast, imagining what I will do to you after I use my leather restraints to bind you.

What I will make you do to me.

You're so ready, your body aching with need, wet, swollen, throbbing with desire. I stand beside you and you turn your head at the sound of my breathing. My clean skin and the hint of my male musk arouses you, sending a jab of lust through your chest to your clit.

I lean down to you and my hair brushes your cheek, the whiskers on my chin tickle your skin, my tongue is wet on your neck where I lick you, my mouth soft at the base of your throat where one day I'll place my collar.

I kiss you very briefly and you taste the anise on my tongue.

I whisper your name and just the sound of my voice makes your body clench. My cologne and a hint of anise on my breath fills your nose. By now, the scent arouses you because I have a shot of the vodka when I come by and have my way with you. You associate the scent of anise with pleasure and your body warms even further, your flesh swelling, your pussy becoming wet.

Leather slides against leather as I uncoil the bindings, which I will use to tie your hands to the headboard and your feet to the base. You'll be open to me, vulnerable.

I've known every part of you – every naked inch, inside and out.

I can't wait to bind you with my leather restraints and make you cry out my name as you come, again and again. Then, I will really kiss you, smothering your moans with my mouth...

I would have loved to read those letters all night but I had an early class in the morning. I couldn't sleep, and since I couldn't run because of my ankle, I got up once more and made a pot of tea, reading the pages of my book until I felt asleep long after midnight.

I spent the next few days going through my daily routine, getting up, going to classes, working on my article, coming home, rinse, repeat. Dawn and I didn't see much of each other because she was busy with her own coursework. Still, as busy as I was, I thought often of Drake Morgan, wondering why he'd warned me off, regretting that he did.

That Friday, I dressed in my prettiest clothes – a cream cashmere sweater and black pencil skirt, black hose and heels, my black leather jacket over top. I sat at the same café where I met Lara, preparing to meet the gorgeous man-god Dom she promised me. She said it was only a few blocks from her law firm's office and so I went once more and waited, sitting at the same small table with my back to the wall, having arrived fifteen minutes earlier so I could calm my nerves. The night before, I read another of the Dom's letters to his new sub. I couldn't get it out of my mind, the words so intense, the promise of pleasure in his description of what he would do to her so enticing.

While I waited, I re-read the letter over, thinking about what I'd ask this Dom I was meeting.

To my new sub.

When we are together, I expect you to surrender control to me in all things. You do so because you trust me completely. You are able to let go of all shyness and self-doubt without fear that I will judge you or harm you. I will only draw out of you what you can give, using your body and your mind to bring us both as much pleasure as we can possibly feel together.

When we part, you are your own woman and I admire your independence. We only meet to slake our thirst for what we give each other, for the special relationship we have established that satisfies our unique needs. For me, that means Dominance; for you, submission.

I expect you to comply with my commands without hesitation. I know your limits for we have already discussed them. You know my desires, for I have already described them. We will establish ahead of time exactly what we will do together so that you are well-prepared.

There will be little need for conversation for we will communicate using touch, eye contact, and only occasionally, a verbal command or word of encouragement, and when necessary, correction. We have discussed your safe word, but I don't expect you to need it for I will not lose control. Of that you can be certain.

Control is what I desire and it is what I am best at.

Why did the Dom's words so arouse me?

I glanced up from my iPhone when the café door opened and Lara walked in. I took in a deep cleansing breath as she made her way to the counter. I put my phone down and watched as she ordered an espresso from the barista then came to my table. She sat down, removing her coat, and glanced at what I was wearing as if to judge whether I met her standards.

"You look nice enough," she said, rubbing the cashmere of my sweater between her fingers. "Classy but not overdressed, nice skirt, hose, even heels. He'll like *you*. I knew that the first time I saw you."

"Why?" I asked, sipping my drink nervously.

"He likes petite women. You're exactly his type."

As we passed the time waiting for the Dom to arrive, we talked about my father.

"You must invite me to a fundraiser one of these days," she said when her coffee arrived. "Making connections is everything in my profession."

"I will," I said, a bit reluctant even though I liked her. What if it got out that she was a Domme?

Lara checked her watch.

"I wonder where he is," she said, her voice a bit impatient. "He's usually right on time."

I took in a deep breath, trying to calm my nerves. As we waited, *he* walked into the café – Drake Morgan, MD. Assistant Professor of Neurosurgery at the Columbia Center for Movement Disorders, Bass Player, Volunteer for *Doctors Without Borders*, the medical charity we both belonged to, the son of my father's oldest and best friend.

What was *he* doing here?

Seeing him once more, I realized that he was perhaps the most beautiful man I'd ever met with those impossibly-blue eyes fringed with thick dark lashes and a few days-worth of stubble on his very square jaw. Fresh from the OR at NY Presbyterian, he still wore blue scrubs under a white lab coat.

He stopped up short, frowning when he saw us, glancing around the deserted café as if in confusion. When Lara stood and waved him over to the table, I got a very bad feeling.

"You're *late*," she said, air kissing his cheeks when he arrived as if she'd been expecting him.

It was only then I realized why he was there.

The look on Drake's face would have been hilarious if it wasn't the most awkward moment of my life.

This was a *disaster*.

"Oh, *God*," I said, glancing away for a moment. Drake was my *Dom*. The Dominant who was going to teach me about the lifestyle. The one Lara thought I could like for real.

"I have to go." I pulled on my coat, gathered up my bag and put on my sunglasses. I walked away, my body stiff, mortified that Drake Morgan was the Dom I was supposed to meet.

"Kate!" Lara called out to me, but I was out the door and on the street hailing a taxi before Lara could call me back. I practically ran away from them – from *Drake*.

Oh, *God*...

The taxi drove down the street and before even a few moments passed, my cell rang. It was from Lara. I refused the call.

When it rang a second time, I answered.

"Before you say *anything*," I said, frustrated, not wanting to speak to her now. "I want you to remind Dr. Morgan that this was *purely* academic. This was research – nothing more. No matter what you think Lara, I'm not interested. This was nothing *personal*—"

"Kate, *Kate*, shhhh," Drake Morgan said, his voice soft. "Don't worry. I *know*. You're a serious student. This is just research. If anything, it's me who should be embarrassed."

I hung up and threw my phone into my bag.

CHAPTER FOUR

I was numb the entire taxi ride back to my apartment, my cheeks hot despite the chill air. The adrenaline shock that went through my body when I realized Drake was my Dominant left me weak.

Drake Morgan?

MD, brain surgeon, bass player, philanthropist, my father's example of perfect *manhood*? Now I knew what he meant when he said my father didn't really know him.

I felt a bit nauseated that he knew I was the one who wanted to meet him. No, make that I felt *completely* nauseated that he knew.

He was a *Dominant*? Dawn said he was dangerous when she saw him in the bar. As usual, she was right.

Holy *crap*... I looked down in my lap. My hands were shaking.

Lara said he liked to tie women up and control their pleasure, fuck them senseless. Mindfucks. The thought of it – even now – even mortified as I was – titillated me. My body couldn't help but respond, a twitch between my legs when I thought of him naked, being all—*dominating*. Like that Dom in the letters.

This was terrible. This was horrible. This was... oh, *hell*, what if my father found out I was looking for a Dominant? Even if it *was* just research for a course paper, if he knew I was really *interested* in the subject...

Total and complete mortification.

Humiliation.

I didn't even admit that I read the books that everyone was talking about when both his wife Elaine and my sister-in-law Christie giggled together about it in front of him.

Oh. *God*. It would be comical if it wasn't so mortifying. I couldn't imagine what Drake thought. *I'm* the one who wanted to talk to him about being a Dominant... About BDSM. About submission. I was mortified by my curiosity and, yes, real interest.

I was already in my father's bad books for changing focus from politics to popular culture and not even going for the internship interview he arranged with an editor friend at the *NY Post*. If he *knew*...

My cell vibrated in my bag again – probably Lara calling back. I fished around in the bottom, searching for it and checked out the call display.

Drake Morgan, MD.

He was using his own phone now. I ignored his call.

No freaking way.

I paid the taxi driver and ran up the stairs to my third floor flat in the old brownstone, slamming the door behind me. I removed my shoes, threw down my bag on the coffee table and paced my tiny apartment. What was I going to do now?

I flopped down on the couch and tried to get control over myself.

He wanted anonymity as well. As Lara said, he was a professional. Top in his field, he didn't want it getting around that he was *kinky*.

Drake Morgan – devastatingly *gorgeous* Drake Morgan – was *kinky*. Not only was he about the most handsome man I've ever laid eyes on, he was wealthy, powerful. And kinky. I felt an uncomfortably warm and swollen sensation between my legs at that thought.

I sighed heavily and glanced around my apartment. It was tiny but I was lucky to get a sublet in a rent controlled building. I insisted on using my scholarship money and work as a teaching assistant to pay for everything, not wanting any of my father's money, although he insisted in setting aside my allowance in a trust fund for when I 'came to my senses'. It meant I lived like a pauper, but it also meant I was independent. I wanted to show my father that I was as good as Heath.

My father *always* favored my older brother over me. Heath had always been the responsible one – the one who always said and did the right thing. Heath would *never* do something stupid like this... He married the right woman, had beautiful children and a respectable six-figure job in corporate finance.

Just when my father was starting to believe I had more to me, I had the breakdown, then fly-boy, and now *this*?

Crap. Just. *Crap*.

Drake Morgan called or texted five more times during the afternoon and evening, but I ignored each one and refused to listen to his voice messages.

Lara must have given him my email.

I deleted the bookmark of the website where that Dom's letters to his sub were posted. I didn't need any more reminders of this. Instead, I read over an article I was writing on social media, determined to put Dr. Drake Morgan out of my mind. I watched stupid videos on YouTube. When that became boring, I watched reruns of *Big Bang Theory*. Those were the kind of men I belonged with.

Not beautiful Dominant Drake Morgan, MD.

Then, I busied myself with cleaning. It was therapeutic. I cleaned out the pantry, throwing out anything past its due date, and then I rearranged my tiny cupboard so that the pots and pans were all in logical order and tidy the way I kept them when I worked in a kitchen during my undergrad years.

Finally, I washed the dishes in the sink, all the while listening to something calming – Faure. *Sicilienne*. I needed something soft and dreamy to make me forget what happened.

It was then someone knocked at my door. He wasn't actually at my *door*, was he? I peered through the peephole.

Crap... Yes. Dr. Morgan himself, his blue eye close to the hole.

Of all the *nerve*.

I pulled back and grimaced, but of course, he couldn't see me. Some idiot must have propped the front door open *again*.

"I don't want to talk to you, Dr. Morgan," I said, my hands still in yellow rubber gloves, soap suds dripping onto the parquet floor. I tried to sop up the puddle up with my foot, but all I ended up with was a wet foot, my pantyhose not thick enough to do anything.

"Kate, *please*, considering everything, call me Drake. And *trust* me. I have no interest in revealing anything about this to anyone. You, Lara and I are the only people who will ever know anything about this."

"Good," I said, relief flooding through me that he understood. "Thank you. Let's just forget this ever happened. *All* of it."

"No, *no*..." he said, and I heard a hint of protest in his voice. "No need for that. We can still do the interviews. You want to research the lifestyle and I'm happy to help in any way I can."

"No *way*," I said, shaking my head vigorously even though he couldn't see me. "I can't. Just forget about it."

"Seriously, Kate," he said, his voice light. I peered out through the peephole and watched him. "There's no need to call this off. I'm quite happy to teach you anything you want to know about," he said and leaned closer to the door as if trying to be private. "About submission. I'll even take you to a fetish night. Lara said you wanted to go. You could wear a mask, and no one would know who you are. I teach at Columbia in the department of medicine. I *love* teaching..."

"No," I said, slicing my hand sideways to cut him off, my hands looking ridiculous in rubber gloves. "It's completely out of the question. It's totally embarrassing."

"*Kate*..." he said, his voice trailing off. "I understand your interest in this completely. I have a lot of experience. You don't have to be embarrassed with me."

"You're kidding, right?" I said, shaking my head, leaning my shoulder against the door. "You don't think this is mortifying?"

"For me, *yes*. For you, *no*. I'm the one who should be mortified, not you. Here I was, hoping to impress you enough that you'd go out with me for a drink some night and you discover I'm a Dom. You're just doing this for a research paper, after all..."

Was that a hint of humor in his voice? He didn't believe this was just research. Lara must have said something.

"I'm changing topics," I said weakly, coming up with the excuse on the spot.

There was a pause.

"What are you going to write about instead?" he said, his voice slightly disbelieving.

"I don't know," I said, stalling for time. "Maybe the Administration's failure to act on climate change."

I heard him chuckle. "Sounds pretty boring in comparison to exploring why women are so excited by the prospect of submitting to a dominant man who knows how to release their inhibitions..."

Oh, *crap*. Why did that sound so – so *erotic* – when he said it? I couldn't help but conjure images of him naked, controlling someone sexually...

Me, for example.

"I should never have even considered it."

"It's topical. It's controversial."

"My father would *kill* me. I don't know what I was thinking."

There was another pause and I heard him sigh heavily. "Listen," he said, his voice conspiratorial. "We could stand here all night and talk through the door but I'm getting really hot standing here in my coat. Besides, it would be far more private if you just invited me in. Then your neighbor across the hall wouldn't keep peeking through the crack in her door and try to find out what we're talking about."

"That's Mrs. Kropotkin. I think her son's with the Russian Mafia."

I watch through the peephole as he waved to Mrs. Kropotkin.

"*Zdrastvooyte*," he said in what sounded like perfect Russian.

Mrs. Kropotkin closed her door, but not completely.

He turned right and then left, scoping the hallway out, his hands on his hips, his coat and suit jacket open, tie loosened. Even through the fisheye, he looked handsome.

"Why do you live in a place like this?" he said. "You come from a wealthy family."

"I don't want my father's money."

"Oh, yes, that's *right*," Drake said, and I could see a grin on his face. "Your father said something about you being a *socialist*..."

"I'm *not* a socialist. I studied political theory. There is a difference. I'm a liberal."

"Of *course*."

I made a face at that. He didn't believe me.

"My father would totally disown me if I joined the Socialist Party. As it is, I'm already a thorn in his side for my political positions and the fact I vote Democrat."

"*My* father was a socialist," Drake said, rubbing his jaw, which was covered by thick stubble, making him look all the more attractive. "A Trotskyite. I vote Republican. My father loved the Anonymous Group. He ate up WikiLeaks stuff. Probably would have stayed in Tent City if he was alive."

"I thought he – that *you* – are really rich."

"I am. He was. His company made a lot of money, but he started it for purely scientific purposes. He was what he called 'an accidental capitalist'. He saw the future in robotic surgery and wanted to help develop it. He was never in it for money. He drove one of those old Soviet cars. A really crappy, shit-brown *Lada*, but he liked the thought it was made in the Soviet Union. One of my favorite memories is of him tinkering with the engine, which was always breaking down. He spent so much trying to keep that piece of crap running."

I laughed at that and watched him through the peephole.

He smiled. "He was a wild man, full of life. Really gregarious." Drake said nothing for a moment. "I miss him."

My throat constricted at the sound of his voice – soft, sad. I missed my mother. I leaned my back against the door.

"What about your mother?" I said, wanting to keep him talking for some reason, remembering what he'd said about his mother leaving.

"She left us when I was ten."

"I'm *sorry*..."

"No, it's all right. I'm over it."

"How do you get over a mother leaving? Did your father remarry?"

"No," Drake said. "He never did. He travelled so much, he just kept the proverbial woman in every port. I had a succession of nannies and housekeepers to look after me."

I sighed. This was really stupid. Even I had to admit that I should let him in. We were having a nice conversation, even if now and then, I got the sense he was amused by me.

"You shouldn't have come here," I said. "It's very forward."

"I didn't want any misunderstanding between us, Kate, and I don't want your father to find out about me. I admire your father and value his friendship. He's like a second father to me. I admire *you*. I," he said, hesitating. "I heard so much about you from your father and others. I'd like to get to know you better."

I ignored that. "You think I would *ever* tell my father about you? I'd have to tell him how I found out about your, you know. *Kink*. No way."

"Kate, why don't you let me in and we can talk? I'm sweltering out here and need some water."

"There's no reason to talk," I said and took in a breath. "I'm not writing about BDSM any longer and so we have nothing to talk about."

"I'd like to hear about Mangaize," he said. "I was in Africa last year but never went to the camps. I was in several field hospitals in the Congo."

"In case you forgot, you warned me off you."

There was a pause. "Oh, *damn*. I did, didn't I?" He said nothing for a moment. "Can I take it back?"

"Nope. My father always said that if a man tells you he's not good for you, you should believe him."

"Your father is a very smart man."

I heard him sigh heavily. It made me want to invite him in. Someone who sighed like that had regrets for the bad things they'd done. They *want* to be good.

"Why *did* you warn me off?"

I watched out the peephole as he shook his head, rubbed his forehead.

"Isn't it obvious? You seemed so innocent, so young, so pure. I was sure you'd be horrified about my," he said, his voice low. "My *lifestyle*. I actually wanted to ask you out but didn't want to with Dave there, and then after the interview, I wanted to once again but I talked myself out of it. You were *Katherine*. Ethan's beloved daughter."

I said nothing. I wasn't horrified by the thought he was a Dominant. I was totally aroused by it but he could never know that. I could tell I'd be like putty in his hands if it ever came to that.

I didn't know what to think. He *did* good and that's really what counted. His father's foundation did many really great things in third world countries. Maybe he *did* like to tie women up and fuck them senseless, but those women wanted it.

Right then, *I* wanted it.

"I'm sorry," I said, and I was truly sorry. "I just can't."

He sighed again. "Well, I should go, then. I don't want Mrs. Kropotkin to learn all my secrets." He had a playful tone but when he next spoke, his voice fell a register so that it was low and deep. As I peered out the peephole, he leaned up against the door, his face next to the fish eye lens. "I'm sorry about all this," he said, his voice soft. Sexy. "If you want to talk – about the article, about me, or the lifestyle – *anything* – you just have to call. Text me."

"I don't think I should," I said, grimacing, regret filling me.

"Okay," he said and sighed once more. "Your call. But if you change your mind and want me, I'm willing. *Very* willing."

Oh, *damn*... That was loaded with meaning.

"Goodbye, Dr. Morgan."

"Good night, Ms. *Bennet*."

I closed my eyes and bit back a smile at the reference to *Pride and Prejudice*. Ms. Bennet. Was he likening us to Darcy and Elizabeth?

I watched out the peephole as he walked down the hallway to the stairs and out of my life.

Mrs. Kropotkin closed her door.

CHAPTER FIVE

A few days passed and I hadn't heard anything more from Drake Morgan. I had to admit I was a bit upset. I thought he'd at least make contact with me, text me, but nothing. Right about then I was starting to regret I'd turned down his request to come in, or go on a date.

Then, I mentally knocked myself in the head. What a silly woman I was... He was no good for me. I'd get into some kind of trouble if I let myself become involved with him. My father would hear about it somehow and I'd have one more big strike against me in his mind.

The following Thursday, I was sitting in my father's apartment, wearing a new cocktail dress he insisted buying for me because this was his first campaign fundraising dinner and he wanted me and Heath to be in attendance. I wore something his campaign stylist brought in for me, chosen from a selection of a dozen expensive dresses, shoes, and jewelry. We had to look perfect as a family. My father's new wife, Elaine, who was only a decade older than me, Heath's wife, Christie, and I made our choices. After the dresses were altered to fit us to perfection, I went to my father's apartment to be 'styled' by the makeup artist and hair stylist he hired to make sure we looked perfect. I wore a silky black dress with a plunging neckline and understated jewelry, my hair down.

She actually spray-painted makeup and eye shadow on my face. I couldn't *believe* it. My father whistled when he saw me, making me blush.

The dinner was catered, of course, and there was a bustle in the apartment as the servers and chef busied themselves setting the table and preparing the food. There was even a bar set up in the large dining room, fresh flower arrangements everywhere and hot appetizers – even Russian caviar flown in from St. Petersburg and fresh Alaskan salmon. An ice sculpture...

Father spared no expense for the event.

Twenty of 'his people' as he called them would be in attendance to discuss his candidacy. They would all be expected to make big donations. They would retire to the study after dinner and talk strategy.

I was given the itinerary. I would stand around with him and Elaine, with Heath and Christie, and have a drink. We'd mix and mingle before dinner. We'd have our meal. Then, the serious business would happen and I'd be excused. My only consolation was that Nigel would be in attendance.

Thank *God*.

I grew up in this old apartment and it held a lot of memories. It had been in my father's family for several generations – since the turn of the 20th century. One day, it would be Heath's. But tonight, it was the setting for my father's campaign event. All I really wanted to do was go home and work on my article on the IPCC's next round of climate talks, but this was family business.

Judge McDermott requested your attendance. You didn't turn Judge McDermott down.

The invitations went out two weeks earlier, and cocktails were set to start at 6:30 with dinner at 7:30. It was now 6:05 and I sat in the living room and checked my iPhone for messages from Dawn. I wanted to invite her but father said no, it was just family and *his people* tonight.

Someone arrived early and I wondered who it was? It was *so* not appropriate for guests to arrive before the allotted time.

Must be a buffoon who was rich but not used to the usual protocol for these kinds of events.

The event planner answered the door and in walked Dr. Drake Morgan looking like a hundred-million-odd bucks.

What?

I froze. Was he invited? I saw the guest list and never saw his name. Maybe he was just popping in? He did know my father...

He looked... *devastating*. While the organizer took his coat, I saw he was wearing a very expensive black suit with a deep royal blue shirt and black tie. His hair was sexy, black and shiny and just a bit wild from the wind outside, falling just below his collar in the back, and there was a fashionably-stylish amount of whiskers on his face. He scanned the entryway and then he saw me sitting in the living area in front of the fireplace. A surge of adrenaline went through me when our eyes met. He slipped his hands into his pockets and smiled, that quirk of a half-smile, his eyes twinkling.

Crap...

I wanted to go to my old bedroom and hide the way I used to when I was a kid, but I was almost twenty-five. I had to stay there and entertain our guests.

Drake just stared at me, as if he was waiting for me to invite him in. I sighed, then I went to him, my hands held behind my back because I just knew that he'd want to kiss my hand the way he had before.

"Doctor *Morgan*," I said, my voice a bit shaky.

"Ms. *Bennet*," he said softly, low enough so that no one could overhear. "You look... *breathtaking*."

I made a face at that, hiding my smile behind a hand. The dress I wore was very feminine. Black velvet with a square neckline that happened to show off my cleavage a bit too much for my tastes but the stylist assured me it was all the fashion.

Of course, Drake extended his hand and it was just then that my father breezed into the entryway.

"Oh, Drake, *there* you are."

I *had* to shake Drake's hand. My father would expect it. I held out my hand and Drake took it and he kissed my knuckles briefly, his eyes never leaving mine. I knew that if my father hadn't been there, he wouldn't have let go. I just *knew*. He was that kind of man – the kind who didn't let you forget that he was male and you were female.

Drake turned to my father. "Judge McDermott," he said, extending his hand. "Thanks once again for inviting me tonight."

My dad shook his hand, his other hand on Drake's shoulder. That meant my father really *really* liked Drake. He only did that with his closest friends or people he wanted to be.

"Drake, please, I insist you call me Ethan," he said in his gravelly voice that made him sound like George C. Scott in *Patton*. "I see you've already spoken to Katherine. Come in and make yourself comfortable." My father turned to me. "I invited Drake here a bit earlier than our other guests so you could give him the tour and show him your photographs from Africa." He turned to Drake. "They're really good and intimate, telling the story of her trip. You want to understand what makes my daughter tick? You see those photos. Very artistic. She has real talent. I have to take a call or I'd join you myself."

I was struck speechless. My father *purposely* invited Drake early so I could spend time with him – *alone*?

"Of course," I said, my voice barely above a whisper.

"Good, good. The others should start arriving in a while. Get Drake a drink, dear. Be a good hostess for me, will you? The bartender had to go get more wine and Elaine is still busy getting ready. Heath isn't here yet."

He left us, a huge smile on his face.

Drake stood there and grinned at me. His blue eyes were made even deeper blue by the shirt he wore. His hands were clasped behind his back.

"Would you like a drink?" I said, dutifully. I pointed to the bar in the dining room.

"Know how to make a vodka martini?" he said.

I went to the bar and found a martini glass and a shaker, some vodka and vermouth. I put in some ice, took out a bottle of Stolichnaya Vodka and poured a couple of ounces. I added the merest splash of vermouth and shook. Then I strained the mix into the martini glass.

"Lime or olive?" I asked, pointing to the small tray of lime zest and olives.

"Lime would be nice."

I put a twist of lime zest into the glass.

"How's that?"

"Perfect." He took the glass and had a sip, all the while staring at me over the rim. He sighed with pleasure, smacking his lips, and then pointed to me. "Where'd you learn to mix a martini?"

"I was a cocktail waitress for a few years during my undergrad. I trained as a bartender."

"That's right," he said. "Dave said you're paying your own way using scholarships and working part-time." He shook his head. "Stubborn girl. You're not having anything?"

"No," I said. "I tend to get a bit argumentative when I drink. Soda and lime for me."

He chuckled softly at that. "I like argumentative."

"I thought you were a Dom."

"I am, but that doesn't mean I like dumb women," he said. "So you get a bit loose-lipped when you drink? That tells me that you usually hold your true opinion close to the vest and only let out your honest thoughts and emotions when under the influence of some kind of mind-altering substance. Alcohol. Serotonin. *Dopamine*..." he said, his voice trailing off. "I'll keep that in mind in the future."

I frowned and pretended to ignore his comment, fixing myself a glass of soda with a squeeze of lime in it. Finally, I turned to him, avoiding his eyes, which I knew would be filled with amusement at my predicament.

"How come you're here? You weren't on my father's guest list."

"I'm one of your fathers biggest supporters. We met in the health club the other day and I offered my support for his candidacy for the House. He said he wanted to repay me after I looked after your injuries at the fundraiser. When I heard you were going to be in attendance tonight, I was only too happy to accept."

"If you think this changes things, you're wrong."

"Changes what, Ms. Bennet?"

I glanced at him. Of course, he was smirking.

"The whole business with the research agreement."

"That's entirely up to you. I'm still all yours, if you want me."

A thrill ran through me at that. What a master manipulator. He had to know how that affected me – offering himself to me as if he were mine to just take. I said nothing for a moment and we each took a big sip of our drinks.

"Kate, I'm so glad your father invited me. I've wanted to meet you ever since I met your father and he started talking about you, but he never brought you anywhere in public. I think I was a bit infatuated with you just from his description of you."

I frowned, not knowing what to say.

"You took photographs while you were in Africa?" he said, his voice soft, sexy. "I'd *love* to see them. See into that mind of yours and what makes you *tick*."

Everything he said took on a dual meaning. Was it me or was he really trying to be suggestive?

I took in a breath. It had been a while since I saw them myself and I didn't look forward to it. They were painful.

"I don't know what my father meant by that – what makes me tick. They're just photos." I started off down the hallway. "They're in the study."

My body was stiff, my cheeks already hot. I didn't want to have to engage him so I said nothing as I led him through the hallways to the study in the south corner of the suite. One entire wall in my father's study was devoted to my photos from Africa.

Drake closed the door behind us and took my arm, turning me around gently to face him. I stared at his hand on my arm and he finally let go.

"I'm sorry if you're unhappy that I'm here," he said and stepped closer to me. Too close. I took a step backwards, avoiding his eyes. "Your father wanted me to come early so that you and I could get to know each other. I'm glad he did."

"Why would he want us to get to know each other?"

"I guess because I said I thought you were a lovely young woman and wanted to get to know you better."

My cheeks heated at that. "I thought you weren't the kind of man someone like me should get involved with."

"You won't let me live that down, will you?"

"It's just that it would have been nice if I knew he invited you beforehand."

He stepped closer again, and this time, he pinned me against the huge mahogany desk. I half leaned half sat on the edge, keeping my glass of soda between us as if it was a shield, my eyes riveted to it.

"Would you have found some excuse not to attend?"

I said nothing, turning my face away from his too intense gaze. Of course I would have. I would have developed a nasty runny nose and cough and bowed out.

"I would have liked the choice," I said. "But of course, my father always has to have things his way."

"He's quite a dominant man himself."

I looked up at him, finally, but avoided his eyes. He smiled just a bit.

"I can't seem to escape them," I said, looking away.

"Maybe that's because you don't *want* to."

That made my back stiffen.

"I left home to get away from him. Listen," I said, pointing a finger at him, focusing on a button on his suit jacket instead of his eyes. "I can't have *anything* to do with you, do you understand? I'm writing my research paper about climate change so unless you know something about that, you and I have nothing to talk about."

He clucked his tongue. "You're trying too hard, Kate," he said, taking my finger in his hand and turning it away as if it was a weapon. Then, he took my hand and opened it, stroking my palm. "Me thinks the lady doth protest too much and that you do, in fact, want to have something to do with me."

I pulled my hand out of his and just stared at his chin so I could avoid his eyes, heat rising to my cheeks – yet *again*. How he made me blush! I was embarrassed by what he thought of me, knowing he was my father's friend.

"I don't like being around you," I said, my voice low.

"I think you *do*," he said, his voice firm, confident. "You *like* me. You don't like the fact that you like me. You don't want to like me but you can't help it."

"I don't *believe* you," I said, my jaw actually dropping that he had the audacity to say that. "You're," I said, fighting to control my emotions. "You're awfully certain of yourself."

I tried to sidle by him, but of course he took my arm once more.

"Yes," he said, his face just a few inches from mine, his expression intense. "I know what I want."

"Well, so do I. And it's not *you*."

What a liar...

I pulled my arm out of his hand and turned to the door, and just then, my father entered. He saw me and smiled.

"There you two are." He rubbed his hands together. "Has she shown you her photographs of Africa yet?"

Drake cleared his throat. "No, she hasn't."

"Come on, Kate. Show Drake your photos. I know he's interested. He's been there many times with Doctors Without Borders. You two have a *lot* in common." He took my hand and then he laid a hand on Drake's shoulder, pulling us both towards my wall of fame.

Ohhh. It's then I got it.

Crap.

My dad was *matchmaking*...

He pushed the two of us over in front of a wall filled with my pictures from Africa.

Then Peter entered the room. "Judge? There's a call for you."

My father raised his eyebrows. "Duty calls. I have to take that, but you two stay here. Kate, show him your photographs. I'll be back when my call is finished."

He left us alone. Drake turned to face me but I refused to look at him. I stood and gazed at the wall, my hands clasped around my glass in front of me.

"You're not really going to make me tell you about my trip to Africa are you?"

"I most certainly am," Drake said, his voice soft. "I'm truly interested. I've been to Africa many times. Besides, I want to see into you, Kate. Right inside. Please, tell me." He waved at the wall and watched me expectantly.

"Nothing's going to happen between us," I said. "The meeting was a mistake so you might as well forget it. There's no reason for you to see 'right inside' me. We're opposites. You vote Republican. I'm a Democrat."

"None of that matters, Kate, when we fuck. All that matters is that we both need what each other has to offer."

I inhaled sharply, shocked at how blunt he was being. "We're not going to...*fuck*," I said, forcing the words out.

"Whatever you say," he said, smiling. "I still want you to tell me about these photos. Your father is really proud."

I turned away and frowned. He had *huge* nerve. Of course, he *was* a Dominant. He was used to getting his way. I didn't want to talk about the photographs.

"There are a lot of painful memories in them."

"Just the happy ones, then."

I took in a deep breath and pointed to a large picture of Nigel and me in the center. Drake leaned closer.

"That's us, the day we arrived in Niger. Our driver took it. Nigel had been there before but I had no idea what to expect and I was so excited."

Drake peered at the picture. Nigel was dressed in khakis, wearing an outback hat with tiny corks dangling from strings on the brim. He grinned at the camera. I stood beside him, my face beaming. I had a huge hat on with a floppy brim and dark sunglasses. We stood on a dirt road and the sun blazed in a heartless sky.

I told him about several others – bright-faced children smiling up at the camera. Aid workers in UN uniforms, stacking sacks of food, others pouring milk into cups or handing out packets of food and bottles of water. Tents and make-shift shacks made out of cardboard and corrugated metal, held together by rope.

I stopped talking when we came to a series of more graphic photos. Inside a medical tent were several babies being weighed. Some of them looked healthy, others were emaciated, their eyes huge in tiny faces. Women waved papers over their babies to keep the flies away. Tiny corpses wrapped up in dirty blankets.

A photo of the open desert, the hard dirt and the sky almost the same beige color, a few bits of scrub brush dotted across the landscape. In the distance, Chinua and Alika and their baby Maya alone against the stark emptiness. Just seeing it brought my emotions to the surface, my throat constricting.

"What's this one?" Drake asked, pointing to it.

I covered my mouth and didn't look at him.

"I can't." I shook my head.

He tried to turn my face towards his but I fought him, not wanting him to see the tears that stung the corners of my eyes. I turned my body away. He touched my arm softly, and then let his hand drop and just that small show of understanding warmed me to him a bit – against my better judgment.

Before we got a chance to speak more about the photos, in walked Nigel and our little bit of private time was over. Nigel strode right over to us and I smiled with relief. I glanced quickly at Drake and put my drink down for the hug that I knew was coming.

"Kate, my *dear*." Nigel bent down to me. "Your father let slip that Dr. Morgan was coming a bit early, and so I thought I'd be chivalrous and offer my services..."

We hugged and he kissed me on both cheeks. I was so glad to see him. He rescued me, and I clung to him as if he were a life preserver.

"Can I get you a drink?" I asked.

"Please." Nigel smiled at Drake but by his sour expression, it was clear he wasn't pleased Drake was here. "My usual."

I nodded and left the two men standing in front of the wall of photographs.

When I returned with a glass of red wine for Nigel, the two men were staring each other down as if in some disagreement. I smiled up at Nigel and then turned to Drake without meeting his eyes.

"How is your drink, Dr. Morgan?"

"Please, call me Drake." He bent down a bit, trying to catch my eye, smiling. "Considering. And it's still fine, thank you."

I caught Nigel giving Drake the stink eye over my head.

What the hell was that about?

Guests arrived over the next half hour and I watched Drake meet and shake hands with two-dozen people. All the while, I tried to stay close to Nigel, but Drake was determined to prevent Nigel from acting as my wingman, stepping beside me whenever I was alone. Then Nigel would come to the rescue and get between us, try to take me over. It was almost comical to watch.

A half-hour in, we stood in the living room when my father pulled Nigel and me back into the study, waving several of the people he'd been speaking with to follow, including Drake.

"Kate has some wonderful photographs from her trip to Africa. Come dear," he said to me, "and talk about your trip."

I frowned, not wanting the limelight he was forcing me into. Once inside the room, the three of us stood in front of the wall of photographs, each one mounted and arranged in several rows.

"Go ahead, dear," my father said to me, ushering me to his side. "Tell us about your trip. Start here, with this one."

I recounted arriving in Africa, of the airport and the questionable plane we took to Niger. I spoke about the UN High Commission for Refugees aid agency I worked for, my term lasting a month and how we distributed supplies and formula to mothers and babies in the camps. I described all the photos with the exception of the one that I couldn't talk about – the empty desert with the tiny figures in the distance.

"Tell them about Alika and Chinua," my father said, touching my back as if to encourage me. He turned to the guests gathered around. "A couple and their baby that Kate and Nigel rescued from the desert."

He turned back expectantly. I tried to force a smile but it pained me to even think of them. Finally, I took in a deep breath, but my voice betrayed my reluctance.

I told the small group about my first trip to the camp, when Nigel and I made our way out to Mangaize, taking the main road there. It was the height of the exodus from the war zone and there were thousands on the road, walking to the camps to escape the bloodshed. We were travelling in a truck, bringing in some supplies.

I shook my head as I told the story. "Each time a vehicle passed, they had to walk down and then walk back up the ditches and they were exhausted, having walked for hours or days."

I turned to Nigel, who nodded as if in encouragement.

He took up the narrative. "Kate finally said, enough is enough. Let's be the one to go in the ditch, and so we did. We drove off the main road and took to the open desert, bypassing the road and the thousands of refugees. We were driving in the middle of nowhere and off in the distance, the driver saw some people and so we went to them, to see if they needed help. They were a young couple with a newborn. They'd been walking for days, and were quite lost, going in the wrong direction. If we hadn't found them..." Nigel turned to me.

I picked up the story, emotions already building. "Chinua, the husband, had given his wife all his food and was..." I stopped and covered my mouth with a hand, shaking my head. Even two years later, the emotions were so close to the surface.

Nigel touched my shoulder then turned to the others, taking over.

"They'd been walking for several days and had run out of food and water. He was so weak, he had to crawl."

I nodded. "He crawled like a crab because his knees were bloody," I said, my voice barely audible. "Alika was carrying her baby. They hadn't named him yet because they weren't even sure if he would live. I thought he was a newborn because he was so small, but he was three months old and starving. Her breasts," I said, my voice a whisper. "She had no milk left. They were like deflated balloons."

Then, I couldn't go on and covered my mouth, forcing a smile, unable to continue. Nigel finished the story for me.

"We put them in the back of the truck and took them to the camp. Once Chinua knew they were safe, and that they had food and water, he up and died despite everything they did for him." Nigel turned to me and squeezed my shoulder. "We were able to save Alika and her baby Maya, though. They got I.V.s and food and the last time we checked, both were doing well."

A murmur went through the people listening, and I smiled, but I felt anything but pleased to be telling the story. I saw the camps only briefly, staying for only a few weeks, but it was enough. At times, they were terrible places of death, especially when the famine was raging and dozens, if not hundreds, died each day.

I wrote objective, journalistic pieces that described in stark language the horror of the wars and human-induced famine. What my pieces didn't reveal was the human behind them, horrified by what I saw, so much so that I had a breakdown.

My father – former Marine – smiled like a proud parent, unaware that I was on the verge of tears. That was how he'd been all my life, blind to my true emotions like an idiot.

"Excuse me," I said and squeezed Nigel's arm. I had to leave the group, who were now speaking amongst themselves and examining photos. I went down the hall to my old bedroom and sat on the bed, trying to get a hold of myself.

Then, the door opened.

Drake.

I glanced away, my cheeks heating – partly in anger that he followed me, partly in embarrassment that he'd see my tears.

"I'd like to be *alone*," I said.

"Being alone is the last thing you need right now." He sat beside me on the bed, close enough that his thigh pressed against mine, his shoulder against mine. Resting his elbows on his knees, he turned to look at me. "I'm sorry. Your father doesn't seem to understand how upset Africa still makes you."

I frowned. Drake *understood*.

"He always sees everything, every event, every word, for its strategic purpose. How it can aggrandize him and our family – or hurt us. He doesn't really pay attention to people. What he said about those photographs being key to what makes me tick? He thinks it means I'm some great humanitarian – some angel of mercy – but really, I was just a student looking for a topic for my honors thesis. I had *no* idea what I got myself into."

"You didn't like Africa?"

I said nothing for a moment, my arms wrapped around myself.

"I hated it – the corruption. It was so hard. Painful. As soon as I could, I changed my topic. I couldn't *do* it. I'm not strong enough, but he can't see that because it would mean *his* daughter isn't up to snuff."

"You saw the worst of the worst." He turned to me, trying to catch my eye. "Where the people have resources, they're full of hope. I see it in the hospitals. The young doctors and nurses – they've been trained in America and they want to raise their countries out of poverty."

He pressed his shoulder against mine. I didn't say anything but I didn't move away either. It was kind of sweet what he did, trying to comfort me.

"I admire you for going. You didn't have to so that does say something about you, what makes you 'tick'."

"You'd be wrong to think that." My voice was bitter. "My father has *no idea* what makes me 'tick'. He practically chose my thesis topic and arranged everything. I *wanted* to do something on the fine arts, but *no*. It had to be political."

Drake frowned. "Your father *chose* your honors thesis topic?"

"You're surprised?" I turned away. "You obviously don't know my father."

"What did *you* want to do?"

I didn't say anything for a moment. Finally, I sighed. "What did *I* want to do? *I* wanted to do a series on young artists in Manhattan, and how they're using social media and new technology in their art, but that was too 'airy-fairy' for him, as he put it. He only sees art for its value as an investment, not for its social or cultural value. I tried to explain but he just dismissed me." I frowned, my emotions so close to the surface. "I was too much of a chicken to fight him and do what I really wanted."

"I'm sorry." He sounded as if he actually meant it. "University should be a time when you explore who you are and what excites you. It shouldn't be a time to please your parents."

I turned and looked at him, and it was one of the few times our eyes met – *really* met. I actually looked into his eyes, like it was for the first time, and it surprised me how much it affected me. I noticed once more how beautiful his eyes were – how blue, his eyelashes long and dark. In that moment, something passed between us. *Attraction*. I felt it in my belly, in my groin. In a moment of irrationality, I wanted him to lean over and kiss me, but he just smiled. Just a brief smile.

Then he glanced away.

The door opened and my father popped his head in.

"Oh, *here* you are," he said and smiled. "I *thought* you two might have a lot in common. Sorry to interrupt, but my dear wife has announced that dinner is served."

CHAPTER SIX

Of course, my father seated Drake next to me. I was on one side of him with Drake next to me and Heath was on the other, with Christie next to him. My stepmother Elaine sat at the other end of the table. Quite the socialite, she knew how to entertain, always knowing the right thing to say.

Drake smiled as he pulled my chair out for me, the perfect gentleman. I could tell he enjoyed this whole situation, amused that my father was trying to match us up. I didn't know why he was so pleased – my father probably saw Drake as prime Grade A marriage material and I knew Drake was *not* into that – not from what Lara told me when she and I spoke after the fundraiser. He had his marriage and divorce and wasn't into romance. He wanted his kinky sex and that was it. He had his work and he had his band and he had his subs. No girlfriends. No fiancé and certainly no wife.

My father was so *wrong* about him it almost made me laugh out loud. Drake must have been chuckling up his sleeve at my clueless father trying to match me up with a Dominant in the BDSM community who only saw women as props for his sexual kinks.

But there was that *moment* when Drake and I were in the bedroom when I felt something resembling humanity from him. No grin, no leer, no gloating superiority.

Like he *understood*.

I was probably just projecting. I couldn't let myself get taken in by his suave exterior. He was a Dom and he wanted his way in all things. He probably figured he could use my father's desire to match me with him to get some kinky sex out of me. I'd have to do everything I could to dissuade him that I was available. I'd have to squelch the stupid physical attraction I had for him and for which I hated myself.

I'd done everything I could to stay away from bad boys since Kurt but I got this crazy idea that I could research this world without getting mixed up in it. Drake was just too damn gorgeous for my own good.

I ate my meal in silence, aware of him next to me, how he turned to me when he spoke with my father, but I refused to engage him. Still, I couldn't help but notice everything about him – at least, everything about him from the neck down. I refused to look in those eyes of his. I always saw him laughing at me, a twinkle of pleasure or amusement in his eyes, and it infuriated me.

Even his hands were gorgeous. Surgeon's hands. His fingers were long and tapered. Not huge meat hooks and I could imagine how they'd feel if he touched me. He was a doctor and knew the human body like no other and that did something strange to me. There was virtually no hair on his knuckles – maybe he scrubbed them so much, it wore off. He had a school ring on his finger and on the other hand was a large aquamarine. He had a leather strap of some kind on his wrist, with what looked like tooling, but I didn't want to look too closely or ask what it meant. I wondered if it wasn't a symbol of his bondage kink. Why else would a surgeon wear a leather strap on his wrist?

The talk was pleasant enough – about the weather, sports teams, the wine, which Drake took pains to praise. He actually sounded like he knew what he was talking about. Boy, he sure knew how to flatter my father, who loved to show how he had refined taste in *everything*.

It was like a love-fest between the two of them and I wanted to slam my knife down on the table and expose Drake for what he was just to see the look on my father's face but I swallowed my anger. If Drake even *tried* to move forward with this stupid agreement, I'd threaten to do just that.

Luckily, Drake didn't try to engage me in a conversation, but my father did several times, trying to get me to tell Drake all about my Master's scholarship, my award for the investigative piece on West Africa, my volunteer work. What he didn't ask me to tell Drake about was what really mattered to me – art, *my* art. It was never any interest to my father, even when my teachers praised me and encouraged me to go into Fine Arts in college.

I sat and steamed, angry at myself for letting my father rule my life.

He was just so damn *powerful*, controlling and certain that everything he believed and did was right. He ran our home like a drill sergeant and his court like one as well. I heard talk of him, and I read some of his decisions. I wouldn't *ever* want to go before him if I was involved in anything slightly morally questionable.

He could accept financial fraud. But moral failings?

No.

It wasn't that he was truly religious. Far from it. Going to Mass was just for show and to make sure he kept the Roman Catholic community behind him.

How he'd *freak* if he knew about Drake...

It almost made me want to get involved with Drake just so I could turn to my father and say, "*Look at your wonderful saint of a man, Daddy. He likes to tie me up and fuck me, make me crawl on my knees to him, kiss his foot.*"

Wouldn't that just about make him *explode*?

I glanced sideways at Drake and he met my gaze, his expression dark, and it was like this current flowed between us.

I tore my eyes away. I could *never* do it.

Just. *Never*.

Finally, dinner was over and those of us not part of my dad's 'people' left for the living room while dad escorted the men into the study for his strategy session. As we left the dining room, Drake took my arm and stopped me.

"Can we talk later?"

I glanced at his hand on my arm. He didn't let go.

"We have nothing to talk about."

"Please? Just hear me out."

I exhaled. My father stood in the hallway, and he kept glancing back to us, his eyes judging. As usual.

"I was going to leave after we 'ladies' have our tea."

"OK. I'll come by your place. Can we talk *inside* your apartment instead of through the door this time?"

He grinned, and that smile made him look so sexy.

"I'd rather you didn't come to my apartment."

"Fine," he said. "Why don't you wait for me and I'll give you a ride home when we're done here."

My dad came over, his eyebrows raised.

"Hey, sweetie, you're detaining Drake. We have important business to attend to."

I looked between Drake and my father. Drake nodded like it was OK.

"We'll just speak in the car." His voice dropped to a lower register, sexy and deep and he had the audacity to hold three fingers up. "I won't come in. I promise. Scout's Honor."

I exhaled. "Very *well*."

He finally let go of my arm and he and my father walked off, my father's arm around Drake's shoulder like they were already father and son-in-law.

If the situation wasn't so upsetting, it would make me laugh so hard at my father for being so out of it.

Later, while I sat with Christie and Elaine, and we finished our tea, Elaine leaned over to me and smiled.

"That Drake Morgan is something. Quite the catch."

"Yes, he is, I guess." *If you're fishing for sharks...*

I laughed to myself. If they only *knew...*

I hung around until my dad finished meeting with 'his people' about his campaign for the House seat that was going to be vacant, all the while trying to talk myself into leaving before Drake came for me to drive me home. I could use my dad's limo service and go home by myself, but I just knew that Drake would come to my apartment and stand outside my door to say whatever it was he wanted to say.

He wasn't some college boy. He was a grown man. Divorced. A neurosurgeon. A Dominant. Trouble, like Dawn said that night in the bar. Oh, how right she was.

I did date a 'nice guy' after Kurt and I broke up, but Greg was *so* nice, so accommodating, so into equality, that he wouldn't even kiss me first. I had to kiss *him* first, and it made me so insecure, like he wasn't really attracted to me, or didn't really feel much desire for me.

Stupid girl insecurities, but I was used to the guy making the moves. At least then you knew he wanted you.

With Kurt, I always knew he wanted me. He said so, *often*. He told me how much he wanted me, and how often and how he wanted to do it. He'd whisper in my ear when we were in public and I'd be so ready when we got back to my apartment that I'd practically melt.

Then, he started increasing the pressure on me, suggesting we role play and that he'd sneak into my apartment one night and be waiting for me to mock-rape me. He wanted to smack my ass while we were having sex. Even though he promised we'd agree to everything before hand, and would only do what I was comfortable with, it *scared* me. Yielding power.

"Come on, *sweet stuff*," he said. "Everyone's adding in a bit of kink in their sex after those books."

I said no. I told him I was just an ordinary girl, with ordinary vanilla tastes. I had no interest in getting my ass hit or being scared to death when entering my dark empty apartment late at night. He did it anyway, one night lying in wait for me, and it scared me so much, I screamed and threw something at him, almost hitting him in the head. I cried, and told him to leave.

Then I called him over and over again, apologizing, asking him to come back and for us to work things out because he made me feel something again, for the first time after Mangaize.

Like I was alive and filled with desire. Like I was wanted.

Really wanted.

He never spoke to me again.

I had to look deep inside of myself to understand why I even tried to get him back, considering he didn't accept my 'no' about the mock-rape and spanking. Was I so desperate for male attention that I'd accept abuse?

My mother would be *horrified*.

Dawn told me to forgive myself, but I had a hard time and for months, I moped around my apartment, dressed in flannel pajamas, watching *Seinfeld* re-runs and eating Häagen Dazs. Now, here I was, with some *other* man hanging around me who liked to enforce his will over women, looking at me like I was a piece of steak he couldn't wait to eat.

Finally, the meeting broke up about an hour and a half after dinner finished and the men left, one by one, shaking my dad's hand and thanking us for the hospitality. I noticed that Drake hung back, taking his time, speaking to Christie and Elaine. Finally, he was the last one and I went to get my coat and bag while he shook my father's hand. The two spoke to each other in hushed voices.

"What are you two conspiring about?" I kissed my dad on the cheek.

"Us? Conspire?" My dad laughed. "Just how to take over the world." He smiled and glanced at Drake. I said my goodbyes to Elaine and Christie, and then Drake escorted me out of the apartment. Once the door to the suite closed, he put his hand on the small of my back and guided me gently towards the elevator.

"I didn't think you'd actually wait for me." He pressed the button. "I thought you'd be long gone, so I'm pleasantly surprised."

"I said I'd wait."

The door to the elevator opened and I entered, Drake behind me. We stood side by side, with him just a bit behind me. He leaned over to press the floor button, and just happened to lean in close to me while he did, brushing against me. Was that a smirk on his face?

"Why are you smiling?"

"Oh, let's just said that I have a hard time riding alone in elevators with pretty women and keeping a straight face these days."

I glanced away, my face heating. Oh. *Right*. The elevator scene...

"Don't get any ideas."

"Kate, I've already had so *many* ideas. And that's what I wanted to talk to you about."

Oh, *God*... How do you handle a man telling you he's had ideas about being with you? A wave of something swept through me, leaving my knees just a bit weak.

The elevator arrived in the basement and we went to the guest parking area and his car. He helped me in, then closed the door for me.

What a gentleman. Opened the door for me, so chivalrous, but wanted to tie me up and make me kneel to him like a vassal to some feudal Lord.

Of course, then I couldn't get the image of me kneeling at his feet, naked, him fully dressed out of my mind. I thought of the movie *9 ½ Weeks* and how the woman crawled on her hands and knees to her lover. I couldn't stop the way my body responded to those images, even as I told myself it would be humiliating.

"Well, talk away," I said, trying to get that image out of my mind.

We drove out of the parking garage and through the streets towards my apartment. A light snow fell, huge flakes drifting down lazily.

"I know it really upset you that I'm the one Lara was trying to match you with for your 'research'. You wanted anonymity and are embarrassed that I know who you are. I think we should still go through with the agreement you wanted – for one reason. Who could be safer than me?"

I frowned. He *wasn't* safe. He was a slippery slope.

"How are *you* safe?"

"I know and admire your father, so there's no way I'd want to screw things up with him. I admire you and don't want you to think less of me than you probably already do. I understand your need for anonymity, at least, for no one to find out what you're doing. You understand my need for secrecy, too. We're not going to expose each other."

I watched out the window, not sure what I thought about what he said. Part of me thought he was right. He would be very careful. He understood.

"Look, I know you're worried about your father finding out about your interest in BDSM," he said, his voice low. "But I'm well-respected in my field and I don't want to screw that up. If people found out I frequent fetish nights and have submissives, it would hurt my reputation. *You* want to learn about the lifestyle and understand female submissives and male Dominants? I can help you. We can *pretend* to be dating, and that way there'd be no reason that we couldn't be seen together. We wouldn't have to make up excuses in case anyone found us together. I won't do anything you don't want me to do. We can write it all out, formally in an agreement, and I'll stick to it. The only way anything will happen is if *you* want it to and specifically negotiate for the agreement to change. I am an honorable man in that respect. You can talk to Lara if you want verification."

We drove along, and I said nothing. He was right, of course. The cat was now out of the bag with us. Both of us knew each other's inclinations, even if mine were purely for research purposes.

Lara said he was absolutely trustworthy.

"Drake, it's just..." I shook my head, my cheeks hot. "I'm so embarrassed."

"I know." He reached out to take my hand and squeezed it before I could pull it away. "How do you think I feel? Your father actually *likes* me. You don't know how much that means to me." Finally, he let go of my hand and glanced quickly at me.

I really didn't know what to say.

"I know you and he don't really get along well," Drake said softly. "But he's like the father I *wish* I'd had. My own father was so self-absorbed and away from home so much that I always felt as if I was just not important enough. He was always, *'Hey, I love you man,'* but I never felt it. If he had loved me, why was he always away?"

He said nothing for a moment as we sat at a stoplight. "Your father is maybe *too* involved in your life but as someone who felt neglected, I envy you that. When I met your father at my dad's funeral, he took me under his wing immediately because he and my dad were such good friends. So, if he found out about *me*..." He shook his head. "I've read some of his judgments. I know what he's like."

"And yet you *like* him."

"He's like a second father to me. He's smart and competent and powerful and has so much history with my dad. And he *likes* me, Kate."

We arrived at my apartment and when the car stopped I got out and started walking up the steps. He followed me quickly to the door.

"*Kate*." He took my arm and tried to turn me to face him. "Don't run away. I want to talk. Straighten this out between us."

"There's nothing to straighten out. We're square, OK? Let's just go our separate ways."

As usual, someone had propped open the door to the building so their cousin or uncle or homey could come in. I opened the door and kicked the piece of cardboard aside that was holding it open, my hands shaking just a bit. I went inside and of course, he followed me before the door closed.

I glared at his chin. "You said you wouldn't come in."

"You said you'd talk to me."

"I did."

"*Kate*..." He put his arm out and stopped me before I reached the stairs, his hand on the wall. I stood there and stared at the leather strap on his wrist.

I waited. He kept his arm like that.

"Are you really going to try to stop me from going upstairs?"

"I want to keep talking."

"Is this what Dominants do? Always try to control things?"

"*Yes*." He exhaled heavily. "I like control Kate. I'm a Dom. It's what I do."

I stood there staring at his arm, at that darned leather strap with ornate carving in it.

"I'm listening."

"Write up an agreement, include anything you want in it, any terms, and I'll sign."

I considered, stalling for time so I didn't have to answer. "What *is* that?" I pointed to the strap. "Is it some kind of kinky *bondage* thing?"

He let his arm drop and fingered the leather strap.

"This?" He twisted it on his wrist so that the carving was on top. "No, it's not some kinky *bondage* thing, although I do have a real leather fetish." He smiled as he stared at the strap, running his finger over the carving. "I love leather, how it feels and smells, and how really fine hide warms when it's against naked skin. I make my subs wear leather corset dresses, naked underneath, but I'm thinking of adding in a garter belt and black stockings with a seam in the back." He grinned at me. "And thigh high leather stiletto boots when we go to fetish parties, but maybe in your case, I'd settle for shorter heels..."

I couldn't hold back a grin and turned my head away. "Not fair," I said, trying desperately not to like him.

"*What?*"

"You trying to make me like you."

He laughed out loud. "See? You *do* like me."

I said nothing for a moment, trying to get my face under control. Beside me, Drake cleared his throat and continued.

"Really soft leather is also nice for restraints, but you have to know how to tie them carefully." He glanced at me and his eyes were intense under those dark arched brows. "But this?" He looked back at the strap. "This was a gift from a patient."

"What does it say?"

"It's French. Here," he said and held his wrist closer. "Do you read French?"

"Just a bit." I took his wrist in my hand and examined the carving.

He cleared his throat. "It's from *Fern Hill*."

I frowned. "I know that poem. Dylan Thomas." I could make out a single line – the last line about singing in his chains like the sea.

"You know it?" he said, his tone surprised. "It's my favorite poem. The end especially."

Then he recited the end of the poem.

I stood there in silence for a moment, a bit shocked that he knew poetry well enough to be able to quote it. I cleared my throat, which felt just a bit choky.

"My favorite line was something about being easy under the apple boughs."

He smiled. "That's the first line." Then, to my surprise, he recited it and I just stared at him, not knowing what to say.

"Do you know the whole poem by heart?"

He shook his head. "I can only remember the first and last stanzas. I memorized the whole thing once, back in college. I loved it because it made me think of my childhood. How happy I was and how unaware that soon, it would all come crashing down."

"How did it come crashing down?" I asked.

He shook his head. "Oh, you know. Life in general." He said nothing for a moment. "I had a patient, a young boy of thirteen from South Africa." He returned his gaze to the leather strap on his wrist. "He suffered from inherited dystonia. A muscle contraction that makes the body contort. He had it all his life. It's hell, but he had such a great attitude. The Foundation brought him here a few years ago to do the operation and we became friends. He made this after he recovered from surgery and went back home. You know – touristy 'native' jewelry sold in the gift shops. I wear it because it reminds me why I became a doctor, and a surgeon."

"Oh, that's..." I said, taken aback by this side of him and a bit embarrassed that I automatically assumed it was about his bondage kink. "That's so... *nice*."

An awkward silence passed between us.

"But the quote? How did he know to include that?"

"He was here for six months and we arranged for him to have tutors. He liked poetry the most of all his classes. He asked me what my favorite line of poetry was and I told him."

He looked at me, his expression thoughtful. Then, he dropped his hand and his face changed. That grin started and the more human moment passed.

"So about our *agreement*. You can include sex if you want, but remember I'm only *so* kinky. I have *limits*..."

There. He had to ruin such a nice human moment by turning it back to sex.

I hesitated, considering. I could write a really great paper on the issue. I had Lara and now I had Drake. Both were ways into this world for me as a researcher and journalist. Plus it would satisfy my own curiosity.

"Give me your phone," he said, motioning to my bag.

"Why?"

"Just give it to me."

I reached into my bag without thinking, handing him my iPhone. He opened my contacts, entering his information.

"There," he said. "At least consider what I've suggested. Draw up an agreement with whatever you want included and send it to me in an email."

I took back my phone and started up the stairs since he was no longer blocking me. He called up after me when I reached the top.

"Remember, send me an email. I'll sign anything you want."

"Goodbye, Dr. Morgan."

"Good *night*, Ms. Bennet."

I rolled my eyes and suppressed a smile.

He texted me before I barely even had a chance to get my coat off.

You seem surprised that I like poetry. What you must think of me... I'm not a Neanderthal, Kate. Write up an agreement between us. Whatever you want. Include as much detail as you feel is necessary. I'll honor it to the letter. Your father would be only too pleased if we were to date and that can be our cover.

At least he thinks I'm a decent sort...

I texted him back a single line.
Imagine how surprised he'd be to find out how wrong he is...
That would hurt and I knew I was being a bitch, but I couldn't help but respond that way to his faux injured tone...
Ouch...
I smiled, but a part of me felt bad. He seemed to really like my father.

After I got into my pajamas, I called Lara to ask her for more details about Drake.

"You won't believe it. Drake was at my father's fundraising dinner tonight."

"He told me he's friends with your father."

"Still, you'd think he could just let this drop, considering how much it upset me. He didn't. He pushed things."

"He's a natural Dom, Kate. He knows what he wants and he does what it takes to get it."

I sighed. "Should I do this?"

"You have to be the one to decide. But know this. Dominants, even the ones into pain, are serious about recognizing and respecting their sub's limits. It's a source of pride for us to know what a sub needs and how far to push to enhance their experience. It's what drives us – having that control and responsibility and giving a sub what they need through satisfying our own needs."

I said nothing, letting that sink in a bit.

"Kate, a vanilla man will never give you what you really need and you'll end up feeling unloved and insecure, unable to respond the way you could with a Dom. A vanilla woman can't give a Dom what he needs. He feels as if he can't be himself during sex, frustrated that he can't take control, make things right – *better*. Doms and subs. We need each other. It's beautiful when it works out."

"It all sounds so nice but can I trust him?"

"You can trust him. Kate, I've known him for *years*."

Much later, as I sat at my desk revising the document I was drafting, I composed an email with the agreement as an attachment. I'd just had a warm bath and was still wet, wrapped in a towel.

I held my finger over the mouse, the little hand hovering over the send button. Then, I pressed send. Immediately, I checked my sent folder and re-read it, biting my nail as I worried I had just made a huge mistake.

From: **McDermott, Katherine M.**
Sent: **November 07, 11:31 PM**
To: **Morgan, D. L.**
Subject: **The Agreement**
Attachments: The Agreement.doc (50 KB)

Drake: I've attached the agreement for you to review and agree to.

Please don't push any of my limits. I know it's in your nature to do just that.

If you do, I'm gone.

Seriously.

Kate

I open the documented and re-read the terms, worried he was going to try to seduce me. I had my father to thank that I knew my way around a legal document.

I printed off the agreement and held it in my hand. After imagining what he'd tell me about his practices and preferences, I realized I was really afraid. It wasn't him I feared. It was fear of myself and how I might just respond to him and to the lifestyle.

I received an email the next morning from him.

From: **Morgan, D. L.**
Sent: **November 08, 5:31 PM**
To: **McDermott, Katherine M.**
Subject: **The Agreement**
Attachments: **The Agreement.doc (50 KB)**

Katherine, I received your agreement and will read it over. We can discuss when we meet.

Drake

That Friday, I sent him a text, deciding I might as well set up a few dates for the interviews.

> *Why don't you send me your schedule so we can set up some dates to meet next week and discuss the lifestyle. We can discuss the agreement at that time. I'm pretty free for the next couple of weeks with the exception of Monday and so I'd like to get started with the interviews.*

He responded within a few minutes.

> *I'm pretty busy all week with my surgical slate and personal commitments... What are you doing on Monday night? What time are you done? I could make a late meal at a restaurant, if you're free after 10 PM.*

I frowned. Monday night was *not* a good night. I was going to Carnegie Hall with my father and his wife to hear Gorecki's

Symphony Number 3. It was very meaningful to me because my mother and I used to go each year.

I'm going to Carnegie Hall with my father and his wife.

A special Veteran's Day performance featuring Dawn Upshaw at the Stern Auditorium, on the Perleman Stage, the concert was part of the Great Singers program. He texted me back in a few moments.

I want to take you.

What? No freakin' *way*. I always cried during the performance, unable to hold my emotions in check and there was no way in *hell* I wanted to be anywhere near Drake Morgan when I was an emotional wreck.

We could meet after. I don't know if I'm ready to start the whole 'dating' ruse yet...

I chewed my bottom lip, wondering if he'd accept my alternate arrangement but he had his own ideas.

> *We could meet there by accident during intermission. I could invite you out for a late meal. I'm sure your father would be pleased. We could start the whole interview process.*

I didn't respond, trying to find a way to say no. As if he sensed it, he texted back right away.

> *I'll have you home by midnight as I have surgery early in the morning. No funny business. Scout's Honor...*

Damn him. I couldn't really find an excuse to say no quickly enough.

> *I'll go for coffee and dessert with you but this is a special family event. We always have a family dinner before the concert.*

He wouldn't take no for an answer.

Can you hold off eating and join me at The Russian Tea Room? I feel like some Pelmeni and blini. Have you been and tried their blini? To die for. I would love company.

I sighed and dialed my father's number.

"Hi, Dad," I said, resigned to this. "Drake Morgan asked if I could go for dinner with him after the concert on Monday."

"That's great," he said, sounding so enthusiastic. "No problem."

"We usually have a special family dinner before..."

"I know you'd rather be with Drake, so go right ahead, dear. You know, you're old enough to date now," he said, laughing. "Why don't you invite him to come sit with us? I know you'd enjoy having some company."

Crap. No help from him, of course.

"I don't think so, Dad. He's probably busy with his band."

I texted Drake back.

My father is very rigid about these things but I told him you invited me to go for a meal after the concert and he said I could miss our usual family dinner. Boy, does he like you... If he only knew...

He texted right back.

He doesn't know and I want things to stay that way. I don't want him finding out about my... pastimes. Just keep that in mind when you worry that I'll push your boundaries. I won't.

I responded immediately.

I'll hold you to that. Good afternoon.

Of course, his response was almost getting predictable.

I'll meet you in the lobby during intermission. Until then, Ms. Bennet...

I couldn't help but smile at that, despite hating him just a bit for it. I could almost see the twinkle in his oh-so-blue eyes...

CHAPTER SEVEN

On Monday night, my father and Elaine and I arrived at Carnegie Hall for the concert. As we took our places in my father's box, I settled in next to the overhang looking out at the seats below and checked over the program. Ms. Upshaw was singing a selection of music, but it was the first part of the evening that I looked forward to the most. *Symphony No. 3 –* the second movement from Symphony of Sorrowful Songs, written about the Second World War, the lyrics comprised of a young woman's prayer written on a wall in a Gestapo Prison in Poland.

Every year, my mother and I would attend a live performance of this symphony somewhere in the country and neither of us could keep a dry eye throughout. We held hands and comforted each other while we sniveled away, tissues at our eyes. My great-grandparents on my mother's side were from Poland and lost several relatives in the war. This was the third year since she died and the first time I attended a performance of the work. I made sure to bring extra tissues in my bag. I got choked up even thinking of it and was glad we were in our box so no one would see me.

Then, Drake appeared at the door to our box and I turned to my father, who made a great show of standing up to shake his hand.

"There you are, my boy. So glad you could make it. Come and join us!"

My father turned to me and smiled, his eyebrows raised as if he'd just given me a present.

Crap...

I stared up at Drake, frowning. "Drake..."

My father stood and moved over so that Drake could sit next to me. Drake smiled and took my hand, leaning down to kiss my cheek.

"I ran into your father at the health club and when he asked me if I was joining you, I told him I was able to rearrange my jam session with my band to another night and was pleased to keep you company."

I sat with my mouth open like a fish out of water. "Oh," I managed. "That's ... good to know."

After he and my father good-fellowed each other for a few moments, he unbuttoned his jacket and sat down beside me. He smelled so good, wearing some really nice cologne. I couldn't place the scent but it was pleasant. I could tell from the fabric and cut that his suit was very expensive. Dark grey silk of some blend with a white shirt and black tie. He moved around to get comfortable, one arm going on the back of my seat, his legs spread wide as if he owned the whole world.

He turned and smiled at me, arching his eyebrow, then leaned closer, his face next to mine, his lips near my ear.

"Don't sound so pleased to see me. Nice move, by the way, forgetting to invite me to sit in your box as your father asked," he said, his breath warm on my cheek.

My father turned back to Drake and he answered my father's questions about his band, his hands animated as he spoke, telling my father about the music his own father used to play and how it influenced him. He took out a pair of opera glasses and talked about them, saying they were his great grandmother's. They spoke together conspiratorially as I tried to figure out what I was going to do about Drake being there.

While my father and Elaine leaned in the other direction with their own glasses, checking out who else was in attendance, I leaned over to Drake but didn't meet his eyes.

"I consider this pushing my limits."

I caught his smile from the corner of my eye. "I'm a good Dom, Kate," he whispered to me, moving closer. "We push our sub's limits. It's the only way they experience anything new or as intensely as they could because they're too afraid on their own."

"You said you'd honor the agreement to the letter."

"It hasn't taken effect yet. Not until November 15th, if I recall correctly. This is just me being who I am."

I sat and stewed. "This is a special event for me," I said, my voice low. "I don't want you here."

"What do you mean?"

"Why don't you ask my *father*?"

I shook my head and turned away. He did exactly that, turning to my father. They spoke for a moment and I listened, waiting to see how clueless my father was.

"Kate said this is a special night for her."

"Oh, yes, that's right. Katherine used to go with her mother each year to hear this performed. *Symphony No. 3* by Gorecki. About the Holocaust. Lost some family on her mother's side in the camps. Isn't that right, dear?" my father said, leaning over to me, a blank smile on his face. "Katherine and her mother used to cry like babies when they listened to it."

I made a face at him and turned away. I wanted to leave. I didn't want Drake Morgan sitting beside me, gloating that he'd weaseled his way into my private life despite my attempts to keep him out. Yes, I had warmed a bit towards him after our little dinner party and how he recited that poem to me after. He wasn't just an empty cad, devoid of personality.

But I didn't want him there.

He sat silent for a moment so I took out my cell phone and sent him a text message.

> *Drake, _please_, can you find some excuse to leave during the first part of the performance? It has special meaning to me and I get very emotional. It has to do with my mother. I'd rather you not be with us. Can't you pretend to get a page about a patient and leave for half an hour? I'm asking you this as one human to another..._please_...*

I sent the text and in a moment, his cell vibrated and he reached into his jacket pocket and retrieved it.

He read the text. I kept my face forward but I could tell he was considering. He typed for a moment and then put his cell away. He spoke with my father, talking about his musical influences, and how he preferred the acoustic guitar but played the bass because his band needed one. He spoke of his dad's guitar collection that he kept, something about his vintage Gibson bass guitar that he played for sentimental reasons, its wood and frets worn with use.

I checked my phone, but there was no reply. I sat there, tense, dreading him being there when the performance started. He was going to ruin it for me and I *hated* him and I hated my completely clueless father for inviting Drake tonight – of all nights!

Just as the lights went down, Drake's pager went off, the buzz audible from where I sat. He made a big performance of taking it off the clip on his belt and checking it.

"Ah, *damn*," he said and showed it to my father. "Gotta run out for a bit. Have a patient post-op who's experiencing complications. I'll run back to the hospital and check on him, but I'll come back as soon as I can."

"That's too bad, Drake. You'll miss the first part of the performance. That's Katherine's favorite part, isn't it, dear?" My clueless father turned to me and smiled.

"That's too bad," I said and turned to Drake, our eyes meeting, his face unreadable. I wanted to thank him, but my father's attention was riveted to me and so I just smiled weakly.

"I'll be back as soon as I can," Drake said, staring into my eyes. "I'm sad I'll miss your favorite part."

He stood and patted my father on the shoulder and then smiled at me briefly before buttoning his jacket and leaving.

I sighed in relief and relaxed back into my chair.

Gorecki – *Symphony of Sorrowful Songs* –written about the Second World War. The second movement, which Dawn Upshaw was performing, always made me cry. It included a prayer to the Virgin Mary inscribed on a cell wall in Zakopane, Poland by an 18-year old girl who was a prisoner.

I was so glad that Drake left me alone for this moment, glad he understood the music had special significance to me. I could tell he didn't like being excluded, but was so relieved that he was willing to go during the performance.

Upshaw entered the concert hall to cheers, the violinists tapping their bows against their music stands. She bowed and took her place. The conductor finally entered after Upshaw, and then, after a brief introduction, the music began.

The opening phrase was simple – three notes, the melody haunting, the strings and piano starting out soft and light, repeating a phrase that was beautiful, almost dreamy. Then the music changed. A darker note taken up by the double bass, the cellos. It repeated, again and again like a funeral bell tolling. Upshaw began, her voice mournful, tearful. She sang in Polish, the lyrics included in both Polish and English in our program.

Emotion built inside me and I tensed, holding my breath, biting my bottom lip as Upshaw sang the lyrics, calling to the girl's mother, asking her not to weep for her daughter. Once, when I used to listen to this, I thought of the family my mother lost in the camps in Poland, but now, I could only think of my own loss, my mother dying after a short battle with aggressive breast cancer. I tried to hold back my tears, but couldn't, and when she sang the last phrase, her voice raised as she called out to her mother, they spilled over and dripped down my cheeks. I wiped my eyes quickly with a hand and then pulled out a tissue from my bag.

I didn't want Drake there beside me, to witness my tears.

My father was so completely *clueless* as if he couldn't understand how personal and emotional this moment was for me – his own *daughter*. This was the first time I heard this since my mother died.

When Upshaw finished the piece, the applause was deafening. A standing ovation followed and I glanced around, the tissue to my mouth, trying to get hold over myself. It was then that I saw Drake. Standing in an empty box by himself, he had his opera glasses trained on me.

I leaned back, trying to hide in the shadows, but it was too late. He'd seen me and I wondered how long he'd been watching me.

Bastard!

Everyone stood, clapping, shouts of "*Brava!*" from the audience. I remained seated, wiping my eyes, struggling to regain my composure.

I could hardly listen to the rest of the music, although it was nice and Upshaw was amazing. At intermission, my father escorted us to the lobby for a drink but I went to the restroom immediately, hoping to fix my makeup before I had to face Drake. When I left the restroom, Drake was already with my father and his wife, a circle of my father's friends surrounding them. He smiled when he saw me. I turned around and went right to the box, refusing to join them.

Barely a moment after I'd been back, Drake arrived and sat beside me, turning towards me, his voice soft.

"How are you?"

I averted my face, looking out over the audience as people began to return to their seats, a tissue twisted in my hands.

"Fine." I said nothing else for a moment, keeping my focus on the audience. "Thank you for understanding and leaving."

"You're welcome." He rested his arm on the back of my seat and turned towards me a bit more. "I've never heard that piece before. It was..." He paused as if thinking of the right word to use. "*Devastating.*"

I glanced at him, checking to see if he meant it, and his face was open, honest. Then he reached into his pocket and pulled out a handkerchief, wetting it with the tip of his tongue. He used the tip to wipe off my cheek. I tried to pull away, but he took my chin in his hand and stopped me, rubbing gently at a spot below my eye.

"Here, let me get this," he said, his voice soft. "Your mascara ran a bit from your tears."

He just *had* to do that – let me know that he was aware that I'd been crying.

I tried to avoid him, but he turned my face so that I couldn't. Finally I met his eyes and I just stared into them, and there was that connection again, passing between us. My emotions were still so close to the surface, and I felt so vulnerable as if he knew exactly what I was thinking and feeling.

Then, he leaned in and kissed me softly, his hands on either side of my face. Just a brief kiss, lips pressed to lips, mouth on mouth, and it felt as if some barrier between us had broken.

He pulled away, and I felt so confused, scared to my core. We remained like that, his hands cupping my cheeks, him staring into my eyes.

My father and Elaine returned and the moment ended.

Drake pulled his hands away and turned to them, standing up and welcoming them both back, his hand on my dad's shoulder. I remained seated, looking away, trying to hide my emotions from all of them, but I had the sense that Drake knew exactly how I felt.

I sat through the rest of the program but I heard none of it. He spoiled it for me. All I could think was that he kissed me – he *kissed* me! I didn't know where he got the nerve, except that he was a Dom as he so eagerly reminded me earlier. He was a Dom and he always tried to get his way. Get what he wanted.

I understood completely what he intended by that.

He wanted me as his sub.

I read the literature. A good Dom pushed his sub's limits to ensure she continued to expand her ability to respond, to experience as much as she could, to be as fulfilled in her submission as they could achieve together. The more she yielded to him, the more they were both satisfied – until they found her true hard limits. Only then would she – and he – be completely fulfilled.

I had no idea what my limits were. I knew what scared me – pain. I knew what I couldn't accept. Humiliation. I could never go to either place. I would never agree to either.

I *was* aroused by the idea of bondage. Leather? Restraints? They excited me. The thought of Drake tying me up and then doing things to me with his hands, his mouth, his cock, making me come the way the Dom in those letters described – I could take restraints, I could handle a blindfold. Not a gag – I had this thing about breathing because I had asthma as a child.

Spanking? I didn't know about that.

It sounded too much like the way you treated a bad child. I read about how pain was just another sensation that enhanced sexual response, but there had never been once in my life when pain led to sexual arousal so I concluded it was just not in me. Luckily, Lara assured me that Drake was not into pain. He was more into bondage and dominance. Mind-fucking, Lara called it.

I inhaled deeply and tried to calm myself, for my heart was racing a bit too fast because of everything. My hands shook just a bit, and I felt as if I couldn't catch my breath.

I had to leave. I had to get out of there.

I stood and grabbed my bag.

"Excuse me," I managed to whisper as I crept past Drake to the aisle and out of our box seats to the hallway. I gasped when I was finally away from them, from *him* and leaned against the wall, trying to catch my breath.

I started walking and found a side exit. I left the building completely, standing outside in the November chill, my arms bare, but the cool air felt good on my skin. I leaned against the building and stared straight up into the sky. It was clear with a few faint stars peeking through Manhattan's light pollution.

The door opened beside me. *Drake... Damn* him.

"Kate, what on Earth are you doing out here? It's freezing out, for God's sake."

He grabbed my arm, but I pulled free and stood my ground. My knees were too shaky to try to walk away, so I just stayed where I was, leaning against the wall, my arms wrapped around me.

"Just leave me. I need some air."

I closed my eyes, for they were starting to tear up again and I hated myself for being so weak. For being a stupid female in front of him. I bit my lip until it hurt and blinked rapidly, turning my face away from him.

He removed his suit jacket, leaving him in his crisp white shirt and black tie. Then, he manhandled me, pulling me away from the wall, wrapping me in his jacket, which smelled of him and was so warm. He tightened it around me, his face dark.

"There," he said and then he tipped my face up so that I had to look in his eyes. I tried to avoid him as if he was some kind of drug, for he was, and I was weak... Our eyes finally met and I felt this jolt of something go through me from my chest to my groin.

"Oh, fuck, *Kate*," he said almost groaning. He pressed against me, his hips pinning me to the wall, his arms on the bricks beside my head. He kissed me, and it wasn't the kiss he gave me earlier in the concert hall, soft and tender. It was passionate, his mouth harsh against mine, his lips parting, his tongue finding mine, searching my mouth. One hand slipped behind my head, the other tangled in my hair, which he pulled out of its clip so that it fell around my shoulders.

The kiss went on and on, my heart racing, his thigh jammed between mine. He dropped his hand to my breasts, his fingers caressing the tops of them, his mouth moving to my neck beneath my ear, his tongue wet against my skin. When his hand moved lower to hike up my skirt, his hand stroking my leg up as if in search of garters, I emerged from the lust-filled stupor.

"Drake, *no*..."

He stopped, his breath coming in short harsh gasps.

"Tell me you don't want me," he said, his voice low.

I glanced away, for his eyes scared me. I couldn't say I didn't want him. My body betrayed me. I was wet and swollen and my heart pounded.

"I thought so," he said and started kissing me again, roughly, his hand on my thigh, then around between my legs, his fingers searching me, pressing against me, the pressure firm against my clit, then lower. "Oh, you're already wet," he whispered, and he made this sound in his throat like a moan. "*Fuck*, I want you right here, right now." He pressed his hips against me and I felt his erection against my groin.

He kissed me again, and I kissed him back, unable to resist any longer. He tried to get his hand into my pantyhose, dipping down beneath my panties to find my clit and it was then that I shocked back to awareness. He had his hand between my thighs, his fingers between my lips, almost inside of me. I pulled away and pushed against him.

"*Stop!*"

He stopped, pulling his fingers away, his hand out from between us, but he leaned with his elbows against the wall, effectively keeping me from escape.

"What?" he said, panting.

"I'm not *ready*," I said, my own breath coming too fast.

"Yes, you are," he said and licked his fingers methodically, one at a time, his eyes not leaving mine. "You're more than ready."

I shook my head and closed my eyes. "No," I whispered. "I'm not ready for this. For *you*. Not yet."

He said nothing, just pressed his forehead against mine. Soon his breathing and my breathing started to slow. I pulled down the skirt of my dress, which he hiked above my hips.

"Well, I'm ready for you." He stood up straight, and adjusted himself, a hand running briefly over his groin. I couldn't help but look down and saw the faint outline of his erection through the fabric of his trousers.

"Any time, Kate," he said, his voice low and husky. "You just have to sign the revised agreement I'm sending to you when I get home tonight." He turned away from me, his hands on his hips and took in a few deep breaths as if trying to calm himself. Then, he went to the door and opened it, pointing inside. "We better go back. Your father will be starting to worry about us."

I walked past him and back into the building.

He stopped and picked up my bag, which I dropped on the ground by the wall.

"Here," he said, and a smile cracked that mouth. "I really must have affected you if you forgot your bag."

I grabbed it from him, and quickly turned away. I wouldn't give him the satisfaction of returning his smile of triumph.

We remained at the rear of the box for the rest of the performance and standing ovation, not wanting to interrupt, me leaning against the wall, Drake leaning over me, one hand on the wall beside my head, his eyes never leaving my face. He caught my eye and passed his fingers beneath his nose, inhaling deeply.

I glanced away, my cheeks heating at his so brazen reminder of how he had his fingers almost inside me. I waited for my father and Elaine to finish clapping. Finally, the applause died and they turned to us. My father smiled, his face bright.

"There you two are!" he said like a proud father of the bride, his gravelly voice ebullient. "I'm so glad Drake went to find you, Katherine. Did he help you calm down a bit? I know that song always gets to you."

No, father. He did anything but help me calm down. Quite the opposite. He had his tongue down my throat and his fingers up my pussy...

"I'm fine," I said, my voice low.

"Good good." My father rubbed his hands together. "Now, weren't you two going out for dinner? The Russian Tea Room, wasn't it, Drake?"

My father looked from me to Drake and back.

"That's right," Drake said. "We have reservations for two in about ten minutes. I could really *eat* something right now."

I caught Drake's eye and his half-grin half-smirk started, his blue eyes twinkling in that way. His words sent a thrill of lust right to my groin. I handed him his jacket and he shrugged it on. Then, he took my coat from the hanger in our private closet and helped me with it, standing behind me, his hands on my shoulders.

His cologne lingered on my clothes and hair.

CHAPTER EIGHT

We walked to the limo that my father had waiting outside the hall and the driver took us to Drake's car, which was parked in a lot down the street.

We said our goodbyes to my father and his wife and Drake opened the passenger door for me. I got inside with reluctance. I just didn't want to go out alone with him, despite my frustrating physical attraction to him as a man.

The car was silent as we drove to the Russian Tea Room. Drake didn't even try to make light conversation to make me more comfortable, as if he wanted me off center, vulnerable.

Finally, I couldn't hold back. "You're not going to talk to me?"

"I'm too busy recovering from our little kiss."

"Little?"

He glanced at me, smiling. I made a face and turned away from him.

"For me it was little," he said. "Maybe for you it wasn't. I don't usually kiss a woman unless I'm in scene and I'm fucking her, so for me, that was nothing."

"If it was nothing, why are you still recovering?"

He grinned. "Touché," he said. "But as I said, I don't usually kiss a woman unless we're fucking, so I'm still a bit uncomfortable. How about you?" He turned to look at me, his eyes dark.

I crossed my arms and looked out the window, avoiding his gaze. "Never better."

"Good. I *knew* you needed some attention," he said, humor in his voice.

I rolled my eyes, trying to hide my smile. He was enjoying himself.

"Do you ever take things seriously?"

"Oh, I assure you, Ms. Bennet, that I take some things *very* seriously. Sex, for instance."

We finally arrived at the restaurant and Drake found a parking spot a block away. He opened my door, then took my hand, his arm around my waist.

The restaurant was still full with late-evening customers, but Drake had a reservation and so the hostess escorted us in to the main dining room, with its dark green walls, gilded fixtures, red leather banquette seating and white tablecloths. We sat at a table with a curved banquette, which meant Drake could sit right beside me. As soon as the hostess left us alone, Drake moved closer to me – closer than I wanted.

"I love these tables," he said, his voice a bit smoky. "If you were already my submissive, I'd have made you wear garters and black fishnet nylons instead of pantyhose. With no underwear on, I'd be able to sit real close and have my way with your pussy while we ate. Your mind would be occupied with what else I was going to eat when we were finally alone."

A thrill of lust went right to my groin at that. I tried to keep a straight face, but my cheeks heated at his words. What possible response could I give to that? Luckily, a waitress arrived and asked for our drink order, and I was spared having to say anything. Drake ordered some blini with caviar to start and then, to my surprise and shock, a shot of Anisovaya for us both. When he said the word, a chill ran through me.

Anisovaya...

"I'm sorry, but we don't have Anisovaya on the menu."

"Tell the bartender that Dr. Morgan is here. He keeps some especially for me."

The waitress nodded. "Certainly."

I turned to him, my mouth open. "You drink Anisovaya?"

"Yes," Drake said and folded his hands on the crisp white linen of the tablecloth. "I love Russian vodka, especially infused with anise."

I sat in silence for a moment, my face hot. "*You* wrote those letters."

He frowned, and then smiled briefly as if recovering, his eyes hooded. "I take it that Lara gave you the link and password."

I nodded and glanced away, not knowing what to say.

He was the Dominant who wrote those letters...

"You weren't supposed to read those," Drake said, moving cutlery around on the table. "They're for my subs to read after we sign contracts so they know what to expect. I feel somewhat at a disadvantage because usually I know what my subs like before they know what I like."

"You read my profile on FetLife," I said, a little too petulantly.

Crap. Drake was *him*.

"Yes, but I want the narrative, not just a list. I want your fantasies so I can fulfill them. Most couples are too afraid to be honest about fantasies, sexual kinks, Kate. The great thing about a relationship like we'll have," he said, leaning closer, "is that you can be totally honest with me. I won't be offended or shocked or jealous or worried about them the way a normal boyfriend would. I'm only here for the sex so I want to make it incredibly good and rewarding. There'll be none of those messy emotions to get in the way of pure pleasure."

I thought about that for a moment when the cocktail waitress brought us our drinks and the caviar, placing them in front of Drake.

"How can you keep emotions out of a relationship? They're bound of leak in."

"Not if you don't let them," he said, as if it was the easiest thing in the world. "I won't let them. Now, down it fast," he instructed, pointing to the shot of vodka. "The Anisovaya goes down smoothly."

"I shouldn't drink," I said, but in truth, I needed something at that moment.

"Oh, you most *definitely* should. I want you to loosen up a bit, Kate. Enjoy yourself. Relax. We need to talk and I want you to be completely honest with me. For a change. Here." He pointed to the shot again. "Pick it up and we'll do it at the same time."

I took the shot and looked at him, reluctant, my hands shaking.

"*Za vas,*" he said in Russian. "To you."

"*Za vas,*" I replied and together, we shot back the vodka. I grimaced. Despite the hint of anise, it was still vodka, straight.

Drake smacked his lips. "*Vashee zda-ró-vye!*" he said. "To your health."

I smiled just a bit, licking my lips. He seemed in such a good mood, now that he had me alone on his own turf. He took one of the blini and smeared sour cream and caviar, then added a few bits of onion to it.

"Here," he said, holding it up to my mouth. "You never drink vodka without eating."

"I don't *know*..."

"A rich kid like you never had caviar?"

"I had a huge aquarium when I was a kid and bred guppies. I couldn't never get used to the idea of eating fish eggs."

He laughed but pressed it on me. "Trust me, Kate. This is so *good*. You'll love it."

I took a bite and chewed, a bit hesitant. Then I raised my eyebrows. The smooth creaminess of the sour cream was punctuated by the sharp little bites of salty caviar and the savory onion. "It's good. I didn't think I'd like it."

"Like I said, you have to trust me. I know what's good. The more I know you, the more intimate we are, the more you can just let go and I'll lead the way."

"You're so sure of yourself," I said. I picked up the menu and examined it. "What's good to eat?"

"I'll order my favorites," Drake said. "Can you trust me?"

I nodded. "Russians don't eat eyeballs do they?"

"No, at least, none that I know."

Drake ate the rest of the blini and then fixed another, which we shared, him feeding me.

The waiter arrived and Drake ordered for us in Russian, requesting the Pelmeni, which were stuffed dumplings, the Blinchik, which were crepes with white truffle, and to start, the famous Tea Room borscht soup.

When the waiter left, Drake turned to me, resting his arm on the back of the seat behind me.

"So, Kate," he said, moving just a bit closer. "You read my letters. How did they make you feel?"

I shrugged. There was no way I was going to tell him. "I don't know what to think..."

"Don't tell me what you *think*. Tell me how you *felt*."

No frickin' way.

"You're a good writer."

"You are so *stubborn*. Look, Kate, this couldn't be easier," he said, moving a little closer. "Your father wants us to be together. We can meet, talk and I can take you out to functions as much as we want, we can do as much as *you* want, explore as much as you want, without having to hide our relationship. No one has to know *why* we're together. They'll all assume they know why, thinking it's because we've *fallen in love*," he said, his tone mocking. "It's great cover."

"I haven't agreed to become your sub."

"No, you haven't," he said and traced a pattern on the back of my hand. "I hope to convince you to sign a modified agreement. I'm going to be honest with you, Kate." He caught my eye. "I want you. There's nothing I love more than initiating and training a new submissive. I think I can satisfy your needs. In fact, I think this is perfect for us both."

"And if I said I just want to write a research paper and interview you? Nothing more?"

"You didn't *feel* like you only wanted to write a research paper earlier. You were nice and wet and for a moment, you kissed me back."

I frowned. "I was overly emotional. You caught me at a vulnerable moment."

He shook his head. "When you're vulnerable, your true feelings come out. It's when you're feeling strong that you're able to hide them. Look, Kate," he said and took my chin in his hand. "There's something between us. I felt it. You felt it. Pure sexual attraction. You want to try submission – I *know* you do. You want to try it with *me*. Why fight it?"

He let go of my chin and I glanced away. "You're so blunt."

"I *have* to be blunt. I have to tell you the truth about how I feel and what I want and what I can give. You have to be completely open with me about what you desire. You have to feel complete trust in me in order to really let go."

"I feel like you're pushing me. I don't like being pressured."

"Kate," he said, turning my face back to him. "This is all about *you*. People think that it's the Dominant who has all the control – and he does, once they're in scene, but to get to that point, it's all about the sub. Her limits. You have all the control. You dictate the terms. I fulfill them. You don't have to be afraid. I'm not going to hurt you, if that's holding you back. I'm not going to reveal anything about this to anyone. It's just between you and me – and Lara of course. She's not going to let anything slip. She's totally professional. All I really *want*," he said and leaned closer, staring at my mouth, before deliberately moving up to my eyes. "All I really want is to do whatever it is you need so I can make you come, over and over again. Is that so bad?"

He licked his lips and I thought – what a manipulative bastard he is. This was one of his mindfucks, him knowing exactly what to say to get me aroused.

"If it's all about me, then let me decide on the pace."

"I will," he said. "This is just me trying to assure you that I *want* you. You don't have to worry about that part of things. This is now all up to you. Like I said, I'm sending you a revised agreement with my preferences later tonight when I get back to my apartment, but if you've read my letters, you already know most of it. I want you to strike off what you don't want to try and include everything you do want. Then we can negotiate."

"How soon would you," I said and hesitated. "Usually start things?"

"We can have sex right away, if you want." He stared into my eyes. "Tonight. But it will take time before you're ready for the bondage. I won't move too fast for you. You'll decide when we start."

"So, we just go somewhere and have sex?"

"My place or yours?" He smiled. "Kate, have you never just had casual sex with anyone? A one-night stand?"

I shook my head. "No. I've always known them first. Dated. Never sex on a first date or a one night stand."

"You've never *wanted* to fuck a man you just met?"

I glanced away, playing with the cutlery. "I've been attracted to men I've met, but I can't just have sex with someone right away."

"Why not?"

"*Because*," I said, frowning. "This is embarrassing."

"Kate, you have to be honest. You have to get over your shyness with me. *Tell* me. Why can't you just fuck me tonight?"

I took in a deep breath. "It's so ...*intimate*." I shook my head, shivering at the thought of just having sex with a stranger.

"Being naked with someone? Letting them touch your skin? Opening your legs to them? Letting them inside your body? It's so ... *you're* so ...*vulnerable.*"

I looked in his eyes. He was a man. He couldn't understand.

"Thank you for being honest."

He leaned in and kissed me softly, his mouth covering mine. I let him. He pulled back when the waitress came with our soup.

"What happened here?" he said, touching my bottom lip with a finger, running it over the small scar where one tooth pierced my lip.

"I fell when I was a kid."

"Don't tell me – wearing your mother's high heels during a dress-up game?"

I shook my head, fighting to hold back my smile. "Stilts."

"*Stilts?* You?" He grinned at that and I couldn't help but smile back, but then I turned my head away.

We ate the rich earthy borscht – the best I'd ever eaten.

"So," he said, spooning some sour cream into my soup, "tell me about flyboy."

"How do you know about *him*?"

"Lara told me."

I frowned. "I'd rather not. Can't we talk about something else?"

"This is important. I need to understand what happened, what he did, how you responded. It will help me know what to do to make you relax and trust me."

I sighed. "I don't like talking about him. He's a bad memory."

"I need to know why your memory of him was bad. Look, he obviously made mistakes with you. He was a total amateur. I won't make those mistakes. Besides, think of this as research. You tell me what he did, and I'll tell you where he went wrong and how I'd do it properly. If we never do anything more, at least you'll understand."

I stirred my soup a bit. "I met him through Doctors Without Borders. He used to fly people into remote camps as a volunteer. He was doing his MBA and we started to date."

"How soon did you have sex with him?"

"A couple of weeks. We went out for coffee a lot at first, and then had dinner. Then we went to a movie and he came over and we had sex."

"What was it like for you the first time? Did you come?"

I exhaled heavily. "Are you going to ask for a moment by moment accounting of our relationship?"

"Yes." He turned back to his soup and took a spoonful. "I need details to understand what your experience was and why it went wrong. So," he said again. "Did you come the first time?"

"No, I didn't. It took a while. But I did eventually."

"What did it?" he asked as I ate my soup. "What was it that allowed you to have an orgasm?"

"You sound like a sex therapist."

He cracked that grin, his eyes mischievous. "That's one way of thinking about me. But seriously, what did you do that allowed you to orgasm?"

"I don't *know*," I said, exasperated, glancing around to see if there was anyone in earshot. "We were a bit drunk, and I just, I don't know... I was more relaxed. He *did* things for a long time and I was more ready."

"How exactly did he work you up?"

"Drake!" I turned to him, frowning. "We're having supper."

He smiled. "I'm not asking because I want to become aroused. I'm asking so I understand what you need. What you like. A Dom must trust his sub to tell the truth at all times. She must trust him enough to tell the truth. Otherwise, it won't work."

"I thought that was what the agreement is for."

"It is but we have to talk openly. I want you to get used to being totally honest with me about sex. You can say anything. *Anything*. I've heard it all."

"Not from *my* lips."

"No, not from *your* lips," he said, smiling. "And I can't *wait* to hear it from your lips in particular. I happen to love your lips, especially your scar. All I can think of when I'm with you is kissing you, licking your scar, sucking your lips, biting them. And I mean both sets." He licked his lips again just for emphasis and bit his bottom lip.

I turned away, trying to hide my heated face. The image of him kissing, licking, sucking and softly biting me aroused me, a twitch of lust in my now-swollen flesh.

"So, enough about your delicious lips that I want to suck and lick and bite. Tell me about flyboy. When did he start to introduce the idea of BDSM into your relationship?"

"After the books came out and it was on the news."

"What did you think at first?"

"I read the books but I didn't want it. I thought BDSM was about men who hated women and just wanted an excuse to hit them and get away with it. I thought it meant I wasn't good enough the way I was. He wanted me to shave. He wanted to do anal. He wanted to spank me. He wanted me to let him mock-rape me."

"And how did that make you feel?"

I frowned. "Upset, of course. I had just started to enjoy sex and then he starts with all this kinky stuff that scared me and made me feel inadequate. Why wasn't I good enough as I was?"

"For someone with a kink, plain old orgasms aren't enough. It's like eating vanilla ice cream after you've had chocolate truffle. You can eat it but it's not the same pleasure."

"You and Lara," I said and couldn't help but smile a bit. "With the ice cream metaphor. Except vanilla ice cream is still sweet. Anal and mock rape aren't."

"They *can* be. It's all in your preparation and build-up. Flyboy should have studied BDSM before he ever tried anything. He should have gone to someone and been trained like I was. I *know* how to do this, Kate. You can relax."

"So, is this dinner and this talk part of how to *do* this?" I said, looking at him, but not in his eyes. I kept my eyes on his chin or his mouth to avoid eye contact. He tipped his head down so that I couldn't avoid his eyes.

"Not my usual MO," he said. "But the general approach is the same. I have to find out what a sub needs and if we're compatible. Sometimes, I have to seduce them a bit."

"So, in your mind, you're seducing me right now."

He smiled. "I hope so."

"What do you *hope* will happen?"

He moved a little closer to me and brushed a strand of hair from my cheek.

"I *hope*," he said, keeping his voice soft. "I hope that we'll continue to talk like this, with you telling me in intimate detail what you did that made you feel pleasure and what he did that scared you. Then I hope you'll agree to take me to your apartment. I hope that you'll agree to let me fuck you tonight so that the first time is out of the way. I promise to make you come at least twice if you do. Nothing will happen tonight in terms of bondage and dominance. It's too soon. But it's not too soon for us to fuck, given our obvious mutual attraction."

"This is all too, I don't know – *clinical*."

"I thought you wanted to understand. I thought if I explained everything, you'd feel more comfortable. I can just *do* it, if you'd prefer. Just train you without explaining."

I said nothing, seriously considering it, a jolt of desire rushing through me from his so blatant words. I couldn't help but imagine what he *would* do to me if I let him.

"You seem to have this all plotted out."

"I do. It's my specialty. I like to study a problem. I like to break it down into its parts. I like to create a strategy for solving it, lay out all the steps. I like to follow through."

"So I'm a problem?"

"I want you as my submissive. The problem is how I can get you to submit. I have to understand you, what you need and want in order to have you, satisfy your needs. Will you at least consider my request?" He wiped his mouth with a napkin and held my eyes.

I glanced away, my stomach all butterflies at the prospect of taking him home with me. "I'm thinking."

"Good. Now, tell me about your love of the fine arts. Do you paint or draw?"

I took another spoonful of soup but suddenly I didn't want to talk about art. "Both. I did a lot in high school, but it was too frivolous for my father."

"Did he actually *tell* you that you couldn't study art in college?"

"Not in so many words, but he made his views known, as he does with everything."

"What about your mother? Didn't she encourage you?"

"You want to talk about submissives? I think that sometimes, mother was afraid of him."

"He wasn't violent was he?"

I shook my head. "No. He just has this *way*... You *know* when he disapproves. He doesn't even have to say anything."

"Sounds like an old bastard. So, now, instead of writing about politics, you're writing about culture and the arts. That's a good compromise. You're a very good writer."

"Thank you," I said, starting to relax now that we weren't talking so bluntly about sex. "It makes me happy to be able to write about what I really love."

The waitress removed our empty bowls and brought the Pelmeni and Blinchik. Drake cut up one of the Pelmeni and held his fork to me.

"Here," he said, "taste this. It's so *good*."

I took the bite-sized piece of dumpling off his fork and he smiled as I ate it. I closed my eyes it was so delicious, rich and savory. "That's so *good*!"

He smiled. "I love that face," he said, his voice a bit husky. "I bet it's like your orgasm face. At least, I *hope* so."

"Do you talk like this to all your submissives?"

"Like what?" He tried to act all innocent, but he knew exactly what I meant.

The cocktail waitress came by and he ordered another round of Anisovaya.

"So," he said, his voice soft and low. "Will you take me to your place tonight and let me fuck you and make you come at least twice?"

I forked a piece of Pelmeni. "I don't know if I can – *tonight*."

"But maybe *some* night? That's a step forward. Look, if you're unsure about sex, just let me come over and see your apartment at least. I'd love to see what your apartment looks like from the inside instead of just what your peephole looks like. Besides, if you make me stay outside, Mrs. Kropotkin might call the cops if she thinks I'm harassing you. You're an artist. I'd love to see your art. "

I couldn't help but smile a bit. "You want to come in and see my etchings?"

"I really do want to see your art. I want to *know* you, Kate. Your art is part of you."

"You don't need to see my art to be my Dom."

"Look, Kate, I *promise* I'll keep my hands to myself. If you change your mind and want to fuck me, you'll have to make the move."

I turned and looked directly in his eyes, searching for how truthful he was, but it was impossible to tell. All I had was Lara's word to go on – that he was absolutely trustworthy. But could I trust her?

After we finished the meal, he fed me some blini with whipped cream and fresh fruit mixed with some fruity Russian liqueur. He seemed to love feeding me and I told myself that this was great insight into what made him a Dom. He really enjoyed taking care of a woman's needs – *all* of them. Chivalry was not dead with Drake. Feeding – I remembered the movie 9 ½ Weeks when the male character fed her while she was blindfolded, trying to heighten her senses.

Drake made everything about control and sensation, as if his life was dedicated to it. I thought about him while he swirled the bit of crepe around in the sweet sauce before lifting the fork to my mouth, his eyes encouraging me to have more. He was a neurosurgeon. He dealt in brains – how they worked and what to do when they went wrong. Neurons, brain structures, neurological responses. He had an undergraduate degree in Clinical Psychology, and studied the mind and how it worked, the unconscious, emotions, personality. It made sense that he would be all about control and enhanced sensation. Maybe it fascinated him on that level.

I opened my mouth and let him feed me the crepe and it was so delicious, I closed my eyes and murmured my appreciation. When I opened them, I saw real pleasure in his eyes.

"I love it when you close your eyes like that," he said as he watched me chew. "But when I make you come, you'll keep your eyes open and focused on mine."

I swallowed hard at the thought. It wasn't just the idea of him making me come, it was how certain he was that he *would*, and that certainty aroused me, my body warming, my flesh swelling. He was so sure of his ability. If he could make me this aroused just feeding me crepes and talking, what would it be like if we were alone and naked? My legs felt weak and I was glad to be sitting down.

Was I that woman – the woman who was so easily controlled by a dominant man? Who got off on being controlled - on giving over complete control to a man?

"What's going on in that too-intelligent mind of yours?"

I frowned. "Why am I too intelligent? You said you didn't like stupid women..."

He laughed and shook his head. "I should have said *too active* mind. Sometimes very intelligent women over-think certain things – like sex and pleasure. You have a very responsive body, Kate. You should just free yourself to feel."

"Women are *always* wet, you know," I said, irritated that he was so certain about me. "You're a doctor. You should know that from your Gynecology rotation."

"Not *that* wet." He gave me that half-grin that was more of a smirk. "Don't be embarrassed. I was hard as a rock so we're even."

He *was* hard as rock. And like Lara said, *hung*. I recalled the feel of him pressed against my belly and how excited I felt knowing he was as aroused as I was. How I wanted him inside of me. While Big was too big for me, I figured Drake would fit.

"You seem so certain of yourself."

"You like that I'm so certain of myself." His grin grew wider and he forked another piece of crepe, picking up some whipped cream and fruit. "If I wasn't, what kind of Dom would I be?" He held the fork up once more and I opened my mouth. "You have to believe that I'm dominant for this to work. If you doubt my ability to take control over you, you'll never be able to yield power. That's key."

"So this is an act to convince me you're able to take control?"

He shook his head and fixed his gaze on me. "This is no act. I'm being as open and honest as I can with you. I *understand* you, Kate. You can relax with me. You can just *be*. Believe me, I won't judge you except when you disobey my orders or don't try hard enough to comply."

Disobeying his orders... Why did that both arouse me and irritate me?

"I'm so conflicted about this."

"I know you are." He reached out and took my hand, stroking his thumb over my palm and even that sent a stab of lust to my groin. "You're afraid. Your modern feminist sensibility thinks this is wrong, that submission is wrong, but that primal part of your brain knows it's right."

He leaned in closer, then he ate a forkful of crepe himself, chewing thoughtfully. He watched me, his blue eyes determined.

"You have to get over your self-judgment and accept this for what it is. Submission for you is just the way you prefer to experience sex. Nothing more, nothing less. There's no deep meaning to it. It just turns you on."

"It shouldn't."

"There you go – that judgmental Superego. Kate, D/s the way we will practice it is safe, sane, and most of all, consensual. That's not just a slogan. I believe it. D/s is not illegal, it's not damaging. It doesn't diminish you in any way. If you sign the contract, we'll have lots of mind-blowing sex in the way that really appeals to us both and you'll sleep really well at night when we part." He forked a piece of strawberry and popped it in his mouth, chewing briefly. "Simple."

I took a drink of water, needing something to distract me from that look of certainty on his face.

We finished the dessert and he described his band members, how often they played and how their gigs at small venues kept him busy most nights. But he had a few open slots a week and would like to see me on those nights, either at his place or mine.

"But tonight, I want to come to your place so I can see who you are when you're not with your family."

"I don't *know*..." I was incredibly aroused, but I was also incredibly afraid.

"If you want, no sex tonight. Just talk. We can go over my personal limits and discuss yours. No touching and no sex unless you initiate it."

"And if I sign an agreement? How much say do I get in what happens between us?"

"When we're together? Sexually? *None*. The purpose of the agreement is for you to give that power over to me to decide what happens. The only out you have is your safe word, but once you use it, that's it. We stop. *Full* stop. So don't use it unless you really mean it. Don't use it unless what's happening is too much for you to bear. At first, you can use 'yellow' as a sign you need to slow down or pause. Red will be only for full stop, and once we're over the initial training. A submissive enjoys some uncertainty, because it's arousing. But real fear and bad pain? That's when you use your safe word. Other than that, other than your hard limits, you leave everything up to me. What, how, when, where, how often."

"I shouldn't need a safe word, Drake, if all we're going to do is fuck. Remember – no pain."

"I told you I'm not a sadist. But sex can get intense. Bondage scenes can get intense. I'm not into pain, but a binding can accidentally get too tight, or you can be emotionally overwhelmed. I will punish you if you misbehave. Sometimes, punishment can be too intense."

"What kind of punishment?"

"We'll have to negotiate that."

"Lara said you'd likely spank me."

He smiled. "Does that upset you?"

"I'm not a child."

"Spanking is merely to reinforce dominance. It's not supposed to be about hurting you."

"How can it not hurt?"

"It won't hurt too much, then."

"How do you know what too much is?"

"I'll show you. You'll tell me. I'll stop at that point."

I shrank in my seat, disheartened. I didn't want any spanking.

"Look, Kate, hopefully, if I do this right, you'll never *need* to use a safe word but it's there just in case."

"I don't know about the spanking part," I said. "We're going to have to talk about that."

"We will," he said, and stroked my cheek. "I won't go too far for you. I want this. I don't want to make a mistake with you."

I sighed. "You won't push me tonight?"

He grinned, his expression mischievous. "I won't push. *Much*. But you have to know that I want you." He leaned forward. "I want to fuck you tonight. I'd love to tie you up and have my way with you, but I know it's too soon. You need to trust me before you can give over your power willingly. But a kiss goodnight would be nice." His blue eyes twinkled.

"I'll consider it."

He paid the check and stood, helped me out of the booth and then escorted me to the coat check. He wrapped my coat around my shoulders, taking the opportunity to nuzzle my neck. And I thought – that was Drake. Constantly reminding me that he wanted me and found me desirable. It was, *he* was, irresistible.

CHAPTER NINE

We drove to my apartment building and the talk was light, of the upcoming election my dad was hoping to win, of Drake's busy schedule practicing with his band. I was still undecided as to whether I'd invite him in. Part of me wanted to. Part of me wanted him to push me, to see how much I could feel just having 'vanilla' sex with him.

Part of me was scared to death.

We walked up the steps to the building's entry and stopped. He stood too close to me, of course, probably hoping to influence me with his animal magnetism. I glanced up in his eyes and he just waited, his eyes half-hooded, the slightest hint of a smile on his mouth. Finally, he sighed.

"Kate, invite me in. *Trust* me. I won't risk anything with you, given who you are and who your father is."

"You won't touch me?"

He bent down and tipped my chin up with a finger. "I may touch you, but I won't force you to do anything. I don't rape women, Kate. I don't like *real* resistance. Only the fun kind. The play kind."

"We won't have sex, Drake. I'm not like that. I don't have sex on a first date."

"I know."

"I'm serious. No sex. I'll think about the goodnight kiss."

I glanced at my cell phone to see what time it was.

"Why don't you call Lara and let her know I'm coming into your apartment. Tell her you'll call her in an hour and if you don't call, she should take action. That way, you'll feel safe."

I dialed Lara's cell. It rang three times before she answered.

"Kate, what's up?"

"I'm standing on the front step of my building with Drake. He wants to come in and just talk, and suggested that I call you so you know I'm alone with him. That I'll call you in an hour to let you know things are OK."

"That's good, Kate. By all means, go ahead. Invite him in. I have complete trust in him to keep his word. Call me in an hour. If you don't, I'll bring Bruno and come right over. Tell Drake that, although I know I won't need to."

I turned to Drake. "Lara said if I don't call in an hour, she'll bring Bruno over."

Drake laughed at that, his eyes merry. He took my hand and leaned down to the cell. "Oh, you're threatening to use the heavy artillery. You've never had to use Bruno with me yet and won't have to tonight."

I pulled the cell back to my ear and heard laughter on the other end. "Have fun, Kate, and relax. You're in *very* good hands, and I mean good. You can trust Drake. Call me in an hour."

"Thanks, Lara."

I ended the call and exhaled heavily. "Who's Bruno?"

"Her Rottweiler."

Even I laughed at that. "Come on up."

As we climbed the stairs, I wondered if I should let him in. I didn't really believe I would, and adrenaline jolted through me because this meant it wasn't completely out of the question that we'd have sex. He promised not to force me, but I knew he'd try to seduce me. He'd seduce me with his words and with his touch. In the back of my mind, I realized I let him in because I wanted what happened between us at the concert hall to continue. I liked his touch. I wanted him to touch me. I just wasn't sure about the sex part. That was too intimate, and we weren't intimate enough yet for me to let him in.

He followed me up the stairs to my third floor apartment, and we stopped at my door while I fumbled in my bag for my keys, muttering to myself about how big it was and how I always lost my keys at the bottom. Just nervous chatter. In the time before I found them, Mrs. Kropotkin opened her door a crack and peered out at us. Drake turned to her and smiled.

"*Zdrastvooyte.*"

She closed her door.

"Did you study Russian in college?" I asked, my voice a bit quivery.

"My father had a cassette tape with Russian lessons on it and I used to listen as a kid." He cleared his throat because his own voice was husky. "I don't really speak Russian well. Just enough to order in a restaurant or make a few toasts."

I had to take in a few deep breaths to get control over myself. Finally, I wrestled the lock open and stepped inside, turning and blocking the doorway before he could enter.

"You'll keep your promise to just talk? No sex?"

He held his hands up, palms out as if to signal surrender. "Kate, it's up to you. You'll be the one to decide what happens. Whatever *you* want."

"We're *not* having sex. Tell me you understand."

"I understand."

I stood in the doorway for a moment, deciding, my hands on the door, Drake outside. I didn't want this night to end. I wanted him to come in and touch me. I was just afraid.

"Come in," I said and sighed.

He stepped across the threshold, turning around, staring at my apartment.

"Kate why do you live like this? This apartment looks like it belongs to a poor kid, not the daughter of a wealthy judge running for election."

"I don't want his money and I don't earn enough even with the scholarship to live anywhere else."

He walked around and the way he was looking at everything and touching all my possessions made me feel as if he were entering my mind and my body.

While I went to the side table in the entry and deposited my keys on a tray, he stood in the hallway and took in a deep breath as if he were smelling me. My apartment had a pleasant scent. With Thanksgiving approaching, I put a few decorations up, a couple of tiny pumpkins on a dish on a small round table in the living/dining area. Vanilla and cinnamon were the main scents from a container of potpourri beside the dish with my keys.

I took off my coat and hung it on a coat tree by the door, then went to Drake. "Let me take your coat," I said, extending my hands. He shrugged off his coat. Then, he unbuttoned his jacket, loosening his tie as well. He kicked off his boots and watched me hang up his coat, and I felt awkward under his gaze, trying to hide my nervousness.

"Do you mind if I take a look around?"

I shook my head without responding, worried that my voice would give away my nerves.

He came to me and tipped up my chin with a finger. "Its OK. I know you're nervous. A bit excited. You know what? So am I."

He sounded a bit nervous, and as if to demonstrate, he took in a deep breath and smiled. I glanced away.

He walked down the hallway that led to the back of the apartment and my bedroom, examining the art on my walls. Stopping at one long narrow picture that I called 'Lady/Knight', he checked it out more closely. A pencil drawing of a couple, a man and a woman, the man in full knight's armor, the woman naked beneath him, her arms outstretched. She strained to meet his mouth, which was trapped behind the metal grill of his helmet, his lips just visible through the grating. He lay on top of her, resting on his elbows, and not one piece of his flesh touched hers.

"You did this?"

I went to stand beside him and tilted my head. I pointed to my initials at the bottom right hand corner. *KMcD*

"I did it in my Freshman year. I took a fine arts elective."

"It's good. Actually technically skilled." He turned to me. "Tell me about this."

"What's to tell?" I said. "It's a pencil drawing of a knight and his lady love."

"And why is she naked while he's in full armor?"

I said nothing for a moment, thinking of how I wanted to explain it. "Our assignment was to show contrasts in textures. I thought that metal and flesh were opposites – almost mortal enemies – and contrasting, kind of like male and female, masculine and feminine. My professor said I took the assignment way too literally."

"Metal and flesh aren't always enemies. I use steel to cut out tumors, open the skull to let pressure off a swelling brain."

I frowned. "I never thought of that. I was thinking more of war."

"It's all in your point of view. Even in war, metal can save lives. Trauma surgeons like my father worked in hospitals on the front lines in Vietnam using steel and cutting flesh to save lives." He turned back to the drawing once more. "Did you at least get a good grade? This is very good."

Technically, it *was* good. My prof said I showed excellent use of shading and perspective.

"I got an A."

"Good. But why a couple? If you wanted to show contrast between flesh and metal, if you wanted the war theme, why not a hand holding a sword? Or were you thinking of a different kind of war – the war between the sexes?"

I was silent for a moment, not wanting to admit the melodrama surrounding it.

"It was after a boyfriend and I broke up and I was all upset about it. You know what it's like when you're nineteen. You'd think it would be the other way around, right? The woman would be covered in armor while the man would be naked, so willing to have sex."

He studied the drawing for a moment.

"Oh, very deep," he said. "He can't really touch her even when they have sex because he wears armor to protect himself. It's symbolic of men's psychological armor. There she is, naked, open, and he can't really touch her even when he's fucking her." He turned and looked at me as if for acknowledgement. "Did you study psychology?"

I kept my eyes firmly on the drawing. "Yes," I said. "I took a course in my Freshman year."

"So you're implying that despite the fact that men want to have sex, they're not really touching the women they fuck. There's always that male armor keeping them from intimacy. Am I right?"

I forced a smile. "You're one of the few to get it."

"I have a degree in psychology. I was trained to look for underlying explanations for behavior."

He took a step to the next painting framed and hanging on the wall. An abstract, all greens and yellows and black lines – I bought it from a friend who went to art school.

"Research suggests that men fall in love more easily than women," he said, his voice light. "Do you really believe that men never let down their armor even during sex?"

"You tell me. You're the expert at keeping things compartmentalized."

"What could you possibly mean by that, Ms. Bennet?" he said, as if surprised. "Are you suggesting that I use D/s as a way to keep my distance from the women I fuck? I assure you, it's quite the opposite. I get right into their minds."

"But you don't love them. You're not really *intimate* with them, despite controlling them sexually."

"I'm *exceedingly* intimate with them." He smiled, but I could see a bit of edge in his eyes. "It all depends on how you define intimacy. Back to you and your difficulty sleeping with men on the first date." He stepped closer to me so that I was forced back against the wall. "You can't open your thighs without being intimate with a man and it bothers you that men can fuck women without being intimate, without actually caring about her the way you *think* they should. Am I right?"

I nodded. "My body is private. How can I get naked with someone I don't care about?"

"My *heart* is private. How can I care about someone who won't get naked with me?" he said, countering my logic, stepping even closer to me, lifting up a strand of my hair, running it under his nose. "What if I was to tell you that your inability to have casual sex was because of your father's and society's influence on you, not because of anything inherent in male-female sex differences? We're both animals with drives, Kate. Society has just controlled women's drives more, redirected them, couched the control in moral platitudes."

I frowned. "I forgot you wanted to be a psychoanalyst. I never did like Freud and his focus on fathers."

"He was right, but in the wrong way," Drake said. "Your father – the generalized father of patriarchal authority – made you believe that if you were purely sexual, if you *needed* to be fucked, you were bad. Isn't that right? He and the Church made you believe you were a bad girl to just want a hard cock inside of you. So you always held back, using this idea of intimacy as a shield – as *armor* against just feeling pleasure for its own sake. You use the demand for intimacy as an excuse so you can maintain the façade of being a good girl when really you're just an animal like me."

I just stood there, turning my face away from his. I could tell he enjoyed how his physical proximity made me nervous but he did nothing. Finally, he turned and walked into the living room, the moment ending but the thought still hanging there.

Was he right? Did I demand intimacy as a way of pretending I'm a good girl?

Why was it not good for me to just want to fuck a man?

After taking off his jacket and laying it on the back of a dining room chair, he removed his tie and unbuttoned the top button of his shirt. He sat on the couch, right in the middle so that I either had to sit beside him or pull up a dining room chair. He leaned back, his arms stretched out on the back of the couch, his feet up on my coffee table.

He caught my eyes. "Am I right?"

"Maybe," I said. "But whose approach is more satisfying in the end?"

Drake shrugged. "I've tried your approach. I was married for five years. You haven't tried mine. *Yet.* Why don't you give it a chance? Then you'll know."

"I can't imagine that meaningless sex can be rewarding in the long run."

He sighed, as if he was growing impatient with talking. "It's not. But it's good enough for now."

I stood on the other side of the coffee table and stared him down. "I only want to fuck someone who loves me," I said. "Is that so wrong?"

"Someone *will* love you, Kate. Do you really want to wait until he does? Is masturbating all alone in your room at night, for what – a year? Is that really good enough for you?"

That *hurt*.

I turned on my heel and went to the kitchen, opening and closing drawers, looking for my tea strainer so I could make some tea for us, but of course, I really just wanted to escape him. He came to me, standing behind me. He probably realized he went too far with that.

"I'm sorry." He reached out and touched my shoulder, softly.

"You're a *bastard*."

"No, I'm not. I'm just being honest." He took hold of my shoulders and turned me around to face him but I did my best to avoid his eyes, because mine were wet. The truth of his words hurt me.

"Kate, you *deserve* to have pleasure when you need it. You're not a bad girl for wanting to feel it. I can give it to you. I *want* to give you the pleasure you need in the way that most appeals to you, deep down inside if you're brave enough to admit it to yourself."

He bent down and tried to catch my eyes, but I closed them.

"Here," he said and folded me into his arms. I didn't stop him, but neither did I melt into his embrace. I was still too hurt to let him comfort me, my body stiff, unyielding.

"I'm sorry I hurt your feelings by speaking the truth so plainly. If this is going to work between us, you have to let me break down those protective walls you've built up around yourself. Otherwise, you won't really experience submission the way you need to."

I looked up at him briefly before glancing away. "So you're telling me you have to be mean to me in order for me to be able to submit?"

"*No*," he said, and tilted my face back to him. "You have to be honest with me about what you need and want. You have to honest with *yourself*."

I just stood there, breathing deeply, fighting with myself.

"Kate, *are* you sexually attracted to me?"

"You already know you're very handsome."

"I didn't ask that. I asked you if you were sexually attracted to me."

I couldn't say it. I felt it, but couldn't admit it.

He tried again, his voice very soft. "Do you want to fuck me? Is there a part of you that just wishes you could right now and to hell with convention?"

Finally, I exhaled. "Yes. But I'm afraid."

"*What* are you afraid of? That you'll have a great orgasm or three?"

"I'm afraid that you'll hurt me."

He sighed, frowning. "I *told* you and Lara told you that I'm not into pain. I don't want to *hurt* you, Kate. I want to make you feel *pleasure*."

"Not that kind of hurt." Of course, he knew what I really meant.

"That won't happen. We'll only have sex. None of that relationship stuff. We won't have breakfast together or go to movies or on dates. We'll fuck. I'll tie you up and make you come until you scream. I'll come. Then I'll go home. You'll sleep like a baby. End of story."

"What if I fall in love with you?"

He shook his head, smiling. "I won't let you."

"That's like saying you can control the weather. You can't."

"I can control the weather, too."

I caught his grin and couldn't help but smile. Reluctantly.

"I know this is all new to you. I know you're afraid." He pulled me against him, his arms around me, his hand caught in my hair, his obvious erection pressed against my belly. He desired me. He wanted me to know. To feel it.

Then, just when I thought he'd push me a bit, he released me and returned to the couch, sitting in the middle once more. He meant what he said. He wouldn't force me to do anything.

It would be my choice, but with him being the way he was – so desirable, so powerful, so... *knowing*, how could I resist him?

I stood in the kitchen for a moment, still debating with myself. I pushed a few dishes around, pretending to wash a cup, but finally, I gave up pretending to be busy and returned to the living room to stand in front of him once more.

"Just theoretical, but if I was really your sub-in-training, what would you normally do at this point?"

He examined me, briefly catching my eye. "I'd suggest that you come and sit with me and we can talk some more."

I sat on the edge of the couch, not touching him, not looking at him, my hands crossed on my lap.

"Did you go to a Catholic school as a child?"

I glanced up, frowning. "Yes. Why do you ask?"

"You have very good posture. Your hands are folded." He pointed to my clasped hands.

I glanced down at them and then unclasped them, smiling a bit ruefully.

"Yes, they expected us to sit properly. The nuns gave us the cane if we were *slovenly* in our dress or behavior."

He nodded. "A good Catholic school upbringing. Making uptight women out of excited little girls full of life and promise. Only the really rebellious ones escaped with their libidos fully intact."

"Yeah, the nuns really did a number on us."

Then he patted his knee. "If you were really my sub-in-training, I'd tell you to come closer. Sit on my lap. So why don't you?"

I frowned. "Am I a child?"

"No," he said. "But I like to sit close together at first. Just touching for a while with all our clothes on. If you decide to stop at any time, you just have to get up. I won't prevent you."

I stood up and moved a bit closer, standing directly in front of him.

"How do I..."

He reached up and took my arms, pulling me down on top of him so that I sat on his lap with my legs to the side, my arms around his neck. It was far too close at first and I trembled a bit to feel his arms slide around me, one arm around my waist, the other resting on my hip. I tried to avoid looking in his eyes as much as possible, and he didn't push, but finally I felt stupid and met his gaze, his blue eyes so gorgeous with those thick dark lashes.

Oh *God*...

He adjusted me a bit, grasping my hips and moving me a couple of inches. My thigh pressed against his erection, which I could tell was now hard as rock.

"Sorry," he said, grimacing a bit. "You're pressing just a bit too hard on my..." He let his voice trail off. He moved his hips beneath me. "That's better."

He wanted me to know he was aroused. I couldn't help but respond, closing my eyes as my flesh throbbed, a pleasant ache building in me.

"You smell so good," he said, breathing in. He slid one hand up my thigh and just let it rest on my hip.

"It's my perfume," I said. "It's called *Mystique*."

"I wasn't referring to your perfume."

"Oh." I tensed. "Maybe I..." I tried to get up, embarrassed that he could smell me but he stopped me.

"I *love* how you smell. Your female scent and the thought of how wet you are makes me so *hard*."

He took my hand and pressed it against his erection, sliding my fingers along its length so that I knew how hard and thick he was. I couldn't help but imagine him filling me up.

That flustered me, and I felt caught between wanting to run away from embarrassment and wanting to stay. Other than my own arousal, a pleasant swollenness, a wetness between my thighs, butterflies in my stomach, I was warm in his arms, comfortable nestled against his chest.

"So we just sit here like this?"

"Yes," he said, stretching out again, his arms on the back of the couch. "We can just talk. With my new subs, I always let them choose the time of our first fuck. If they want anything to happen, they have to make the move. If they want me, all they have to do is kiss me. But I warn them. If they do, I take that as a sign they want to fuck me and I take over. I take control and I fuck them. If they change their mind, they have to use a safe word. If they do, it all stops right then, and I go home."

I relaxed just a bit, knowing that I had ultimate control over whether and when we would fuck the first time. It would be my choice.

He caught my eye for a brief moment.

"So be warned. Don't kiss me unless you mean it." He held my gaze, grasping my chin when I tried to look away. "I can sit here like this for as long as you want and talk if that's all you want tonight. Sure, I'm hard as rock, but it will fade eventually if nothing more happens. But if you *kiss* me, I'll take it to mean you want me to fuck you. I'll take your clothes off and I'll eat you and then I'll fuck you. I'm not a frat boy, Kate. I don't like to play games."

My cheeks heated at that and I stiffened. "I thought you *liked* playing games. Isn't that what people in the lifestyle call it? Playing?"

"*Fuck* games, Kate. Not emotional games."

We sat like that for a few moments as his warning sunk in, his arms on the back of the couch, me nestled against him, my arms around his neck. He wasn't touching me. I was touching him. If anything was going to happen, I had to make it happen.

And the thing was, I *wanted* it to happen.

He had me right where he wanted me. He knew exactly how to manipulate me, knew what to say, how to get me to think and feel the things he wanted me to think and feel.

He *was* a Master. I could see that now.

Sitting on his lap like that, his body warm beneath mine, his shoulder muscles beneath the expensive white shirt solid under my hands, his aftershave masculine, his slight male musk intoxicating. His very large and very hard erection pressing against me was a reminder of how aroused he was.

He was *mine* – this gorgeous powerful man – if I wanted him. I had never felt this much lust for someone and I felt almost out of control, my body warm, swollen, my breathing shallow.

Yet, I had ultimate control. I decided if anything happened. But I decided only if he would fuck me or not. Once I kissed him, he'd take over and have his way with me.

He was right. I always felt guilt for wanting sex. I always felt bad when I fantasized about sex with men I'd just met or seen – like it was wrong for me to just feel horny. When I *did* have a boyfriend, even then, I couldn't really let go. Orgasms were so hard and took so long because I always felt insecure, unsure if my noises and movements and preferences would turn my lover off. Like how I was feeling – my body's arousal – was somehow unsightly and offensive.

He made me feel as if my body and my desire were intoxicating to him. As if he knew what to do when it came time for sex. I wouldn't have to worry.

All I had to do was kiss him and he'd take over. If I didn't kiss him, we'd just talk and then, when it came time to leave, he'd go.

"Why do your subs need a safe word if the first time is just vanilla sex?"

"It's always good to have a safe word. Things get passionate. Heavy. Hard. Fast. If I overwhelm the sub and she can't handle it, I need to know. But Kate," he said and turned my face to his. "Using red as a safe word isn't a request just to slow things down a bit or to adjust things. It's a signal for a full-stop. Once they use it, it's over. So I warn my subs not to use red unless they really are unable to go on."

"What exactly do you mean by heavy? Hard?"

"*Kate...*" He smiled indulgently, as if I were a child. "Have you never had really passionate sex with a man before? A little desperate? He's pounding into you from behind, grabbing your hips, thrusting hard and fast?"

Oh, *God...* Those words and the thought of how big he was made me clench.

I swallowed, my throat dry. I looked in his eyes, and I could tell he was a bit amused at my inexperience, but even *his* cheeks were flushed. I took him in all at once as he leaned back against the couch – his face so symmetrical, his jaw square with a day's growth of whiskers, his eyes so blue and fringed with thick dark lashes. His mouth was soft, his lips parted. His black hair a bit mussed, collar open, shirt undone just enough to see his chest.

He was the most desirable man I'd ever seen.

"Red is a stoplight," he said. "You say red, everything stops."

"How do I know you won't run a red light?"

He closed his eyes and smiled. "Unlike flyboy, I'm not into rape, Kate. Not even mock rape. If I do it, it's because my sub needs it and asked for it." He opened his eyes again and now they were so intense, his brows furrowed. "I can only get off with a woman who wants it. Who wants *me.*"

I stared at him. Everything inside of me, my body, my emotions, my heart, was pushing me towards him. The only thing holding me back was that annoying sense of propriety that my father and the nuns created in me.

Damn them...

"*I* want you."

He just waited, watching me with those eyes. He was so calm, patient. I didn't know what held me back. Why was it so hard for me to just lean over and kiss him?

Finally, he exhaled as if he'd been holding his breath.

"Then *kiss* me."

I closed my eyes, feeling utterly frozen in place. "I can't."

"Oh, *Kate*..."

Then he wrapped his arms around me and pulled me on top of him as he lay down on the couch, his head against the armrest. I couldn't help but straddle his hips, my thighs on either side of his, my hands holding me up, my face poised directly above his. He pushed my hair away from my face, tucking it behind my ear, then he slipped his arms around my waist, pulling my hips against him so that I could feel his erection. It actually made me tremble.

I closed my eyes and leaned my head down, my cheek pressed against his.

"Oh, *God*." I practically panted in his ear but I just couldn't force myself to *kiss* him. If I did, it would be game over. This would really happen and it scared me *so much*.

"*Jesus*, Kate, are you that repressed that you can't even *kiss* me?"

"You said it yourself," I managed to say. "If I kiss you, you're going to fuck me."

"You said you want me, so just *do* it."

"Why are you making *me*?" I said, emotion filling me. "You already kissed me *three times* tonight. Why do I have to be the one now?"

"You *have* to be the one."

"Why?"

"You have to say yes. I have to know that you want me to fuck you. That this is what you *really* want. What you really *need*. I don't want any doubt."

"Then, *yes*, for Christ's sake, *yes*," I blurted out, tears of frustration actually springing to my eyes. "I *want* you to fuck me. I *need* you to fu—"

Before I could say the words, he pulled me down to him and forced me to kiss him, and I did. I *kissed* him back and when I did, I felt him relax completely beneath me. With the exception of his erection, his body was yielding instead of hard, his arms no longer tense, no longer pulling me against him. He *let* me kiss him. I cupped his cheek, my fingers threading through his hair while my mouth moved against his, my tongue searching and finding his.

The kiss went on and on, all the while my body grew more aroused, if that was even possible. I ground my groin on his erection, needing to feel it against me, my heart pounding in my ears, a delicious stab of lust racing through my body at the thought of him entering me, pounding me from behind like he'd described.

Finally, I pulled away, confused at his lack of – well, of *anything*.

"I thought," I said, gasping as our lips parted. "I thought you were going to take control after I kissed you."

He smiled slowly, his eyes half-hooded. "Who's to say I haven't?"

"I don't understand. You said—"

"Stop talking."

Then he *did* take control, rising up, forcing me to sit up as well. Instead of me lying on top of him, he pushed me down on the couch and now he lay on top of me, his body heavy on mine. He didn't kiss me. He watched me as he pressed against me. Resting on one elbow so that his body was poised above me, his eyes never left mine. He trailed his fingers over my cheek, over my bottom lip, then down the side of my neck to my throat. His fingers traced the upper curve of my breasts, making me shiver, then he squeezed one breast through the silky fabric of my dress, his finger and thumb unerringly finding my nipple and tweaking it, making me gasp, my back arching.

He smiled and spread my thighs open with a rough knee, hiking up my dress around my hips, his hand grabbing my mound, his finger searching for my clit through my pantyhose and panties. Then he pulled his hand away and ground his erection against me until I groaned, my eyes closing.

"Keep your eyes open."

I opened my eyes to find myself staring into his determined ones.

Then, he rose up between my thighs and reached for my pantyhose, grasping the waistband and removing them, pulling them down and off me.

"From now on, you're only wearing garters and nylons when you're with me. No underwear."

When he reached for my panties and pulled at them, I took in a deep breath, my heart racing, knowing this was it. He pulled them off me and I was bare from the waist down. Instinctively, I drew my knees together, but he deliberately spread them again with his hands until my thighs were wide open, exposing myself to him, the air cool on my heated flesh.

"Oh, you're so nice and *wet*."

At that, I tried to cover myself up, embarrassed that I was so wet. I wanted to run to the bathroom and wash myself.

"I should take a bath..."

He made a face. "What? *No*. Kate, you're supposed to be wet. Your scent makes me rock hard. I can't wait to taste you."

Then he stood and pulled me up as well so that we were standing by the couch. I felt dizzy, my head spinning just a bit at the abrupt transition. He turned me around and undid my zipper, pulling the shoulders of my dress down from behind. He pushed my hair out of the way, his mouth on my neck. He bit my shoulder but not hard enough to hurt. My dress slipped off and down my arms so that I was standing in my bra and nothing else. While still behind me, he ran his hands over my hips and around to my belly, then up until he cupped each breast briefly, squeezing them through the lacy black fabric. I leaned back against him, my eyes closing as he touched me so gently, his erection still pressed against me from behind. His fingers pulled the lacy cups of my bra down so that my breasts jutted out over top of the fabric, my nipples puckering in the cool air. The palms of his hands grazed my nipples and I couldn't help but gasp.

He embraced me from behind, one hand below my breast, the other sliding down my skin over my belly and then lower to my mound, barely touching me, then down to my thighs.

"Spread your legs," he said, his tone authoritative, but his voice still warm.

I complied and his hand moved back to my labia very lightly without touching my inner lips or clit. All the while, he licked my neck, sucked the skin on my shoulder, biting me softly.

Then he pulled me around to face him and removed my bra, unclasping the hook in front so that my breasts spilled out. He threw the bra on the floor, and just stared at me, his gaze moving over my body from my face to my thighs and then back.

I couldn't help but move to cover up, but he stopped me, his hands holding my arms.

"Don't cover yourself," he said, his voice firm. "You look so delicious, I want to lick you. I want to run my tongue over every inch of you."

He did nothing, just stood there staring at my naked body, letting that sink in and the thought of his mouth on me, of him licking me, sent a stab of lust through me.

He'd barely touched me, but I was more aroused than I had ever been before.

"Undress me."

I swallowed and stepped closer, reaching for his shirt. His eyes never left my face as I pulled his shirt out of his pants and then unbuttoned it. I took each hand and unbuttoned the cuffs, then pulled the shirt off him, leaving him bare-chested. His abs were well-developed, a washboard six pack, his pecs large but not overly, a trail of dark hair leading from his navel to beneath his trouser waistband. His erection pressed against the fabric of his trousers, and when I started to unbuckle his belt, my fingers grazed it and he made this sound in the back of his throat. I unzipped him, his pants dropping and he stepped out of them. He wore boxer briefs in black, and I almost gasped when I saw how large he really was.

I hesitated when it came to removing his briefs, but took in a breath and pulled them down so that his erection sprung out, heavy and thick and long, the head smooth and wet with fluid that had leaked out, leaving a spot on his briefs. He stepped out of them and now all that remained were his socks. I rolled each one off his foot, my face next to his cock, unable to avoid looking at it.

He was so beautiful, his skin pale. His cock was beautiful, long and thick and pink, a prominent vein running up the shaft.

"See how ready I am for you?"

I glanced up into his eyes, which were dark, no trace of humor in them now. I quickly stood and waited for his next command.

"Touch me. Feel how hard I am because of you."

I did, grasping him, stroking up his length to the head. He *was* hard and my body responded to the feel of him in my hand. I imagined how he'd feel inside of me, filling me up, the pressure intense.

He was almost as big as Big.

"Kneel down and lick me. Taste me," he said. I did, kneeling as he instructed, and with one hand, I grasped him and directed the head to my lips, licking the head all around, his fluid salty.

"Suck me."

I took the head into my mouth with soft lips, my tongue rolling around the head, stroking the underside and he gasped. At the sound of his pleasure, my body responded, a thrill racing through me.

I felt his cock jump in my mouth and I sucked the head in further, moving my wet lips over him slowly. He let me do this for a few moments, then reached down and guided my head, increasing the speed, pushing inside my mouth a little deeper. His breathing became more intense and he thrust his hips just a bit each time, pushing deeper into my mouth but not so deep that I gagged.

I glanced up at him with his cock in my mouth.

"That's so *good*, Kate."

Then he pulled me off him and kissed me, dragging me with him back towards my bedroom.

"Do you have any condoms?"

I shook my head. "No," I said, embarrassed. "I haven't had sex for a long time. I wasn't planning... "

"That's all right," he said, stopping by the coat tree, reaching into a pocket inside his lapel. "I honestly didn't really think we'd end up here, but I brought a couple just in case lady luck smiled down on me." He pulled out a couple of condoms in foil packs and smiled. "I prefer bareback and we will once we're both tested and clear. Are you on the birth control pill?"

"Yes," I said. " I'm on the pill and I was tested a few months ago. There's been no one for a year."

He ran his hand through his hair. "Look, Kate, I get tested regularly and I make sure all my partners are tested. I'm clean." He shook his head. "But until we both get the all clear? We have to use these."

I nodded. "You're the doctor."

"Doctors still get HIV."

"I trust you."

He took my hand and led me to the bed. Sitting on the edge, he directed me between his spread thighs, burying his face between my breasts. He wrapped his arms around me and pulled me against him, then his mouth claimed first one then the other nipple, his tongue wet and warm against them, the tugging as he sucked sending a delicious thrill through my body, making me gasp. He squeezed my breasts while he sucked, working me up even more, my body feeling so swollen and aching.

He turned me around, pushing me onto the bed so that I lay back, closing my eyes, letting him have his way with me. He lifted my thighs so that they were spread wide, then he opened one of the packs and held the condom out to me.

"Put it on."

I sat up and held the condom, unsure how to do it. "I've never..."

"You've never put a condom on a man?"

"They always did it."

"Hold the top between your finger and thumb and then place it over the head. Unroll it over the head and down as far as it will go."

I followed his instructions, amazed at how big he was, my breath shallow from arousal. Then he pushed me back against the bed again and kissed me as he slid his cock against me, rubbing the head against my clit while he held my hands firmly in one of his above my head. My heart was beating so fast, my face hot, my thighs trembling.

"You're so nice and wet, Kate," he said, sliding the head of his cock up and down against my clit and it felt so good I groaned out loud, unable to stop myself. "Oh, you like that do you?"

He kept rubbing me like that, the pleasure building inside of me. Then he pressed the head against the entrance to my body, sliding it just an inch inside me, then back up and around my clit, repeating that over and over again, entering a bit deeper each time.

"It's been a while, hasn't it, since you had a cock inside of you."

I didn't say anything. I wasn't going to mention Big, although I'd never managed to get Big more than a couple inches inside. With that, he shoved himself a little deeper into me, the pressure intense. He was bigger than anyone I'd been with before.

"You're so nice and *big*." I gasped, the pleasure building as he entered me just a couple of inches and then withdrew, teasing my clit with the head before plunging back inside me again.

"You're so nice and *tight*." He closed his eyes and thrust deeper. He remained inside me this time, his thumb against my clit, stroking all around it while he just kept still. I couldn't help it. I wanted to feel him move inside of me, a little deeper, and I thrust my hips up, trying to increase the sensations.

"Feels good, doesn't it? So *sweet*..."

He thrust a bit, still only a couple of inches inside of me, his thumb rubbing my clit. Straight fucking with other men had never felt that good before and I'd always only come through oral sex. Now, with all the workup, with everything that happened since the concert hall, all the nerve ending inside of me seemed to be on fire, and every time he thrust, I felt closer and closer to going over the edge.

"I feel," I said, my eyes closing as the sweetness built, " that feels *so*..."

I watched him from under my eyelashes and his eyes were closed as he thrust slowly inside of me, still so much of him outside of my body he was so big. This was just teasing me with his cock. He wasn't really thrusting deep or fast. Just slow, pulling out every couple of thrusts, stroking over my labia to my clit and then back inside. But it was enough and my body started to tense as my orgasm started.

"*Ohhh*." Waves of pleasure spread out from my center, up into my belly and down my thighs. "Oh, *God...*" I gritted my teeth, my eyes closing from the intensity.

"Don't come yet," he said, stopping his movements. "This is too fast. *Breathe*, Kate. Wait and it will be even better."

I couldn't speak, caught in the waves of pleasure, gasping when his movement stopped, depriving me of the stimulation just when my orgasm started.

"Oh, *baby*, you're already gone," he said, and began thrusting harder, faster, entering me deeply, pushing me back over the edge once more.

CHAPTER TEN

I came *hard*.

When he realized I was already gone, he entered me completely, right to the hilt and my eyes rolled back in my head. He leaned over me while he thrust, watching my face. Then, when I was done, when the last waves of my pleasure retreated, he just stopped all motion.

"What are you doing?" I gasped, wondering why he stopped.

"I like feeling you clench around me." He was grinning as if he couldn't hold back his laughter.

"Why are you laughing at me?" I covered my face with my hands.

"Oh, *Kate*," he said, and tried to pull my hands away from my face. "I'm not laughing at you," but even as he said it, I could hear the mirth in his voice.

"*Don't*," I said and turned my face away, mortified, my eyes filling. He pried my hands away from my face and forced me to look in his eyes.

"No modesty allowed with me." He moved slowly inside of me and it made me clench again. "That was just so *fast*," he said, amusement in his voice. "You really needed a hard cock in you."

I struggled with him, trying to turn away, cover my eyes again, my cheeks hot.

The beep-beep beep-beep of Drake's cell alarm pulled my attention away from him.

"Oh, *fuck*. Lara..." Drake withdrew from my body and went to his jacket for his cell, his cock still rock hard.

"Hi, it's me. We're in the middle of things..." He listened. "Just a minute." He came back to the bed where I was lying on my side, hands covering my face, mortified that he was able to manipulate me so well and that I came so fast with him barely doing *anything* to me. He crawled onto the bed beside me and handed me the phone. "It's Lara. She wants to talk to you, make sure you're all right."

I pushed the phone and his hand away, not looking at him. "I'm fine," I whispered.

"She says she's fine."

Then he leaned down and tried to turn my face towards him, but I fought, my hair covering my face, my hands over my eyes. What the fuck was wrong with me? My eyes stung with tears.

Drake left the bedroom, and I watched as he went to the living room and stood in the darkness. I got up and pulled on my nightgown, a tiny black lacy thing and stood at the door, listening. He spoke quietly, but I could still hear him.

"Lara, she's a bit *emotional* right now," he said, his voice almost inaudible. There was silence for a moment as he listened to Lara. "I barely even had it *in* her. Seriously, I hardly did anything. Like, two minutes..."

I bit my lip to gain control over my emotions.

"I'm not an idiot *frat boy*," I heard him whisper. "I *did* take it slow. Christ, She was just so ready..."

A pause. "I will. *She* will," he said. "Thanks for understanding."

I went to the bathroom before he returned to wash my face and get hold of myself. I closed the door behind me, but there was no lock so he could come in if he wanted.

He knocked at the door. "Kate, let me in."

"Just *go*."

"Don't be like that. Let me in. We have to talk."

I didn't respond and then he came inside. I stood at the vanity holding a wet washcloth to my eyes. He put his arms around me from behind, just pressing his body against mine as if to comfort me. He was still semi-hard but he didn't push or make any kind of sexual move.

"Kate, *why* are you crying?"

"I'm not."

He turned me around and took the washcloth out of my hands, wrapping his arms around me, forcing my head onto his shoulder. I was just mortified at how easily he was able to arouse me, and how fast I'd come. It shocked me.

He pulled me into the living room and made me sit on his lap once more, straddling his hips, his still semi-erect cock lying to the side, condom covering him. I gave in, my arms slipping around his neck, my head resting on his shoulder. I didn't say anything, and he didn't force me to.

"I should have been more aware of how you were doing, Kate. I was just so aroused myself, too busy enjoying myself to notice, a little shocked. That was sloppy of me and won't happen again. I really didn't think anything would happen..."

"You were laughing at me."

"No, *no*," he said, shaking his head. "I wasn't laughing *at* you. I was delighted *with* you. I was ecstatic. You're so *responsive*." He tried to catch my eye but I avoided him. "Look at me." He took my chin in his hand and turned my face. Finally, I couldn't avoid his eyes and I felt that connection between us again.

He took in a deep breath. "I didn't think you'd come so fast and so easily. I didn't even get to *taste* you."

"I'm so *embarrassed*," I whispered. "You barely did *anything* to me. I've never been that fast before."

"Don't be. It means you can come many times in a session. You don't know how pleased that makes me." He brushed hair off my cheek. "Sweet submissive Kate. You really are a sub, little one. I just proved it without even trying."

"What do you mean?"

"I didn't really even have my Dom hat on with you – not fully – and you were totally responsive to me and what I was doing and saying and how I was touching you. You have no idea how that kind of response is so addictive."

"You didn't," I said, glancing down at his erection. "You *know*..."

"No, I didn't *come*," he said, smiling at me. "Way too fast for me. Next time you can do me twice in payback."

I tried to hide my own smile by tucking my face into the crook of his neck. "Won't you get blue balls or something?"

He laughed softly. "I'll be fine, Kate. But I did want to ask you something. Do you always come during intercourse?"

I shook my head. "No, never with a partner."

He frowned. "What does *that* mean, with a partner?"

"Well," I said, my cheeks reddening when he pulled back to look me in the eyes.

"What?"

"I do with..." I said, shrugging one shoulder, my voice barely audible. "You *know*."

"With what? Tell me, Kate. You can't shock me. Your fingers?"

I shook my head, embarrassed. "I got this gift at a bachelorette party *and*..."

This look came over his face – I couldn't tell if it was amusement or incredulity. "A dildo or a vibrator?"

"The first one." I couldn't even say the word.

"You use a *dildo*?"

He pushed me back down on the couch, leaning over me, grinning like an idiot. "Sweet little Ms. *Bennet* using a dildo to get off? Oh, *God*..." He bent his head next to mine, his mouth beside my ear. "I won't be able to sleep tonight imagining it."

He pulled back and I covered my eyes, smiling, my face hot. "I can't believe I admitted to that!"

"Oh, you *have* to admit to things like that with *me*, Kate. I have to know these things. You *are* a little kinky after all. A dildo? How big? What color?"

I bit my lip and turned my face away, not able to look him in the eye.

"Come on, *tell me*!"

"I looked it up on Google," I said, stifling a laugh, covering my mouth. "It's flesh colored and called," I said, breaking out in giggles. "Mr. *Big*."

He laughed out loud at that. "Well, then, I'm perfect for you!"

We laughed together for a few minutes, me giggling almost uncontrollably, tears in my eyes I was laughing so hard, relieved that he wasn't horrified. All my anxiety seemed to dissipate with the laughter.

"So, tell me details," he said, pulling me back up so that I sat straddling his hips in his embrace. "When did you start using it? Was it before or after flyboy? How often do you use it?"

"*Drake*!" My face was so hot from embarrassment. "I can't talk about this!"

"Oh, yes you can. You *must*. This is like Pandora's Box. Once you mention it, you have to tell me everything. Did you use it before or after flyboy?"

I sighed. "After," I said, remembering. "My friend's bachelorette party about eight months ago. We all got one. It was a Carrie *Sex in the City* party."

"And? Details. Come on."

I shrugged my shoulder a bit. "I tried it, but it was too big. So I just kind of played with it a bit. You *know*..."

"No, I don't know. You have to describe it."

"I *can't*..."

"I'll make you show me right now if you don't tell me," he said.

"No way!" I shook my head. "I do just what you did. You know, just playing around a bit outside, going in a bit but not too deep at first... Eventually, I got the hang of it and I think I found my G-Spot."

"You sure *did* get the hang of it."

He pulled me against him and took in a deep breath, kissing my neck. "Oh, sweet Kate, don't be embarrassed about that. You don't have any idea how much men want to learn something like that about their lover."

"It's embarrassing."

"Oh, no, *baby*. There isn't a heterosexual man alive who'd think less of you if he knew. In fact, he'd be pleased that you can come from his dick alone. That's not all that common."

"I wanted to be able to. It frustrated me that I couldn't. I only used to be able to through oral and it felt like there was something wrong with me. So when I got *Big*, I decided to try..."

He smiled and stroked my cheek. "You call it *Big*?"

"After *Big* on Sex and the City. Carrie's boyfriend. We used to joke with each other about it. *Has Big visited you lately?*" I said, raising my eyebrows suggestively. " *How's Big doing? Still such an upright kinda guy? Still as reliable as ever? Never lets a girl down.*" I smiled sheepishly. "That kind of thing."

He laughed and then pulled me against him, and I could feel him smiling against my neck, his cheek raising. We sat like that for a few minutes, not speaking, just basking in the post-laughing jag high that released all my anxiety over coming so fast.

"Come," he said and pulled me back into the bedroom and I was certain that he was going to fuck me, finish the job, but instead, he pulled me onto the bed and under the covers. Then he pulled me on top of him so that I lay on his body.

I waited for him to do something but he didn't, just held me, stroking my hair, his other hand stroking the skin on my back.

"You don't want to..."

"To what?"

"You *know*..."

"Fuck you?" He glanced at me, smiling. "It's getting too late and I don't like to rush." Then he glanced at his watch. "It's almost past the witching hour," he said and turned my face to his. "I have to go in five. Have an early morning in the OR but I wanted to just lie here for a while with you. Make sure you're OK."

"I'm fine," I said, my voice stronger now, a tiny grin on my face. He kissed me softly. He was still semi-erect. "Are *you* OK? You're still a *bit*..."

"I'll be fine," he said, humor in his voice. "It's not the first time I've left a woman half-erect and won't be the last time."

"You don't want to *just*..."

He squeezed me. "Just have a quickie? A quick ram from behind?"

I nodded, my cheeks heating.

"I'm tempted but no," he said and rolled over on top of me, watching me as he stroked my cheek. "I don't want to use your body like that right now but next time?" he said, frowning. "Next time I *will* use your body for my pleasure entirely. I intend to fuck you without you coming, just a straight desperate fuck so that we're even."

That made me clench.

"Why not now?"

"Not now – not the first time. The first time is all about you. We don't have time to get you back in the mood after that laughing fit. As fast as you were, I know you won't be that fast again and I don't have time. I can wait until next time."

We lay like that for a while longer and I just relaxed, my cheek against his shoulder, my arms around his warm body.

Finally, he sighed. "I have to go."

He rose up and I followed him to the bathroom, watching as he unrolled the condom from his still semi-erect cock. He threw it in the trash. Then he took a pee right in front of me. I turned away, embarrassed.

"I have no shame, Kate, about anything to do with the body. You shouldn't either. Not with me."

Then he washed his hands and I followed him out to his clothes, watching as he dressed. He came to me and tipped my chin up with a finger, kissing me, a sweet kiss.

"Until next time," he said, his eyes meeting mine. "There will be a next time, I hope? You'll give me another chance?"

"Yes, please," I said, not intending to sound so formal.

"I look forward to it. I'm going to edit your agreement and send you a revised copy in email tonight. I want you to read it and consider it. Sign it. I want this for real, Kate. I think we're a good match." He kissed me again. "Promise me you'll consider it."

"I will."

While he finished dressing, I watched, admiring his physique. I handed him his coat and he pulled it on. He kissed me softly, stroking my cheek with a thumb, his fingers threading in my hair.

"Call Lara now, so I know you have. She'll be waiting."

I retrieved my cell from my bag, dialed and then waited.

"Hi, Lara?" I said, looking at him. "It's Kate. I'm fine."

He nodded to me and then left the apartment, the door closing softly behind him.

"Tell me what happened," Lara said as I closed the door behind Drake.

"He seduced me is what happened. I didn't plan on us having sex tonight but he has this *way*..."

She laughed on the other end of the line. "That he does. He's a great mindfuck, Kate. That's his specialty. He knows how to get into your mind and uses that to get what he wants. Keep that in mind when you're with him. He's *very* smart."

"He is. Especially in *that* way. You know, psychology."

"It's how we met. Abnormal Psych course in my senior year. We actually studied BDSM and I think that's what got me started in the lifestyle, but Drake remained outside, just interested intellectually. He didn't get back into it until after his divorce."

"Did he come to you about it?"

"Yes. I taught him everything he knows, but he's a natural. But I think he was a bit sloppy with you tonight. Tell me why you were crying."

I exhaled and bit a nail, thinking about it. "I don't know," I said. "I was embarrassed. I came so fast, and he was grinning at me, almost laughing and I thought he must think I was really stupid."

"Oh, *no*, Kate, you have to realize that's a bonus for a man like Drake."

"Why?"

"He *wants* to make you come, a *lot*. It's his way of feeling power. You just proved yourself capable. With new subs, especially novices, it takes a while to work out the differences between you. You have to learn how they respond to things, what they like and need. See how compatible their needs are with what you need. It can take a while to get in sync. The fact you came so quickly means he *gets* you. He understands you and what you need. I just don't think he realized how *much* he gets you and was able to affect you. And," she said, "how much you affected *him*."

"I was surprised as well. I mean, I never came through intercourse alone before. Not with a man, I mean. Just a dildo."

"Oh, you use a dildo?" She said nothing for a moment, but I could hear a bit of a laugh on the other end. "That explains it."

"I thought I was ruining myself using it. It was so big I couldn't even get it inside of me completely."

She chuckled. "Drake could ruin you for other men, so watch out."

"He's big."

"He's *delightfully* big," Lara said, her voice filled with humor. "If he wasn't a Dom, I'd have made him my own sub."

"You trained him? Doesn't that mean he had to take the submissive role?"

"Yes, but every Dom has to learn. I showed him how to top someone. I taught him how to use toys and implements. I taught him safety procedures. He's a natural, Kate. He understands this at a really deep level. As a novice, you couldn't be in better hands. Usually, he would have just let you go if there'd been any personal connection between you and him so I'm surprised he's pursuing you. He really shouldn't because he doesn't like any messy personal stuff in his sexual life. And I think he really likes you, but don't tell him I told you that. "

"Oh, I wouldn't dream of it."

"Good. He usually keeps his distance with his subs. He doesn't see them socially. He doesn't really talk to them about anything outside the lifestyle and sex. He's already seen you socially a couple of times so this is not usual for him, nor is it usual for him to screw up like this."

"It was kind of unavoidable, given who we both are. He and my dad are so close."

"Usually, he compartmentalizes very well. He has his work, his band, his charity, and his subs. But I have a feeling you're just his type. Maybe too much if all you want is instruction and to write your article."

I frowned, wondering why she was warning me. "That's all I want," I said, but of course, Drake was so attractive and so desirable in every way, a part of me couldn't help but hope we became more than just fuck partners.

She was silent for a moment. "Kate, I'll tell you the truth. When I learned you two knew each other personally, I told him to stay away from you."

"You did? Why?"

"You're too messy. He should only be with experienced subs who know that this is just sex."

"Messy?"

"Too much crossover in your lives. Doctors Without Borders, your father, Africa. You're both in the same social circles. I'm warning you. That's not what Drake wants, so don't expect anything from him."

"I won't," I said, but it hurt to say that.

"He's been alone since his divorce. All he's had are his subs, which he's not emotionally connected to. *Still...*" she said, as if debating with herself. "I wonder. Did he kiss you? I mean, aside from during sex? Did he kiss you goodnight?"

"Yes," I said, frowning. "He kissed me, um," I said, counting it up mentally, "at least five times. Maybe more. Why do you ask?"

"Don't get any romantic ideas, because he's not able to go there. This is just sex, Kate. Keep that in your mind. Don't let yourself go beyond that."

"I *won't*," I said again, frowning.

"Well, I'll let you go. Sweet dreams, Kate."

"Good night, Lara. Thanks again."

I ended the call and just sat on the couch for a while, remembering the very brief and almost whirlwind events from earlier. I covered my mouth with a hand as I thought about what happened from the time we were outside the concert hall to him kissing me goodbye.

Lara warned me and I had to take that warning to heart.

He said he didn't kiss women unless he was fucking them. He kissed *me* several times without fucking me, both before and after. Lara seemed really interested in whether he kissed me as if it meant something. I didn't know him well enough to understand *what* it meant, but men always kissed you a lot when they were trying to get you into bed. Once they did, the kissing seemed to stop.

I wondered if it would be the same with Drake.

Thing is, I *loved* kissing. It seemed so intimate. I craved it. When it stopped being so important, once you were really into a sexual relationship, I always felt deprived. The couple of men I slept with before always seemed to want to get right to the meat of the matter, right to the sucking and fucking and kisses stopped being so important.

If I was going to enter into this D/s relationship with Drake, I hoped he would still kiss me, but I expected we would only meet to have sex so he would kiss me then, based on what I read from his letters to his subs. Lara warned me. I had to be content with just really *really* great sex.

After a warm bath, I went to my laptop and checked my email, looking for the agreement he said he'd email me when he got home. It was half an hour since he left and I expected to find an email from him but nothing. Maybe he was busy editing it or something.

I yawned and made a pot of decaf Blackberry Tea. Then, I curled up on the couch with a soft blanket, watching the late night talk shows to pass the time. I couldn't wait to read Drake's contract, to see exactly what he expected from me sexually and in terms of behavior.

Later, an hour after he left, I checked again, but there was still nothing from Drake, so I just shut out the lights and went to bed.

CHAPTER ELEVEN

The next day, just before lunch, I got an email from Drake while I was at Columbia. I was surprised that he waited so long to send it. He said he'd send it when he got home the night before.

I opened it eagerly and read the contents.

From:	**Morgan, D. L.**
Sent:	**November 12, 11:31 AM**
To:	**McDermott, Katherine M.**
Subject:	**Your Submission**
Attachments:	**The Agreement.doc (120 KB)**

Kate:

I've attached a revised agreement for you to review. If you have any concerns, note them and we will discuss later tonight. I have a practice session with my band from 8:00 p.m. until 10:00 p.m. but will drop by after. Then I'll use you the way I promised.

Drake

That made my heart rate increase just a bit. I opened the contract PDF and sat at my desk in the teaching assistants' office, reading it on my iPad.

The first part seemed what I expected, and similar to what Lara showed me:

SUBMISSION AGREEMENT BETWEEN

Drake Liam Morgan (hereinafter referred to as "Master")

AND

Katherine Marie McDermott (hereinafter referred to as "slave")

Said Submission Agreement, hereafter referred to as "the Agreement", refers to total dominance and control of Master in his sexual relationship with said slave.

1.0.0   Slave's Role

> *The slave agrees to submit sexually to the Master in all ways. This applies to all situations in which the Master and slave interact sexually, both in private and if applicable, in public. Failure to obey will result in punishment as the Master sees fit with the exception of the slave's veto right (section 1.0.1). Once entered into the Slavery Agreement, the slave's body belongs to the Master, to be used as He desires, within the guidelines defined herein. When they are together, the slave exists solely to please the Master and will do so to the best of her ability.*

1.1.0   Slave's Veto

The slave may refuse to comply with any command or act that is illegal or would result in permanent bodily or psychological harm to said slave, that would shed blood or involve breaking of any law.

I was really interested in what it said about Drake:
2.0.0 Master's Role

Once He signs the Agreement, the Master takes on full responsibility for the slave's body and is given license to do with her sexually as He sees fit, under the provisions determined in the Agreement. The Master will care for the slave, arrange for her safety and well-being, as long as He owns her. The Master commits to treat the slave properly, to train her, punish her, and use her as He sees fit.

3.0.0 Punishment

The slave agrees to accept punishment the Master chooses to inflict. Failure to comply with Master's demands immediately and properly will result in discipline, until it is performed satisfactorily. Refusal to comply with Master's demands will result in punishment, to include any of the following: bare handed spanking, denial of orgasm, denial of attention.

4.0.0 Others

The slave may not seek any other Master or lover or relate to others in any sexual or submissive way without the Master's permission. If the slave does, it will be considered a breach of the Agreement, and will result in termination of the Agreement. The Master will not give the slave to other Masters.

So, he wanted exclusivity. I was glad to see that clause. I had no interest in being shared with other men. I had a hard enough time being with one man, let alone more than one.

The final section included his limits, which I was most interested in reading to see if we were compatible.

5.0.0 Limits

The slave agrees to the following activities, which the Master shall engage in at His discretion:

- All forms of sexual intercourse, oral sex and play, anal sex and play, masturbation, mutual masturbation, vaginal fisting;

- All forms of bondage with the following: Rope, leather, and other suitable restraint materials, and other restraints as the Master sees fit;

- The use of appropriately designed sex toys, including but not limited to vibrators, dildos, anal training toys, vagina beads, etc.

Anal sex? Anal training? Vaginal fisting? How could he include anal sex, knowing that it was one thing I freaked over with Kurt? I *told* Lara that – I assumed he understood when we talked that it was off limits.

All of a sudden, I didn't feel quite so positive about this agreement.

He *did* say I could strike things off the list, but he also said it was his role as Dom to push my limits. Would I end up doing the things I didn't want to just to please him? Would I hate doing them, but do them anyway so he'd be happy, and nice to me, keep being my Dom?

I remembered reading *The Story of O* and thinking how horrible O's existence was. How her submission was nothing more than an excuse for the men to abuse her and get away with it.

Drake was so desirable, so powerfully persuasive, so knowledgeable about how to manipulate women, including me, that I feared I'd do almost anything to please him if I let myself.

I thought back to my experiences with him – all the touches, the eye contact, the sound of his voice, soft at times, harsh at times, low, sexy... How blunt he was about some things, and yet, how he knew when to be soft.

I could still rip up this agreement, send him an email and tell him that I'd changed my mind.

Indecision gripped me. All afternoon in my tiny office at Columbia, I dithered about the agreement.

Later, after I arrived home from work, I printed the agreement off and sat at my desk, examining it.

My phone rang. I checked caller ID and it was Dawn.

"Hello," I said, chewing a fingernail, undecided whether to talk to her or not.

"What's up? How did the concert go?"

I sighed and settled back on the couch. How did it go?

"Dawn, what can I tell you? Drake Morgan was there..."

Fifteen minutes later, she was at my door.

She sat on the couch and I told her about everything that happened between us – without the mention of Drake's kinks or the idea that we'd enter into any kind of D/s agreement.

"I don't know, Kate. I said he was trouble... How did he get invited to the concert?"

"He's friends with my dad. Dad invited Drake when they were at the health club they both belong to. He's really quite sweet, Dawn. He's just an alpha male, that's all."

She shook her head. "Out of the frying pan, into the fire is what I see. Just take it slow with him, OK? "

"Look, he really likes my father. He wouldn't do anything to harm his relationship with him." She shrugged. In the background, my kettle whistled. "I'll make us some tea."

I left her in the living room and went to my kitchen, finding my tea ball and loose tea. While I poured the water over the tea, I remembered the previous night and how Drake had forced me to make the first move, to admit how I felt, to tell him point blank that I wanted him to fuck me. Even now, it sent a thrill through me, remembering the feel of his body on mine when he finally pushed me back on the couch and took over.

I fixed a tray with cups and my cream and sugar bowl from Ireland called Belleek porcelain my mother used to use. It was one of her many possessions I claimed after she died, and when I used it, I felt closer to her.

When I returned to the living room, Dawn was standing at my desk, some papers in her hand. It was then I realized what she was reading – *the agreement*.

I almost dropped the tray in my rush to get to her and take it out of her hands.

"Give that to me," I said, after I put the tray down and went to her side.

She let go of it with reluctance, her eyes wide. "Holy *fuck*, Kate. What the hell are you thinking?"

I made a face. "You weren't supposed to read that."

"Slavery? Vaginal fisting? What is he? A neurosurgeon or a failed obstetrician?"

"I've read about it," I said, my face hot. "It's supposed to be about trust and gives a woman a really powerful orgasm."

"Trust? Sounds more like it's about torture. Can you even get Big inside of you? Can you imagine *his* fist?"

"You don't understand." I plopped down on my couch, frowning, not really wanting to explain what I'd read. "I can veto anything I don't like."

"Oh, *yeah?*" she said, standing in front of me, her hands on her hips, her face red. "How do you know he won't do it anyway? What would you do if he did?"

"I'd use the safe word. It's Red. I say that and everything stops immediately."

"Yeah, *sure*..." She shook her head, her face pale. She sat beside me on the couch. "How do you know he'd stop? *God*, Kate. What's wrong with you? Why would you even consider this? This says slavery. Ownership. This says you'd be his possession, his slave."

"It's not enforceable. It's just psychological to have an agreement."

"Those books were fantasy land, not real life."

"Some people do this for real. He *does*. He's not a sadist."

"Anyone who wants to shove their fist inside of you is a sadist, Kate. Don't fool yourself. Have you ever had anal sex? It hurts like *hell*..."

"Maybe whoever did it to you didn't know how. *Drake* said—"

"Listen, you can't trust *anything* he says. He's not disinterested. He obviously wants you to be his submissive – his 'slave'. He'll tell you anything to get you alone, so he can fist you and fuck you in the ass."

"He *had* me alone, Dawn. He had me entirely *naked*. *He* was naked. He stopped after I, you know, finished and was upset. He didn't even get off."

"Probably because he *couldn't* get off without hurting you or something kinky." She moved closer beside me and took my hand. "Kate, you have to listen to me – *this* is scary. I know what abuse is. I watched my sister get beat up by her boyfriend when I was a kid."

"This isn't *abuse*. It's consensual. He's not a sadist."

"You can't *do* this. You can't choose this, Kate. If you do, there's something wrong with you. Send him an email right now and tell him you don't want to go through with this," she said, pointing to the agreement. "Tell him you came to your senses and have no interest in his kinky lifestyle. Then, come and stay with me. You shouldn't be alone so much. We'll find you a *real* boyfriend."

"But I *like* him, Dawn. He's actually sweet when he lets down his front."

"More like when he puts *up* his harmless front... Kate. *Listen* to me. This is a big mistake. Didn't jerkface Kurt teach you anything?"

I sat there, my heart pounding, so confused. I *wanted* Drake. I wanted to have sex with him. Just plain old vanilla sex. But I also wanted to try bondage. I wanted to be like those women in his letters, waiting alone in my apartment for him to come to me, make me feel something so intense. I didn't know what else I wanted, but I knew I wanted those things. I had never just felt such an overwhelming need to fuck a man before. Just fuck him.

What was so wrong about that?

The way Dawn sounded, Drake was a monster and I was off my rocker.

I covered my eyes and bit back tears of anger and frustration.

"See?" she said, wrapping her arms around me. "He's got you so confused you can't think straight. He's *dangerous*, Kate. I told you that the moment I laid eyes on him in the pub that night."

She *was* wrong. I wasn't confused. I was *certain*. Her response made that clear to me. One thing I was also certain of was that Dawn could hurt Drake if she wanted to.

"You can't say anything to anyone about this. He's a friend of my father's. He's got a respectable job. He does charity work. He saves patient's lives."

"Probably because he feels guilty about the things he does. What do you think your father would say if he knew you were with him and if he knew what Drake was? What would Drake's patients think if they knew he tied women up and fisted them vaginally?"

"No one knows what people do in the privacy of their bedrooms. Why should it matter if it doesn't affect their jobs? This is between consenting adults."

"Why would anyone *consent* to this?" She just shook her head. "You're over the edge, Kate. Not thinking right. Send that email right now. Tell him you changed your mind."

"I'll think about it," I said. "I'm not doing anything right now."

"I'm not leaving until you do."

"Dawn, this is *my* decision. I have to do what I think is right."

"Do I have to call your father and warn him?"

Then, I regretted telling her anything about Drake. One more mistake on top of the many others.

"Don't do that. I'm asking you as my best friend. Don't say *anything*."

"When I was a little girl, I couldn't do anything about my sister. I won't stand by now and see you abused."

"I'm not *being* abused," I said, frustrated and afraid. "It's not abuse if it's consensual. If I want it."

"No, you're just *sick* if you want it." She stood up. "I *will* tell your father if you don't tell Drake to get lost."

"Dawn, I'm pleading with you – don't do this! At least meet with him and talk to him yourself."

"So he can try to smooth-talk me? No way. I saw everything I needed with that agreement. Send him a text. Email him – I don't care what. I'm doing this as someone who loves you."

I sat with my eyes closed, fighting my emotions. Dawn's expression was intense, her mouth determined.

If I didn't break it off with Drake, she'd call my father. Who knew what my father would do. He could get Drake in a *lot* of trouble...

I sat at my computer on the desk against the wall and composed the email, tears in my eyes.

From: **McDermott, Katherine M.**
Sent: **November 12, 5:31 PM**
To: **Morgan, D. L.**
Subject: **Re: Your Submission**

Drake, I read your agreement, but I'm afraid I just can't go through with this. I made a mistake and I'm going to just put this behind me. I'm sorry but this isn't going to work between us after all.

Please don't come over or contact me again.

Goodbye.

Kate

I stared at the send button. Dawn leaned closer and read over my shoulder.

"Send it now," she said.

I craned my neck and glared at her, angry that she was forcing me, but what could I do? If I didn't send it, she'd get

Drake in trouble with my father. Drake said himself he wouldn't want my father to know.

"I'll send it," I said, struggling not to cry, "but then I want you to *go*."

"What? *Why?*"

"You're blackmailing me, forcing me to do this. It's none of your business or my father's business what I do or what Drake does. So you can leave, and don't bother to call me either."

"Kate, he's got you all confused. *I'm* your friend," she said, jamming her thumb into her chest. "*I'm* looking out for your best interest. He's only out to get his rocks off."

"You can leave *now*."

"I'm not leaving until I see you hit send."

I hesitated, wiping my eyes.

"*Do* it."

I sent the email. "There, I did it. Now, go!" I said, shouting at her.

She stepped back from me, frowning. "You're crazy. He's got you hypnotized or something, like a cult. If I hear you've been with him, I'll call your father."

"Just *leave*."

She did, collecting her coat and bag, then going to the door. She took a look back at me from the open door and shook her head before pulling the door closed behind her.

I stared at the computer screen, at my inbox, wondering whether he'd reply and if he did, what he'd write. It was just before dinner and he'd probably be in the O.R. until seven and then he had his jam session. He might get the email in between, which could mean any time between then and eight.

I sat with my head in my hands, waiting. I couldn't drink my tea, for my hands shook and my stomach felt sick. After about half an hour without any reply, I got up and went to the kitchen, washing dishes to keep myself occupied. I got out a bucket and filled it with hot soapy water and scrubbed the floors in the kitchen on my knees with a scrub brush. Then I cleaned the oven and took some Windex and paper towels and cleaned the windows.

I checked my email to find one from Drake, which arrived just a moment earlier.

From: **Morgan, D. L.**
  Sent: **November 12, 6:46 PM**
  To: **McDermott, Katherine M.**
  Subject: **RE: Your Submission**
I'll be right over.

I chewed a nail and debated what to say in response. Finally, I replied.

To: **Morgan, D. L.**
Sent: **November 12, 6:48 PM**
From: **McDermott, Katherine M.**
Subject: **Re: Your Submission**
No, please don't. I don't want to see you ever again.

There was no response. I wrung my hands. He called my cell, again and again.

Finally, I had to block his calls, my hands shaking. I deleted his voice messages without listening. But I saw his texts.

Kate, what happened between last night and lunch?
Tell me.
Let me talk to you. Please...
I want you.
Oh, *God...*

I debated whether to reply. If I did, it would only encourage him, but I felt bad just cutting him off like that.

This is just the way it has to be for your own good. Please stop calling and texting me. It won't do any good.

He responded immediately.
For my own good? What does that mean?
Kate, don't do this...
I put my phone away.

I sat in my quiet apartment, my phone shut off completely and sitting on the coffee table. At any moment, he could knock on my door, so I decided to leave. I picked up the cell and ignored the message notification indicating I had five messages waiting to be read.

Five?

He was persistent. I ached to read them, but I knew if I did, I'd crumble. Instead, I called my father.

On the third ring, he answered, his voice sounding distracted, but still pleased.

"Hey, sweetheart, to what do I owe this pleasure?"

"You're at home?"

"Yes, I'm on leave so I can plan for the election. What's up? Is everything OK?"

I chewed my nail, wondering what to say. "Can I come and stay there for a few days?"

There was a silence on the line as if he was processing what I said. When he spoke, he sounded more engaged, his voice low and soft.

"Of course, Katie. What's the matter?"

He called me *Katie*. He only called me that when I was a child and then when I was sick after Africa. I knew then he was worried, wondering if I was having a relapse. "I just need to get away for a while."

"Do you want me to send a car?"

I sighed. "No," I said, glancing around my apartment. "I'll find my way over. I could use some air so maybe I'll walk."

"It's a long hike and it's dark."

"I need to think."

"Your bedroom is always waiting for you. We'll hold dinner until you get here."

"Go ahead and eat, Daddy. I've had something."

"See you in a bit."

CHAPTER TWELVE

I made the trek to my dad's apartment from mine, walking south and then east beside Central Park and then south again to his apartment building. This time, I went in the front entrance, carrying my backpack filled with my MacBook and clothes, makeup and a few personal items. I took the small elevator up to his suite and used my key to enter the front door.

The living room was empty. Elaine was nowhere to be seen, so after I took off my coat and placed my backpack in my old bedroom, I went to the study. My father was sitting at his huge desk, on the phone as usual. He saw me and waved me over while he kept talking. I went to him and waited.

"Yes, certainly, I agree," he said, turning his cheek for me to kiss. I bent down to kiss him. "That's the tack we'll take."

He waved at me to sit on the chair across from him. I did, staring at the pictures on the wall from my trip to Africa. He seemed as if he were trying to end the conversation with whoever was on the other line and finally, said goodbye. He put the phone down and made a face at me, rolling his eyes.

"Long-winded sonofabitch. Sorry, dear. I had to finish that call."

"That's all right."

He stood and came around his desk, leaning against it, directly in front of me, his eyes intense and focused on me, his half-eye glasses in his hand.

"So tell me why you needed to get away from it all. Does this involve Drake in some way?"

I nodded and my throat closed up a bit as emotion filled me. I covered my mouth for a moment, unable to speak.

"Now, you see, I *thought* things were going well for you two," he said, shaking his head. "You seemed really intense at the concert. What happened? Lover's quarrel?"

"Something like that," I said, getting hold of myself, surprised that my father thought we were lovers.

"Tell your old man what happened. I know Drake is a very eligible bachelor, but you're a very lovely young woman, accomplished and intelligent. Did he want to move the relationship forward too fast? Is he getting too serious?"

"*No*, Daddy, nothing like that. It's just we're not really compatible, I guess."

He frowned. "Here I thought the two of you were so well-matched."

"Why did you think that?"

He shrugged, pursed his lips. "You're both attractive, intelligent, civic-minded. You both *love* music. You both share Africa."

"He's a Republican," I said, trying to come up with some reason.

He laughed. "I know, and you don't know how surprised I was to find out. His old man was a flaming socialist, but I guess kids have a tendency to go the opposite way from their parents. You know, in rebellion..." He shook his head, smiling. "What an idealistic fool Liam was, but I loved the crazy bastard anyway. He was a heroic sonofabitch. I don't know how many of us he saved." He shrugged, his hands clasped. "So you're not on the same political page. Liam and I were best friends over in 'Nam. Stranger things have happened before between political opposites. In fact, sometimes, they make the best matches. Opposites attract, you know. *Yin/yang...*"

Yin/Yang? The Drill Sergeant talking Tao? My father had never talked to me like this. I never heard him describe me before.

"Yin/Yang?" I said, wanting to probe him a bit, since he seemed so talkative.

"Yes, you know. Light/dark. Positive/negative. Active/passive. Male/female. It's what makes the world go round," he said, winking at me.

"Daddy, I've never heard you talk like this. Is this Elaine's influence on you?"

"Good Lord, no. I'm not a spring chicken, Katherine. I've been around the block a few times. Why, once upon a time, I too was a young man out pitching woo." He grinned.

"Pitching *woo*," I said and smiled. I exhaled, my cheeks a bit heated at what he'd said. "Things just can't work out between us."

"I thought you two were so right for each other," he said. "That's why I invited him to the concert. Why, I've been told by women who know about these things that he's very attractive." He wagged his eyebrows at me and smiled. "I could tell he was attracted to you at the dinner party, the way he kept following you around like a dog after a bone. When we were at the health club, he raved to me about your writing, especially your piece on Africa. You know how important Africa is to him. I thought he might bring you out of your shell. Lighten you up a bit. You've been a bit reclusive since your mother passed and since that business after Africa..."

That business after Africa. My father couldn't admit that I developed clinical depression.

"Kurt was obviously a jerk, but I though Drake was more your type. Strong. Confident. Competent."

"You were matchmaking for me, Daddy?"

He smiled. "Someone's gotta do it. You don't seem all that good on your own. I wanted you and Drake to meet for quite some time, but you've been so reclusive and Dawn isn't much better. Didn't she join a nunnery or something?"

I laughed, in spite of my sadness. "No," I said, smiling just a bit. "She volunteered in India with Mother Theresa's charity. She's trying to set me up, too."

"The Greg fellow? He was a bust."

"Daddy! He was a nice young man. He just finished his MFA..."

"Extremely milquetoast, if I recall..." my father said, shaking his head. "Not your type."

I frowned and examined him closely. "What *is* my type?"

He picked up his glass of scotch and took a sip. "Someone like Drake Morgan, I'd say. Or at least I thought so, which is why I encouraged it."

Someone like Drake Morgan...

I sat there, frowning to myself, surprised at this turn of events.

"And what is Drake Morgan like?"

"He's very intelligent, capable, strong, confident, professional. He's a man's man, but he knows how to treat a woman, I'd say, judging by the attention he gave you at the dinner party and the concert. I know him very well, Katherine, and I thought he was just about perfect for you." He shrugged. "But I guess if you don't like him, I was wrong. Usually, I'm a very good judge of character. I pride myself on it, given I have to judge people all the time."

"I *do* like him, Daddy. It's just not going to work out."

"Shame." He drank the rest of his scotch down. "Why don't you get your old man a refill and get yourself something to drink? The sun's over the yardarm. There's a girl."

He handed me his empty glass and I nodded, returning to the living room and the bar. As I refilled his scotch, I felt such conflicting emotions. My father actually thought about the kind of man I needed...

He thought Drake was that kind of man.

After a casual dinner with Elaine, we three sat in the den and listened to music, something way too abstract for me, modern classical, chatting about nothing in particular. I forced myself to stay with them as long as possible, the sadness building inside of me. Finally, I couldn't take it any longer and faked a yawn and stood, ready for escape.

"I'm going to bed early. I've had a busy day and I've got lots of work on my plate tomorrow."

"Good night sweetheart," my father said when I leaned down to kiss him on the cheek. "Sweet dreams. I'm sure things will all work out with Drake."

"I don't think so, Daddy."

"Well, these things have a way of working out for the best eventually."

I went to my room, a sickness in my gut that this was *not* going to work out between Drake and me the way my father thought. I was tempted to check my mail to see if Drake had written or texted me, but I fought the urge. After washing my face and brushing my teeth in my old bathroom off my bedroom, I crept onto the huge four-poster bed and under the quilt. I lay in the darkness, thinking about Drake. He *was* strong, competent, professional. He did know how to treat a woman. Make her feel as if she was the center of his attention.

I tossed and turned for quite a while, wondering if I'd ever see him again, finally dissolving into tears at the thought I might not.

I skipped classes the next morning, deciding to work on my paper instead. I tried to work at my father's apartment, but had left an important file at my apartment, so after lunch, I said goodbye to my father as he sat in his study, on the phone. I went to my front door and of course, someone had propped open the door. I kicked the cardboard out that was used to prop the door open and went up the stairs. Inside, I found my files and put them in my backpack. A light flashed on my answering machine on the landline, and I checked the record of callers. Drake showed up several times as did Dawn's number.

Finally, I took out my cell and sat on the couch, checking my email and texts.

There were several from Drake.

Kate, please call me.

Kate, what happened? You were fine when I left you...

Will you at least answer my texts so I know you're OK?

The last one was from just a few moments earlier.

Kate, I'm coming over to talk to you. Please give me the chance to make it right...

If he came over, if I got within arm's reach of him, I knew I'd cave and if Dawn caught wind of me still seeing him, she'd get him in trouble. I grabbed my coat and backpack and left the apartment, rushing down the stairs to the back alley. I slipped along the streets, and then doubled back, going to my favorite deli across from my apartment building, entering from the back door on the alley. I went to a small table in the bay window so I could watch in case Drake arrived. I sat with my cup of tea and kept an eye on the street.

Sure enough, in about ten minutes, Drake's sleek black car drove up. He double-parked and then he left the car and ran up to my building's front door. He was wearing his scrubs and lab coat, a little blue scrub cap still on his head. He stood at the door and jiggled it, but couldn't get inside. There was no buzzer system so he was out of luck. As I watched, he took out his cell, tapped on the screen and then held it up to his ear.

Seconds later, my cell buzzed. I checked it and the call display read *Drake Morgan, MD*.

I refused the call, sending him to my voicemail.

My heart sped up to see him, and I felt a real pang of guilt and sadness at what happened but I couldn't see any way out of it. I had to just end it. I was mortified that I was so careless with the agreement that Dawn found it.

He sat on the steps and just redialed. Again and again. As I watched out the window, he typed on his cell.

> *At least tell me why you don't want to be with me. What was it? Did the contract scare you? Don't be afraid, Kate. You can strike off anything that you don't want to do. I just included those things that I know probably upset you so you'd have something to cross off. I don't need to do them. I don't need to do anything that you don't want to do. I want to be with you.*
>
> *Please, give this time.*

My heart actually hurt as I read his text, like a knife in my chest and my throat choked up. At that moment, I hated Dawn so much...

> *Drake, I'm doing this for you. To protect you. I can't say anything more but you have to stop trying to see me. You have to just stop for your own good. I can't say more....*
>
> *I'm sorry...*

Then I shut off my phone and watched him. He persisted for a while but then stopped, going to his car and driving off. I bit my lip to stop my tears.

I just lay around my apartment all afternoon, spending time there after Drake left, lying on the couch watching stupid soap operas. Finally, before supper, I walked back to my father's apartment. I went right to my bedroom and closed the door, sad that I was not going to be with Drake. I sat on the bed and just wiped my face as tears flowed, unable to stop them now that I was back at my father's apartment. After a few moments, I heard a knock at my door.

"Sweetheart? Can I come in?"

"No," I said, my voice breaking.

"How come? You sound like you need to talk."

"I need to be alone."

The door opened and he came in anyway, sitting next to me on the bed. He put his arm around me and squeezed me, and that only made me cry even harder.

"There, there, *doll*," he said, grabbing a tissue off my night table. "This Drake misunderstanding has really upset you."

"It's not a misunderstanding. It's just not going to work out."

He just sat with me for a moment as I finally got hold of myself.

"Look, you have some time off next week. I was thinking you should come down to the Bahamas with us for the weekend. Get away from it all. Sun, sand, white beaches, lots of tropical drinks. You've been working like a dog for years, Kate. Some R&R would be good for you. What do you think?"

"When would you want to go?"

"Next Wednesday over the Thanksgiving weekend. Will you be able to sneak away?"

I thought about it. I did have some time off and really, the idea of getting away from everything appealed to me.

I nodded. "I just have to hand in an article to the student newspaper."

"Good. We'll get a ticket for you. We'll get a couple of suites at the British Colonial Hilton in Nassau, on Paradise Island so there's more than enough room. We can do some snorkeling, scuba diving, or nothing at all. Whatever you want."

I smiled and leaned against him, surprised that he was being so attentive and thoughtful.

The following week went faster than I imagined. I ignored and deleted all of Drake's and Dawn's texts and emails unread. To my surprise, Drake didn't show up at my doorstep and I was sad but relieved. At least I wouldn't have to deal with him.

He must have finally given up.

Each night I tossed and turned in my bed at my father's house, remembering everything that happened between Drake and me before falling into a fitful sleep. Each day I went through the motions of my life, rushing through things in the hope that one more day would be over and I could go back to sleep – a dangerous state I'd been in after my trip to Africa. I recognized the symptoms of depression and couldn't wait for a change of scenery. I figured going to the Bahamas would provide me an escape from the reminders of what almost, but didn't quite, happen between Drake and me.

I spent an all-nighter getting an article finished for *Geist* on Tuesday. I packed a small bag with summer clothes from storage, sundresses, sandals and a bikini and bought some sunscreen and sunglasses at the local drugstore.

The Wednesday evening flight took us right to the Bahamas and a limo drove us to beautiful resort on the water. The British Colonial Hilton looked like a huge plantation with white sand beaches and palm trees. We arrived late that night and went right to our rooms, which were adjoining, each suite a one bedroom with separate living areas.

I was exhausted. Maybe just the thought that I was away from everything, my article written, with no work ahead of me for four glorious days, made me collapse into bed. I fell asleep in minutes, the bedside lamp still on.

I slept late and my father didn't wake me as he usually would have for an early morning walk on the beach. Instead, there was a note from him slipped under my door. They let me sleep in, not wanting to wake me on the first day of my very short vacation.

Katherine,

Take your time this morning and just rest. Go for a walk on the beach. We've already had breakfast and have gone for a boat ride. Meet us at the restaurant at noon for lunch. Then, we'll go scuba diving in the afternoon. We have lessons booked. Tonight, we'll have a nice Thanksgiving Dinner. The hotel puts on a great spread for American guests.

Love, Dad and Elaine

It was 11:00. I got up and went to the window to look out over the ocean. The weather was perfect, the sky clear, the water azure, the sand white. Palm trees swayed in the breeze and people took their places on the beach.

After a shower, I put on my white bikini and favorite piece of clothing for summer – a little white eyelet sundress with thin straps. I was white as a ghost, my fair skin guaranteed to burn unless I slathered on copious amounts of sunscreen, which I did. Before I met with my father and Elaine, I slipped out the front door to the beach and took off my sundress, holding it as I walked along, hoping to soak up a few rays of sun, avoiding the tourists, ankle-deep in the surf. I kept my face in the sun to get some color. I intended to only be out on the beach for ten minutes, but I got busy wading along, holding my sundress up, my legs in the cool water. It was so quiet and peaceful, I just walked and walked, stopping now and then to pick up a stray shell or examine a piece of driftwood that washed up on the shore.

Finally, realizing I'd been gone for longer than I intended, I turned back and made my way to the hotel. My cheeks were already hot from the sun and the fact I'd left my sunhat in the room, not planning to be away for so long. I could already see a bit of red on my exposed skin despite the sunscreen.

I put my sundress back on and went into the hotel to the restaurant, for I was already late. It was then I saw a billboard in the lobby with a list of conventions being held at the hotel that week. A variety, but most had a medical theme. One in particular caught my eye:

Deep Brain Stimulation in Pediatric Movement Disorders – Lower Level, Empress Room

Drake did deep brain stimulation. He treated pediatric cases and I remembered the story he told of the small boy from South Africa who gave him the tooled leather wristband. I stood staring at the billboard and wondered if it was possible... Surely he wouldn't be at this hotel of all hotels in the world.

I heard some laughter and conversation from guests who were ascending the staircase that led up from the lower levels. Men and women dressed in casual clothes fitting to a resort in the Bahamas – khakis and white shirts, sandals.

Bringing up the rear was Drake Morgan.

He was dressed in white and looked devastatingly gorgeous – white linen shirt, sleeves rolled up, neck unbuttoned and tail untucked over white Dockers and black leather sandals. His hair was a bit mussed, and his face slightly tanned with a bit of scruff on his jaw. He was with a woman as tall as him, with fashionably long blonde hair pulled back in a ponytail and a nice tan. She was wearing something casual but still fashionable – a shirt and skirt that looked straight from the outback. They laughed together as they talked, his hands animated.

He was already with someone new? Was she his sub? Would he bring a sub to a convention?

He saw me and stopped in his tracks, blinking. His companion stopped and stared at me, a smile on her lovely face.

"Excuse me," Drake said to her. I turned on my heel, my stomach in my throat, adrenaline washing through me.

"Kate!" he said, and then I heard him speaking to her in a low voice, but couldn't make out what he said.

What the *hell*... Did my father arrange all this, hoping we'd run into Drake?

I was *mortified*.

I made it to the elevator but he was right there beside me, his hand on my arm.

"*Kate*," he said, stopping me when the elevator doors opened. "You arrived."

I turned to him, completely flustered. "I *arrived?*"

"Yes," he said and let go of my arm. "I was expecting you."

I got on the elevator and he followed me, closing the door and pressing the close button before anyone else could get on like he wanted to be alone with me. Then he cornered me, his arm on the elevator wall, his body so close to mine I could smell a hint of coconut, as if he'd put on some sunscreen recently. I avoided his eyes, unsure if I could control my emotions.

"Was this all a set-up?"

He said nothing, so I glanced up at his face. He was smiling softly.

"You could call it that."

"You and my father?"

"Me and your father. He thought it might be a good idea for us to get away from it all, work through this 'difficulty' we're facing, I think he said. I agreed."

I frowned, something building in me, feeling like it would explode any moment. "What did you tell him?"

"Oh, I made something up about how you were concerned about my schedule, and how busy I was, thinking I wouldn't have time for you. That kind of thing. He bought it completely." He moved a bit closer, running his fingers over my cheeks. "You're a bit burnt. Your skin is so fair..."

"I told you we can't be together."

He leaned down and caught my eye. "You said you were doing this for my own good. I have to know what you mean by that or else I can't accept it. I'm the one who should decide what's for my own good."

"Drake this can't happen."

"*Shh*. When I told your father about a conference I had to attend and that I was *not* looking forward to it because I was worried about you, he offered to bring you here for a bit of a getaway. Of course, I thought it was a *spectacular* idea..."

When the elevator door opened, he stepped away and I made a beeline to my suite, using the keycard to open the door. I went inside and he followed me, coming to stand beside me as I watched out the window.

"*Kate*..." he said, taking my shoulders in his hands, turning me to face him. "Come *here*."

"Who was that woman you were with?"

He frowned, then grinned. "Her? That's Doctor Laurisse Marchand, from Quebec. She does the same work I do and we've collaborated on a paper we're presenting. She's very happily married with kids and is a few years older than me. She also has a very dominant personality, like me. In other words, not my type so don't even let your mind go there."

Of course, I flushed even more deeply at that, if it was even possible. Just being alone with Drake was enough to make my knees weak.

"Nothing can happen between us, Drake."

He took my hand and pulled me over to the couch. He sat in the middle, and like that first night, he pulled me down onto his lap so that my face was just inches from his.

He tilted his head. "You look absolutely ravishing. I want to ravish you."

"I'm serious. We have to end this. For your own good."

"Tell me how ending this would be for my own good."

"You have to trust me. Someone knows about you. Your kink. They threatened to expose you if we kept seeing each other."

"What?" he said, frowning. "*Who?*"

I shook my head. "I can't say."

"You can't or won't say?"

"Both."

He exhaled heavily. "Kate, I can't just end 'this' like you seem to think we have to. You're an unanswered question. You're unexplored country and I very much want to explore you. Every single *inch* of you, inside and out."

That sent a surge of something through me and I felt as if my whole body flushed.

He nuzzled his face into my neck, his mouth warm on the skin beneath my ear. His lips brushed my earlobe when he spoke.

"Unless you can tell me who is threatening you so I can understand it, and agree or not, find a way around it, I am *not* giving you up. You said you'd sign my agreement last week. I don't think anyone is threatening you. I think you read my limits and you're afraid. What was it that shocked you? Was it vaginal fisting? Anal sex? I *told* you I put those in specifically so you could strike them off and feel some degree of control."

I glanced away. Those did shock me, to be honest, but I was willing to strike them off the list as he said I could.

"It wasn't that. I'm telling you the truth."

"Then, who is it? Tell me or I won't believe you."

"Drake, I *can't*" I pulled myself out of his arms and stood, moving away, because sitting on his lap like that, feeling his warmth beneath me, his face so close to me, his mouth on my neck made me dizzy with lust.

He stood and came close to me, and I backed away, but only ended up wedged against the table. He had me cornered.

"Tell me, or I'll keep after you. I won't give up on you, Kate."

"Why not? Barely anything has happened between us. It would be a lot easier to end it now rather than later when we're forced to after you've been disgraced because of my carelessness."

"What about your carelessness?"

I shook my head, dread filling me at the thought of telling him.

"I," I said, fumbling for words, so embarrassed that I was hoping to be a journalist who was supposed to prize informant confidentiality and I was so sloppy with the agreement that Dawn found it. "I left the agreement on my desk and someone found it."

He closed his eyes and exhaled heavily. His lips pressed thin and when he opened his eyes, I had to turn away, so afraid of his anger.

"*Who* found it?"

"Just someone who doesn't want me to be with you, OK?"

"Nigel," he said. "It was Nigel, right?"

"No!" I shook my head.

"Don't protect him, Kate. I know he doesn't really approve of me."

"What do you mean? Why wouldn't he approve of you?"

"Did he force you to stop seeing me? He knows that I'm in the lifestyle." He shook his head and then he seemed to relax. He stroked my cheek, then his fingers fell to my chest and he brushed them against the tops of my breasts. "I can talk to him, assure him that I mean you no harm."

"It wasn't Nigel. Does Nigel know about you?"

"Yes."

"How does he know?"

"I can't tell you how he knows. That's private. He just knows. I thought he was OK with it, but if you're protecting him, you have to let me know. I'll have to speak with him if he's pressuring you."

It was then I realized that Drake must know Nigel through the BDSM community. I didn't know a lot about Nigel's personal life. I knew he had a long-time partner – an actor who did off-off-Broadway.

"Nigel's *kinky?*" I said and frowned.

He rubbed his forehead, then ran his fingers through his hair.

"I can neither confirm nor deny that statement," he said, his expression serious. "It's not my place to out people. I take this seriously. Kate, I've known people who've lost their jobs and their lives because of adverse publicity around BDSM. All I can say is that he knows about me. Please, just tell me who's threatening you so we can figure this out."

"I can't and we can't just figure this out. This person will not back down, no matter what. This person is very morally judgmental. And irrational. If they think we're together, they will tell my father about you. Now, you'd better go. This can't happen."

"Who is it?"

"It's someone who doesn't understand BDSM. They never will. Listen, this is just too much trouble, Drake. Why are you so *insistent?* "

"Because I *want* you."

"That doesn't *matter.*"

He sighed, his expression frustrated, his brow furrowed.

"Look, I won't touch you, if you really don't want me to. I promise we'll just talk."

I shook my head. "It's not that I don't want you to touch me. I *do*, God do I want you to, but you're in danger. Can't you understand?"

His face changed. "So you *do* want me to touch you," he said, moving even closer. He put his arms around me, slipping them under my arms and pulling me against him so I had to embrace him.

"*Drake...*"

"Sorry, you said the operative words. I need to finish what I started that night before we were so rudely interrupted by my cell phone alarm."

And then he kissed me, his lips on mine, his mouth opening and his tongue finding mine, his hands all over me, one hand squeezing one cheek of my ass, while the other grabbed a breast a bit roughly, but not too roughly that it hurt.

"*Fuck*, I need you." He actually pressed me down on the table, knocking the gift basket of fruit and chocolates off so that they fell to the floor and rolled around on the carpet. His mouth trailed down my throat and then he pulled my dress up and off me, throwing it onto the floor beside the fruit. He just took me in, lying on the table dressed only in my little white string bikini, my breasts far too exposed and falling out of the top. "God, you're *luscious*. I want to eat every inch of you."

My heart pounded in my ears, my body responding to his urgency, my flesh aching in need. He untied my bikini top and pulled it down to expose my breasts entirely.

"You're sunburnt, you bad thing. As your doctor, I must chastise you severely for that."

"If you're my doctor, isn't there some kind of ethical issue with becoming involved with a patient?"

"Fuck ethics," he murmured against my skin. He began kneading my breasts, squeezing them, sucking my nipples one after the other, his tongue circling them, his lips tugging at them. His teeth bit them softly, sending delicious jolts of lust right to my clit.

Of course it was then my father decided to knock on my door.

"Katherine? Are you there? We have reservations for lunch."

I almost gasped out loud, my body tensing for Drake had moved down my belly and he had spread my thighs and was biting me through my bikini bottoms, tonguing my clit through the fabric.

"Drake!" I whispered. He exhaled and rested his forehead on my belly, his mouth still above my pussy.

"Fuck, *Ethan*," he whispered back. "You have *horrible* timing." Then he rose up and laid on top of me, grinning. "So close and yet so far."

I couldn't help but smile back.

"Katie? Are you OK sweetie?" my father said through the door. "We were worried about you." He jiggled the door.

"*Katie*?" Drake whispered, grinning. "You better answer him. Tell him we'll be right down."

"I'll be right down, Daddy. Give me five minutes, OK?"

"All right, dear. We're waiting."

We held our breaths for a moment and then Drake buried his face between my naked breasts. When he lifted his head, he kissed each nipple.

"Jesus *Christ*," he said, staring into my eyes. "Am I ever going to get to actually *come* inside of you?"

"You want to?" I grinned.

"Right now, there is absolutely *nothing* I want more in this world. An end to poverty? World peace? Human rights for all? No. I want to fuck you until I come inside of you. Bareback."

"We haven't been tested yet..."

"I have been. I'm clean. I'm know you are as well. You told me and I trust you. I want to see my come dripping out of you."

"*Drake!*"

"Seriously," he said. "You've brought out the animal in me, Kate. We're talking caveman. Warlord claiming territory, plundering." He grinned so wide he started laughing.

"*Plundering...*"

Then he rose up over me, propping himself on one elbow. He brushed a strand of hair from my cheek and then grazed his fingers over the tops of my breasts and my nipples so that they puckered.

"Once we're alone, once we're *finally* alone, I'm going to fuck you and come inside your body and I'm not even going to worry about making you come, because you owe me one, remember? After that, I'll bathe you and shave your sweet little pussy, and I'll tie you up and make you come three times. Once with my tongue and mouth. Once with my fingers, and once with my cock."

"Oh, *God.*" I closed my eyes, desire washing over me.

"You like that idea, do you Kate?"

I opened my eyes and his were so intense, his nostrils flaring as he breathed in deeply.

"Yes," I whispered.

"You want me to tie you up and make you come?"

"Yes."

"Yes, what?"

I shook my head, not knowing what he meant. He waited, and then I remembered. Did he want me to say Yes, Master? Or Yes, Sir? Neither one felt right.

"Yes... *Sir?*" I said, hesitantly.

He closed his eyes and leaned down, pressing his forehead against mine, smiling. "No, *no.* I want you to say the words." He kissed me, and I could feel his smile against my lips. "Just say what I said. That you want me to tie you up."

"Oh," I said, understanding. He wanted it acknowledged. He wanted me to give him permission. "Yes, please tie me up and make me come, Drake."

"You're not ready for *Sir* yet," he said, his gaze moving over my face. "You don't feel it yet. But one day you will be ready and you will feel it. And I will *enjoy* hearing that word come from your sweet lips while you beg me to let you come."

I exhaled, closing my eyes. His words affected me so deeply. I *wanted* to feel it – that he was *Sir*.

I wanted it to feel right.

He stood up, running his hands down my inner thighs to my pussy. "*Damn*. You're so nice and wet. But we better go or Ethan will be back with firefighters to break down the door."

He pulled me up so that I stood in front of him, my head tilted back to look in his eyes. He leaned down and kissed me.

"I like that you're short," he said. "Petite. It brings out the Dom in me."

"I like when the Dom in you comes out."

"Oh, Kate, you ain't seen *nothing* yet. All you've tasted is vanilla ice cream."

I frowned a bit, unsure if he was warning me or trying to entice me.

"Don't frown," he said, stepping closer. "If you like it now, all I mean is that you'll like it even more when we actually play."

I nodded. "I better change," I said and pointed to my room.

"I'll wait, although I feel like I need to go and jerk off in the bathroom to get rid of this," he said, grasping his still-hard cock, taking my hand and placing it over his length. "But I want to save it for you."

I took in a deep breath, my body responding from the feel of him in my hand.

"I wish I could help you with this," I said, my voice a bit quivery.

"You will. *Later*."

"You know, I still haven't signed anything."

"You will. *Later*," he said, grinning.

"You're so sure of yourself."

"No, I'm not," he said, pulling me into his arms. "I'm just sure of what I want." He kissed me, tenderly this time. "I want you."

I sighed and pulled reluctantly out of his arms. "I better freshen up..."

I went into the bathroom and brushed my hair, applying a bit of makeup and then I got my bag. Drake was standing at the window, talking quietly on his cell. When he saw me, he motioned me over and pulled me against him.

"Yes, I'll meet you at 1:30. We can review the slides once before 2:00."

Then he ended the call and put his cell away.

"Business?" I asked.

"Just preparing for our presentation this afternoon at the conference. My colleagues and I are presenting the results of a three-year study on pediatric neuro-electrophysiology. Dr. Marchand and I are doing the presentation at 2:00."

I nodded.

We went to the dining room where my father and Elaine were seated.

"Look who I ran into on the way over here," I said, pointing to Drake.

My father's face lit up like a floodlight. He stood and started glad-handing Drake, who of course, glad-handed back like they were old buddies.

"Drake, how nice to see you again."

"You can cut the act, Daddy," I said, smiling. "Drake already told me you two conspired to bring me here so I could 'get away from it all'."

My father looked between Drake and me and then laughed in his gravelly voice. "Guilty as charged. I confess."

We sat down and had a very nice meal and all the while, I watched my father and Drake talk about business, about the election, about Drake's presentation, about his plans to go to Africa later in the New Year for a stint as a surgeon, about all of us scuba diving later after his presentation. My father had already organized a training session and then a dive at one of the local tourist traps. Drake was already certified as a diver so he was excited to be going with us and eager to escape the afternoon session after his presentation was done.

It felt surreal to think my father was actively trying to push us together. If he knew Drake was a Dominant and engaged in kinky sex with submissives that he tied up and blindfolded, and that he wanted to do those things to me – and that I *wanted* him to...

I shuddered for a moment to think of the consequences. And that was the real issue. Not whether I wanted him or he wanted me. That was pretty clear already. This thing between us – this intense sexual attraction – if we indulged in it this weekend, I knew it would be next to impossible for us to end it when we got back to the real world.

It would be a really huge risk for Drake. We'd have to be exceptionally careful that Dawn never found out.

I sighed and put my spoon down, my gut in a knot over this. Drake must have heard my sigh for he reached over and took my hand, squeezing it for a moment, and it was so sweet it made my throat choke up a bit. I glanced at my father and he was smiling to himself, as if pleased to see the show of affection between Drake and me.

If he only knew...

CHAPTER THIRTEEN

White Beach Diving Adventures was located a way down the coast from our hotel. We drove down the winding road in a limo my father hired, which deposited us at the small diving business on the ocean, that housed a wharf and boat launch, a small wooden shack with equipment and a room for instruction, changing rooms for suiting up.

We took the hour-long instructional course designed for tourists, Drake sitting beside me, his arm on the back of my chair, his legs spread. We went over safety techniques, how to wear the gear, the itinerary for our short dive, and then it was time to suit up. A group had already gone out in a boat before us, and so we were going as our own small group, just Drake and me, my father and Elaine and our instructors. My father had grown a bit portly and they had a bit of trouble finding the right suit to fit his belly. Elaine was tall and slim and fit nicely into a woman's suit. Drake was well-built and looked very delicious in his wetsuit. It was me who was the real problem.

Of course, I already made one mistake, wearing my bra and underwear instead of a bathing suit. I hadn't thought to bring a one-piece and all I had was the white string bikini. I didn't think it was appropriate to wear it so I wore my skin-colored lace bra and panties, not thinking that they would get wet and still be wet after the dive was done. My instructor smiled and said I wasn't the first person to wear underwear. Some people didn't wear anything. He'd seen it all.

I was petite and small boned, the smallest woman's size left was too big in the body and too small in the bust.

The instructor held up yet another wetsuit for me to try.

"This is all we have left. It's old."

It had a front zip and fraying fabric. It was the only suit left that had any chance of fitting but it was worn, the zipper a bit rusty.

"Maybe I should just stay behind."

"Nonsense," my father said. "Suit up and let's go."

I went behind the curtain and tried once more, hoping this suit fit me well enough. It was a the best so far, but when I tried to zip it up, the rusty zipper stuck about half way up at my waist.

I struggled with the zipper with no luck.

"Um, I need a bit of help with this zipper..."

Elaine was getting dressed herself so Drake came in the change room where I was struggling with the zipper.

"It's a bit rusted," I said, trying to hold the two sides of the zipper as close together as I could so that the zipper was less stretched. Of course, the suit was still too tight in the bust and my breasts were squeezed together. Drake leered at my chest and smiled while he took hold of the zip loop and pulled, but it didn't budge. He jiggled the zipper up and down, but it was completely stuck.

"That's what you get for having such luscious breasts," Drake whispered as he gave one strong jerk on the zipper latch. "Squeeze them a bit more, pull the two sides closer."

I did, feeling like some exotic dancer putting my breasts on display.

"Christ, you're going to give me a boner, Kate."

"You better not get one," I said. I glanced down and was shocked at how big he looked already, the wetsuit thin and showing his ample length. "You look like you already do."

He glanced down. "No, I'm soft. I'm just a *shower*, not a *grower*."

"A *what?*"

"A shower. I *show* my length all the time, and only thicken up and harden when I get an erection. Most men are growers. They're smaller when soft and grow in length when they have an erection."

"*Oh*," I said, amused at his clinical description of the categories of men's dicks. "So what I see is what I get?"

"More or less," he said. "In terms of length, at least." Then he leered at me, his eyes hooded. "As you learned from Big, length isn't as important as girth when it comes to a woman's pleasure..."

"Drake!"

He just grinned and gave one huge tug and voila – the zipper went up.

"There," he said, smiling at me. "Confined." He eyed me up and down. "I might be convinced to put you in some latex at some point. A nice black latex cat suit would be really delicious..."

I adjusted the suit a bit, and it was too tight but better than all the others.

"We have to get going," the instructor said through the door. "Those suits are thin but if you wear them for any length of time in this warmth, you'll overheat. Most accidents in triathlons are due to people overheating while waiting for their wave of swimmers to leave the shore."

We emerged and made our way to the boats, where an assistant instructor was loading up our gear. Since he was already certified, Drake took over as my buddy, helping me with my equipment and swimming with me on the outing.

The dive itself was pretty cool, even if half of it was spent just getting used to the equipment, trying out various safety procedures, and practicing. Finally, we took the boat out a bit near a line of corals and we all dove down and spent time just swimming over them, exploring them and all the sea life they held.

After about half an hour, we returned to the marina and when it came time to get the suit off, it proved just as hard to get off as on. I struggled alone with the zipper for a while in the change room, not saying anything. Finally, my father called to me.

"Sweetie? Do you need some help?"

"Yes," I said. "Its just as hard to unzip."

Drake came in and took hold of the zipper and gave it a few good yanks, but to no avail. We tried every imaginable way to make the zipper budge but nothing. The instructor came in with some oil and drizzled it over the zipper, but that did nothing to help matters, just made my hands and Drake's hands all slippery.

Drake was in his board shorts and sandals, his chest bare. Dad and Elaine were back in their street clothes, and there I was, in that old worn suit that was too small in the bust, and I was starting to get really hot.

"Phew," I said and waved my face with a hand. "I'm getting hot."

"We need to get you out of this," Drake said, his brow furrowed.

"Is everything all right in there?" my father called out.

Drake went out, leaving me in the change room.

"There's a problem with the zipper. It'll take a bit but we may have to cut her out of the suit. Why don't you two go back to the hotel and we'll meet you back there for a drink before dinner?"

My father agreed. "I'll send the limo back. Are you sure everything's all right?"

"No problem," I heard Drake say.

Meanwhile, I was starting to seriously sweat, a trickle of moisture running down the back of my neck and forehead.

Drake and the instructor came in and both took turns yanking on the zipper, but to no avail. Then just when the instructor was going to get a pair of scissors to start cutting me out of the suit, Drake was able to get the zipper down about six inches, right below my bust.

"Maybe you should take the top off so you can cool off," Drake said. I tried to pull the arms off but it was too tight, the zipper not down far enough.

"*Goddammit*," he said, frustration in his voice. I held the top of the suit and he pulled and jerked it but nothing.

"I'm feeling a bit faint," I said, the sweat now running down my neck and face.

"*Christ*," he said, his voice low. "We have to cut you out of this – *now*."

The instructor brought the pair of scissors but they weren't up to the job and so they had to find a box cutter. The instructor went out to his truck for a tool box, searching through his tools for one. Luckily, Drake was a surgeon and was as good with box cutter as he was a scalpel. He was able to cut around the zipper and down to my crotch, peeling the suit off me. I wobbled a bit from dizziness, and just about fainted. Once the suit was off, they had to lay me on a bench in the equipment room. The instructor brought in a fan and Drake poured water over me, and in a few minutes, my heart stopped beating so fast and my hearing started to recover. But I lay there in my lacy bra and underwear, soaked through to the skin, my pubic hair and nipples visible through the sheer wet lace.

I was too sick to be very mortified, and the instructor just kept his eyes averted as Drake fanned me and held a cool cloth to my forehead.

When I was finally cool enough, I sat up and just rested for a moment, to make sure I didn't faint when I stood up. The instructor brought me a bottle of fruit juice and some ice cold water and soon, I was feeling better. I put my sundress on over my wet bra and panties and Drake and I left the marina as another group of hopeful trainees entered the building.

We took the limo back to the hotel, and Drake pulled me into his embrace while we drove back.

"You scared me," he said, running his fingers through my hair, which was starting to dry. "You were overheating and could have developed hyperthermia if we hadn't gotten you out of the suit. Plus, you have quite a sunburn."

"I'm just glad it's over. I thought I was going to faint."

"You almost did."

He tilted my head up and kissed me, softly, and I felt completely protected and cared for.

"I feel really tired," I said once we were back at the hotel. We went up to my room and my father and Elaine came right into the room through the adjoining door.

"What took you so long?" my father said.

"We had trouble with the suit and had to cut Kate out of it. She overheated a bit."

"Is she OK?"

Drake nodded. "She just needs to rest. Get some more fluids into her."

My father came over to where I lay on the bed. "Maybe you should stay in your room for dinner. Drake can order something in for you. They could send up some turkey and fixings."

I nodded. I felt incredibly fatigued as if I'd just survived an ordeal. I didn't want to go to the dining room.

"I'll just stay here and watch TV."

Drake put his hand on my father's arm.

"I'll make sure she's all right. She needs to just rest. We can order something from room service when she gets hungry. You two go ahead."

My father and Elaine came by and kissed me on the cheek and then left us alone.

"I'm hungry," he said, checking out the menu. "What would you like to eat? Do you really want turkey? Or something local, fresh?"

I shook my head. "Whatever you want. I'm just going to close my eyes for a bit."

I heard him talking on the phone, his voice soft. Then he came over and sat beside me on the bed. He took my wrist and felt my pulse and then leaned down and kissed my forehead.

"Just rest a bit. I'll watch some headlines."

He stretched out on the bed beside me and turned on the television, switching channels until he found the international news. I closed my eyes and just drifted, the sound of some news anchor's voice lulling me into a pleasant dreamlike state.

I woke up to find Drake spooned against me, his arm around me, his hand flat under my left breast. I rolled over onto my back and he adjusted himself, his eyes a bit sleepy. He kept his hand on my breast.

"You like keeping your hand there?" I said, and smiled.

"I was just taking your pulse, making sure you were OK."

"Yeah, *right...*"

"Seriously," he said, his face poker-straight. "You overheated. I wanted to make sure you were all right. I was feeling your apical pulse, just under your left breast."

"Oh," I said, feeling a bit silly. "I didn't realize doctors did that."

He leaned in, grinning and nuzzled my neck. "No, you sweet thing, I was just kidding. I just like squeezing your lovely breast. But I did also feel your pulse and it was perfect. I *could* have felt it here," he said, slipping his hand down my body from my pubes to my inner thigh. "It's called the femoral pulse, but I thought that might be a bit dangerous..."

Just then there was a knock at the door. Drake jumped up. "That's room service with our meal."

He opened the door and a waiter came in with a cart covered in white linen, with several dishes covered with metal domes to keep the food warm. Drake signed for the bill and gave the waiter a tip. When we were alone, he lifted the domes and examined the food.

"What did you order?"

"Fresh fish and vegetables, some salad. Not much of a turkey man. Hope you're hungry, because I sure am."

My stomach did feel empty as I sat up, watching Drake as he arranged our table, setting out the dishes and pulling the chairs into proper position.

"Come," he said, motioning to the food. "You need some food in you, get your blood sugar up. I'm going to keep you busy tonight and you need your strength."

That sent a rush of desire through me. "You have it all planned out?"

"You know it."

He pulled a chair out and motioned to me so I got up and smoothed my hair and my sundress and sat beside him. Then, he proceeded to feed me my meal, the fish delicious and cooked in some very simple herbs.

"Do you always feed your subs?"

"I don't usually eat meals with my subs, but I enjoy looking after them."

"Why?" I asked as he spooned some rice pilaf into my mouth. "Why don't you eat with them?"

"The relationship is just about sex."

"Eating is too personal?"

He nodded. "But I like taking care of a sub's needs. *All* of them. It also reinforces my dominance, which is necessary for submission to work. A sub needs to feel totally cared for, totally safe and cherished if she's going to submit completely. That, your complete submission, is what I want."

I let him feed me, enjoying the look of pleasure on his face as he did.

"Have you figured out why you want a woman's complete submission?" I said and watched him eat. "I imagine, given your training, you'd have some theories..."

He shrugged a shoulder and cut up some fish, picked a piece and held the fork up to me. "I need control. I *love* having a woman completely under my control."

"What does that control give you?"

"When she's tied up completely, willingly, waiting for me to do what I want to her, I am," he said and paused, taking in a deep breath. "Completely *satisfied*. It also makes me incredibly hard. Hearing her moans of pleasure, seeing her response to my touch, my words? Nothing else can get me off as well. But it's that she *wants* it, that she *chooses* it, that she trusts me completely to have her under my control that gets me off."

"Lara said she taught you to top someone. You can't get off if the woman takes control?"

He chewed his food for a moment, his head tilted to one side.

"I can, and did when Lara topped me. I actually tried out pain, but it did nothing for me personally, either giving or receiving. Lara even got me subs who were painsluts to see if I enjoyed it, but it did nothing for me. I always felt bad for damaging such lovely flesh. A surgeon is used to cutting into the body, but it's always to heal, fix, improve. We create wounds, yes, but the patient never feels pain while we do it and we pride ourselves on a patient who experiences the least pain possible post-op. I'm curious about sadists and masochists, but in an entirely clinical way, not sexual."

He stopped and looked at me pointedly. "You don't have to worry. There isn't a sadist hiding inside of me, waiting to get out. I had ample opportunity to see if there was, and no."

"I'm not worried."

"Good. Don't *ever* be."

I sighed. If only Dawn could understand...

"What was that sigh about?"

I shook my head. "I just wish this person could understand, Drake. I can't see that they ever will. They had a very traumatic experience and that's made them unable to understand. You and I? We can want each other and be good for each other, satisfy each other's kinks, but this will always be dangerous for you. You have to really think seriously about this. We'll have to really be extremely careful if we carry on when we get back to Manhattan."

"*If* we carry on? You mean, *when* we carry on back in Manhattan. I'm not giving up on you that easily. I have yet to plumb your depths, Kate. I want to plumb them. See how deep you go."

That made me very warm, the thought he wanted to take me as far as I could go.

We finished up the meal and I felt perfectly satisfied.

"Let's go for a walk along the beach now that the sun is down," Drake said.

I put on my sandals and we went out to the beach, the last rays of the sun orange-yellow on the ocean waves. The air was markedly cooler and it felt good on my sunburnt skin.

We walked along and he told me about his band.

"Just a bunch of guys from college," he said, his arm around my shoulder. "We started to play during our Junior year and never stopped. We found our niche and even though we're older than most bands, we enjoy playing."

"I'd like to hear you some day, or is that also off-limits for your subs?"

He said nothing for a moment, watching the ocean as we stood in an embrace.

"You may not like our music."

"Retro-psychedelic rock?" I said, forcing a smile, feeling a bit hurt that he'd have to think about it. "British Invasion? I heard you talking to my dad at the concert. I like some of it. I've heard my father play it before on those Oldie Goldie satellite radio stations. I don't have to hear you play, if it makes you uncomfortable."

He said nothing for a moment, but I could feel a change in him. The mood shifted entirely.

"I tend to keep things separated. The different parts of my life don't intermingle, Kate."

"I know. I'm sorry. I won't expect anything."

We started walking again, but I felt incredibly sad that he wanted to keep me separate from other parts of his life. He told me that early on. I knew that from Lara. It was just hard to accept.

I felt a bit emotional all of a sudden, a tinge of regret.

As if he felt it, he stopped before we got back to the hotel.

"Lovely *Katherine*," he said, stroking my cheek. "I've already gone off my usual routine with you, broken my own rules. Let's play things by ear, OK?"

I looked up into his face, but couldn't really see much detail because it was almost completely dark.

"OK. You're the one in charge."

He stroked my cheek.

"Thank you for understanding."

We went back inside and I went to my father's suite to say goodnight. They weren't there, so I assumed they were out dancing or something. When I got into my room, I checked my cell and sure enough, they were down at the lounge and were going to do some touristy thing and said goodnight.

I was surprised my father was so unconcerned that I was alone with Drake. Did he think we would sleep together? It felt weird. It felt *good*, as if he truly saw me as an adult now. I thought he'd disapprove of me being sexual with anyone, but he really must like Drake if he just left me alone with him.

Back at my hotel room, I felt a bit of anticipatory excitement about what would happen next. Drake said that he was going to use my body tonight and I felt myself warm to that thought, my flesh throbbing in response to the very idea of him using me that way, just taking his pleasure in me. It surprised me. I couldn't explain why it thrilled me but it did. Maybe it was the thought that he needed me, wanted me, wanted to just get his pleasure in my body that did it. I didn't know why and hadn't really thought about it before.

But it aroused me completely.

I wanted to watch him fuck me and come. I wanted to watch his face and body as he did.

While he checked his own email, I went to the bathroom and brushed my teeth, feeling a need to freshen up.

"I'm just going to zip to my own room for a moment," Drake said. "I have to get a few things, but I'll be right back."

I nodded from the bathroom door. I finished washing my face and put on my little black nightie before he returned.

When he saw me, he raised his eyebrows.

"You look lovely," he said and ran his fingers over the tops of my breasts. "Come with me. I want us to talk about the agreement."

I followed him into the living room. He had a briefcase and an overnight bag. Out of the briefcase, he removed a document. It was the agreement he'd sent to me the previous week.

"Come here and sit on my lap," he said, patting his lap.

I complied sitting across his lap as I had before, his body firm and warm beneath me, my hands on his shoulders. He held the agreement in his hand and then pointed to it, once I was comfortable.

"I want to talk about what upset you when you read it the first time."

I took the document in my hand and read it over. "Do you have a pen?"

"Yes, but before you sign, you have to tell me what you want removed. How you feel about the limits I've listed."

"Where's your pen?" I said again. I looked in the pocket of his shirt and there was one inside. A beautiful ornate fountain pen with a polished burled-wood barrel, expensive looking with a gold nib.

"This is beautiful."

"That was my father's pen. He was so old fashioned about some things. Felt that disposable pens were bad environmentally."

"You're so sentimental, Drake."

He smiled. "I guess. So," he said and pulled me closer. "Tell me about what parts of my limits bothered you when you first read it. We can negotiate. I want you to feel completely secure when you sign."

I nodded. Then I stood up, extracting myself from his arms. I went to the desk against the wall and opened the two-page document to the second page where the signature lines were located.

"Is this where I sign?"

He came to me and stopped me, his hand on mine.

"Kate, you haven't answered my questions. You can't sign until we've gone through each item."

"I've already read this. I've thought about it ever since I received it." I signed my name.

"Kate," Drake said, his head tilted. "I know you were concerned about something. Tell me. I won't sign until you do."

"I trust you, Drake," I said, turning back to him and handing him the pen. "You won't hurt me. I'm OK with the agreement the way it is."

"What about this?" he said, pointing to the mention of anal sex. "And this?" He pointed to the reference to vaginal fisting.

"I trust you, Drake," I said again. "I know you'll keep me safe and only go as far as I can handle."

He just stared at me, shaking his head slightly as if he was surprised. Then, he took the pen from my hand and signed in the appropriate spot. He put the lid back on the pen and turned back to me, pulling me against his body, his arms around me, pressing my head against his shoulder.

"Oh, sweet *Katherine*," he said softly. "You surprise me. But you've made me very happy."

I looked up at him, into his eyes. "I want to make you happy."

He leaned down and kissed me, softly. It was so tender, it sent a surge of something through my body. I expected him to go all Dom on me and take me roughly as he said he would, but he didn't.

He pulled me into the bathroom and took off my nightgown, staring at me as I stood naked before him.

"Your burn is getting worse." He went to his bag on the floor by the desk and pulled out a shaving kit. He came back to where I stood on the cool tiles of the bathroom floor. "Here," he said and removed a razor and some shaving cream. "I'm going to shave you and then I'm going to eat you and fuck you. Are you ready?"

"Yes," I said, my voice a bit quivery from excitement.

"Yes, what?" he said, looking at me, his expression a bit dark but I could tell he was forcing the look, and didn't really mean it.

"Yes, whatever it is you want me to say."

"You signed the contract," he said, his eyes hooded. "What does it say?"

"Yes, Sir," I said, smiling just a bit.

"Don't you smile when you call me *Sir*, or you'll ruin the whole effect. When we're together, I want you to consider us in scene. I'll call you either *Katherine* or slave, depending on how I feel. When you call me Sir, make sure it has a capital 'S'. Do you understand?"

"Yes, Sir," I said, fighting to keep a straight face but failing. "Why Katherine, if I may ask?"

"It's what I first knew you as – *Katherine*. It's more formal and will keep me in proper Dom headspace. I'll give you a bit of leeway at first with proper forms of address," he said and I could tell he was fighting a grin as well, "but if you continue to be saucy, I'll have to spank your delicious little ass. Do you understand?"

"Yes, *Sir*," I said. I kept my face solemn. But in truth, the idea of him spanking me didn't scare me anymore. In fact, I wanted him to, just so I could try it out, see if I responded and how I responded. "What if I said I wanted you to spank me, just so I could know what it felt like?"

He shook his head, his brow furrowed. "I'll be spanking you soon enough, Katherine. There's no way with that mischievous look in your eyes that you won't need one. But first, I'm going to fuck you the way I want." Then, he ran a bath while I stood there and examined the bottle of aloe gel on the counter.

"Come and sit in the bath. We need to soften up your pubic hair before I shave you."

I complied, sitting in the warm water. While I sat, he arranged his implements on the vanity. A razor, some shaving cream in a bottle, and an electric wet/dry shaver. He ran hot water in the sink and threw in a couple of washcloths.

"Stand up," he said, sitting on the toilet beside the bathtub. I did, the water dripping off me. He turned on the shaver and he proceeded to shave my pussy and inner thighs. "Spread your legs wide," he said, his voice a firm command.

I did, and rested my hands on his shoulders while he shaved me.

"Put one leg on the side of the tub," he said, pointing to me. I did and that exposed me to him, my cheeks hot with embarrassment and arousal that he was so close, touching me and examining me like that. Then he added more shaving cream and used the razor to get the rest of the hair, between my thighs. Soon, I was naked, my skin smooth.

"Perfect," he said, running a washcloth over the area, then his fingers. He glanced up in my eyes. "Nice and smooth. I can see everything now." He stood and took my hand. "It makes me hard as rock."

A thrill went through me as I imagined what he would do next.

"Now, I'm going to eat you the way I wanted since I first met you, when you were on the bed with your garters and nylons showing. Before I do, I have to apply some of this," he said and pulled out a small bottle of green-looking gel.

"What's that?"

He glanced at me, his brows raised.

"I'm sorry," I said, realizing I hadn't called him Sir. "What's that, Sir?"

"It's aloe vera. It's for your burn. Can't be fucking you roughly if your burns are hurting."

He then proceeded to rub the aloe over my burned skin, my cheeks, my shoulders, the tops of my breasts, the front and back of my arms, my belly, and the tops of my thighs.

"Are you being Doctor or Dom now, Sir?"

"Doctor Dom," he said, cracking a bit of a grin. "Now, stop being so cheeky, Katherine, or I'll have to put you over my knee and teach you about punishment."

I covered my mouth with my hand to hide my huge grin.

"Oh, *you*," he said and pulled me into an embrace. He kissed the top of my head. "I can see I'm going to get nowhere with you tonight, Ms. Bennet. If you were any other sub..."

"If I were any other sub what?" I said. "Sir, I mean."

"If you were any other sub, I wouldn't be smiling."

"Smiling is good, Sir. I read that it releases good brain chemicals."

"That it does. Now, *Katherine*," he said and pulled away, his face changing from amused to stern. "No more talking. Time to submit and become my slave as you agreed in the contract."

He took my hand and led me back into the bedroom. We stood beside the bed, him behind me, his lips on my neck and shoulder.

"Close your eyes," he said as he touched me, his voice soft and low, almost a whisper. He pulled my hair away and over to one side, his lips at my ear. "Just give yourself over to me."

I did, trying to relax completely, not thinking any longer, only feeling. His hands were warm on my skin, his lips and tongue soft against my shoulder as he bit me gently. His hands stroked down my arms to my hands, which he took in his, our fingers briefly entwining as he continued to kiss my shoulder and neck. Then, he searched my body with his hands, his fingers sliding down over my hips and across my body, his fingers grazing my naked pussy, just barely touching me. One hand covered my mound completely while the other slid up and over my belly, sending jolts of lust through me, making my breath come faster.

With one hand, he cupped one of my breasts, tweaking my nipple softly. The other hand remained covering my pussy, as if claiming it for his own. An ache began to build in my groin from his touch, and the sound of his voice in my ear, so calm but firm, his tongue sliding up and down my neck to my ear, his breath on my cheek.

After sitting on the edge of the bed, he pulled me between his thighs so that his face was at the level of my neck and he just held me for a moment. His hands moved over my naked skin and his touch sent waves of lust through me, my pulse increasing, my stomach full of butterflies. His breath was warm on the skin of my neck, his hands kneading my buttocks, then slipping around and cupping my breasts, tweaking my nipples, pulling them into hard points.

He was just touching me all over, his face in the crook of my neck and I was getting so aroused just from his light touch. I closed my eyes and gave myself over to him, letting him do whatever he wanted, not expecting anything, not feeling any pressure to do anything but respond.

"I told you I was going to use your body for my own pleasure, Katherine, and I'm going to. You're not allowed to come, do you understand?"

"What if I can't help it?" I said, my eyes closed as he sucked one nipple, a jolt of lust rushing through me as his teeth grazed the puckered areola. "Sir," I quickly added.

"A simple yes or no is all that's required."

"Yes," I said, my voice husky. "*Sir.*"

"You have to learn that you're only allowed to come when I want you to. I know when you're ready and when you deserve an orgasm. If you feel like you're going to come, you must tell me immediately."

My eyes almost rolled back into my head when his fingers slipped between my labia to find my clit.

"I don't want you to come this time, Katherine. I want you to just feel well-used. I want you to get used to being an object for my pleasure."

"Then why are you arousing me, Sir?"

"Shh," he said, a finger on my lips. I could feel his cheek raise in a smile against my skin. "No talking. I want you to feel how I felt the other night when you came so quickly and we were rudely interrupted. You have to yield up every bit of power to me, Katherine, when we're together. I decide everything. What we do, how we do it, if and when you come, and how you come." His fingers continued to stroke my clit, then slipped a bit deeper, teasing the entrance to my body.

"You've probably spent most of your life trying to keep quiet when you have an orgasm, Katherine. I want you to be loud. I want your eyes open and staring into mine."

I gasped when his fingers stroked inside of me, his thumb on my clit, my body clenching in pleasure around his fingers.

"You're so nice and *wet*, Katherine. You're almost ready for me."

I kept my eyes closed as he continued to stimulate me, and in truth, I felt as if I could come just from his fingers alone.

Then he pulled his fingers out abruptly and pushed me down onto the bed so I lay on my back.

"Crawl up farther," he said as he removed his shirt and shorts, so that he was standing in his boxer briefs. I did, pulling myself back on the bed.

"Are you going to tie me up?" I said, breathless, excited about the prospect.

He frowned.

"*Sir*, I mean."

"Katherine, a slave doesn't ask her Master what he plans. She merely submits happily."

"But you said..."

"Shh," he said and took my hands and placed them above my head. "Keep your hands together like that. Imagine that they're restrained and tied to the bed frame. Don't let go no matter what."

"Why aren't you going to restrain me for real?"

"*Kate*," he said, his voice a bit frustrated. "You have to let *me* decide these things."

I complied, holding my hands, my arms stretched above me.

"Now, close your eyes and keep them closed until I tell you to open them. I don't want you distracted by anything besides how your body feels."

I nodded.

He spread my thighs and lay between them, his mouth at my neck and then my breasts, sucking each nipple, squeezing my breasts as he did. My face was hot, my heart pounding, my groin aching. I knew he was going to eat me, as he said he would, and the anticipation was killing me, sending waves of desire through my body.

He moved down to my groin, to my shaved pussy, and licked it all over, the external labia, and around my inner thighs and it almost drove me crazy. When he finally licked my inner lips and clit, I groaned out loud, then inhaled sharply as he sucked them into his mouth.

"Remember," he said, pulling off me. "You can't come this time. You have to tell me if you feel like you will."

I said nothing, my eyes closed, my body so ready. He slipped his fingers into me and placed his mouth over me again, sucking me, licking me and soon, I felt that sweetness that always came before an orgasm.

"I..." I gasped, my hands in his hair. "I'm going to..."

He pulled off and removed his fingers, and I just lay there panting, so close. Without any stimulation, my impending orgasm waned and I panted, swallowing, my mouth dry.

"Good *girl*," he said. "Keep your eyes closed."

He stood up and pulled me back to the edge of the bed, my legs spread, my feet on the edge. "Put your hands above your head again. Now, I'm going to fuck you until I come inside of you. You're not allowed to come this time."

I nodded, licking my lips, my brain fuzzy from lust.

He then proceeded to stroke my clit with the head of his cock, repeating what he did to me that first night at my apartment, teasing me with it, poking the head into me just a bit before withdrawing and stroking my labia and clit slowly. He was deliberately arousing me again, building me back up to an orgasm, and when he entered me part of the way, I felt it start again.

"I'm going..." I said, gasping as he pulled out, my thighs quaking. Again, he just waited. I felt hot all over, my body tense. After a moment, when my breathing slowed, he started once more, stroking his length over my pussy, then pushing in an inch, maybe two.

I gasped. It felt so good, I thought I was going to pass out. He stopped moving and leaned over me, his cock still inside of me. His face was just above mine.

"Open your eyes," he said, his voice firm. I did, staring into his. "I'm teaching you patience, Katherine. You have to get used to obeying me. You have to turn your body and mind over to me completely. Just *feel*."

I nodded.

"Now close your eyes again."

I did. He started to thrust inside of me, slowly, agonizingly slowly, entering me a bit more with each thrust. He didn't touch my clit, just fucked me, until his entire length was in me. It felt so good as he withdrew completely and then entered me again, slowly, over and over again. Then, he stroked my clit softly, lightly, and that additional stimulation was enough and I knew I'd come if he didn't stop.

"I'm going to..." I said, gritting my teeth, trying not to but the sweetness built in my groin, deep inside me. He didn't stop. Instead he leaned over me again, his arms on either side of me.

"Open your eyes," he said quickly. "Look in mine."

I did, expecting he'd stop fucking me, but he didn't.

"Oh, *God*..." I said, gasping, but he didn't stop and then I went over the edge.

"Say my name," he ordered. "Say my name when you come."

My body took over as my orgasm started and I tried to keep my eyes open, I tried to say his name, but it was almost impossible. He started thrusting deep and fast, his face just over mine.

"*Say my name.*"

I tried but could barely speak above a whisper. "*Drake...*"

And then I was lost to it, waves of pleasure washing over me, my body tensing, arcing against his, breathing through gritted teeth, my eyes locked on his. He thrust harder, faster, watching me the entire time. I felt his cock become even harder inside of me and finally, he grimaced, his eyes closing briefly before opening again, grunting with each thrust as he came, his face inches from mine, his eyes locked on mine.

Then he collapsed onto me, his face in the crook of my neck, gasping for breath in my ear. His cock throbbed inside of me and I clenched around him, my arms still above my head. I slipped them down and around him, my legs wrapping around his waist. His skin was warm against me, his body weight comforting.

It was such a powerful orgasm and I felt almost faint, my hearing dulled, my mind drifting as if I was riding on a wave of bliss as he kissed my neck.

Finally, when I recovered enough to think, I couldn't hold back.

"I don't understand," I said. "I thought you didn't want me to come, but you made me come on purpose."

He pulled back, his face over mine, his eyes locked on mine. Finally, he smiled, his eyes crinkling at the corners.

"Kate, my whole reason for existence when we're together is to make you come."

"But then, why did you tell me..."

He kissed my neck once more and then rose up. He took my legs and spread them and watched as he pulled his now-softening cock out of me.

"Perfect," he said as he watched and I remembered him saying he wanted to see his come dripping out of me.

I smiled and covered my face with my hands, a bit embarrassed at his carnal pleasure in the evidence of his orgasm. It amused and interested me at the same time. I always thought it was messy and a bother, but he found it satisfying, like he was marking his territory. It was just one more clue to Drake, and how his mind and libido worked.

"Why did you tell me I wasn't supposed to come?" I asked again.

He leaned back down between my thighs, his face above mine, and he stroked my cheek.

"I have to learn your body like it was my own because I want to own it. You have to get used to taking orders from me. You have to get used to me controlling your response. I watched you get closer and closer with what I did to you so I could learn to judge when you're no longer able to hold back. I watched your body and your face. I listened to your breathing for how erratic it became when you started to come, watched your skin for how it flushed when you were ready, saw your nipples as they puckered when your orgasm started, how your belly tightened as your muscles tensed. They're all clues that let me know how you're feeling, how you're responding to each thing I do to you. Eventually, I'll be able to tell you're close without you having to tell me. But you'll still have to ask permission. I want to control your orgasms, Kate. It's my kink."

I nodded. He wanted me to be completely in his control. To give up my will to him so he could make me do what he wanted. He wanted to make me come, not just accidentally during sex, but purposely.

I closed my eyes and just lay beneath him, bliss filling me, my arms and legs heavy. I didn't have to do anything except respond. I didn't have to think. I didn't have to worry. I didn't have to try to do anything.

It was liberating.

"I want your every orgasm to be mine."

"Why?" I said, opening my eyes.

He just stared at me, shaking his head.

"Why does it matter?" he said, his face serious. "I just do. There's no big mystery. It gets me off. When I really feel your complete submission, that moment when I know you are completely mine, it will be," he said, pausing as if searching for the right words. "Bliss."

"Bliss," I said, wondering what bliss felt like, but pretty sure it felt close to what I felt when I was in the throes of my orgasm.

"Hopefully, when you do submit completely, you'll feel it, too."

"I thought I did."

He smiled. "No, not even close. We're just starting, Kate. I have to learn every inch of you. I have to learn all your little kinks. All the things that send you over. I have to feel you give more and more control to me. Unquestioning. You have to do things without a thought and you're still thinking. It will take a while. But it will be so worth it for us both."

He kissed the tops of my breasts where I was burnt and laid his head on them, his breath warm on my nipple.

I couldn't imagine it getting any better than this.

To my surprise, we didn't fuck again. I thought he intended to make me come three times, and I began to wonder if he didn't use his sex talk as a way to ramp up my desire. I smiled to myself as I lay in his arms in the dark once we'd both brushed our teeth and crawled under the covers. He knew how to work me up.

I was also surprised that he decided to stay with me.

"Why are you sleeping here with me?" I asked, when he snuggled against me, his arms around me, one hand under my breast as if he was feeling my pulse. "I thought you'd go back to your own room."

He was quiet for a moment. "I thought I'd stay with you tonight, make sure you're all right after the day you had. You've got a bad sunburn, and you had a touch of heat stroke."

"So you're in charitable doctor mode?"

He kissed my shoulder. "Something like that." He said nothing for a moment, but then he sighed. "To tell you the truth, I've gone a bit off the reservation, so to speak."

I rolled over onto my back and looked at his face in the darkness. I could just make out his cheekbones and a glint in his eyes from a sliver of light from under the curtains.

"Off the reservation?"

"I've broken my own rules with you."

"How?"

He stroked his hand over my shoulder and down my arm. "I told you. I keep things in their own place. I don't like them to mix."

"Why? Were you one of those kids who kept their food on separate parts of the plate, not letting them touch?"

He chuckled for a moment. Then he was quiet and I just listened to him breathe.

"It gets messy."

"*What* gets messy?"

"*Katherine...*" He kissed my forehead. "Is this twenty questions?"

I felt a bit hurt at that. He didn't want me to question him. "You want to understand *me*, Drake. Why can't I want to understand you?"

"That's *not* how it's supposed to work. You're supposed to just let me do the thinking. Let me do the knowing. You just let go of control when you're with me and relax. I should remain this dark and powerful enigma."

"Dr. *Enigma*," I said, smiling just a bit. "I think I get it. You want to stay a bit mysterious so I feel more submissive when I'm with you. Am I right?"

"Something like that. Now, shush. Go to sleep. I'm going to fuck you first thing before the conference starts and I want you all bright eyed and bushy tailed. Fair warning."

"*Bright eyed and bushy tailed...*" I said, a stab of desire going through me at his warning. "How will I be able to sleep after you tell me that? Too bad I didn't bring *Big* along..."

"You've got the real Big right *here*," he said and thrust his pelvis against me. "Don't you try to get me all hard again, Katherine." He nuzzled my neck and I could hear the smile in his voice. "I have to present my paper tomorrow morning in another session. I have to *sleep*."

I sighed. "Good *night*, Drake."

"Good night, Ms. *Bennet*," he said, humor in his voice. "I'm beginning to think that name suits you to a tee and I should start calling you *Elizabeth*."

"Did you read *Pride and Prejudice*?" I said, surprised.

He shifted on the bed beside me, snuggling a bit closer. "Dave isn't the only person in the world to take a Victorian Lit course in college. I read *Pride and Prejudice*, but I'm more a Brontë *Wuthering Heights* fan."

I lay in the dark, Drake's arm around my waist, and thought about him as a young student, maybe twenty-two or twenty-three, studying Victorian Literature and reading Ms. Austen and the Brontës.

"Why did you like *Wuthering Heights* so much?"

"*Kate...*" He yawned beside me. "Tomorrow. I promise that, after I fuck you, I'll tell you all about my love of Emily Brontë over breakfast..."

"*Wuthering Heights* is so ... depressing. Tragic. *Pride and Prejudice* is happily ever after."

"Shh," he said, squeezing me. "I don't believe in *happily ever after*, Kate. I've studied psychology. I've been divorced. Now *please*. Women's brains have this tendency to become more active after a good fucking. Men need *sleep*. Very strong *hint...*"

That sent a stab of something through my chest. I just lay still, barely breathing. I understood what he just did. He just reminded me very clearly that this was just a contractual agreement. What I so eagerly signed was meant to limit our relationship to kinky sex. He might have gone off the reservation somewhat with me, but this was as far as he was going to go.

I thought about *Wuthering Heights*, about Heathcliff, the tragic anti-hero. How Catherine was the only light in his darkness, how his enduring love for her drove him to do terrible things. How Catherine couldn't deny her love for him and how their love ended in tragedy.

I shivered, and it wasn't just my sunburn. Beside me, Drake breathed slowly and deeply, already asleep.

CHAPTER FOURTEEN

I woke really early, just as the sun was rising. Drake had rolled over onto his back and I was lying all alone, shivering, the sheet off me. My skin hurt where I was burnt and so I got up and quickly put on my nightgown, intending to put some aloe on my burns to ease the pain. I snuck out of the bed and tiptoed to the bathroom, taking my bag with me. I sat on the toilet to have a pee and took out my cell only to find an email message from Dawn. The subject line read

*Read this **now**.*

I hesitated. I did *not* want to open it and read anything bad from her. But I did anyway.

> *Kate, I know you're in the Bahamas with Drake. I asked Heath where you were and he was only too happy to tell me that you'd snuck down there for the holiday weekend to be with Drake, so bad planning on your part if you were trying to hide this. I also know that Drake is not what you think he is. He's not some sweet harmless man who likes to have some control during sex. Maybe you should ask why his ex-wife had a restraining order against him. Seriously, Kate. I did a background check on him. You think he's not a sadist but the police report I have suggests otherwise. If you don't come to your senses, I think the prospect of an anonymous letter with this police report included to the Head of Surgery at NY Presbyterian might convince you to end this very dangerous relationship.*

I covered my mouth with a hand to stifle my gasp and texted her instead of sending an email.

> *Dawn, why are you doing this? Have you decided you'd rather lose my friendship than see me happy? I'm <u>happy</u> with Drake. Just give this a chance. Please, I'm begging you. He's not what you think...*

She responded immediately.

> *A restraining order, Kate. I wonder what he tried to force on his ex-wife? Do you suppose he wanted to fist-fuck her? One day, you'll thank me for this. I can wait.*

I held my head in my hands. Drake's ex-wife had to get a *restraining* order against him? A shock went through me, making me feel a bit dizzy. I was sure there was a good reason, but still, it made me slightly nauseated.

A noise at the door drew my attention away from the message. It was Drake, standing naked in the doorway, his hair mussed, his eyes sleepy.

"What's the matter? Are you feeling OK?"

"Drake, I'm taking a pee..." I said, putting my cell in my bag. "Can you give me a moment?"

"Sorry," he said and stepped out of the bathroom doorway. "I was worried you were feeling sick from your burn."

I wiped myself, flushed and washed my hands, wondering what I'd say. He came in and stood beside me. When I avoided his eyes, he tilted my chin up with a finger so I couldn't avoid him.

"Are you OK?"

"My burn hurts," I said, my voice a bit quivery. "I thought I'd put some aloe on it."

He nodded and ran his fingers over the burn on my breasts. "Let me do that."

"I can do it," I said, pushing his hands away.

"I *like* to do it," he said, insisting, taking the bottle out of my hands and turning me around, lifting me so that I sat on the vanity, my back to the mirror. He was strong enough that I couldn't resist so I didn't. I just gave in and let him, my mind in a whirl over what Dawn said in her email.

A *restraining* order?

Drake leaned closer between my thighs and pulled down one of the straps to my nightgown. He squeezed some aloe out and smoothed it over the burns on my shoulders and breasts.

"This is going to make me hard."

"It's still really *early*..."

"Six hours of sleep is my usual," he said, cracking a grin. "You're so delicious in that black lace. But even more delicious out of it." He hiked up the hem so that my thighs were exposed and of course, my newly-shaved pussy. Then he poured a bit of aloe gel on my thighs where the burn was worst and spread it over. "Oh, I am definitely getting hard because of this."

"I need to take a shower first," I said.

He put the bottle of aloe down and leaned against me, his mouth at my throat, kissing my neck.

"This is waterproof," he said, his fingers sliding up my inner thigh to my groin. "Oh, you're so nice and *smooth*..." he said when he touched me.

I swallowed hard, in the grip of conflicting emotions. Desire rushed through me at his words and touch, but anxiety did as well. I *had* to find out what happened before I judged him. Dawn sent a PDF of the restraining order in her email. I wanted to read it but I had the feeling I wouldn't be able to until Drake and I fucked. He wouldn't let me alone now, not in the state he was in with a delicious-looking erection standing up between our bodies. Just seeing it sent a stab of lust through me, thinking of how good it would make me feel once inside of me.

"I'll turn the shower on. You get naked."

He turned away and started the shower, and I admired his delightfully round and firm ass, his strong, wide back. His skin was so smooth and fair although he did have a bit of a tan on his arms and legs. I undressed, resigned to what was going to happen, wanting it, but still, so afraid of what I'd find when I opened that PDF...

The shower stall beside the bathtub was tiled and large enough for four people. There were two safety bars on the walls and after I got in and was completely wet from the warm spray, Drake maneuvered me into the corner and proceeded to wash me. He took a bar of soap out of its box and lathered up really well, his eyes intense as he began to slide his soapy hands over my shoulders and breasts, his fingers circling my nipples, drawing them into hard points. I grasped onto the two bars on either side of me, and closed my eyes, letting him just do what he would to me. I tried to block thoughts of the restraining order out of my mind. I tried to just focus on his fingers and what he was doing to me, so expertly working me up.

His soapy hands trailed down my body over my belly and down to my thighs. He slipped his fingers between my labia and thighs, gently, and then around my back to my ass and his touch sent thrills of desire through my body. He slid his hands around my hips and soaped between my cheeks before turning me around so that the water rinsed the soap off me.

"There," he said, turning me back, lifting one of my thighs so that warm water ran down my body and between my legs. "All clean."

He turned the shower off and knelt down on the floor, taking my leg, placing it over his shoulder. He glanced up at me, his eyes intense. "I'm going to eat you, Kate. Put your leg over my other shoulder. Hold on to those bars for support. Remember to tell me if you feel like you're going to come."

I did as he said, my thighs shaking just a bit to see his mouth so close to me. He worked his hands up and around my thighs and spread my labia, then began to lick me all over, his tongue circling my clit, then going lower to the entrance to my body. It felt so good, his tongue so soft and warm against me, but when he lowered one hand and slipped two fingers into me, I clenched around him.

It didn't take long and soon, my arousal built and I felt the unmistakable signs deep inside me of an impending orgasm.

"Drake, I..." I whispered, but he didn't stop. He kept licking, sucking my clit into his mouth, his fingers stroking inside of me. "Drake, I'm going to *come*..."

This didn't stop him, but seemed to encourage him and he thrust a third finger inside of me, and the increased pressure combined with the sensation from his tongue on my clit pushed me over. My orgasm started, my whole body shaking, my thighs tensing around his head. I breathed in through gritted teeth as waves of pleasure overtook me, and I moaned out loud. "Oh, *God*..."

He kept licking and thrusting his fingers inside of me, my body quaking, clenching around his fingers.

He finally stopped after I almost let go of the safety bars in my near delirium. He pulled his mouth away and stared into my eyes as I gasped above him, my arms shaking.

Then he let each of my thighs down from his shoulders and stood up, his rock-hard dick pressing against my belly.

"Turn around," he commanded and I did, knowing what came next. I bent over and spread my thighs without him even telling me, gripping the safety bars once more and he entered me from behind, his length easily sliding inside of me, I was so slick from my orgasm. I thought he'd just fuck me quickly and come himself, but he didn't. He slid his hand around my body between my thighs and began to stroke my still very-sensitive clit while remaining still, his cock feeling so nice and big inside of me. His fingers were soft at first, but soon, he increased pressure as he began to thrust inside of me, very slowly, stroking inside the entrance to my body and a couple of inches so that he hit my sweet spot over and over again.

He was so good at this, it felt so good, so sweet that soon, I was ready to come again.

"Drake," I said, breathless once more, "I'm going to come again."

He didn't stop, just kept sliding inside of me just a few inches, his fingers never stopping their slow, agonizing tease. I was breathing rapidly, my body so close once more and I felt that any moment my orgasm would start. I tried to speak, barely able to get it out.

"*Drake...*"

"*Come* for me," he said, his voice hoarse. He started thrusting faster, entering me all the way. "Say my name when you come," he whispered, biting my shoulder. "Say my *name*."

I gasped as my orgasm started, the sensations so intense, jolts of pleasure down my legs and up into my belly. My face felt hot, and I had to grit my teeth.

"*Say my name*," he said again, his voice a harsh whisper.

"*Drake...*" I groaned as I shuddered, my whole body quaking.

He was right behind me. He pulled his fingers away from me, and gripped onto my hips, thrusting harder, grunting in my ear as he came as well, gasping with each thrust, pulling my hips against him. Finally, he stopped and just leaned against me as I bent over, still grasping the safety bars for support, my thighs now shaking.

"*Fuck...*" he gasped in my ear, his hands stroking underneath me, down from my neck and over my breasts, then to my pussy once more. "That was so good."

I clenched around him when he touched my clit and he groaned. He just stood like that for a moment, his cock still pulsing a bit inside me, his breathing and mine starting to slow. Finally, he slipped out of me. He turned me around and grasped my shoulders, bending down to kiss me, pulling me into his arms as he did. I just melted into him, trying not to think, trying to just feel *him*, feel this moment. The other moments when I had to face reality, when I had to face what Dawn sent me in her email, would come soon enough.

"There," he said, stroking my cheek. "That's two for one, I think."

I smiled and closed my eyes, biting back sadness that started once more when I thought about Dawn's email. "Are you keeping track?"

He leaned down and pressed his face in my neck, kissing me, and I felt his cheek rise in a smile.

"I'm greedy that way."

After we ate a quick breakfast in our room that Drake had ordered the night before, Drake went back to his own suite to prepare for his conference session. I sat alone in front of the open window and read my email, examining the copy of the restraining order.

It named Drake and was taken out by his former wife, Maureen. A temporary order of protection for "forcible touching" and "harassment". The order was dated almost five years earlier and I wagered it was after he and his wife split.

Forcible touching... Harassment...

Not quite what I thought at first. I thought he'd assaulted her. I could understand if a husband who had just been told by his wife that she was leaving him tried to touch her, tried to stop her from going through with it.

I could see Drake, maybe not quite understanding his Dominant nature, trying to control her and getting too insistent. I could see there being misunderstandings over this and a he-said she-said situation. Then I feared I was trying too hard to find an excuse for him. Maybe the split came out of left-wing for him and he freaked. It didn't seem like the self-confident controlled man I knew but perhaps he was really heart-broken by the split. Would he really hurt his wife?

Maybe that was what drove him to compartmentalize his life so carefully, keeping women at arm's length using submission contracts.

I sent Dawn a text.

Dawn, that was during his breakup with his wife of five years. He was probably upset and maybe overreacted but he wasn't cited with assault of any kind. He probably didn't want her to leave him. He has mentioned how broken up he was over their split. Can't you understand that he is not dangerous? He is not into pain! He just likes control and I happen to like it when he takes control. Is our friendship worth nothing? Can't you give me the chance to prove to you that he's a good man?

She responded in a couple of minutes.

I have to follow my conscience. He likes to tie women up and fist them and anally fuck them, Kate. Doesn't that scare you? How much farther from that is rape? Even if you let him willingly, what's wrong with you if you want that? It's sick.

I sat and held my head in my hands, grief washing over me that she couldn't listen to reason. Was she going to actually try to ruin his career over this?

Don't do this, Dawn. Don't ruin him. He hasn't hurt me. He's only cared for me.

She replied right away.

I won't wait around until he does hurt you. Kate, this is for your own good. End it now before it goes any further and he either breaks your heart or hurts you for real. If you don't, I <u>will</u> send this to the head of surgery along with his FetLife profile. Do you know he calls himself Master D? I asked around the nurses at NYP and I heard an earful. They say he's a controlling bastard. Who knows what else I'll find if I have my PI dig a bit deeper... End it Kate. I don't care if you hate me. I have to do this to save you from even worse pain.

I didn't respond. I just dialed Lara. She answered on the second ring.

"Hey, Kate. What's up?"

"Lara, I'm in trouble. I need your advice as a lawyer."

"Uh, *oh*. Can I assume it involves Drake?"

"You assumed right," I said and related what happened. I didn't use Dawn's name but told Lara that it was someone who knew Drake in his professional life.

"What happened with his wife?" I asked, cringing, not sure if I wanted to know.

"Oh, that was overblown," she replied. "He tried to stop her from leaving the night she announced she wanted a divorce. He wanted to keep talking and she just wanted to leave. He stopped her physically. Didn't hurt her or anything, but by then, she was so cold to him, she didn't care how he felt. When he persisted, calling her, wanting to get counseling, try to keep the marriage together, she took out the order of protection. It was only temporary, so no big deal. It wasn't a permanent order so the judge didn't think he was a real danger. Drake had been so busy with his work, with establishing his career, he didn't understand how far apart they had grown until it was too late.

She just couldn't deal with him, had a new boyfriend and just sprung it on him out of the blue."

"Poor Drake," I said. I felt really bad for him.

"Christ," she said, sounding exasperated. "What did you tell Drake about this?"

"I tried to break it off with him last week, but he wouldn't accept it. He said he wants to stay together and that we would just be really discrete, but this person was able to find out that we were both in the Bahamas. She found a Private Investigator and did a background check on Drake. I didn't tell him any of this yet. I'm afraid for him."

There was a silence on the line. "I was a bit concerned about Drake. He's gone a bit native with you, Kate."

"What do you mean?"

"You know, a bit wild. Like the old Anthropologists when they stayed too long with the tribe. Not following his usual routine. He *never* sees his subs outside of the lifestyle. I don't know what he was thinking with you, but he saw you at the fundraiser, at your father's campaign fundraiser, at the concert, and now he's there. That really surprises me. He's not being sane about this. His reputation is far more important than training a potential sub."

"I tried to talk to him, but he's just not listening. How bad would it be if the existence of a restraining order was made public, say to someone in the hospital?"

"I have no idea, but it would depend on the optics of it and the person who received the information. Some people might completely ignore it. This happened five years ago after all. But add in the whole kink element, his profile at FetLife... That might be too much."

I sat and chewed my nail. "What should I do?"

She was silent for a few moments. "What do you *think* you should do?"

"I don't want him to be hurt because of me."

"Then end it."

I closed my eyes. "I already tried that."

"You didn't try hard enough. Listen, Kate. I know Drake Morgan. You want to end it with Drake? Tell him he doesn't do it for you. Tell him you don't feel it. Or better, show an interest in meeting another Dom who might be better able to get you to submit. Technically, he should have just kept things totally professional with you and not seen you outside of establishing this D/s relationship. He screwed up. You can use that, claim that he feels too much like a boyfriend, not a Dom."

"I couldn't do that! He *does* do it for me. He *knows* that..."

"Kate, you two have only known each other for a few weeks. Just cut him off. Be mean. Believe me, there are any number of subs who would be entirely grateful to have a Dom like him. I'll set to work finding a replacement for you. She'll be there to assuage any sadness he feels over your broken agreement."

"You really think I should do this?'

She was silent for a moment. "I think that this shouldn't have happened. I think whoever found out about you and Drake is an evil person to threaten this. I'm so sick of the public's ignorance of this lifestyle and intolerance. Drake is my close friend. I think you have to put Drake's career before your own hopes for this D/s relationship. He's a wonderful man, Kate. He does really wonderful work as a neurosurgeon. Don't let your desire for him ruin his life."

"I know."

We said goodbye and I ended the call. I sent a text to Dawn.

> *You win. I'm ending it with him tonight. I'll be back in Manhattan as soon as I can get a flight.*

Then I cried my eyes out.

CHAPTER FIFTEEN

While Drake did his presentation, I went with my parents for a boat ride, all the while holding back my emotions, forcing a smile for them every so often. After our trip, we came back to the hotel and there was a note from Drake saying he had a lunch with his colleagues but hoped to be back around mid-afternoon.

We went down to the restaurant and sat on the patio, eating our lunch in the shade of a huge umbrella.

"How are things, sweetie? You seem a bit... distant this morning."

I shrugged my shoulder. "Fine."

"Things OK with Drake?"

"They're all right."

"Just all right?"

"He's very self-absorbed."

"He's here to present his research, Kate," my father said, his voice a bit impatient. "He's probably just focused on his work."

"He's really a nice man," I said. "He's just always a bit preoccupied. I don't feel like he's really with me even when we're alone."

I sighed. I wanted to lay the foundations for our breakup with them so they didn't fight me.

"He's a busy man," my father said. "He's busy now with work."

"I'm bored," I said. "I think I might go back early. Is there any way I can get my ticket changed?"

"Katherine!" he said, frowning. "What are you thinking? You just got here..."

"It's just not working out, Daddy. Maybe he's too old for me. I don't know... I want to go out and party. He just wants to sit around and listen to music or watch television and I just don't do that. I mean, he was already in college when I was still in primary school."

My father just shook his head. He was not pleased and I'm sure he thought I was being a shallow bitch. My heart was breaking, but I knew this was for the best.

Later, Drake came to my room using the key card I gave him to enter my suite as I was lying on the bed. I was busy rehearsing in my mind what I was going to say to Drake and pretended to be sleeping. I had a plan in mind and it was a cruel plan. If Lara was right, I had to make Drake think he wasn't, as she said it, 'doing it for me'. That would be hard. It would require a real acting job on my part.

He came right over and laid on the bed beside me, pulling me into his arms. I pushed against him a bit.

"Drake, I was *sleeping*."

"Sorry," he said, stroking my hair. "I missed you all day. I've been thinking of you, planning what I was going to do to that luscious body of yours when I was finally finished with the conference, which is, *now*."

He nibbled my neck, and the touch of his lips sent a stab of pleasure through me, but I stiffened instead of melting into his arms.

"Not now," I said, pushing him away again.

He pulled back and leaned on his elbow. "What's the matter?"

I sat up on the bed and wrapped my arms around my legs. I yawned. "I didn't sleep well I guess."

"I know how to wake you up," he said, that half-smile starting. He ran the backs of his fingers over the tops of my breasts and it made me shiver.

"Ow, my burn," I said, although my burn was quite good by then.

"Sorry," he said, frowning. He lay back on the bed, his hands behind his head. He just watched me for a moment. "What have you been doing?"

"We went for a boat ride and then had lunch. I've been sleeping."

"What would you like to do?"

I shrugged my shoulder again. "I don't know..."

He sat up closer, so that he was sitting next to me, and kissed my shoulder. "Kate, I know something's wrong. I can tell. What is it?"

I yawned again. "I don't know. I'm a bit bored, I guess."

"You're probably not used to leisure time, having nothing to do. Your father said you've been working like a dog for years, working on your degrees and for *Geist*."

"It's just that most of the people here are older than me. There's no one here my age. I feel like I'm in an old-folks home or something."

He just watched my face, a strange expression on his.

"Would you like to go out to a bar? The locals have some nightlife. Dancing."

I made a face. "Whatever." I actually didn't want to go out somewhere. I wanted to just cry. "Not really. I don't know if I want to be out among *the locals*."

"Come here," he said, holding his arms out.

"Why?"

"I need to hold you."

I shrugged and climbed onto his lap. Of course, I felt incredibly sad doing so, because I wanted his arms around me, and I felt so sad about what I had to do.

He tilted my head up and just looked in my eyes, his face perplexed. "Kate, what's wrong?"

"I don't know," I said, trying to sound bored. "Just bored, like I said."

He kissed me, and I tried hard not to kiss him back, but he was insistent. He started to search my body with his hands, pulling me into his arms. I had to do everything I could not to respond to him. I thought about the ugliest things I could to stop my body from responding. I thought about the scent of dead bodies in the graves outside Mangaize. I pictured worms in a grave crawling through a decomposing body. I thought about never seeing Drake again, and a surge of sadness filled me, making my throat choke up.

Drake pressed me back on the bed and lay on top of me, his arms cradling my head while he kissed me, one of his knees between mine, pushing my legs apart. He kissed me intently, completely focused, his breathing becoming more intense. He pressed his hips against mine and I felt his erection. It felt delicious and my body couldn't help but respond, so I thought immediately of Kurt, and how he scared me that night we broke up.

Finally Drake pulled back. He just stroked my cheek, silently giving up.

Then, his cell rang and he pulled it out of his pocket and checked the ID.

"Crap," he said. He answered. "Hi," he said and listened. "Not tonight. No. I have something planned." A silence followed. "Sure," he said. "Tomorrow before the plenary. See you then." He ended the call and turned back to me, his brow furrowing.

"You really are tired," he said. "I'm not feeling the usual response in you."

I yawned and stretched. "Maybe," I said, wracking my brain for how to do this. "It's just so dead here. Nothing to do."

"I can think of lots I want to do."

"Yeah?" I said, keeping my face blank. "Like what?"

He smiled but it seemed forced. "Do I even have to say?"

"Oh," I said and crawled away from him, standing up. "*That.* I'm thirsty. I'm going to get a drink." I took my bag and went to the vending machine down the hall. I bought a drink, needing to get away from him, from his strong warm body, from the scent of his aftershave, the look on his face.

I just stood in the hallway and opened the drink, taking a sip, wanting to delay this, not sure how I'd be able to do it.

"Kate?" Drake leaned against the doorjamb. "You want to go somewhere?"

I shrugged and returned to the hotel room, walking past him, trying to avoid touching him. He followed me into the living room. I took the channel changer and switched on the television.

"Wonder what channels they get here?"

He sat on the couch, right in the middle, his arms outstretched on the back, just watching me as I stood and flipped through the lineup of shows.

"Come here," he said, his voice low. I turned and looked at him and he was so devastatingly beautiful in his white button-down shirt, open at the neck, his tan Dockers, black sandals. His hair was shiny and a bit wild, his jaw covered by a layer of stubble. I shrugged and put the channel changer down and went to him, sitting beside him. He patted his lap. "I mean here."

I sighed and climbed onto his lap, my hands resting on his shoulder. I bit my lip until it hurt to control my emotions.

"What?" I said.

"What's wrong?"

I shook my head. "I don't know, Drake. I'm just not *feeling* this."

"What do you mean?" His eyes narrowed.

"This," I said pointing between us. "Submission. It's just not there. This feels too much like a traditional relationship. You know. Boyfriend / girlfriend."

"You seemed to enjoy yourself this morning."

"Yeah, but it was just ordinary sex. You rub my clit the right way and I'll come. I could do that with any man. There was nothing kinky about it." I raised my eyebrows. "Maybe we're just not working out. Now that we're alone, it's just not really," I said, searching for the word. "Exciting. Lara told me that sometimes, a Dom and sub just aren't compatible. You must really *feel* it. I just don't feel like we're the right match. I want to *feel*, I don't know... really possessed. I *don't*. It's like, I can't even call you *Sir* and feel it. I mean, Nigel's a Sir. He's an actual Knight and I don't even call *him* 'Sir'."

I watched him, his face changing in front of me. He didn't say anything. He just looked in my eyes, blinking rapidly. His breathing increased a bit, but he said absolutely nothing.

"I'm sorry," I said. "I just don't feel it with you. You're really sweet, Drake. Maybe Lara has someone else who I won't have any history with. Someone really anonymous. I might be able to feel it more with a stranger. You know how this works. What do you think?"

He said nothing, just looked in my eyes, his gaze moving over my face but his skin blanched.

Finally, he spoke, his voice controlled, low. Very calm. "I think you might be onto something."

I nodded. "I *knew* you'd understand. You've been doing this for a long time and have lots of experience. I already talked to my parents. I think I'll go back tomorrow morning, try to salvage a couple of days of my vacation."

"And this has nothing to do with the person trying to keep you from being with me?"

"*No*," I said and frowned. "Of course not. Like you said, we could just keep this agreement under wraps."

"Why did you sign the contract?"

"I have to admit I was a bit shocked by your contract, but I thought, you know, maybe I needed to just sign the damned thing and take a risk, give it a shot. But once I did, it was like all the thrill was gone. So maybe I expected more than I should have. You know, it was just straight sex after all."

I stood and went to my drink on the table. I took a long sip. He kept sitting there, his arms out on the back of the couch, watching me.

His face was pale under his tan, his mouth thin.

"Well, then," he said and stood, his body stiff. "I guess I'll go to the bar after all and meet my colleagues. Have a good trip home."

He left, taking his bag and shaving kit with him, closing the door behind him without another word.

I sat down on the floor and covered my mouth with my hands.

Later, after I sat with a cold washcloth over my eyes to bring down the redness from weeping, I met my dad and Elaine in the restaurant. I had to eat something and I had to show a brave face to the world so that they believed me when I insisted I wasn't upset. As I went by the bar, I glanced in and saw a group of people sitting around a table, recognizing the woman Drake had said was his co-author. I checked the table out quickly, but Drake wasn't there. I walked by the front doors to the other side of the hotel where the restaurant was located and as I passed, I glanced out to the beach, which was about twenty feet away. Drake was standing there alone, watching the sunset, his hands in his pockets.

I hurried into the restaurant, my stomach nauseated, biting back tears. I didn't know how I'd be able to eat. I sat with my parents and they were both pleased to see me, looks of concern still on their faces.

"Sweetheart, are you sure you're all right? You look a little pale. Your eyes are red. Were you crying?"

I shook my head. "No, I'm fine. It's my allergies. I'm just a bit disappointed, that's all. You know how it is when you have high hopes for a relationship and it doesn't work out."

"We've all been there before Kate," Elaine said, smiling at me, her expression sympathetic.

"Drake came by just a few minutes ago," my father said. "Asked if you were OK. You told him you were going back tomorrow?"

"Yeah," I said, trying to sound nonchalant. "He agreed."

"He seemed really upset, Katherine." My father just shook his head. "Guess I was really wrong about you two. Maybe I should hang up my matchmaking hat."

"Oh, don't do that Daddy. I'll meet the right man some day." I forced a smile that I didn't feel and picked up my menu.

I tossed and turned all night, unable to sleep, my mind going over everything again and again. Should I just go to him and tell him the truth? What would he do? I had the sense he'd ignore it and push on, arguing that we'd just be really careful. But Dawn was *not* going to let up either. I knew she'd watch me like a hawk. If she'd been determined enough to hire a PI to track down info on Drake, she'd have someone follow me. She was really moralistic at times, and we'd clashed in the past over issues, but we'd always found a way through the disagreements because of the sheer length of time we'd been friends.

Back in Manhattan, nothing changed. I arrived in my apartment late that night and crept right into bed. I slept in most of the next day, unable to get out of the bed except to go to the bathroom. I felt as if I'd been hit by a truck, my body aching, my stomach sick. I just closed the drapes in my bedroom in some ridiculous attempt to block out the world. I had one more day off before I had to go to work.

I told myself that it was for the best. I didn't want Drake to be disgraced because of me. I couldn't live with myself if my selfishness led to harm of his career or reputation. He was an important neurosurgeon. He did really great things for people. If he was disgraced because of me, because of Dawn's moralistic crusade, I could never live it down, and there would be nothing I could do to fix things.

This was just the way it had to be.

It didn't make it any easier to bear. I wanted him – so *much*. It was so good with him, even just the vanilla sex. I couldn't imagine what it would be like if he really had his 'Dom hat' on with me. I remembered how much those letters he wrote to his subs affected me.

I went to my history and found the website and logged in so I could read another letter.

To my new sub:

> *Don't be afraid, little one. You're safe with me. You can just relax in my embrace and know that I will protect you. I will learn you inside and out – what you like, what you dislike, what you need and what you don't need. Then, I will give you everything you desire.*
>
> *I will approach you like a wild animal in need of being tamed to hand. I will tame you. You feel out of control now, but one day, I will come to you as you wait for me in position, your blindfold on. I will whisper your name, my mouth next to your ear, my breath warm on your naked skin, my hands caressing you. When I bind your hands with my soft leather restraints, when I tie your feet to the bedposts, you'll be completely controlled and all your anxiety will be gone. You don't have to make any decision from now on when you're with me. I*

will make them all. Every decision will be about your pleasure for that is my pleasure.

One day, you will purr like a contented kitten as I stroke you, running my fingers over your naked skin, exploring every inch of you with my eyes, my fingers, my tongue, my cock. For the first time, you'll be free of all your fears, all your insecurities and doubts. You know how much I desire you by how hard I am when I'm with you, how much I enjoy every inch of your body, your scent, your touch, your every response, your every gasp, your every moan of pleasure.

Once we cross the threshold into our special world where just we two exist, you can leave all your fears behind. You turn over your will to me, and when you do, you will feel as much desire as you are able, as much lust as you can possibly feel. I want it all.

I can handle you.

Why did that affect me so deeply? Drake had that effect on me. I felt as if he knew what was going on in my mind, what I needed, how to touch me, what to say. He felt so certain and confident, his body warm and firm. Strong.

But he accepted what I said. He believed me. He let me go. Did he really think I was bored? Did he really think I was interested in meeting someone else?

If he did, then he didn't really know me as well as I thought because inside I was dying.

I barely ate anything, my stomach sick, my head aching. By Sunday night, I felt entirely hopeless. Drake didn't even *fight* for me. He just let me go.

I must not have meant much to him after all.

I realized that despite his so attentive treatment of me when we had been together, he really *did* see me as a project to study and plan and carry out, nothing more. If he had felt anything for me beyond just a new project, he wouldn't have let me leave.

As each hour passed without him even sending me an email or text, a phone call, agonizingly slowly, that sunk in even more deeply. I had been so delusional to think he was more than just a Dom to me. That I was more than just a new sub to train.

I hadn't taken a shower or brushed my teeth for two days. I took a sleeping pill and went to bed Sunday night before the sun even set.

On Monday I couldn't face work. I couldn't face getting up and having a shower. I just dragged myself out of bed and sent my boss an email saying I was sick and needed a day off. That I'd be in on Tuesday. But in truth, I felt like Tuesday would feel just the same as Monday.

On Monday afternoon, my father called. I woke up and checked my caller ID. I had to answer. I didn't want him worried.

"Hey, sweetheart. How are you? We expected to hear from you."

I swallowed, licking my dry lips. "I must have caught something. I'm home sick. Been sick all weekend."

"What's the matter? A cold? Is there a flu going around?"

"Must be. I stayed home today, but I'll see how I am tomorrow and go to work if I feel better."

"Are you sure everything's all right? Do you need me to get anything for you?"

"No, really. I'm fine. Thanks, Daddy."

"Take care, doll."

I hung up, and just lay back in bed, covering my face from the light.

The next morning I called in sick again and slept in. Around eleven, the phone rang again. I checked the caller ID and it was Lara.

"Kate," she said, her voice sounding concerned. "I had to fess up to Drake that I talked to you about all this. He's coming over to speak to you as soon as he's done with surgery this morning. Please, keep in mind what I said and don't listen to him. He's being irrational. Just get out of your apartment, don't be there. If you do run into him, be hard and say you've come to your senses. I know you're upset about this. Drake told me he talked to your father about you, and your dad said you were sick and that he thought you were upset that things didn't work out. I couldn't lie to him. Please, do the right thing."

"Lara..." I said, shaking my head. "I miss him so much."

She exhaled loudly. "You are both *crazy*. Don't say I didn't warn you but seriously Kate, if you care about Drake you won't encourage him. Do you understand?"

"I know you're right," I said, exhaling in exasperation. "I'll make sure I'm out of the apartment when he comes by."

"Thank you. His reputation is worth more than one sub. Kate, I've seen too many powerful men fall over a simple affair. It's not *worth* it. Think of the guilt you'll feel if anything happens to him because you encouraged him."

"I won't be here when he comes by, Lara. Don't worry."

I hung up and went to the shower. If I had to go out, I had to at least clean myself up enough that I didn't look like an escaped mental patient. I quickly dressed and dried my hair and gathered up my bag. It was 11:45 and I expected that Drake would be done his surgery soon. I had to leave.

I went across the street once more to the deli and took my place in the window seat, ordering a cup of tea and toast with jam, the first thing I'd eaten beyond Cheerios and milk for three days.

At about 12:20, he drove up and once more double-parked. He went to the door, and just then, a resident exited the building and Drake took the handle and went inside.

Damn... They shouldn't have let him in, but I suspected when they saw his scrubs and lab coat, they let him in, instinctively trusting a physician. After a few moments, he came back out and pulled out his phone and entered something. In a moment, my phone buzzed and I took it out.

Drake Morgan, MD.

I ignored the call. He called back. He sat on the steps and called, over and over. Then he texted me.

> *Kate, I know everything. I talked to Lara and she confessed that she guilted you into saying goodbye to me. I was confused the other day when you claimed not to feel anything for me. I tried not to respond – to respect your wishes. In truth, I was hurt.*
>
> *Talk to me. Please. I'm not letting you run away just to protect me from something that might never happen. It's up to me what risks I take in my life, not you.*
>
> *Your father is worried about you. He says you've been sick all weekend. You know what I think? I think you're upset about this. Maybe as upset as I am.*
>
> *Kate, please... Don't give up on this – on us – without a fight.*

I felt incredibly sad to see him sitting on my steps, texting me when I was sitting across the street, watching him. I thought about what Lara said – that it would be on my conscience if I encouraged him. That I would regret my decision to be with him if anything happened to hurt his reputation but his words made my eyes tear up, my throat constrict.

He was upset. I hurt him by what I said.

I scanned the street, checking to see if Dawn was hanging around, but they were pretty empty.

I'm in the deli across the street from you.

He glanced up and my heart did a flip when I felt his gaze come to rest on me, sitting there in the bay window at a tiny table for two. He stood up and made a beeline for me, his expression so intense, his face so dark, it almost scared me.

CHAPTER SIXTEEN

Drake entered the deli and came right over to my table, pulling up the rickety chair beside me. He sat next to me, his knee wedged in between mine as if he was trying to block my escape, prevent me from leaving. He leaned close to me, taking my hand in his. He kissed my knuckles. His face was pale, his brow furrowed.

"Drake, you can't *do* this," I said, almost whispering, trying to pull my hand away from him, wiping my eyes. "We have to just end this. Better to do it now before any damage is done."

"It's already been done. I *want* you. Don't you want me?"

I said nothing, sighing, emotions building in me. Of course I did. "It doesn't matter what we want."

"*Tell* me that you don't want me."

I exhaled and tried to avoid his eyes.

"*Tell* me, Kate. If you don't want me, I'll leave right now."

"It's not that I don't want you," I said, staring at the leather strap on his wrist, the story he told me about it making my heart break for him. "I *do* want you but we can't be together. It's for your own good."

"If you still want me, we'll find a way to work around this, whatever it is. Tell me who knows? What did they say?"

"I can't *tell* you," I said, leaning back a bit from him, his gaze so intense. I couldn't extract my hand from his. "Look, barely anything has happened between us. We had sex a couple of times. We should just let this drop. I'm sure there are other subs with far fewer ... impediments than I have."

"*Impediments*..." he said, smiling just a bit. "Something happened between us, Kate. I know it's only been a short time, but I don't want this to end, especially not in this way because of someone else forcing us. If we stop seeing each other, it should be because of how *we* feel, not someone else's judgment."

I just stared at him. He was so sure of himself.

"This person told me there was a restraining order against you. Your ex-wife..."

He closed his eyes and bowed his head, his hands still grasping mine. Then he glanced back up at me, his blue eyes pained.

"That was a long time ago in a different life."

"You can understand why they, and why I, might be concerned... You *are* into BDSM."

"Not the SM part. Kate, I didn't injure her. I tried to prevent her from leaving our home. That's all. I prevented her from leaving for a while. I wanted to talk to her. I wanted to try to work things out. She wasn't listening."

"Why? What happened between you? Why did your marriage fail?"

He sighed and just stared at me as if deciding if it was worth it to tell me.

"Why does any marriage fail?" He shook his head. "Because the couple are no longer in sync. *We* were no longer in sync. I wanted more control. She didn't want me to have it. I was so ambitious about my career, traveling around the country doing conferences, presenting papers. We grew apart, and when I did finally try to assert more control, she was already gone emotionally."

"You were just starting to recognize your Dom tendencies?"

"Yes, but not very clearly. Look, I may have been a self-centered asshole, but I never hurt her. *Never*."

"Why were you a self-centered asshole?"

"I spent too much time away. You know..."

"No I don't."

"I was like my father, Kate. I was too busy and neglected her."

I just stared at him.

"Why? Didn't you love her?"

He shrugged, exhaling as if exasperated. "I don't know. Part of me thinks I did still love her. Part of me thinks I had no idea what love was." He looked away as if he did know but didn't want to admit it. Finally, as if drawing on some deep reserve, he looked back up at me. "I neglected her and she fell out of love with me. She said I was a self-centered prick who cared only about myself."

"Do you agree?"

He nodded but didn't say anything for a moment. "I didn't know what it took to make a relationship work. I'd never seen a marriage. Never knew what a woman wanted, what she expected. I can do sex, Kate. I do it really well. Everything else in a relationship? Not so much."

I nodded. That's why he kept it to his submissives. No love. No romance.

"What happened in court? Lara said you got off really lightly."

"Lara helped me. She's very rational and saw what was happening and set me on the right path. I started training with Lara at that point."

"You already knew her?"

He nodded. "Yes. We were old acquaintances and took classes together during our undergrad years. When I needed a lawyer, I called her. When I needed to be taught how to do this properly, she trained me. Kate, I've never hurt anyone purposely except during training and that was consensual. If anything's happened otherwise, it was an accident. Incidental to what was happening."

"What happened?"

"A binding a bit too tight. A bruise or abrasion on a wrist or ankle. Nothing permanent. Nothing inflicted on purpose. I've always chosen my subs very carefully. I don't *want* anyone into pain. If a sub needs pain, I refuse to sign. Just D/s. Just pleasure. You can ask Lara for more details if you need them. I'll tell you anything you want to know." He glanced at his cell. "Look, I hate to rush this. I know you need to process this but I have a surgery in a very short time. I want you to come with me. I don't want to leave you alone right now."

"Come with you where?"

"To the hospital. You can sit in my office while I take care of this procedure. It's pretty short – only about forty-five minutes. Then I have an hour off before my final surgeries of the day. I want to figure this out."

"I can go back to my apartment and wait there."

"*Come* with me. I don't want you out of my," he said and hesitated. "Out of my *reach* right now."

"I'm not going to disappear..."

"Kate, for all I know, you might. Come with me. Wait for me. Then we'll figure this all out."

I sighed. "I shouldn't go anywhere with you. If anyone saw us."

"No one is going to see us."

I exhaled. "OK."

He still hadn't let go of my hand. He squeezed it, and then he leaned in and kissed me. I let him and a stab of desire filled me at the touch of his lips on mine.

"Come," he said, standing, pulling me up. He wouldn't let go of me as if I'd dematerialize in front of his eyes. We walked to his car, our fingers entwined, and he opened the door for me. I got in and we drove to NY Presbyterian, to the wing where his office was located and parked in a spot marked "Doctors Only". He was quiet on the way there as if he was deciding how to handle this – how to handle me.

We walked hand in hand through a maze of halls to his office, which was very comfortable but clinical looking with a window, a desk with two computers and a filing cabinet, and a huge flat screen television on the wall. A small couch and two chairs on either side of a coffee table. I imagined that's where he met with patients and family members.

"Here," he said and pointed to the couch. "Have a seat and make yourself comfortable. I have a collection of out of date magazines to read." He went to the huge screen, turning it on. "There's a coffee and vending machine down the hall if you get thirsty or hungry. You can watch the surgery on the screen if you want. We're recording all procedures and you can watch live feed here."

"I can watch you operate?"

"Yes," he said. "I do really specialized robotically-assisted procedures and record every case for my clinical course in neurosurgery." He held up a remote. "You can use this to turn the volume up or down. If you get bored, you can switch to cable and watch television." He brought up a screen that had three views, one with a slightly elevated view of a high-tech looking OR theatre, another directly above a gurney, and a third staring at what resembled an open CT scanner. A number of gowned and masked people walked around, moving equipment.

"That's your OR?"

"For the procedure this afternoon, yes. It's a really advanced OR suite equipped for neurological procedures like I'm doing this afternoon." He pointed to a machine that looked like a CT scanner. "That does real-time images of the brain for really delicate surgery."

"What are you doing?"

"Implanting electrodes in a man's brain to stop Parkinson's tremor. That's for imaging the brain during the procedure. The patient will be sitting with his head inside the machine so we can watch as the electrodes are inserted to make sure we get them in the right location. Speaking of which, I have to get ready or I'm going to be late. Gotta go scrub in."

After he handed me the remote control, he bent down to kiss me. I raised my head and let him.

He touched my bottom lip, my scar, and then stared into my eyes, frowning. "Wait for me?"

I nodded.

"I'll be forty-five minutes, maybe an hour, depending on how things go. OK?"

"I'll be here."

He went to the door and looked back at me. "I won't be long."

I smiled and I waved at him.

He closed the door and left me alone.

I removed my shoes and tucked my feet under me, stretching out on the couch to watch Drake perform brain surgery.

As I watched, activity began to increase in the OR. A couple of gowned, masked and gloved technicians moved equipment around, positioned tables and trays, and arranging implements. I heard music start and turned up the volume. In the background, I just made out Led Zeppelin. *Black Dog* played over the speakers, and I remembered what Dawn said that first night in the pub when she pointed Drake out. He played Brit Invasion music in his ORs during surgery. I thought that was just TV surgeons, expecting that real ones needed quiet for their very delicate procedures.

Apparently, not.

Soon, a patient was wheeled in and then several people transferred him to a chair like structure. He already had this metal halo-like device on his head. They leaned him back into a semi-reclining position, his head between the arms of the CT.

On the walls were monitors that showed various perspectives on his brain.

Several people in full scrubs milled around, moving things into place around the patient, speaking to him in low calm voices. I imagined they were OR nurses and surgeons for they worked on the patient, getting him into position, checking over his shaved head. Then, one of the surgeons started to cut his skull with a drill, the high-pitched whine audible over the music. It wasn't Drake – the man's voice was foreign sounding – East Indian.

Then, two gowned and masked figures entered the OR, holding their gloved hands up and in front of their bodies. They had safety glasses on and what looked like binocular lenses attached.

Drake must have been one of them. I watched, wondering if I could tell which one. One of the two approached the patient and spoke to him, and it was then I knew that was Drake.

He spoke to the camera for a moment, describing the procedure to treat Parkinson's Disease. Mr. Graham was a sixty-two year old man otherwise in good health who began to experience tremors on the left side of his body. Since that time, the tremors increased, and now, he was unable to carry out the most simple tasks of everyday life. He went on to describe the surgery, using lingo I couldn't quite catch. Finally, he went to the patient's side.

"How are you doing, Bob?" he said, his voice firm but warm. "Ready?"

"Cut away, Doc. Great tunes, by the way," Mr. Graham said. "When you asked me, I didn't really believe you'd play Led Zeppelin in the OR."

"I find music relaxes patients. Luckily, we have the same taste in bands."

"You're too young to like this music."

"It's my father's music. I love it, too."

The music was loud, but not too loud so that the audio picked up every word Drake and his team said. Drake consulted the CT images, checking to make sure everything was in proper alignment. He described what he was doing, his voice firm and warm, instructions given for the benefit of his students. As I watched, he explained how he was threading an electrode into a precise position in the brain, guided by a CT-generated image on a screen beside the operating table.

"When I stimulate the section of the brain where the electrode has been placed, Mr. Graham's hand should stop shaking. Slowly at first, maybe not completely, but there will be noticeable improvement."

I watched Mr. Graham as Drake worked. His head was imprisoned in a metal cage. He lifted his hand at Drake's instruction and it shook wildly. It was clear he could do nothing with it.

"We are now going to send a charge down the electrode to the *subthalamic nucleus* and the *globus pallidus interna*, the structures responsible for motor movement."

In a few seconds, Mr. Graham's hand stopped shaking. Slowly at first but in about ten or fifteen seconds, it was almost perfectly still.

"Oh, God, *oh God*," Mr. Graham said, his voice breaking. "Oh, *God* I can't believe it."

I couldn't help but smile to myself, the emotion in his voice bringing tears to my eyes.

"*Thank* you, Doctor," Mr. Graham said, his voice breaking. "Thank you, *God*."

Drake bent over Mr. Graham, but he kept his hands away from the man. I had the sense he wanted to touch Mr. Graham but of course, he had to keep sterile.

"I *love* my job," he said, his voice soft. "I can't believe they pay me to do it."

About twenty minutes later, after they sewed up Mr. Graham's incisions and wheeled him out of the OR, Drake entered the office in his scrubs, his cap still on his head. He glanced at the screen and saw the technicians cleaning the OR. Then he turned that intense gaze to me.

"How are you?"

I went to him where he stood beside the door and put my arms around his waist, squeezing him.

"What's this?" he said, smiling, his arms slipping around me, a bit of a surprised look on his face.

"That was amazing."

He closed the door to his office and removed the cap off his head, throwing it on the trashcan by the desk. Then he pressed me against the door.

"Mmm, Ms. *Bennet*," he said, his voice low and sexy, one of his knees between mine, his hips pressed against me, his arms on the door beside my head. "I hope this show of affection means you've reconsidered and you're planning on giving this a chance."

"I still want you," I said, running my hands up his chest, his muscles firm under the blue scrubs. "I never stopped. If anything, I want you even more. But if this person finds out that we're seeing each other, they'll tell my father about your involvement in the BDSM community and send the restraining order to your boss."

He just watched me, his gaze moving over my face. "You won't tell me who?"

"I can't."

"If I talk to them, maybe I can assure them I won't hurt you and..."

"I *can't*. You *don't* understand. They're serious and completely irrational about this."

He pulled me over to the couch and we sat down. He moved next to me, his arm around me.

"So, it's back to the secret affair? We can't see each other in public?"

I nodded.

"Well, at least you *want* to try."

"I do."

A look came over his face at that, like relief. "I have a jam session tonight but I'm done at 9:00."

"I can't be seen with you, Drake. I can't go to your apartment. You can't come to mine. I don't know where we'll meet. A hotel?"

"No, that's too..." He brushed hair off my cheek. "Too cliché. I have a small apartment on 8th Avenue near Columbia from when I was in school. It was my dad's when he was a student. He bought the whole building when he started to make serious money and I decided to go to Columbia. We could use that. I spent a lot of years there and it has some of my old junk from when I first lived away from my father. I store a lot of his stuff there as well."

"This person works three nights a week. Every Tuesday and Thursday for sure. One night on the weekend. On those nights, I could probably go there. I might be able to make excuses for a night now and then, but this person is determined to watch me. I have to make them think we've truly broken up so they stop."

"You seem so much more positive about this. What happened?"

I shook my head and just looked at him – at the blue eyes, the jaw, the mouth... I thought about what my father said to me about Drake. I thought about Drake's letters to his subs and how much they aroused me. I wanted to feel that excitement waiting for him to show up.

"This made me face up to what it was that I wanted. Having to say goodbye to you made me realized that I *want* this," I said and ran my hands up his chest to his shoulders. "I want *you*."

He leaned closer and kissed me, softly.

When he pulled back, he stroked my cheek. "Look, I only have an hour. Will you come with me? Surely this person isn't tailing you? We could go to my place on 8th Avenue but we'll have to hurry because of traffic."

"Why don't we just stay if you only have an little while. We can talk here," I said and brushed hair off his forehead.

"Ms. *Bennet*," he said, grinning. "I don't want to *talk*." Then he leaned down and kissed my throat. Desire washed over me at that and I felt a bit lightheaded, gasping as his mouth moved over the tops of my breasts.

"Do you think it's advisable?" I said, when he pulled me over to the couch and onto his lap so that I lay across him, my arms around his neck. "I mean, do you think someone might come in? One of your nurses? Or maybe..."

"Enough talking." He pressed me down on the tiny couch and kissed me, his kiss starting off tender, but slowly building in passion until we were both breathing hard. His hand searched my body while his tongue searched my mouth, his fingers slipping under my sweater to cup a breast through my bra, stroking the flesh that spilled out above the fabric. Then his hand travelled down over my belly and down my thigh, pulling up my jean skirt until he found my mound.

"I'm going to lock the door and fuck you right now," he whispered, pressing his fingers against my clit through my tights. I gasped and couldn't help but press against him. Then he got up and went to the door, turning the lock. He came back and lay beside me again, kissing my neck, pulling open my sweater, running his tongue over the tops of my breasts. When he pulled the fabric down to expose one nipple and sucked on it, sending a thrill through my body, I gasped.

He stopped sucking and pulled on my nipple. He took my hand and ran it over top of his scrubs so I could feel his erection.

"See what you do to me?"

I smiled coyly. "That was your own doing." Then, I heard voices outside the door. "Drake, is this a good idea? Will you get in trouble if someone comes? Maybe we should stop?"

"Shh," he said. "You signed the contract. No resistance." He kissed me again, leaning over me, stroking my cheek, his fingers running over my bottom lip. "I want you *now*."

"Do you," I said, barely able to speak as he nuzzled my neck. "Do you think it's a good idea before surgery? Won't it, like, sap your vital essence or something?"

I felt his cheek raise in a smile against my neck, then his mouth moved back down to my breasts.

"*Quiet*. You talk far too much. I'm going to eat you," he said, taking my hand again and moving it down over his balls. "*Right now*."

Then he pulled away and bent down, taking my feet and removing my shoes, before unzipping my jean skirt and pulling down my tights and underwear. He finished undressing me so that I was completely naked, sitting on the couch. Still fully dressed, he knelt down and examined me.

"I'm going to have to shave you again tonight," he said. "I look forward to it."

Then he buried his face between my spread thighs, his fingers opening me up, his mouth and lips and tongue finding my clit. I leaned back and just closed my eyes, for he was an unstoppable force. My last coherent thought as he slipped two fingers inside of me was that I tried to warn him, so if anything happened, I did my part. Then, I just let myself feel what he was doing to me.

He worked me up, his tongue stroking all over my aching flesh until my heart was racing, my breathing fast and shallow, pleasure building in me. Just when I thought I might come, he withdrew his fingers. He pulled me up and turned me around so that I leaned over the couch, my knees on the seat and my body over the back. After unzipping, he stroked me with the head of his cock for a few moments. When he entered me, moving slowly inside of me, just a few inches, it felt so good I gasped. Then, he bent over me, one arm around my waist so that he stroked me with his fingers.

"Tell me when you're close."

He kept his fingers on me as he thrust and soon, I was ready, the sweetness growing in my groin.

"Drake, *I...*"

He increased his tempo, and soon, my orgasm started, the pleasure building and then almost exploding through my body, my face hot, my thighs quaking. He thrust even harder as if he could tell I was coming, and it wasn't long after my own pleasure subsided that he came as well, thrusting deeply, his mouth at my ear, grunting as he did.

He leaned against me, breathing hard, his hands covering mine on the back of the couch.

"*Fuck*, I needed that..." He kissed my shoulder and bit it gently. "I needed *you*." Finally, he slid out of me but when I tried to turn around, he stopped me.

"No, stay like that so I can admire you. My come is running down your leg."

I smiled to myself. Drake Morgan, MD, neurosurgeon, bass player, philanthropist, enjoying the evidence of his orgasm inside of me. No matter how intelligent and accomplished he was, he was still a man. A *kinky* man.

I said nothing, waiting for him to have his fill of examining me in that position. He sat on a chair across from me and just stared.

"Um, my legs are a bit shaky," I said.

"I know. I like seeing you shake because of what I did to you."

Finally, he turned me around, using several tissues to wipe me up. Then he pushed me down on the couch, lying on top of me.

"This won't affect your surgical performance, will it?" I said, unable to keep a grin off my face.

He laughed out loud at that, his eyes crinkling in the corners. "Probably. Might improve it."

"I thought men got all sleepy after an orgasm."

"Sometimes, but it depends on the time of day. Right now, I feel great. I was feeling very *deprived*, Ms. Bennet. Very unhappy so a few extra pleasure endorphins will only help." He closed his eyes and sighed, pressing his forehead against mine. "You just have no idea how *relieved* I am. When I went up to your apartment, I made poor Mrs. Kropotkin so frantic I thought she was going to call the police. It took every neuron I ever made studying Russian to convince her I didn't have ill-intent. I was really worried about you."

"I'm sorry," I said, my voice soft, feeling guilty for ignoring his messages. "Lara asked me to think about what was more important – my happiness or your career. I left the apartment because she told me you were coming over."

"You were planning on not seeing me ever again?"

"I was afraid I'd hate myself if I did meet with you." I nodded and even then, the thought of it physically hurt. "I knew I wouldn't be able to resist you if I got within a foot of you. I was right."

He smiled. "I can't resist *you*. I don't want to. Kate, I can't leave this thing between us hanging. I have to *know*. I have to know how far I can go with you."

A surge of something went through my body at that. "I just don't want anything to happen to you because of me."

"If anything happens, it will be because someone else made the wrong choice, not either of us. It will be because you're important enough to me to take that risk." He kissed me then stroked my cheek. "Your father was glad to see me and even he encouraged me to go to your apartment and not give up."

I smiled. "He said he thought we were really intense with each other and well-matched."

Drake nodded at that. "We are." He kissed me softly.

"Maybe I should leave you alone for a while before your next surgery."

He sighed. "Probably. I don't want you out of my sight though."

"I'll go back to my father's for the rest of the afternoon. I'll make an excuse to go back to my apartment for the night. Then, we can meet at the apartment on 8th Avenue after your practice."

"Maybe I'll cancel tonight."

"*Don't* because of me. Your music is important to you."

He stroked my cheek with the backs of his fingers. "I don't want you out of arm's reach, Kate."

"I can't stay here all day," I said, smiling. "We can spend the evening together at your secret hideaway. *After* your practice."

"Tonight." He kissed me again, softly.

"I should go now," I said. "Let you focus before your next surgery."

"I wish I could cancel that, but I can't. Poor man's been waiting for a while to get the procedure."

I stood and started dressing once more, pulling on my underwear and tights. Drake helped, handing me my jean skirt, zipping it up for me, buttoning the button. He helped me on with my bra and fastened the front clasp. Then he pulled the sweater on and around my shoulders and buttoned it up.

"You like dressing me?"

"Dressing and undressing a woman is a total turn on and pleasure." Finally, he smoothed my hair before leaning down to kiss me once more. "Where should I pick you up tonight?"

"I can meet you – it's probably better that I don't get a ride with you anywhere. I'll take a taxi."

"I don't like leaving you alone. I don't like loose ends, Kate."

"Just give me the address and I'll meet you there."

"Give me your iPhone."

I reached into my bag and pulled it out. He took it and called up my GPS, entering in the address and directions from my father's apartment. "There," he said. "You can find your way there easily with that."

I took the phone back. 8th Avenue a few blocks away from Columbia, where I went to school. It would be convenient. I lived just a dozen blocks to the north in Harlem.

He walked me to the door of his office. "Are you sure I can't drive you back to your apartment?"

I shook my head. "No. I can take a taxi. I don't want to be seen in your car just in case we run into anyone. We already risked a lot coming here."

He exhaled. "OK, but I don't like this, leaving you alone now. You can always call me and I can pick you up if you change your mind. Text me and let me know you're on your way, OK? Otherwise, I'll worry."

"I will."

He kissed me once more before I left him. Then he watched me at his office door as I walked down the long hallway to the exit.

I hailed a taxi and took it back to my apartment in Harlem, happy that we had made a decision, even though a sense of guilt flooded through me. Lara would not be pleased.

CHAPTER SEVENTEEN

The rest of the day couldn't pass quickly enough. I went back to my father's apartment as I promised I would and was smiling like an idiot thinking of my meeting with Drake later that night. I had to bite my lip to stop the grin from getting any larger and took in a deep cleansing breath. I put on my best glum face and popped my head into his study. He was sitting in his chair, his tie undone and his shirt open at the collar, sleeves rolled up. He had his black reading glasses on and was studying a paper.

"Hi, Daddy."

"Hello, dear," he said, putting the paper down. "You're back. I was so worried about you."

"I thought I'd come by. I'm lonely..."

"Is everything OK with you? You look a bit flushed."

I shook my head. "It's cold out."

"Are you feeling OK?"

"Still a bit disappointed."

He stood and came over to me, his hands on my shoulders. "Are you sure you know what you're doing? Breaking up with Drake? You two seemed so happy together while we were out scuba diving. What changed?"

I sighed and turned away, feeling bad to be lying to him, but I had no choice.

"I think I was just a bit infatuated but when we were alone and away from everything, it just became apparent that he's too old for me."

"Nonsense, Kate. I'm twenty years older than Elaine and we're very happy."

"Maybe you're younger at heart than Drake, Daddy. He's a bit of a fuddy-duddy."

"A fuddy-duddy?" He frowned at me. "I never would have thought that about Drake..."

Oh, Daddy, if you only knew how far from an old fuddy-duddy he is...

"Will you be staying here all night?"

"No," I said, hoping I wasn't overdoing it with the Drake dissing. "I'm better. I'll stay for supper if it's OK and then go home. I have to go to class tomorrow so I need a good night's sleep."

He nodded. "You're welcome to stay here as long as you want. I know Elaine enjoys having you here. I do, too, but I'm really busy with the campaign."

"Thanks, Daddy. I have to get back to my life."

Dinner was quiet, but I had to submit to Elaine's questions about Drake and how I was feeling and my father's pointed stare as I answered. It was like he didn't believe me and kept frowning when I spoke about why Drake and I weren't right for each other.

Finally, I yawned about eight o'clock and said I needed to go.

"Take the service," he said. "Why spend your money on a cab?"

"If you insist," I said, because he wouldn't let up. "I can afford cab fare."

"Nonsense," he said, accepting no refusal. "Why have an old man with money if you can't take advantage of it now and then?"

He bundled me up in my coat and handed me my bag. I kissed him on the cheek as was our usual practice. He pulled me into a hug, which wasn't our usual practice.

"You know what I think?" he said, his voice soft. "I think you don't really want to end it with Drake. If you change your mind, I'm sure – in fact I *know* he'd be only too pleased. So don't do this if you really don't want to. Life is too short. People come into and go out of your life and sometimes it's only when they're gone that you realize how you felt about them. How much you cared."

I sighed. "Do you mean Mom?"

"And Liam." He squeezed my shoulders. "Good night, sweetheart."

I took the limo service back to my apartment and went inside. I had a quick bath and examined my pussy with a faint growth of hair emerging. He was going to shave me again tonight and I felt my body respond to the very thought of it.

I changed my clothes, putting on the garter belt and a pair of nylons Dawn had brought over that night we went to the bar. I wore a black cashmere sweater that buttoned up in the front, a lacy black bra and the black lace garter belt. I wore no underwear, remembering Drake mentioning that if I became his sub, he would expect me to not wear any underwear when we were together. It thrilled me to imagine what he'd do when he found out I was nude under the skirt except for the garter belt and nylons. I hoped it would please him to know I was thinking about what he'd like.

Then, I stood in the shadows of the entryway, checking the street to see if there was anyone watching the building. Just to be safe, I went out the back exit and walked down the alley to the street and hailed a cab, giving the driver directions to Drake's apartment on 8th Avenue. Luckily, the driver didn't try to make light conversation with me and I was able to focus on the meeting with him at his old apartment. I sent him a text when I was a few blocks away.

I'm on my way. Be there in 2.

He texted back immediately.

I am so ready for you, Ms. Bennet...

I smiled, hiding my grin behind my hand in case the driver was watching me in the rearview mirror.

I was so curious to see his place – both of them. His current apartment I wouldn't get to see, but I could imagine it was all dark wood and leather furniture and smelled of him.

This old apartment – Drake said his father, and then he himself, lived in it during their school years at Columbia Medical School and I wondered why he kept it. Sentimental reasons? That just added another dimension to the image of Drake Morgan, MD, I was getting to know – bass player, philanthropist, Dominant. He liked old sixties Brit Invasion music. He was a certified scuba diver. A vodka aficionado with a taste for all things Russian. A man who loved his job as a highly specialized neurosurgeon and did it because he enjoyed it and because it was rewarding. He didn't have to work because of his father's wealth and the still-profitable company Liam founded. A man who made junkets to war-torn parts of Africa to do delicate surgery, risking his own life to do so.

A man who liked to tie women up and dominate them sexually, controlling their orgasms, making them look in his eyes and say his name while they came.

One thing he didn't do was romance. He made that clear to me in the Bahamas and that night at my apartment. We wouldn't do Sunday breakfast in bed, or meet for lunch, or do other romantic relationship things. We'd meet like we were going to tonight. He'd tie me up and fuck me. I'd come several times. We'd each go our separate ways and I'd sleep like a baby.

That had to be enough for me.

The thing was, he was so *much*. There was so much *to* him. I already knew too much about him to think of him as just a Dominant stud service and I knew I was on dangerous ground. If I let myself slip just a bit, I could fall.

Hard.

When I looked at him, I already saw too much inside of him – that strap on his wrist, the letters he wrote to his subs, his preferring the tragic Heathcliff and Catherine of *Wuthering Heights* to *Pride and Prejudice's* Elizabeth and Darcy. Yet, he playfully called me Ms. Bennet or Elizabeth.

I swallowed back this nagging sense of something I didn't want to think about and exhaled, trying to blank my mind of such thoughts. I was going to meet with Drake Morgan to be well-fucked and to explore this fascination with submission that wouldn't let up. My body responded to the very thought of what he might do to me. Would he tie me up tonight? Would he blindfold me?

I signed his contract and had to expect anything, but I had a feeling he was going to move very slowly with me. So far, he'd only made me hold my own hands together and close my eyes despite me wanting more. Would he soon start to use real leather restraints and a blindfold?

I *hoped* so. I wanted to feel totally possessed the way I imagined his subs felt when I read his letters.

After the taxi drove up to Drake's building on 8th Avenue, I paid the driver and stood in front on the sidewalk. A corner brownstone walkup with ornate windows and wrought iron window boxes with faded ivy, the building was very old. Browning ivy crept up the building's façade so that it looked like it belonged in London instead of Manhattan. There was a buzzer system and I noted that the penthouse was listed as *Mr. L. Morgan*. I wondered why it was in Liam's name, but it was his building so I imagined Liam bought it for Drake when he was at Columbia and Drake never changed it.

I buzzed and the door clicked open when I pulled. I stepped over the threshold into the dim entryway with three mailbox slots and a recycling box beneath it. There was a plaid rug to wipe your feet on and someone had chained a bicycle to a metal pole of some description beside the stairs to the basement. I heard a door open up the staircase and footsteps coming down, the wooden stairs creaking.

Drake – he must be coming to meet me. I smiled and started up the stairs, butterflies in my stomach. When I got to the second floor landing he was there, barefoot, dressed in some faded jeans and a white linen shirt unbuttoned and untucked to reveal his washboard abs and the thin black trail of hair leading down from his navel. He looked so... *desirable*, his black hair a bit mussed and a growth of whiskers on his jaw and chin. He smiled when our eyes met and a jolt of something went through me when I realized this was *it* – I was going to be completely in his world. Under his control. I'd signed his contract, giving him almost total license with me. All I had were safe words and trust that he'd respect them.

"There you *are*," he said and came to me, pulling me into his arms. I rested my head on his shoulder and inhaled, enjoying the familiar scent of Drake – his cologne and a hint of soap as if he'd just bathed.

He tilted my face up and kissed me and I felt weak, desire flooding my body when our tongues touched, my flesh already aching.

"You may have to carry me up the rest of the way," I said, my voice a quivery from excitement. "I feel a bit weak-kneed."

"Ms. Bennet, are you nervous to be alone with me?"

"Yes," I said. "But the good kind of nervous."

"Good. I want you a little nervous." Then he bent down and picked me up, one arm under mine, the other under my legs.

"Oh, no, *don't*," I said when he started up the stairs. "I was just kidding! Put me down, please! Let me walk."

"I don't *think* so, *Katherine*. I think I *want* to carry you up and into my *lair*."

He grinned at that, his eyes twinkling with a look that promised so much...

I gave in and buried my face in his neck, smiling, a thrill going through me at the thought of being in *his lair*. His place.

We went through the doorway and it was like a loft instead of a typical apartment with separate rooms. The unit was open concept and bookshelves covered all the walls, filled with thousands of books. Because it was a corner unit, it had windows on three walls and would be bright during the day. Now, it was dark outside, and only a single table lamp provided light. The floors were hardwood planks with antique-looking Persian carpets of various sizes scattered here and there. In the front was a combination living room / den and in the center of the apartment, the kitchen was on one wall and open to a dining room. In the back, through the only door, I could just make out a bed.

The windows were huge and ornate with multi-paned windows looking out over the street. In the living room six old guitars stood on stands, acoustic and electric. Posters of old bands covered the walls without bookshelves – the Beatles, Led Zeppelin, Deep Purple, The Who. I took it all in while he held me in his arms.

"Are you going to put me down?"

He smiled. "I don't know *what* I'm going to do with you, Ms. Bennet. I haven't decided yet. One thing I *might* have to do, if memory serves me, is kiss you to keep you from talking."

He did kiss me as he stood there with me still in his arms. A soft kiss, just lips on lips. Then he pulled back and his eyes were so intense that I felt my breath hitch.

What that look promised...

"I *must* be getting heavy..." I said softly, for I didn't like being held.

"You're light as a feather."

I sighed and gave in to him. "You have so many *books*. And all these guitars..." I glanced around. "I want to explore your apartment."

"I want to explore *you*."

That sent a jolt of lust through me. "You do, do you? I think you already did after lunch..."

"Ms. Bennet, there's so much more of you to explore. So much more of your body. So much more of your mind."

I swallowed at that, my mind immediately going to the clauses in the agreement, but he did put me down. He removed my coat and I took off my boots, leaving them on the mat by the front door.

"Take a look around. I'll get us a drink."

I put my bag down on the table and walked around while Drake went to a small sideboard in the living room. Dark wood paneling gave it a masculine feel. More bookshelves lined the walls, an ancient leather couch and wing chair sat beside a small fireplace, and leaded glass windows faced the street. I wandered around, looking at the posters on the walls, the guitars, the piles and piles of magazines on every flat surface with titles like *Guitar*, *Rolling Stone*, *Bass Player*, and then scientific journals – *Annals of Internal Medicine*, *Lancet*, *JAMA* and others.

I peeked into the bedroom at the rear of the apartment to see a huge four-poster bed covered in a thick coverlet. The room was light, with white walls and sheer curtains at the windows. There was a small bathroom off the bedroom with an old claw-foot bathtub and pedestal sink. When I returned to the living room, Drake was there with two tiny crystal glasses etched with a delicate filigree design. Inside was a clear liquid.

"Here," he said, handing me one. "These are my father's glasses that he got from an old woman named Yelena Kuznetzova, who was rumored to be Stalin's housekeeper at his dacha in Soviet Georgia. This is Anisovaya. Drink up."

"I should have *known*," I said, smiling. "Stalin's housekeeper?"

"It was one of my father's favorite stories. Probably just his bullshit wishful thinking."

"He was a Stalinist? I thought he was a Trotskyite."

"He was a Sovietophile. Anything Russian, especially Soviet. He was sad to see the Soviet Union fall. Said it was their folly in Afghanistan."

I nodded. "It was probably Afghanistan."

"Anyway, *Za vas,*" he said in Russian. "To you."

"*Za vas,*" I replied and we shot the vodka back. I grimaced a bit and he smacked his lips.

"Oh *korosho*, that's so good." He smiled, a wicked smile. I couldn't help but smile back.

"This is a nice old apartment."

He took my empty glass back and looked around. "My father bought it for me when I started college. Until then, I lived in Baltimore with him. He worked at the University of Maryland Shock Trauma Center until he died."

"So you came to Manhattan and lived here all by yourself?"

He nodded. "He hated that I was moving away, but I wanted to come to New York to Columbia, get away from Baltimore – and him."

"Why him?"

He shrugged. "He wanted me to become a doctor like him, and I was in rebellious youth mode at the time. I wanted to study psychoanalysis. So I came here. When he couldn't talk me out of it, he made sure to come here and buy me a place to live. He wanted me to live here because he'd been so happy here and so he made the owner an offer way over its market value. It was his only real splurge despite his wealth. He approved because it was a rent-controlled building and he let the other tenants stay, not raising the rent once. Such an idealistic socialist..."

"It's yours now," I said. "Have you raised the rent?"

He shook his head and smiled. "Nah. I'll let the current tenants keep the units until they decide to move out. Rent controlled units are so rare, it's a shame to lose them. I keep this place just for the memories."

"Sounds like a bit of his socialism rubbed off on you." I raised my eyebrows.

He grinned. "It's just lazy rich boy, actually. I can't be bothered to change things." He glanced around. "I don't want to."

While he put the glasses down, I stood in the center of the dim apartment beside an old leather wing chair next to a fireplace. I was completely surrounded by Drake's things from his life – his music and his books and his father's old possessions. I felt like I was seeing right into his mind.

I *liked* what I saw.

He missed his father. Couldn't part with his things. The living room was crammed full with furniture. I just *knew* it was his father's for it looked like it belonged in a man's home – all leather and dark wood and overstuffed. There was a huge old wooden desk up against the window and one of those wooden office chairs on rollers. Taped up boxes sat stacked high in one corner, marked with *Dad* on them.

"Is this your father's furniture?"

He smiled briefly. "Yeah, I know. Sentimental, right? When he died, I couldn't bring myself to sell it or give it away so I closed up his apartment in Baltimore and had it shipped here."

I smiled to myself. "How often do you come here?"

"I practice here," he said, standing a few feet away, staring at me. "Luckily, old Mr. Neumann downstairs is practically deaf, so it doesn't bother him."

"You practice here with your band?"

"No, just me. I come here when I have time off and just play."

"Do you ever have time off? You sound so busy... Your surgery. Your band. The foundation. Your subs..."

"I'm rich. I only work as much as I want to. Interesting cases only. I keep busy."

"Do you play this?" I went to an old acoustic guitar that was attached to an amp standing next to the desk and wall of books. "I thought you played the bass guitar."

"I play lead and acoustic as well."

On the table beside the guitar was a piece of sheet music. Something by Simon and Garfunkel. "*Old Friends/Bookends*". On the top of the sheet music was a hand-written note.

'To Liam. From your 'old friend'. E'

It looked like my father's handwriting, the E for Ethan. I held the piece of sheet music up and beneath it was a faded Polaroid of my father as a much younger man and a man who looked very much like Drake, with dark hair and a jaw covered in stubble. Both wore fatigues and had dog tags around their necks. They stood side by side smiling at the camera, their arms around each other's shoulders. It looked like it was taken in Vietnam for the background was jungle.

"Oh my *God*," I said, staring at the Polaroid, a hand covering my mouth. "This is *them*." I turned to him and he nodded, smiling softly.

"Your father gave that photo and sheet music to my dad a long time ago. I remembered them when I came here tonight and found them so you could see."

I looked both over, amazed. "They really *were* friends." I glanced up at him. He had a strange expression on his face. "Somehow, I didn't really believe it. Like it was just a story my father told me about this crazy doctor friend of his from 'Nam."

He came to my side and took the photo out of my hand. "They thought they'd be friends forever."

That made my throat constrict when I thought of Liam dying in a plane crash. How this apartment – the furniture – the Foundation – were Drake's way of keeping his father with him.

"Will you play this for me?" I held the sheet music out.

He shook his head and took the sheet music away. "I don't think so."

I frowned. "Why not?"

He smiled and put the sheet of music down on the desk, but his smile was a bit forced. Then I got it. *Of course.* This was too personal. We were just D/s partners. Would-be Dominant and submissive.

"I understand," I said, grimacing. "That's getting too personal, right?"

"No, it's just that I had other plans when inviting you here..." He raised his eyebrows at that.

Emotions battled in me. I was a bit hurt that he wouldn't play it for me. I didn't believe for a moment that the reason he wouldn't play was because he wanted to have sex with me.

"I get it, Drake." I sighed and went to the window, looking down at the street below. "You don't want us to cross that line. I'm sorry. This is just new to me. This *fucking* without emotion thing."

He came up behind me and wrapped his arms around me, his hands taking mine, our fingers threading together.

"Oh, there's lots of emotion, Kate. Just very contained and appropriate."

I nodded. "I know. You want to keep things compartmentalized. Your food in all the right spots on the plate. No messy mingling of flavors. I'm used to piling everything on the fork all at once. I don't know if I can do this."

"Shh," he said, his breath warm in my ear. "Stop over-thinking. Just *feel*. Feel this," he said and pressed his erection against me, reminding me of why we were here. "I've been imagining fucking you all afternoon. You don't know how difficult it was to blank you out of my thoughts because I kept thinking of your tight wet little pussy and getting hard. Not quite a good thing when you're supposed to be focused on delicate brain surgery..."

I smiled and leaned back against him, closing my eyes, trying not to let sadness dull the excitement I felt. "You're exaggerating."

He chuckled, and nuzzled my neck. "Maybe not *during* surgery but in between."

I nestled into his arms, enjoying his warmth. "I apologize if I intruded in your thoughts."

"No apology necessary."

We just stood there at the window, the faint light from the street filtering through the wrought iron trellis covering the window, his arms around me, his body pressed against mine.

"And *now*," he said. "Now that I have you all to myself, alone in my *lair*, it's time for you to put that signature on the agreement into effect. You understand what that means?"

I swallowed hard, a thrill of something between excitement and fear going through my body right to my groin. "Submission?"

"Yes," he said, his lips at my neck. "No hesitation. No questions. Just comply."

"What if—." I said, but he stopped me, his finger on my mouth.

"Shh," he said. "No *what ifs*. You know the safe words. Yellow if you need me to slow down. Red if you absolutely have to stop what's happening. You also know what red means."

"Full stop and I go home?"

"Yes. But remember – I don't want to go too fast or scare you. I want you to trust me. I want this to work so I plan on keeping a very close watch over you and how you respond to me and what I'm doing. You don't have to be afraid. *Much*. Do you understand?"

"Much?"

"Kate, a little fear is arousing to a sub. A little uncertainty about what I'll do to you. What I'll make you do to me. Admit it. It makes you wet."

I closed my eyes, my cheeks hot, my heart rate increasing just a bit.

"*Admit* it," he said in my ear, his mouth on my neck, his arms tightening around me as if to reinforce his power over me. "You have to learn to be completely honest with me. It arouses you. I can tell, Kate. Your heart rate just increased. Your breathing is fast and shallow at the thought. If I was to slip my fingers between your lips, I'd feel how wet you are. Tell me I'm right."

"Yes," I said softly, his firm arms around me, his lips at my neck, his breath on my skin making me feel so aroused.

"Yes, what?"

I hesitated. He wanted me to call him something. To acknowledge he was a Dom and in control. "What do you want me to call you? Sir? Or Master?"

"What do I *want* you to call me? I want you to call me *Master* when we're in scene. I know you don't feel it yet. If you say it enough, if I make you *feel* it, eventually it will be second nature. I'll enjoy that. But more than that, I will enjoy you calling me Master even if you don't feel it."

"Why? Don't you *want* me to feel it?"

"Of course. That's what I long for. But I also just want your submission. Your obedience. I know you don't feel that I'm your Master now, but your willingness to just do what I command will please me in itself."

"Yes," I said, and swallowed "*Master.*" I scrunched my face up because it just didn't feel right, but I did it all the same. I *wanted* to feel it. Maybe saying it would ensure one day that I did really feel it.

"Good *girl*," he said and stroked his hands over my body, over my shoulders and down my arms, then over my breasts.

"When we meet from now on, after you cross that threshold and I kiss you the first time, it's a signal that we're in scene and I expect obedience. I'll call you Katherine or slave, you call me Master. Now, no more talking. No hesitation."

The shift in the atmosphere was palpable and I felt as if something descended over him, changing him subtly. Instead of just Drake with the guitars and dead father, he was Drake the Dominant, Master D, establishing control over the situation and over me.

That shift in him thrilled me.

He caressed my breasts for a moment through the fabric and then moved lower over my belly and to my thighs. Just his touch over my clothes aroused me, and I pressed against him, his erection hard against my buttocks. Desire welled up inside of me when he slipped one hand beneath my sweater to cup a breast, making my legs weak. The other hand slid up under the hem of my skirt and then he felt the garter belt.

"Mmm, I *like* this, Ms. Bennet..."

I smiled to myself, for he'd already messed up by calling me Ms. Bennet.

I was glad that I thought to wear the nylons and garter belt. Then his fingers moved and he felt my naked flesh beneath the garter belt.

"Oh, I *really* like this," he said, his voice low, husky. Sexy. "I like that you remembered and thought about this and how to please me." His fingers slipped between my labia and down lower to the entrance to my body. "I really *really* like that you're already so *wet*."

He kissed my neck while stroking my clit and I gasped, inhaling when his fingers penetrated me. He was tall enough so that he could reach down and slide his fingers under my skirt to feel the garters attached to the tops of my nylons. Then, he released me and turned me around to face him.

"Take your clothes off except for your bra, the garters and nylons."

Then he backed away and turned the wing chair around, sitting on it, his arms on the arm rests, his legs spread wide. His face was shrouded in darkness for the only light in the entire apartment came from a dim yellow bulb on a small table lamp by the fireplace and through the window from the street.

"Undress, Katherine. *Slowly.*" He licked his lips as if his mouth was dry. "Touch yourself while you do."

I took in a deep breath and tried to squelch the usual shyness I felt about getting naked with a man. He'd already seen me naked. But I wasn't quite comfortable yet.

"It's a shame that you don't have some nice high heels, but I know you're not good on them."

I couldn't say anything, my throat was so dry. I started with my sweater, unbuttoning it slowly. When it was fully unbuttoned, I pulled it down over my shoulders, letting it hang for a moment before removing it from my arms. I dropped it on the coffee table. Then I ran my hands down my body and over my breasts, cupping them briefly before moving down to the zipper in back of my skirt. I unzipped it slowly.

"Turn around and do that."

I frowned, but complied, turning around so that my back was to him. I pulled the skirt down and over my hips, bending down as I did. I knew this would give him a good view of my ass, my face heating as I did.

"Oh, Ms. *Bennet*..." he said and exhaled loudly. "I like this view very *much*..."

"You said you'd only call me Katherine or slave,' I said, smiling to myself.

"Shh," he said quickly. "A slave never corrects her Master."

I stepped out of the skirt and turned back, dropping it on the coffee table as well. Finally, I was there as he requested in my black lace garter and bra, sheer black nylons. I stood quiet, waiting for his next command.

He just stared at me, his gaze moving over my body. Then, he twirled his fingers. "Turn around, slowly. Let me see you from all angles."

I did as he commanded, turning around slowly, his gaze on my body making me so aroused.

"Lift your hair up, hold it up as you turn."

I did, pulling my hair up above my shoulders.

"Come here and straddle me on the chair."

"Don't you want to shave me first?"

"*Slave,*" he said and shook his head. "No questioning my decisions. Besides, I'm going to send you to get waxed. It lasts longer."

I gritted my teeth, wondering how much pain that would be. Then I went to him and complied, one knee on either side of his hips, my arms resting on his shoulders. He looked me up and down, at my bare pussy, my thighs spread wide, and then up to my face.

"Your cheeks are nicely flushed, Katherine. You're nice and wet as well. I suspect you're also nicely swollen inside. Almost ready for me."

I didn't say anything, waiting for what he would do to me. Finally, he pulled the fabric of my bra down to expose my nipples and tweaked each one, before pulling me up and leaning in to suck one, pulling on the areola gently with his teeth, the tiny bit of pain making me gasp but then he sucked and the pleasure immediately after went right to my clit.

"Stand up."

I did, standing with a foot on either side of him on the cushion so that my groin was level with his face. I knew what was coming next, my pulse increasing at the thought. He reached up behind me and squeezed my ass, pulling me closer.

"Put one foot on the arm rest," he said. When I did, he began licking me all over, slowly, agonizingly slowly, biting me softly before slipping his tongue between my lips to find my very swollen clit. I had to prop myself on the wall behind the wing chair while he bit and licked and sucked me, the sensations making me dizzy with desire. He slipped a couple of fingers inside of me while he sucked and licked and my thighs began to tremble.

"Tell me if you feel close. Remember, you can't come until I say you can."

Soon, I could feel the faint stabs of pleasure building deep within me, my face hot, my breathing faster.

"Drake, I *think*..." I said, then realized I'd used his name. "I mean, *Master*..."

He didn't stop what he was doing. If anything, he increased the tempo, adding another finger, sucking me into his mouth so that I had to moan out loud.

"I'm *going to*..."

He still didn't stop and my orgasm started, waves of pleasure spreading outward from my groin, down my legs and up into my chest. I could barely keep my eyes open, my body clenching around his fingers, my thighs quaking.

It was too much. "Oh, God, please *stop*..." I gasped.

Finally, he stopped his motions and I just leaned against the wall, breathing deeply, my forehead resting on the hard plaster.

"Should I get down?" I said after a moment. I tried to pull away but he stopped me with one hand, keeping the other where it was, his fingers still inside me.

"No, wait. I like to feel this."

I stopped, my body clenching involuntarily every few seconds in the aftermath of my orgasm.

He covered me once more with his mouth, his tongue flat against my throbbing clit. I inhaled deeply for I was still so sensitive.

Finally, when my thighs were shaking too much from maintaining the position, he pulled his mouth off me, taking my hips in his hands and pulling me down so that I was back sitting on his lap, straddling him. He kissed me and I could taste myself on his lips and tongue, the slightest hint of salty flesh.

When he ended the kiss, he pulled back and just looked at me, his gaze moving over my face.

"My turn."

CHAPTER EIGHTEEN

I couldn't stop the smile that spread across my face. "I thought I got two for every one of yours."

He made a mock face of affront. "That's a *very* saucy mouth you have." He touched the scar on my bottom lip. "I might have to just silence it with something."

"Not a ball gag," I said, pulling back, a bit of apprehension filling me.

"That's not *quite* what I had in mind..." He grinned. "And remember your manners..."

"Oh, sorry," I said, grimacing. "*Master*..."

"Good girl," he said, his face becoming stern once more. "Now, on your knees."

I slid off his lap and on my knees between his spread legs, my hands on his muscular thighs.

"Take me out and lick me."

A thrill went through me at the sound of command in his voice and the dark look in his eyes. I reached to his jeans and unbuckled the belt and top button and then unzipped, to find he was naked under them. His cock was thick and so hard and sprang out once I pulled the material aside, the head smooth and wet with his fluid. I held his shaft in both hands and began licking him, starting as low as I could get and up his shaft to the head, my tongue circling it before lapping off the fluid that leaked off it.

"That's very nice, Katherine. Now, take me in your mouth and suck."

I did as he commanded, the head large and smooth against my tongue and cheeks. It was difficult to take him all in he was so thick, but I managed, sucking as I moved my mouth over the head, up and down, while I stroked his shaft with my hands.

My hair fell over my face and he pulled it back, holding it up, twisting it in his hand.

"More," he said, guiding my head just a bit. "Deeper."

I tried, but he was huge and it was difficult. I was able to get him in deeper, but only the first few inches and then, when he pulled my head down a bit too far, I gagged. He let up, not guiding me as firmly and his grip on my hair lessened.

"That's good, Kate," he said as if to encourage me. "Stroke with your hands."

I did, taking him as deep as I could with my mouth, stroking with both my hands. I felt his cock become harder under my lips and tongue and then he tensed, but he stopped my motions completely. He breathed in deeply as if to ward off his orgasm.

"Pull off, *now*," he said, his voice urgent and I did, licking the head once before I looked up at his face, waiting for his next command. His face and neck were flushed, his nostrils flaring as he breathed in deeply several times. "Good *girl*," he said. "You have a sweet mouth, but I want your other lips on me now."

He pulled me up and then stood. "Undress me."

I pulled the shirt off his shoulders and down his arms, then dropped it onto the pile of my own clothes. Next, I pulled his jeans down and he stepped out of the legs so that he was naked in front of me, his magnificent cock jutting out, wet from my saliva.

He took my hand and led me back to the bedroom, practically picking me up and throwing me onto the bed so that I lay across it sideways on my back. He loomed over me, his hands on both sides of my shoulders. He leaned down and kissed me, rubbing his cock over my pussy. When he pulled away, he just looked at me, his gaze moving down over my face and lower to my body lying beneath him.

"Are you're going to tie me up?" I said, breathless, waiting.

He frowned briefly. "Kate, a proper submissive doesn't ask questions about her Dom's plans on how to top her. And she makes sure to use the proper form of *address*..."

I covered my eyes with a hand. "I'm sorry, *Master*. It's just that I'm *curious*—"

He silenced me with his mouth, kissing me in mid-sentence. Then, he pulled back, examining me like I was a problem he was trying to solve, blinking rapidly.

"I don't want to move too fast with bondage so I didn't bring any gear," he said, his voice soft. "It can be very arousing but also scary at first. But maybe just a bit for now. Your hands perhaps..."

He rose up and went to an armoire, sorting through his belts, testing them one after the other, but he seemed unhappy with them all. Then he examined a hanger with several ties on it, selecting a black leather tie. He returned to the bed and held it out in front of me so I could see it. Thin and flexible, it was from a by-gone fashion era. I couldn't help but grin as he examined it. He caught my grin and turned to me.

"Ms. Bennet, that grin is entirely *inappropriate* to the mood I'm trying to create..."

I covered my mouth, trying to hide my huge smile. "Master, I'm sorry," I said, my voice betraying my amusement. "But I was imagining you wearing it when you were a college student... So hip with your thin leather tie. I bet the coeds were all over *you*."

"Oh, I was very *groovy*, Ms. Bennet, in my day," he said, grinning finally, his blue eyes twinkling.

Then, he very roughly took my hands in his and held them over my head, his grip a bit too firm as if he was trying to re-establish dominance, his face becoming stern once more.

"You are too cute, *Katherine*, and able to distract me too well, but I want you to focus on what I'm doing here and *now*."

I swallowed hard, shocked back into the moment, the smile fading on my face. I didn't want him to be unhappy with the way things were going and exhaled heavily. How quickly the mood could change between us...

"I'm sorry, *Master*," I said, barely able to whisper.

His eyes burned into mine. "If your mind wanders, I'll have to bring you back with me. I want you here, with me, mentally and emotionally, Kate. With *me* in the moment. Focused."

I nodded, unable to speak, feeling a bit like a bad little girl getting disciplined. Then, I realized I *was* being disciplined. He kept staring in my eyes as if waiting to see compliance in them.

That look in his eyes – stern, demanding, in control – sent a thrill of desire through my body. Finally, I breathed in deeply, letting go of my attempt to control anything, my mind or my body. As if he sensed my release, he sighed.

"Good *girl*," he said. He held my hands above my head with one hand and reached down to touch my bottom lip with a finger, stroking the tiny scar there. Then he leaned down and kissed me and my body responded, my heart racing, pressing against him, a little groan escaping me when he ground himself against my pussy.

He pulled away and stood, taking my hands in his and binding them together with the leather tie, the knot tight but not so tight that it constricted them or was uncomfortable.

"Test them. Feel them. They won't get any tighter than that, no matter what you do. I've used a special knot so don't worry. They should be fine no matter how you pull on them. But if they do get tighter, tell me right away if it becomes painful in a way you can't tolerate."

I nodded and tried to pull my wrists apart. Then, he pushed me back onto the bed and fastened the other end of the leather tie to one of the spindles in the headboard. There wasn't much give. I pulled at the tie to feel how secure it was. I wouldn't be able to get free if I wanted to and I realized then that I was truly confined now. I was here until he released me. I couldn't run away.

That did something to me, that knowledge, and heat rose in my body, up over my chest and to my face. I panicked a bit, my heart racing, breathing faster. But even with the bit of panic, my body responded, my clit throbbing, a trickle between my thighs. He had one hand on my neck as if feeling my pulse, and he watched me intently, his brow a bit furrowed, his gaze moving over my face.

"Now you understand," he said, his voice husky. His own breathing had increased, his cock jumping against my groin as if the knowledge he had me tied up and totally helpless made him even harder. "You're completely mine now, Katherine. All you can do is kick me and scream, but I can easily gag you if I want, and besides, Mr. Neumann won't hear you."

"Are you *trying* to scare me?" I said, my eyes stinging just a bit.

"*No,*" he said softly. "But this is serious now. You have to trust me completely to let me do this." He let that sink in for a moment. "*Do* you? If you don't, we'll stop right now."

I searched his face. If I didn't know him, his expression and the position I was in would scare me to my core. But I *did* know him. I knew him as a man. I *did* trust him.

Completely.

He would never hurt me purposely. He'd shown that time and again.

"Yes," I said, relaxing fully, forcing my body to go limp beneath him. "*Master...*"

Then he kissed me, his eyes still open, one hand cupping my cheek. The kiss started off soft, tender, but soon became more intense, more needy, his tongue finding mine, insistent, searching. He finally closed his eyes and sucked my tongue into his mouth, then licked my bottom lip, biting it before moving down over my chin and neck, stopping over my carotid as if to feel my pulse again to monitor my level of excitement.

He squeezed my breasts, kneading them, pulling the lacy fabric down once more so that they jutted out. He started sucking my nipples, biting them gently, before sucking them once again, increasing the pressure on his teeth each time, always licking and sucking afterwards so that my nipples were almost excruciatingly sensitive. Each nibble and each suck and each lick sent thrills through me right to my clit as if the two were connected. His bites were just on the verge of pain but never going too far over and the way his tongue pulled on my nipples after just heightened everything.

"I don't like *pain*," I said, almost in a delirium. "*Master*," I added quickly, my voice shaky.

"I'm just seeing how far I can go with you," he said, his breath warm on my skin. "You don't really know yet what you like and what you don't like if you haven't really tried. I can tell you *like* what I'm doing now by how your body responds," he said, thrusting two fingers between my labia to see how wet I was. "I won't go too far. Now keep completely still or I'll have to tie up your feet as well."

I closed my eyes as he moved lower, his mouth and tongue tracing a trail down over my belly to my pussy. He began to lick me all over again, slowly, pressing his tongue flat against me, not making direct contact on my clit just yet and I longed to thrust my hips up but tried to keep still like he commanded. Finally, my flesh throbbing, aching for contact, he spread my thighs and ran his tongue up and over my clit, making me moan out loud.

When he slipped several fingers inside of me, I clenched around him, unable to control my body. I was so close to orgasm, I knew I wouldn't last long if he moved his fingers at all.

"Master, I'm so *close...*"

"Good *girl*," he said, his voice sounding pleased. He pulled away from me and got up onto his knees, then lifted me, turning me over so that I was in doggie position, my weight borne by my elbows and knees, face to the side pressed against the bed. He just remained behind me, his hands moving over me, stroking up and down my back, and down my thighs. Then, he slipped fingers between my labia and began stroking slowly up and inside me. When his thumb made contact with my anus, I tensed completely.

"Please, *no...*"

"Shh," he said, leaning over me, his fingers still inside of me, thumb pressed against me. "You signed the contract, Kate. This is part of it. I won't penetrate you now. Just getting you used to the sensation. *Relax.*"

I remained tense for a moment, unsure of the sensations, my anxiety about any anal contact overriding the sensation of his fingers inside of me. He wrapped his other arm around me and played with my clit, and soon, the pleasure from the contact combined with that of his fingers inside of me did overcome my reluctance and I relaxed. As if he could feel it, he kissed my shoulder, then bit it gently.

"That's my good *girl*," he said. "No moralistic judgment of what you enjoy allowed, Katherine. Just let yourself *feel.*"

He kept stimulating me in that position, fingers on my clit, fingers stroking me just a few inches inside, his thumb moving in a circle over my anus, and he once again brought me right to the brink of orgasm, the pleasure almost reaching the point of no return.

I gasped, barely able to speak. "I'm *going to...*"

He immediately withdrew his fingers and just remained in that position, his hands on either side of me, his body covering mine, his cock pressed against my pussy but unmoving.

"Just breathe, Kate," he said, kissing my neck and shoulder. I did, breathing deeply and soon, the sensation subsided and I just waited, my body so ready, my mind almost blank to everything except the feel of his body against mine.

I wanted him inside of me. All of him. Every inch.

Finally, he turned me over, kneeling on the bed, pulling my hips into position on his lap, spreading my thighs with his hands. He stroked the head of his cock over my labia slowly, circling my clit each time. He began that familiar tease, slipping the tip of his cock just inside of me, then pulling out, stroking my clit, repeating it over and over again, building back up so that I was breathing hard and fast, my cunt so in need of him inside of me.

"What do you *want*, Katherine?" he said, watching my face. "Tell me what you want. *Beg* me."

I could barely think coherent thoughts, let alone form words.

"Please, Master," I gasped, licking my lips, my mouth dry. "*Fuck* me."

He slid into me, pressing his entire length inside of me, his fingers on my clit and I groaned because it felt so sweet, the pressure so good, so satisfying.

"Yes, you like that, don't you?" he said, pulling completely out and stroking my clit again with his cock. Then he thrust inside all the way again and kept thrusting, his fingers light on my clit and soon, I was there once more, my mind lost to the sensations, and I couldn't even speak. I gritted my teeth as the sweetness started, spreading out from my clit and vagina, through my body.

He leaned over me, sliding into missionary position quickly, his hands on either side of my head, his face over mine. "Look in my eyes," he said, his voice harsh. "Say my name when you come."

I could barely keep my eyes open, the pleasure was so intense. As my pleasure crested, I tried to speak, but could barely gasp out his name. He thrust faster, harder, until finally, he came as well, grimacing, his own eyes closing briefly before opening again, boring into mine.

His whole body tensed, his hips thrusting and then he kept himself deep inside of me, withdrawing to repeat the deep thrust, grunting as he ejaculated. Then he collapsed against me, his face in the crook of my neck, his breath coming in gasps against my skin.

For the next few moments, we both recovered, not saying anything. He kissed my neck, my shoulder, my face, and finally, my mouth, the kiss warm and tender. Once again, he rose up, his cock still inside of me and slowly withdrew, watching my body as he did and I couldn't help but smile, turning my face to the side.

"What's that smile about, Ms. Bennet? Does my kink amuse you?"

I didn't say anything, mirth building in me, afraid I'd burst into laughter if I spoke.

"*Well?*"

I looked at him and he was grinning, his blue eyes twinkling, but I couldn't say a word.

"I can't wait to see it over other parts of your very delicious body. Maybe your luscious breasts. Or that smirking mouth, which I'm going to kiss right now, just to wipe that smile off your saucy face."

He did, lying back on top of me, kissing me again, barely able to keep the smile of his face when he did. He pulled back and looked in my eyes. "A Dom isn't supposed to lose control of the scene so easily. I may have to spank your delicious ass to remind you to show proper respect for your Dom's *kinks...*"

My eyes widened at that. "Now?"

He shook his head. "Oh, no. Not *now*. Your first spanking will only come before a good fucking. I wouldn't want to waste getting you all wet. I'd only spank you when I was going to fuck you immediately afterward. And my spanking would make you very wet."

I swallowed at that, my mouth dry, imagining it.

"We're still two to one," he said, smiling. "I won't be really happy until it's three to one."

"Three?" I said, closing my eyes as he nuzzled my neck. "I don't think I can do three."

"Of course you can. If you can do two, you can do three. You're young and you're multi-orgasmic."

"I don't think so," I said. "Two seems to be the most I can have in one encounter."

"You've just set me a challenge, Ms. Bennet," he said, grinning. "The kind a neurosurgeon like me can't resist."

Then he began nibbling at my neck again.

"Please, no," I said, gasping just a bit when he moved down to my nipples, which were extremely sensitive from his teeth. "I'm too sensitive."

He rose up briefly and frowned at me. "*Katherine*..." There was no smile on his face. "You signed. Is this truly a red-light matter?"

I blinked rapidly, considering. I shook my head. "It's just," I said, softly, not wanting to argue but unable to imagine any more stimulation. "I'm so *tender* right now..."

"All the better to make you come again," he said. "Women are different from men, Katherine. You have a very minimal refractory period and can orgasm again almost immediately if you relax and let me take control. The way you *agreed* to..."

"What if I don't *want* to?"

"You gave control over your body to me. *I* want you to. I thought you understood that."

I sighed and closed my eyes, turning my head to the side.

He crawled up until he was directly over me, took my chin in his hand and held my eyes with his.

"What is it, Kate? Why are you resisting this?" He shook his head. "It's not like another orgasm is a bad thing."

I shook my head in return. I didn't *know* why. It just seemed like the purpose of all this was for us to enjoy each other and I just didn't feel I *needed* to come again. It was more of a challenge to him rather than wanting my happiness. Then I realized something: his ability to exert control over me made him happy. As his submissive, *my* happiness was supposed to come from pleasing *him*.

I *did* want to please him. I wanted *him*. I wanted to be his submissive – to wait for him with anticipation the way he described in his letters to his subs, to watch him use me, make me feel what he wanted to make me feel – intense pleasure. To be totally controlled. When I signed the contract, I agreed that my body, my response was *his* to control and enjoy. Making me come three times would please him. My willingness to let him try would please him.

"*Slave*," he said, his voice firm. "Are you mine?"

I inhaled deeply. "Yes," I said, finally yielding. "*Master*..."

In the end, it turned out that I could come more than three times. In all, five. He made me come five times without stopping, using his fingers, his tongue and his once-more erect cock, as if to prove a point and reinforce that I wasn't to resist him, no matter what, unless what was happening was a red-light matter. Coming five times was not one.

By the time he was finished with me, I was almost incoherent, my mind in a kind of strange drifting bliss, my groin pleasantly achy, my clit still throbbing from all the stimulation.

"I'm going to be sore tomorrow,'" I said, closing my eyes as he untied my hands.

"Good," he said, and rubbed my wrists where I'd pulled at the leather tie. Then, he lifted me up into a seated position in his lap and began massaging my shoulders. "I want you sore. I want you to remember that you came five times. That *I'm* the one to set limits for your body, not you. You're far too timid and fearful to do so. You're too inexperienced. You don't know yet what you're capable of sexually, Kate. Let me be the one to discover how far you can go. That's what a D/s relationship is all about."

"I'm so tired..." I said, my eyes closing. "I have to get home. I'll call a taxi..."

"Shh," he said, cradling me in his embrace. "You'll stay here tonight. You need to recover. Just lie with me."

"If I'm not at home and," I said, almost using Dawn's name before catching myself. "And that person comes by, they may become suspicious."

"*Katherine*," he said, his voice firm. "When you're with me, I make the decisions. You're with me. I've decided you're staying the night."

I exhaled and just relaxed into his arms. "It's your neck, not mine..."

"It is." Then he laid me down on the bed and went to the bathroom, bringing back a warm washcloth that he used to wipe me off, starting at my face and then moving down over my body to my pussy, touching it gently to wipe away his come, the touch of the washcloth on my sensitive skin causing me to gasp just a bit.

He smiled, as if he enjoyed the thought I was uncomfortable.

"Does that please you?" I asked. "The thought I'm in pain?"

He stopped what he was doing and frowned. "Is it truly pain? Or is it just discomfort from a very thorough and enjoyable fucking?" He waited for a moment, watching me.

"Answer me, Katherine. Is it because you were well-fucked? Remember the rules..."

I watched his face, trying to decide. "Yes, *Master*," I said finally, a tiny bit of annoyance in me despite how languid my body felt, my eyes closing.

"Yes, *what*?"

"Yes, Master," I said, too sleepy to open my eyes. "It's because I'm well-fucked."

"Good *girl*," he said and kissed me as if to reward me for good behavior.

"Can I ask why you call me a girl? I'm really not, you know. I'm almost twenty-five." I said while he continued to wipe me off. "A quarter century." I opened my eyes to see his response. He didn't stop what he was doing, but frowned again as if considering.

"I know you're a woman, Kate. You're an intelligent, passionate, caring woman. I respect you. I would never fuck a girl. The essence of a D/s relationship is power exchange between consenting adults. The submissive has to trust the Dominant enough to give over total control to him. In order for you to trust me, you have to *feel* that I truly am dominant in personality. That I can exert total control over you with confidence." He stopped his motions for a moment and turned to me, his eyes holding mine.

"You sound like a professor giving a lecture."

"I *am* a professor."

"Of surgery..."

"Of surgery, but I could teach BDSM. I do give lectures sometimes. You wanted to understand, Kate. You have to feel submissive for this to work. If you don't, you won't yield control to me. I have to use every weapon in my arsenal to ensure you feel it because that mind of yours is just too intelligent, too busy. When I call you *girl*, that reinforces the difference between us. I'm thirty five so I'm older than you. I'm more experienced. I'm more knowledgeable about sex. Most importantly, I'm able to control myself. Therefore, I'm able to control you. You can trust me to do so and you can just release yourself completely to feel whatever I decide you should feel."

He continued wiping off my body, his expression thoughtful. I said nothing, just watched him, enjoying the look of care on his face. He was totally involved in cleaning off my body, in caring for me, and that surprised me.

"Why are doing this?" I said, curious. "I could clean myself off. Isn't this a servant's job? Shouldn't I be cleaning *you* off?"

He paused and caught my eye. "Are you in any kind of condition to wash me?" He smiled briefly. "You turn yourself over to me completely, Kate. You allow me to restrain you, elicit intense emotions in you, make you feel strong passions and sensations, to use your body as I want to use it. You're my responsibility. My *complete* responsibility when we're together. Your body needs to be cleaned and tended. Your mind needs to be calmed and comforted. Doing so is my responsibility as well. Submissives can be very delicate emotionally after an intense scene. They need to be cared for. It's called *aftercare*. I enjoy doing it."

"So is our *scene* over now? We're back to normal people?"

He stroked the cloth over my thighs. "I'd prefer that when you're here, we stay in scene. Usually, I don't have a sub stay overnight, but in this case, I don't think you should go home."

"Why don't you let them stay? Potatoes and gravy mixing with meat a bit too closely?"

He smiled but kept his eyes focused on my body as he wiped my calves. "Something like that."

"So, technically, I should still refer to you as Master."

He nodded. "I'll give you a bit of leeway since you're new." Then he threw the washcloth across the room into a laundry hamper. He knelt on the bed between my legs, his hands on his hips. "But next time, I expect perfect compliance with the terms of the contract or you'll get a spanking."

"Promise?" I said, unable to stop my smile.

"Oh, *you*..." He laid on top of me, his face in my neck. "That's called topping from the bottom and deserves a spanking in and of itself. Or perhaps orgasm denial..."

"Yes, please, no more orgasms tonight!" I said, giggling. Then he rose up above me, a gleam in his eye, a half-grin on his mouth.

"Ms. Bennet, I can see you need a lesson in proper submissive *behavior*." He reached down between my thighs to touch my clit and I gasped, cringing away from him, for I was still far too sensitive.

"No, please, Drake, *don't*..."

For whatever reason, my emotions were still far too close to the surface and my eyes filled with tears. I bit my lip and turned my face away. How could I move so quickly from laughter to tears?

"*Shh*," he said, rolling over, pulling me on top of him. He held my face in his hands, his thumb wiping my tears off my cheek. "I *won't*. But don't tell me what to do and what not to do. Don't even tell me what you *want* unless I ask you. It's not your place, Kate," he said and then added, "*Katherine*..." as if he, too, was having problems keeping to the terms of the agreement.

I nodded. "I'm sorry *Master*."

He pulled me down so that my head rested on his shoulder, one hand stroking my back gently, one hand stroking my hair. We remained like that for some time, until the strange sense of sadness drained out of me completely and a peace settled over me instead.

Soon, I dozed in his arms, immersed in the warmth of Drake's embrace, waking only briefly later, checking the alarm clock beside the bed. An hour had passed and Drake was covering us with the blankets. I closed my eyes once more.

I woke in the middle of the night and was alone in the bed. The clock radio read 3:30 a.m. and light from the moon filtered in through the sheer curtains onto the floor. I rose and peeked inside the bathroom, but it was empty. I cracked open the door leading to the living area and saw Drake sitting in the living room on a stool, his back to me, the acoustic guitar in his arms, headphones on. He was playing, but the sound was muted for the acoustic guitar was electric and was hooked into a small amp at his feet. I could hear the faint sounds of his fingers on the metal strings, sometimes sliding up and down, the sound of his fingers strumming or plucking strings.

I went up behind him while he played. He was wearing his jeans but was bare from the waist up. I glanced over his shoulder and saw he was playing the music from earlier that my father gave to his – *Old Friends / Bookends*. When I rested my hands on his shoulders, he startled a bit and stopped playing. I went around and stood in front of him while he removed his headphones.

"You woke up."

I nodded, my arms around my own waist, facing him, acutely aware of my nakedness.

He looked me up and down as I stood before him. "You are a vision of loveliness in the moonlight."

A blush rose up my neck and face at that and I tried not to cover up. "You couldn't sleep?"

He shook his head and strummed the guitar absently. "I woke up and my mind wouldn't stop. Sometimes, playing helps."

"You still won't play for me?"

He exhaled heavily.

"No, it's OK," I said, hurt. "I understand. Potatoes and meat..." I sensed that this was too much – asking him to play for me.

But then he unplugged the headphones and started to play, the guitar soft. After a brief musical intro, he started to sing, his voice surprisingly good, although soft.

Emotion welled up inside of me as I listened, the image of the old men sitting on a park bench like bookends so sad. I could hear the muted sounds of the city described in the lyrics, see the old men disappearing into overcoats, their collars up, their wisps of white hair blown by the wind.

I had to bite back tears, thinking of him losing his father, keeping all his old furniture and guitars here as a way to hold on. No matter that the relationship might have been strained or imperfect, to lose your father is to lose your rudder. This was Drake's way of preserving his memories – playing his father's music, using his old guitars, keeping this apartment, his father's old furniture.

I thought of his father and mine – how the two shared an uncommon hell over in Vietnam and how it must have cemented a bond between them despite the differences in their politics. How my father thought they would grow old and still be friends.

He finished and looked up at me, his eyes guarded. I went to him as he sat there with the guitar in his arms, his eyes on mine and took his face in my hands. I kissed him, my eyes wet.

"Thank you."

I left him alone with his music and went to the bathroom, unable to stay there with his face like that, so vulnerable, as if his heart was open for me to see right inside of him. He brought the music and photograph out specifically for me to see, but he didn't show them to me, as if he had second thoughts. He let me find them. I wondered if he would have showed them to me on his own, or if he would have left them alone. I had the sense he would have left them if I hadn't found them.

They were far too personal.

I held a wet washcloth to my eyes, breathing in deeply to control my emotions.

He wanted to keep me separate from the other parts of his life – his work, his charity, his family, his music. I was just to stay in the kink part. Now, he'd failed at all four. He let me see the photograph, the music from my father, let me hear him sing and play – it muddied the careful order he had established over things.

I wasn't sure I could do this – stay in this one corner of his life.

I heard him in the doorway to the bathroom. "Come back to bed," he said, his voice soft.

"Just give me a minute." I was barely able to speak from the emotion choking my throat.

Then, I felt him behind me, his arms slipping around my shoulders, pulling me against him. He said nothing, just rested his chin on the top of my head for a moment. Finally, he leaned down and kissed my shoulder before turning me around, embracing me.

"Sweet *sweet Kate*..." He tilted my head up and looked in my eyes, wiping moisture from my cheek. "Why the tears?"

I shook my head, breathing in, trying to control myself, but that song, although so simple, was so filled with meaning.

"It's so beautiful and so sad. They were old friends with so much history. My *father*..." I swallowed back emotion. "I can't imagine losing my father."

He nodded, his face emotionless. He brushed hair off my cheek. Then he led me back to the bedroom and pulled back the blanket, pointing to the bed. I crawled in and he followed me, spooning against me from behind, his arms around my waist.

"Close your eyes."

I exhaled and tried to relax, but my eyes wouldn't close and instead of sleeping, I watched the motes of dust drifting in the beam of moonlight filtering in through the curtains, thinking of old men sitting on a park bench in Central Park.

CHAPTER NINETEEN

8th Avenue became my refuge from life, my entire existence focused on getting through the next day and night until it was time to meet him again. After that first night, I'd enter the apartment and he would be waiting for me instead of me waiting for him as I once imagined. It just seemed to work out that he was already there waiting for me when I arrived.

I'd open the door and breathe in deeply, his cologne, the scent of leather and old wood coming to symbolize Drake to me, arousing me before I'd even make it through the door. He'd have a shot of Anisovaya waiting for me in Yelena Kuznetsova's crystal glasses and we'd drink a toast to each other before falling into our respective roles. He'd take the glass from my hand and place them both on the sideboard. Then, he'd come to me, wrapping me in his arms, his chin on the top of my head for a moment and that was a sign I had to shift into submissive mode.

It became easier and easier, the word *Master* less awkward on my lips.

The week that my period was due again, I tried to bow out of seeing him. The last time I had my period, we were separated out of necessity when I broke it off because Dawn found the contract. This time, there was no excuse. He was standing at the doorway on Sunday morning before I left, examining a wall calendar.

"I'm free Monday, Tuesday, Thursday and Saturday this week," he said. "I hope you can make all four nights."

I shook my head and stood beside him, examining the calendar. "I'm due on Tuesday," I said, touching the date. "It will last until Friday. I can't make Saturday night because this person doesn't work that night. I guess we have to take a week's break."

He shook his head. "I don't like that, Kate," he said, frowning. "Just because you have your period doesn't mean you can't come to me."

"I don't *think* so," I said, holding my hands up, stepping away from him and his frowning expression. "I have bad cramps and on the day before and first day, I'm what my father calls a hellcat."

"No, I still want you here. You said you had every Tuesday and Thursday for sure and one day on the weekend that you'd *always* be free so I want you here then if I can't have you on Saturday. Monday as well. I have many techniques guaranteed to tame beasts, hellcats included."

"*Drake...*"

"*Katherine*," he said and pulled me against him, but my body was rigid. "You forget, I was married for five years to a woman who had periods. I'm also a doctor, unless you also forgot that fact. I even did an OB/GYN rotation and delivered babies, did C-Sections, cut out uteruses. Why, I even had my whole hand and part of my arm inside a woman delivering a breech twin..."

I made a face and right away, thought about that clause in his contract about vaginal fisting.

"There's no reason to be together if we can't do things," I said, trying to wrestle free from him, but he held me tight, nibbling my neck playfully.

"What do you mean, we can't do things? We can *always* do things. Besides, a good orgasm will help your PMS and cramps."

"I could *never*," I said, making a face. "I'm way too uncomfortable. I can't imagine it."

"You can and you *will*," he said. "*Submission*, Katherine. It's what I want. I don't want to be away from you for so long."

"But it's *disgusting!* Haven't you heard about masturbation?"

"Why should I masturbate when I can have you? You are *such* a good Catholic girl despite being a socialist..." He reached down to my waist and tickled me.

"I'm *not* a socialist!" I said, laughing despite myself, squirming in his arms. "I'm not a good Catholic girl. If I was, I'd still be a virgin and wouldn't let you tie me up and fuck me."

"And I'm so glad you're a bad Catholic girl, Kate. If you weren't, I'd die of blue balls."

He chased me around the apartment, and I almost fell on one of his small carpets that slipped beneath my feet when he almost cornered me. He caught me from behind and held me firmly.

"Now, no more arguments about it. I want you here on Tuesday and Thursday. I won't fuck you if you really don't want me to, if it really upsets you that much, but I *will* make you come and you will make *me* come. No more arguments."

Finally, I gave in.

I didn't know what to expect when I arrived at the apartment on 8th Avenue that Tuesday night, but it certainly wasn't what I found waiting just inside Drake's door. He was there, dressed in football equipment, elbow and knee pads, shoulder pads, a helmet on and a cup over top of his jeans. In one hand was a bottle of wine.

"Oh, my *God*," I said, covering my mouth with a hand, laughing at him. He grinned from ear to ear under the helmet's faceguard grill. He even had a mouthpiece in.

"I thought I'd be prepared for a hellcat," he said, mumbling around the mouthpiece. Then he spit it out. "You don't look too hard to handle."

"You are so *bad*," I said, laughing as I removed my coat and boots.

He came to me and embraced me, the equipment hard and bumpy against my body. He was laughing so hard, trying to kiss me, but unable because of the helmet. Finally, he just held me, his body still shaking with mirth.

"You're not going to keep that on, are you?"

"I don't *know*," he said, still chuckling. "Kinda feels a bit kinky. You could get some pompoms. Shake your booty a bit..." He grinned, his blue eyes twinkling in that way. "Maybe I'll keep them on just until I see how *hellish* you are."

"What's that?" I asked, pointing to the wine. I was less tense due to the laughter, but still, I felt a certain amount of trepidation about the evening's events.

"A nice Pinot Noir," he said, a bit more in control. "Red wine is good for menstrual cramps. Helps stop the prostaglandins that cause your cramping." He leaned down and whispered, but he couldn't get close because of the face guard. "I'm going to get you good and drunk and then fuck you."

I stepped backwards, trying to escape his arms. "You said you wouldn't, Drake. I'm holding you to that."

He let me go and started to peel equipment off so that he was left in his white button down shirt opened at the neck, untucked over a pair of faded jeans.

"I said I wouldn't if you really didn't *want* me to, but," he said, pulling me into his arms, putting on a fake German accent, "*Ve have vays to make you vant me to...*"

"You are a dirty conniving *bastard*," I said and sidled away from him when he tried to prevent my escape. "I have a headache and can't drink wine."

"Just had a shower so not dirty. My father was definitely married to my mother when I was conceived, so not a bastard. I am *not* conniving. I am *calculating*. I plan. I analyze a problem, breaking it down into its component parts, then I solve each problem so I can have the outcome that I want."

I escaped and ran away but he chased me, lunging at me, smiling as he grabbed me.

"I *want* to fuck you. As to your headache, an orgasm will help you with that."

"*Drake!*" I said, trying to avoid his grasp.

"*Kate*," he said, his tone chiding. "I said I want to *fuck* you. You're resistant because of outdated sense of bodily modesty that is entirely inappropriate in a D/s relationship. I must break down your resistance. How better to do so than to get you good and drunk?"

"Why are you doing this?" I said, trying to keep him away, slapping his hands away only half-playfully. "Why are you pushing me?"

"That's what I *do*, Kate. You know this. You signed the agreement. There wasn't any clause that said you wouldn't fuck me when you had your period."

"I didn't think there *had* to be." I just stood there, my eyes closed, my hands fisted. I was close to tears, despite his playful tone.

"*Kate*," he said and put his arms around me, enveloping me in his warm embrace. "Just *trust* me..."

"You can't even go one week without sex?"

"There's no reason to," he said, his voice soft, his lips at my ear. "I don't *want* to go a week without fucking you. You wait. It will be so good for you. You'll have a nice orgasm and you'll feel so much better. I *promise*..."

"I won't be able to enjoy it."

"Let's have a bet," he said and pulled back, touching my bottom lip with his thumb. "You don't enjoy it, and I have to fuck you twice in your favorite position next time. You enjoy it and I get to fuck you twice any position I want."

"That sounds like a win-win for you," I said. "No bets."

He laughed and pulled me into the living room and made me sit on the couch while he poured us each a glass of wine.

"That's because you know you'll lose. How *are* you feeling? I mean your cramps?"

"I took some Tylenol. It doesn't do much."

"You need something different – Ibuprophen's best." Then he motioned to my glass. "Drink that all down. You need the alcohol to dull your cramps."

I took a big gulp, wishing we'd keep talking about nothing instead of him preparing me for sex that I didn't want to have.

"So you prefer old music," I said, hoping to distract him.

"Yes, there's more than enough great music from the sixties and early seventies. My dad was a collector and has thousands of albums."

"What's your absolute favorite piece of all time?"

"Drink it *all* down." He motioned to the glass again. "I want you silly drunk and giggling."

"You must have a favorite," I said, wanting to keep him talking.

He shook his head. "Drink up. No more delaying, Kate."

I exhaled in frustration, and drank down the rest of the glass of wine, a warmth building in my limbs and stomach from the alcohol.

"I'm a really cheap drunk," I said, smiling a bit. "I get drunk very quickly. No tolerance to alcohol."

"Good." He poured more wine into my empty glass. "Drink that down as well."

I took a gulp. "You aren't drinking."

"This is just for show." He held the glass up. "I have to stay sober so I can have my way with you." He wagged his eyebrows.

"I don't want to do *this*," I said, pouting. "Why are you making me?"

"When we're in scene, it's not about what you want, *Katherine*. It's about what *I* want. I want *you*. *Tonight*. I've been hard all day waiting for you." He took my hand and placed it on his erection. I closed my eyes. Just the feel of him in my hand made me respond, a thrill going through me.

"How can you stand to have sex with a woman when she's bleeding?"

"I'm a surgeon, Kate. A little blood doesn't scare me."

"It's gross."

"Oh, Ms. *Bennet*," he said, smiling, pressing me down so that my wine almost spilled. "You don't know what gross is. *You* could never be gross. You are an entirely delicious morsel of womanflesh and I can't wait to partake of your delights."

"You're going to make me spill," I said, trying to be mad at him.

"Drink up." He took the glass and moved my hand closer to my mouth. "Drink it all."

I did, squinting a bit, unused to guzzling wine. "You are so *bossy*."

"I *am*," he said and grinned, nuzzling my neck. "You love it."

I did. *Most* of the time. Not this time. My sense of propriety prevented it. I was mortified at the thought he wanted to fuck me now.

"It'll be so messy," I said, closing my eyes as he moved my sweater off my shoulder and bit the muscle. "I'll be horrified."

"Kate," he said and took my chin in his hand. "Have you *ever* fucked during your period?"

I shook my head, my face heating.

"No? Don't tell me how you'll feel. *I'll* tell you. You'll be orgasmic and won't notice the blood. In fact, think of the blood, what little there will be of it, as extra lube. I'm *big*. You're deliciously small and *tight*. I can use all the help I can get."

I sighed, the alcohol starting to make my mouth feel a bit rubbery. "It really doesn't bother you?"

He grabbed my hand and held it against his erection once more. "Does this feel as if it bothers me? Believe me, Kate. It *really* doesn't bother me."

"Is this a kink of yours?"

"No, it's not a *kink*. It's just not a deterrent."

He poured even more wine into my glass. I took another big gulp, wanting to get drunk so I wouldn't notice.

"Oh, *fuck* it," I said, leaning back. "*Whatever.*"

"Don't you *whatever* me, Ms. Bennet, or I'll have to smack your round little ass."

I closed my eyes and smiled. "Promises *promises...*"

In the end, it wasn't as bad as I thought. I'd drunk enough wine so that my head spun a bit and he tied a blindfold around my eyes so I couldn't see anything. I laughed as he ran a bath and tried to maneuver me into it without me falling and cracking my head. Then he washed me carefully, his hands lingering on my clit, and I knew he was trying to arouse me. I had no idea how much blood there was anyway.

I *did* have a very intense orgasm as he fucked me from behind, his fingers on my clit. I did feel better afterwards. He didn't remove the blindfold until I was completely cleaned off. When he did, he kissed me.

"See?" he said, running his thumb over my bottom lip. "That was good, wasn't it?"

I nodded. "I didn't call you Master once," I said, smiling, my mouth feeling a bit cottony from the wine.

"You're drunk. I made allowances."

I went to the bathroom and inserted a new tampon, then I slipped into my black lace nightie.

Ordeal *over*.

He dragged me to the living room and he put some music on the sound system – something folksy, from the sixties. He said it was The Turtles, *You Showed Me*, the music dreamy, about falling in love. We sat together on the couch, me on his lap, my arms around his neck. I rested my head in the crook of his neck. I *did* enjoy what he did to me. I did have an intense orgasm. I felt better, just like he said I would.

"I should go home now," I said, yawning. "I'll call a taxi."

"You're not going home drunk," Drake said, shaking his head. "You'll stay here with me."

"I really shouldn't," I said, frowning. "What if..." and I almost said Dawn's name. "What if this *person* tries to come by my place and I'm not there?"

"Shh," he said and squeezed me. "No arguments. I bought some eggs and spinach and some nice feta cheese. We'll have what my dad called a 'hangover omelet' in the morning, to fight the one I know you're going to have."

I sighed and gave in. He'd have his way with me one way or the other. He got up and put another album on the old turntable.

"Who is this?" I asked, the music very different from the other songs.

"Nick Drake," he said. "This one's called *River Man*. I like it because the guitar's in 5/4 time and in standard tuning. I play it with the band. My dad named me after him."

I listened for a moment. The lyrics were hard to decipher.

"What's it about?"

"Can't say for sure," he said, examining the album cover. "He's dead and didn't say. From what I read, it's supposedly about Wordsworth's poem, 'The Idiot Boy' about a mother with a mentally disabled son, but I think it's about Hesse's book, *Siddhartha*. It's really just the feel of the piece and the guitar I like."

"There are scratches," I said, noticing the occasional hiss. "You don't mind? Don't they have re-mastered versions?"

"Sure," he said but shook his head. "Real vinyl enthusiasts like the sound better. It has a certain quality that can't be caught in digital. I don't mind a few scratches to hear the original. This is a really rare album. I paid a lot for it."

"You don't like any modern music?"

He sat beside me, one arm going around my shoulders.

"I like some," he said. "But you're one to talk about liking old music. How old's Gorecki's piece?"

"Seventies."

"Touché,' he said and smiled. "What do you like? Anything modern?"

I shrugged, taking a small sip of my wine. "Some. Mostly classical. Don't ask me why."

"Your absolute favorite piece of music ever? Besides Gorecki?"

I took in a deep breath. "Barber's *Adagio*."

"That sounds familiar. Where have I heard that?"

"It was in the movie *Platoon*. I saw it with my dad and it upset him so much. One of the few times I saw him with tears in his eyes."

"Oh, yes." He frowned for a moment. "I remember that movie. My father wouldn't go. Said the Hollywood capitalists were glorifying war or something." He said nothing for a moment, running his hand over my hair.

"What else? What's next?"

"After Barber?" I said and frowned. "Not much better, I'm afraid. Music from Master and Commander. *Fantasia on a Theme by Thomas Tallis* by Vaughn Williams."

"I saw that. What piece?"

"The one that played during the scene when they have to cut the young man loose and let him drown."

He nodded. "I remember that." He said nothing for a moment. "Gorecki, Barber. Williams. Awfully depressing music you like."

"It makes me actually *feel* something."

"Yes, but incredible sadness..."

"It's better to feel sadness than nothing at all."

He turned to me. "You don't feel anything unless it's sad?"

"Not for a long time. Not after my mother died."

He just stared at me, and then I hated myself for mentioning her.

"You were ill after you returned from Africa."

I nodded, not wanting to talk about it.

"Tell me."

I shook my head, forcing a smile I didn't feel. "I didn't cry when she died," I said. "I felt nothing. It was like everything just shut off and I couldn't feel anything. My doctor said everyone grieves differently, but how could I not cry? I just went through the motions, day in and day out."

He squeezed my hand.

"Then you went to Africa?"

I took a sip of wine. "Yes," I said, remembering. "I tried to keep busy. I think I was in denial. So I went to Africa even though I probably shouldn't have. I didn't cry until Mangaize. Then it was like I couldn't stop." I turned to him. " Why could I cry for complete strangers and not my mother?"

"You were crying for yourself."

I nodded. "I was. I didn't think I deserved to feel sorry for myself. But those people in the camps? They deserved it."

We sat in silence for a while and I felt so bad, talking about my depression. "Sorry to be such a downer."

He shook his head quickly. "No," he said and smiled softly. "*Don't* be. I asked."

I snuggled into his arms. There seemed to be no barrier at all between us anymore. I couldn't imagine being any closer to a man than I felt at that moment with him.

That Thursday night, as we lay in bed afterwards and Drake was wiping me off with a warm wet cloth, I asked him about going to a fetish night.

"You want to go?" he asked.

"Yes," I said, watching him, enjoying his aftercare, not as drunk as I was on Tuesday night. "When I read about them, I always wanted to go."

"Voyeuristic are you?"

"Maybe. I don't really know yet. I *don't* think I'm an exhibitionist. The thought of people watching me makes me a bit queasy."

"I'll keep that in mind but you have to know that people who host these events sometimes host play only parties where you have to do something."

"Like what? I don't want to have sex in front of people."

"We'd have to do something. I might tie you up, blindfold you, demonstrate some bondage, that kind of thing just so no one complained."

I cringed a bit. "I don't *know*..."

"Let's play it by ear. There's a very private and exclusive pre-Christmas dungeon party in Yonkers I thought we could go to. Would you like to go? It's the Saturday before Christmas."

The idea of going with him to a dungeon party thrilled me. The idea of him tying me up thrilled me. The idea of people watching? It gave me little butterflies in my stomach.

"OK," I said. I didn't want to deny him.

He kissed me. "Thank you. I want to take you. I have something special in mind for that night."

"What?"

He just smiled and shook his head. He finished wiping me off and after I inserted a new tampon, I came back to the bed and he pulled the covers over us, snuggling down against me from behind.

"What about you?" I asked, feeling so relaxed that I forgot to use the proper term. "Do you like to watch other people or have other people to watch you?"

"I like to watch, yes. I can go either way when it comes to exhibitionism. I have done some tutorials and demonstrations of bondage and I can perform if I have to. I tend to like my sex private. I'll expect you to be dressed appropriately and I'll have to put a collar on you and we can do whatever you feel comfortable with."

"A collar?" I felt my neck and imagined how a thick leather collar would feel. I turned around in his arms so that I was facing him, the contours of his cheek and jaw highlighted by the light from the window.

"Would you like that?" he said, brushing hair from my face. "I'd have to make sure no one else tried to touch you or even approached you. I'm very possessive like that. I don't share my subs."

"I wouldn't want to have sex in front of people, though," I said, my hands on his chest, his arms wrapped around me. "I'm not into the whole poly scene. I'd like to watch what other people do, but I'm too shy to have people watch me fuck or have an orgasm. And I can't easily just fuck anyone."

"I *know*," he said and nuzzled my neck, playfully biting my shoulder. "I like that."

"You *do?* I thought you saw it as a failing in me."

"I did when I wanted you to fuck me that first time, but now, I see it as a definite plus. I don't want to think of you with anyone else..."

I smiled and kissed him, amused by the contradiction.

"But when we *do* go," he said, his voice chiding. "I'd expect you to remember to use the proper form of *address*..." I saw his grin start despite the darkness. "If you don't in front of other Doms, I'd have no choice but to punish you."

Then I realized we were still in scene, as he called it, and scrunched my face up. "Oh, sorry, Master. I've been very bad."

"That's all right," he said, trying not to smile. "I'll let it go tonight but I won't always be so tolerant."

"What *would* you do, Master? If you had to punish me?"

"I'd bend you over my lap and spank you with my bare hand. And then I would have to fuck you, but it would be in private."

He still hadn't administered one of his spankings I'd been so eager to experience. I wanted to suggest it, but of course, that would be topping from the bottom and I wasn't going to do that.

"I want to go, Master," I said, whispering. "I want you to have to spank me."

He pulled me against him, nuzzling my neck. "You are such a bad girl to tempt me like that, Katherine. You've been very good. Except for the occasional lapse in your use of terminology, I've found no good reason to spank you. I like it that way. We have so little time together, I don't want to *have* to punish you, no matter how you might enjoy it."

I nodded and wrapped my arms around him. It would happen eventually – maybe at the dungeon party. Until then, I was still far more enamored with exploring bondage with Drake. Exploring Drake period. I knew I wasn't supposed to concern myself with what made him tick. That was his job. My job was just to submit and let him take me where he wanted me to go, but I couldn't help it. I was so curious about him and what made him want to control me so carefully during sex, why he had to compartmentalize his life. I was curious about his wife and why they broke up.

"You never told me much about the restraining order."

"For a reason, Kate. I don't like to talk about it. It was a mess."

I nodded, not wanting to push him, but still curious. I turned away, trying to hide my disappointment.

He took in a deep breath. "Have I once hurt you in any way, intentionally, that scared you or made you upset?"

"No," I said, having to admit it.

"Then please, trust me that it had nothing to do with any kind of abuse."

I sighed. He *had* been biting me a bit, on the shoulder, on my nipples, my labia, but it never was a real hurt, just the good kind. At least, what I thought of as the good kind – the tiniest bit of hurt that reminded me that his mouth had been there, pleasuring me. Still, he had worked a small bit of pleasure/pain into our sexual experiences. It was more than I thought I would ever want or like, and so he was right. If he didn't push me a bit, I would never have suggested it on my own, too afraid of what it might mean about me.

"You're *not* a painslut," he said after one night where he bit my labia after licking me and I was a bit upset, thinking there was something wrong with me that I liked it. "You never will be, Kate, so get that crazy idea out of your sweet little head. Think about the pain you get after a good workout. Your muscles ache because they've been over-worked. You get lactic acid buildup in them that causes the pain and muscle tissue is actually broken down, then rebuilt. You welcome that pain because it means you're building new muscle. The tiny bit of pain you feel when I bite you just makes the pleasure all the more welcome and intense. Think of it as providing contrast which enhances the real purpose of the act – pleasure."

It made sense to me in a neurological way, but psychologically, it still made me feel uncomfortable. I was now getting used to being totally restrained, hand and foot, my eyes covered with a blindfold while he played with me, eliciting more and more response from my body and mind. In fact, I might have been too eager for Drake, for he seemed to want to proceed more slowly than I did. He told me I had to learn patience.

That he knew how fast and how far to go.

If there was one negative to our relationship, it was just that it was so constrained by his desire to keep things so compartmentalized. I had one role in his life – being his submissive. It was also difficult being unable to be open about what limited relationship we did have, to sneak around, not seeing each other outside of 8th Avenue. It made the old apartment all the more special, but at the same time, a sense of grief often filled me when I left. I knew that this relationship was probably doomed to die a natural death once we'd explored everything and reached whatever limits we both had. I also felt sad that I couldn't share the rest of my life with him. Christmas was coming and I'd be alone at the very time when I wished I had someone with me to celebrate. Drake had no family left, except a long-lost mother who he never saw.

I had to shut that thought off, push it into the back of my mind. For the present at least, I was in a state of near bliss, going through my day on the days I would meet him aroused, breathless, butterflies in my stomach thinking of his strong warm body and hands claiming me once I was completely under his control.

I trained myself not to think of ever seeing him outside of the apartment and relating to him as anything other than his play partner and submissive. I just shut that part of me off as best I could. But the sadness lingered, a tiny part of me watching myself from the outside as I walked up the steps to the old brownstone, sad for myself. Pitying myself that I'd found such a wonderful man but couldn't be his completely, couldn't have him completely as my own.

CHAPTER TWENTY

Drake was waiting for me when I arrived at the apartment on 8th Avenue on Saturday night. I'd made an excuse to stay at home alone when Dawn called me wanting to go see a film. I claimed to be sick, and luckily, she called Jill instead and I was off the hook.

I ran up the stairs, excitement building in me that tonight was the night – our first fetish party together and I wondered what he had planned. He said he'd been out to one of the leather shops in Manhattan to look for appropriate fetish wear for me and I'd gone on Friday to get waxed, so I was smooth, the way he liked. No wacky design left in the pubic hair like the attendant suggested. No heart, no landing strip. Just pure bare skin. Luckily, my skin and hair seemed the type not to react badly to the waxing and I loved how smooth I felt to the touch.

Drake stood in the doorway, smiling. He wore a really nice pair of low-slung black leather pants and nothing else, his chest and feet bare.

"There you are," he said, pulling me into his arms once I had my coat off. He rubbed his face in my hair and breathed in deeply. "You smell so good."

I wrapped my arms around his waist, my hands sliding up his strong back, over his smooth skin, and then down to cup his ass through the leather pants.

"I think I really *really* like the pants. What are you wearing underneath?"

"Commando," he said, grinning against my neck, his cheek raising. "I have to be ready to fuck you at the drop of a hat."

"Oh, *God*..." I said, gasping when his hands slipped under the hem of my dress to feel my naked pussy.

"Oh, God is *right*," he said, murmuring against my neck. "I don't know if I can wait until later to fuck you but I want to at the club."

I pulled away and looked in his face, in his eyes, which were already dark with lust. "But not in front of anyone, right?"

"*Katherine*," he said, his voice a bit hard. "We're in scene."

I inhaled deeply and nodded. "Forgive me, Master."

"Forgiven," he said. "As if I could ever *not* forgive you." Then, he frowned a bit. "As for what happens tonight, do you *trust* me? Do you trust me to know what you need and what you can handle?"

I looked into his blue eyes. "Yes. Completely." He frowned and waited, and I realized what I'd done. "Yes, Master."

"Good girl. I decide what happens tonight, not you. Your one out is to use the safe word."

"I never want to use it, Master," I said, frowning, my voice wavering from nerves.

"Neither do I," he replied. "Now, I see I'm going to have to wipe that frown off your face." Then he turned me around in his arms, tickling me from behind. I giggled and tried to wrestle out of his arms, but he was too strong. Finally, when I was in near hysterics from his fingers, he let me go.

"Off to the bathroom," he said and smacked me on the ass. "I have something for you."

I mock-screamed at his smack, which didn't hurt at all, and ran to the bathroom as he chased me, his hands reaching out.

I stopped inside the bathroom and leaned against the vanity, wondering what he had for me. He entered with a box in his arms. It was from the leather shop and I knew what it was – a leather corset dress as he said. He'd taken measurements of me the last time we were together and said he'd pick something out for me to wear.

"Take off your clothes."

I complied immediately, eager to try on whatever he had in the box. He was busy unwrapping it and when I was completely naked, I stood waiting, excitement building in me.

He glanced up from the contents of the box and smiled. "That's what I like to see." He came to me and wrapped his arms around me, pulling me against him. He kissed my neck, bit my shoulder just a bit and then stepped back.

"I got you a very nice black number," he said. "But first, there's this." Then he reached into the box and pulled out a thick black leather collar. It was lined with felt on the inside and had a silver buckle and a padlock.

"My *collar*," I said, reaching up to feel my neck. I smiled and held my hair up so he could put it on.

"Wait," he said, holding up a hand. "There's more to it than just putting it on. This is symbolic, Katherine, of our relationship. It signifies that you're mine, completely and totally, when you wear it. Do you understand that? Completely and totally mine."

He held my gaze, his eyes intense.

"Yes, Master," I said, my throat a bit choked. "I understand."

"Good girl," he said and kissed me. "It means no hesitation from now on when you wear it. No questioning my decisions. No avoiding what I order you to do. You obey immediately and completely without thinking or reservation. You only think of how to please me. If you don't submit fully and with pleasure to what I demand, you have to expect that I'll punish you. Up until now, we've been just playing a bit with D/s. This is serious now. Do you understand?"

"Yes, Master," I said a bit too quickly, eager to have him put it on.

He took my chin in his hands, and caught my eye. "*Katherine*, I want you to focus. Tell me what this means. When I put this collar around your neck, what does it mean?"

I inhaled, blinking. He was really serious about this part. I had to rein myself in and think clearly.

"It means I am yours totally. I obey you completely without hesitation."

He looked long in my eyes.

"*Master*," I said, grimacing.

"Good girl. But it's more than just a symbol of possession. It means I've *chosen* you and you've chosen *me*. I'm offering this to you – being your Dom. You've accepted with all that means. It means we're exclusive. People take collaring very seriously in the lifestyle. Do you understand how serious this is? It's not given lightly. It's not just for show."

I swallowed and looked in his eyes. He was very serious, his face almost grim.

"Yes, Master."

He nodded but kept looking at me as if searching my face for a sign that I *did* understand.

"Now turn around and hold up your hair."

I did and he stepped closer behind me, kissing my shoulder first, then he wrapped the collar around my neck, watching in the mirror as he fastened the closure and secured the tiny padlock. Then he held up the key. The black leather was shiny, thick.

"Slave," he said, his voice serious. "This key is mine, just as you are mine when you wear my collar. When I put this on and close the lock, wherever we are, you must obey me immediately, and fully. No hesitation, no complaints. If you do hesitate or complain or fail to comply, I must punish you. Do you understand?"

I nodded, swallowing hard. "Yes, Master."

I examined myself in the mirror. The collar was thick, but not uncomfortable, the soft grey felt buffering the feel of the hard leather.

"You look delicious, slave. I want to eat you. In fact, I think I will eat you before we go. But first, I'm going to dress you."

Then he slipped the black leather corset dress out of the box and I stepped into it. The skirt was far too short, barely covering the tops of my nylons, and the bodice far too big, but I realized that he could tighten the corset with ties in the back.

He pulled the ties and soon, the top fit more tightly, the boned bodice pushing up my breasts, squeezing them together so that I was a bit uncomfortable.

"How's that feel?" he said, his voice a bit husky. He ran his hands over the tops of my breasts which spilled out over the leather cups.

"It's a bit tight," I said, adjusting my breasts against the leather.

"Can you breathe?"

I took in a breath. "Yes."

"Good. That's perfect. You look..." he said, eyeing me up and down. "*Delicious.*" Then he reached into the box and pulled out a black lace garter belt and black fishnet stockings. "Put these on. Then I'm going to eat you."

I complied, my body warming to the thought he was going to make me come. I pulled the garter belt on and then sat on the edge of the tub and pulled on the stockings, one after the other. He knelt down and fastened each garter to the stockings. Then, before I could move, he forced my legs apart and I had to grip the back of the tub for support as he lifted one of my thighs over his shoulder.

I wedged the other foot against the wall, and when he kissed me, I almost jumped.

"Oh, God, Master, I don't know if this is a wise position..."

"Don't argue with me, slave. Tell me if you feel like you could lose your grip."

"Yes, Master," I said, closing my eyes as he began licking me all over, his fingers spreading me open.

"I'm going to be very fast, Master," I said, barely able to speak. "I've been aroused all day."

He glanced up at me. "Good. Just remember to ask permission to come."

I nodded, my heart rate increasing as he slipped a finger inside of me.

"Nice and wet," he said, then he started licking me again, slowly, agonizingly slowly, before covering me with his mouth and sucking me inside. It didn't take long after he slipped several fingers inside of me before I was ready to come, and I had to suck in air to be able to pull myself out of the moment.

"Master, I'm ready..."

"You're what?"

"I'm going to..."

He stopped his motions, leaving my body and flesh aching with need. "I'm not sure if you deserve it. I think I want to hear you beg."

"Please, Master. May I come now?"

"I'll think about it."

Then he began licking me again, his fingers fucking me slowly. My impending orgasm began again and I gasped.

"Master, I..."

He once again pulled away and my orgasm stopped. I groaned, my thighs quaking, my flesh aching, needing more stimulation.

"*Please*, Master," I said, my arms shaking just a bit.

He licked me again, then sucked my clit between his lips. I clenched around his fingers, my body so ready, just needing a bit more stimulation. When he moved his fingers in me, stroking me, that was it and I gasped.

But he stopped again, glancing up at me. "I didn't hear you ask nicely enough."

I breathed in deeply as the sensations subsided.

"Please, Master, let me come," I said, my voice shaky.

"I don't think so. I think I'll leave you in need. Aroused. You'll be all the more aroused by what happens at the party."

I groaned, wanting to protest, but I remembered what he had just said to me about submission and so I swallowed my need, my flesh swollen and achy. He withdrew his fingers from me and stood, leaning over me, holding me in his arms and kissing me so that I tasted myself on his tongue.

We stood up, but my legs were shaky and he had to practically hold me up. He stroked his fingers through my hair.

"You'll be so ready later," he said, taking my hand and stroking it across his erection. "And so will I. Perhaps some of your inhibitions will be overcome."

He was hard as rock, his erection trapped behind the leather pants. I sighed, content to wait and see what he had planned. Then I watched as he slipped on a crisp white linen shirt, leaving it untucked, and then his socks and boots. Finally, he pulled on a black tuxedo jacket over top.

He looked amazing.

The drive to the mansion where the fetish party was being held took almost half an hour. On the car stereo, Led Zeppelin, *Sunshine of Your Love*, played in the background while Drake described what would happen when we arrived at the home of a wealthy investment banker who hosted the once-monthly exclusive and very private dungeon party and fetish night.

"Will we wear masks?" I asked, a bit nervous. "Master?" I added, catching myself.

"No need for this party," he said. "These people will be more afraid of you knowing them than you should be of them knowing you. These are some of the wealthiest and most powerful players. I'm already a member of the host's inner circle, but you'll have to sign a disclaimer, agreeing to keep private anything you see at the party, not revealing any names to anyone, and if you see anyone on the street, you'll ignore them unless you're in a social situation and it demands that you acknowledge them. This is to protect the people who attend, many of whom are very powerful people and could be harmed if word got out about their involvement in BDSM."

"What if someone knows me?" I said, still nervous.

He reached out and touched my lips with his finger.

"Master," I said quickly. "Who is the owner? Would I know his name?"

He shook his head. "No. Just a very powerful banker with lots of money he made himself. He doesn't run in your father's old money circles. You might see his name on the Forbes 500 list, but not in the news. These people are very private."

"How did you meet him, Master?"

"Someone who knew him and knew me introduced us and I got an invite. After he watched me for a while, I was offered membership. Lara is a member as well. She may even be there tonight."

"Master, Lara will be mad that we're together."

He nodded. "I've smoothed things over with Lara."

"Are these all the kinky types from the one percent?"

He laughed at that but then he reached over and touched my lips with a finger. "Remember your manners, Katherine. You're being a bit lax because of excitement but I can't be lenient tonight as I usually am. If you disobey me in front of my very powerful and wealthy friends, I'll have to punish you."

"I'm sorry, Master. I'll do better."

"They're not all from the one percent. Some are there simply because they're good at what they do, kink-wise. Like Lara. She has several very powerful submissives, which is why she's invited. Men who run this country, but who like to be dominated in the bedroom."

We drove through a heavily wooded area in Yonkers to a mansion set high on a hill, surrounded by a security fence with remote control cameras spaced along the perimeter. A guard at the gate accepted Drake's ID and checked his name on a list and then waved us through.

My heart rate increased as we drove to the front entrance. A valet opened my door and helped me out. Then Drake came to my side and took my arm. He handed the valet his keys and we walked in the front door, into a luxurious foyer done all in rich marble and mirrors, a huge crystal chandelier in the center of the room suspended from a vaulted ceiling. Drake pulled an invitation out of a pocket in his overcoat and handed it to a shaved-headed security guard dressed in a business suit, a wireless earphone in his ear. The guard examined it and then checked me out, eyeing me up and down.

"She's new, Sir?"

Drake nodded.

"Sir, she'll have to sign," the guard said. He pointed inside the entry to a table set up with an older brunette dressed in a black corset and mini skirt, thigh-high stiletto boots. She wore no collar. We went to the table and the woman smiled at us.

"Master *D*," she said, making eye contact with him. I took it from how she greeted him as an equal that she was a Domme.

"Mistress Innes," he replied. "Good to see you again."

"You know the procedures. Your submissive will have to sign." She handed me a sheet of paper and a pen. "You can read it over there and sign. I'll get one of the Attendants to witness."

Drake led me to an ornate side table with a chair that had a tapestry seat. I sat and read over the document, which was as Drake had described it. "Master," I whispered. "Is this legally binding?"

He nodded. "*This* is. It's a non-disclosure agreement. The Attendant is a notary public and can legally witness. You break the agreement's terms, you can be sued."

I signed and dated the document.

The Attendant was collared and dressed in leathers, his torso bare except for straps that crossed his chest. He wore a black leather hat and huge leather boots. Tattoos marked his chest and arms.

After he introduced himself, he turned to me. "You understand that you are now legally obliged to keep secret what you see here and the names and identities of those who you meet?"

I nodded. The Attendant signed in the appropriate spot and pointed to a room off the left. "You can leave your coats and overshoes in the coat check. Fetish wear is required. If you have none, you will be able to choose from what is in stock or else you'll have to leave."

Drake nodded and we went to the coat check. Drake removed my coat and handed it to a scantily dressed coat check girl who also wore a collar, indicating her status as a submissive.

"Thank you, Sir," she said. She took my coat and hung it up. Drake removed his overcoat and suit jacket and handed it to her as well. He pointed to my feet.

"Take those off," he said. I hesitated for a brief moment but then removed my boots.

"Master, what do I wear on my feet? I forgot shoes."

"Nothing. Submissives wear bare or stocking feet."

I raised my eyebrows at that. He smiled. "It's psychological."

I nodded. The coat check submissive gave Drake four tiny tokens. "Sir, you're aware of the two drink per person maximum," she said. "Drinks are being served at the bar. The dungeon is downstairs, but there are stations set up around the main floor for demonstrations. There's dancing in the ballroom. Have an enjoyable evening, Sir."

She smiled at us and pointed to huge ornate double doors.

"Thank you," Drake said and took my hand, leading me through the doors and into another world.

We stood just inside and took in the scene. Perhaps fifty people stood around in small clusters, men and women dressed in leather and latex, some with collars on, various body parts exposed depending on their status as Dominant or submissive. Classical music played in the background from a small trio of a pianist, a violinist and a bass player. All wore fetish wear.

"These people are the movers and shakers," Drake said as he stood behind me, one arm around me, resting on my hip.

"I hope I don't see anyone I know through my father," I said.

Drake squeezed me from behind. "*Katherine...*"

I closed my eyes. "Oh, sorry. *Master*. I'm just so nervous."

"I know," he said. "Let's get you a drink. I need you relaxed but still aware of the rules."

We went to the bar and Drake ordered us two shots of vodka. We held them up and toasted each other as we always did and shot them back. Then Drake kissed me after I'd barely swallowed the vodka as if he wanted to taste it on my tongue.

"This is going to be a great night," he said.

We wandered around the main floor, and surprisingly, I was only introduced to a couple of men with their submissives. The greetings were short and although friendly, none of the men tried to engage Drake in any substantive conversation. It seemed as if everyone was here for the show. At various places on the main floor we saw what looked like home-made gymnastic equipment – a re-designed miniature pommel horse, a narrow balance-beam like structure and a wooden X on the wall with manacles at the end of each of the arms. There were tables with whips and floggers and everywhere, there were spray bottles and towels. It was like a gym or exercise room mixed with bondage gear, set against an eighteenth century salon with ornate furniture and a huge marble hearth.

I shivered. This was the BDSM that I had a difficult time accepting, but these people were submitting to this and doing this because they wanted it. For whatever reason, pain and humiliation and submission pleased them. These people gave each other what they needed and could get nowhere else.

"Why do these people like this? All of this – domination, submission, pain and humiliation, Master?"

"*These* people, Katherine?" he said, his eyebrow cocked. "You happen to be one of *these* people now. Maybe you're not into pain or humiliation, but you're into submission. It's not illegal so don't judge, Katherine. *Understand*."

I thought about Drake, and how he needed control, sexual control, over his lovers. How he enjoyed having me tied up and completely helpless. Was it because he was afraid a woman wouldn't allow him to do what he wanted unless she was completely tied up? Or was it the trust, as he said?

It was hard to know. I tried to connect the dots in his life – his failed marriage, the restraining order, the bondage, the sexual control. Was it as simple as him feeling this was the only way to keep a woman? Tie her up and make her come over and over again?

As if he could sense my unease, Drake led me to a couch by a huge bay window and sat me down, while he remained standing in front of me.

"What's going on in that mind of yours, Ms. Bennet?"

"Master, I was just wondering why people are attracted to BDSM. Why you are. Why I am."

He sighed heavily. "In the end, does it matter? I've tried to understand why I am. Understanding why doesn't change things. I still want it."

"So you understand why, Master?"

He looked away, inhaling deeply. "Perhaps."

I didn't push for any answers. It wasn't my place to ask. He'd tell me if he wanted me to know but I doubted he did. I had a suspicion. All his life, he'd been abandoned by women.

His mother left him when he was ten and then he had a succession of nanny and housekeepers. He would get close to them only to have them leave again. Then, he married and his wife left him. That had to be the reason. Was it that simple?

Was Drake that easy to understand? He tied up women and controlled their sexual response as a way of feeling control for once?

A surge of affection for him went through me as he stood in front of me, so attractive in his leather pants and white shirt, his hair a bit mussed as always, his blue eyes intense.

I *wanted* to submit to him fully, to give him whatever it was he needed to feel. I felt so bad at what I'd said to him in the Bahamas when I tried to leave him, abandoning him as well like all the other women in his life.

But this thing between us was so dangerous. If Dawn found out...

I shoved that thought to the back of my mind. I smiled at Drake and was rewarded with a beautiful smile back.

"I'm just glad to be here with you tonight, Master," I said, emotions filling me for this beautiful man with a need to tie me up and dominate me. "I'll do whatever you want me to do."

He reached down and took my hand, pulling me up and into his arms. "You make me very happy, slave."

He kissed me and it was a purely tender kiss, his lips soft on mine, his fingers threading through my hair, one hand on the small of my back, pulling me against him.

Then, he pulled away and brushed hair off my cheek. "But we're being observed. We have to do something public to merit participation in this evening. It also puts us at as much risk as others. It's the only way we'd be trusted to keep identities secret. I'd like to demonstrate an over the lap spanking of you in public, and then, I'd like to fuck you in private."

I blinked, pleased that finally, he'd spank me, but in public?

"I don't know if I like that..." I said, shaking my head, adrenaline surging through me. "You said you'd just tie me up, demonstrate bondage..."

At that, his eyes narrowed. "Katherine, are you refusing me?"

"It's just that it wasn't what I thought of when you promised me you'd spank me..." I glanced around at the people in the room. I didn't want them watching me get a spanking. I wanted a spanking that would make me aroused and want to fuck Drake. Not one with people watching and Drake using it as a teaching moment.

To my surprise, Drake grasped my hand, then pulled me towards an empty spanking horse. He stood me in front of it, standing behind me, his hands on my shoulders.

"I'm giving you a choice, slave, which I wouldn't usually give a submissive. You can have a barehanded over-the-lap spanking in front of everyone over there," he said, pointing to a black leather cushioned divan in the corner, a couple of feet from the wall. "Or you can have a spanking using this spanking horse. Choose."

I looked at the horse. It looked like a repurposed pommel horse except it had places for manacles. The choice was clear, but I didn't like that I had no choice to opt out of the spanking – without completely walking out of the evening. I was going to be spanked, one way or the other.

"Over the knee, please, Master."

"Stay here." Then he went to an Attendant, who stood on the sidelines, his arms crossed. They spoke for a moment and the Attendant nodded, pointing to the equipment. Drake returned and stood in front of me, his hands resting on my shoulders. He caught my eye, staring into mine, a frown on his face.

"This slave has displeased me," he said, his voice rising. "I'm considering what punishment I have to administer."

Immediately, several couples turned to us, standing a few feet away as if at some kind of unspoken buffer zone.

Drake turned me around to face the people who stood and stared. He had his hands on my shoulders.

"She's new and isn't yet quite as careful in her obedience as she should be. I have to keep reminding her not to hesitate or question my commands. Frequently, I have to remind her to use proper forms of address. I'm going to administer punishment for her failure to obey immediately and without question. Since she's new, and since we've never done this before, I have to go slow. I thought this would be a good time to demonstrate how to spank a novice submissive the first time, over-the-lap."

My face heated under their assessment. There were a few appreciative nods from the onlookers. Drake turned me around, his voice firm and loud enough for others to hear.

"The first thing to do with a novice submissive like this one is to acquaint her with the purpose of the act, telling her what she will experience. This will ensure she doesn't panic at any unfamiliar sensations and doesn't view it in the wrong way. You want your submissive to obey and to accept her punishment without protest, so going through each step first will help prevent that. Later, when she's more used to punishment, you can just carry it out without detailed explanation, quickly, to make a maximum affect on her state of mind, which isn't properly submissive. But the first time, a wise Master always explains what is going to happen. This isn't about pain. This is about obedience and reinforcing submission, demonstrating to her how she has given up her power entirely and is not permitted to protest or hesitate to obey an order, unless it is to use the safe word."

He turned back to those watching. "A bare hand is good for over the lap spanking but you can also use an implement, such as a paddle or tawse. Whatever works well given that you'll have only one hand available. The spanking horse is best if you want to use floggers or a tawse or riding crop, depending on your preferences. For this submissive, I'm going to use my bare hand, so over the lap is best."

He turned to me and pointed to the black leather divan. "When I sit, you are to lay over my lap." He tilted my head up so that I had to look in his eyes. "Are you clear on what will happen, slave?"

I nodded, my throat choked up.

Drake turned to those watching, his eyebrows raised. I heard a titter go through them and realized I hadn't used *Master* when responding.

"You can see I've been a bit too indulgent with this slave. She needs to learn her lesson on how to properly address her Master, and how to submit to an order without question."

He turned back to me, frowning. "I said, are you clear on what will happen, slave?"

"Yes, Master. My apologies for not using proper form of address, Master."

He nodded. "Good girl."

Then he sat facing the group, and pulled me down over his knee. My hair spilled over my face, and I was glad no one would see me. I realized that my skirt would ride up a bit, exposing my garters and nylons.

"Master, my skirt..." I tried to reach back, but Drake held me firm, one hand on the small of my back. Of course, he was planning on exposing my ass. He was going to spank me in front of everyone.

"Did I ask for your opinion on what is happening, slave?"

I swallowed and just forced myself to do whatever he said, with no comments.

"No, Master. I'm sorry." I made my body go limp. As if he felt my submission, he removed his hand from my back.

"Good girl," he said softly, then he took my hands in one of his, and with the other, he held me down, his hand on the small of my back. He turned to those gathered around us. "This submissive is not into pain, although she doesn't yet know her true limits. She has been pestering me to spank her so she will know what to expect. I have to ensure she understands that this spanking is done to punish her, not to reward her curiosity or give her pleasure." Then he bent down to me. "Are you ready?"

"Yes, Master."

My heart was pounding. I wanted this, just so I'd know, but at the same time, doing it in front of others had me anxious. I wasn't sure if this would ruin it for me or make this better. I had to just let Drake take over and decide. I had to trust him.

Surprisingly, my arousal from earlier in the night before we left 8th Avenue re-emerged and I felt an ache building in my flesh. Would the pain from the spanking squelch it? Or would I want him to fuck me right away?

Then Drake spoke to the crowd. "The first time, let the submissive become familiar with the position. Don't rush things or you'll cause unnecessary panic. The Dominant's purpose is not to create fear and anger in the sub, but to reinforce the direction of power in the relationship, to teach her what is expected of her, and to help her become a better submissive. By losing all control in this way, the sub is reminded who has the power. Generally, any man is stronger than most women, especially in upper body strength. It should be fairly easy to restrain her, and keep the struggling to a minimum. But a Master enjoys a bit of struggle. The pain from the spanking should be equal to the amount of pain necessary to make the point, but no more. This isn't about sensation play. This is punishment. Keep reinforcing that."

Then, Drake pulled up my skirt and I knew that my buttocks – and more – were completely exposed to all those who cared to watch. I gasped, my face heating.

"*Master*..." I whispered, unable to stop myself.

"*Shh*," he said, and rubbed one of my cheeks with his hand.

After a moment, he spoke to the others. "This is virgin ass in every way. Never spanked properly. Never claimed. I aim to do both, but one thing at a time."

A murmur went through those who watched, and someone said, "Lucky you."

I heard Drake chuckle. He was enjoying this. He said he liked to teach...

"As I said, this particular sub is new to the lifestyle and has never been punished before, nor has she experienced a sensual spanking, anal play or penetration. She has expressed her eagerness to be spanked several times and each time I have refused. I want her to understand that *I* choose when an act will be performed, whether sexual or punishment. She imagined I was just going to demonstrate some minor point of bondage tonight, but earlier, she questioned one of my commands and so I decided to use this opportunity to demonstrate how to properly punish a new sub who is not into pain."

He kept running his hands over my ass, cupping each one, slipping his fingers between my cheeks, then he slid one finger inside of me and I tensed, my face hot with embarrassment. I couldn't believe I was letting him do this to me in front of people but it seemed to please him. I was also shocked that despite everything, or perhaps because of it, I was aroused. I never thought I was into exhibitionism. Was I?

"This slave is very responsive sexually. She's aroused by this, even though it conflicts with her self-image as a proper Catholic girl. I've enjoyed breaking down her barriers. This is just one more that I will cross."

He kept rubbing one ass cheek softly. He bent over and spoke softly to me.

"Now, slave, I'm going to spank you. I don't want you to protest or make a sound. Just take the punishment. You know the safe word. Remember what happens if you use it."

"Yes, Master," I managed to whisper.

Drake spoke to the others. "The first time you spank a sub, do so just to let them know how it feels and to reinforce submission. The point will be made even if you stop long before you would in a normal session of punishment."

With that, he struck my ass cheek, his palm hitting low on my buttock, a loud smack resulting. It stung a bit, but was more of a shock than painful.

I could take this.

I relaxed a bit, letting my body go slack. Drake didn't say anything at that point, but he must have felt my compliance. He smacked me harder this time and I tensed a bit. He rubbed my buttocks softly as if to soothe them, slipping his fingers between my cheeks each time.

"She thinks she can handle this level of pain and is relaxing. You have to up the pain in order to find that amount that is just beyond comfort level, both physically and psychologically. This is not a sensual spanking. It's punishment and should hurt enough. *Just* enough, but not more. This is to make a point, to reinforce her submission. She should just give in and take it, and if you're lucky, she'll go into what is termed 'subspace'. You must watch a sub carefully to see if and at what point this happens. At that point, you have to rein yourself in a bit, because she won't feel the pain and you could hurt her beyond her tolerance, or even do permanent damage. A Master must be exceptionally attentive to his slave during such an encounter."

I tensed at that, unable to stop myself. Hurting me just beyond what I can tolerate? I wasn't sure about that.

"My slave has just tensed in response to what I've said. Such is the danger of demonstrating a technique. The slave can undergo anticipatory arousal or anxiety. At that point, it's good to reassure her."

He bent down to me, his mouth next to my ear. "Do you trust me, Katherine?" he whispered.

I said nothing for a moment, blinking, trying to calm myself. He stroked my hair, then down my back. "Katherine, I won't do more than you can take. Do you trust me?"

Finally, I inhaled. "Yes, Master."

"Good girl," he said and began stroking my buttocks again, his fingers lingering between my cheeks, slipping down to my pussy.

"This slave is nervous, but also excited sexually. Some arousal, even when being punished, is inevitable simply because she is submitting and that is arousing to a submissive."

Then he smacked my buttock again, harder than ever, and it stung quite a bit. Soon, several more blows fell on my ass, alternating between buttocks, several in a row, before he stroked each buttock softly.

"You can see her skin is very fair and fine. She's already getting quite a delicious blush to her nice little ass from the spanking. I'll have to be mindful of that. I don't want to draw blood, but a bit of warmth and tenderness will remind her of her punishment when she sits for the rest of the evening."

Then, he rained down a volley of smacks, each a bit harder and more painful than the last, and I began to wonder if he'd stop and when. My ass was starting to hurt. It felt hot, and my heart was pounding but I was determined not to cry out or respond, biting my lip, pulling at a small bit of loose skin to distract myself.

After several more smacks, and me biting down hard to prevent crying out, I did let out a gasp, despite my best efforts, tears blurring my eyes.

Drake stopped immediately, and rubbed my ass tenderly. He leaned down and whispered in my ear.

"Have you learned your lesson, slave?"

"Yes," I said meekly, a sob in my voice. At that moment, I think I hated him just a bit, but at the same time, something was building in me, a sense of elation that I submitted, that I didn't fight and I didn't use the safe word, despite it hurting me beyond what I thought I would tolerate.

"Yes, what?"

"Yes, Master," I gasped, crying now in earnest.

"Good," he said and bent down to kiss my buttocks, one after the other, resting his cheek against one. "Perhaps you'll be a bit more careful in your behavior when I give an order."

Then he sat me up and turned me to face him. I tried to wipe away my tears, which I knew would make my mascara streak.

"Oh, *Kate*," he said, his voice aghast. "Your lip..."

CHAPTER TWENTY-ONE

He touched my bottom lip and his finger came back bloody. I just covered my eyes with my hands and cried quietly, no sound coming out of my mouth, not wanting to look in his eyes because I just *lost* it. It didn't hurt that much – not really. It was just so *intense*, the way I felt. I couldn't explain it. I *had* to cry as if some kind of dam had burst within me and I had to let the emotions out.

He pulled me into his arms and kissed my shoulder, stroking my hair and I knew he felt truly bad about my lip, even thought it wasn't really his fault. Then he pulled back, removed my hands from my eyes, and shook his head softly.

"I'm sorry," he said. "You were too strong and I went a bit too far, waiting for you to make a sound to indicate you'd reached your limit." His face was ashen, his brow furrowed as he touched my lip. Then he leaned in and kissed me, taking my bottom lip between his, licking off my blood. Then he pressed my head to his shoulder and spoke to those who stood there watching.

"This slave was trying so hard not to use the safe word that she bit her own lip, drawing blood. Drawing blood is one of my hard limits and hers, so I inadvertently crossed it. This was a mistake on my part, and is due to my failure to recognize how stubborn she is and what a high pain threshold she has. We're still getting to know each other. Don't let your position as Dominant or Master prevent you from apologizing when you recognize you've crossed a line or performed inexpertly. It's the only way to regain your slave's trust."

Then he pulled me back from his shoulder and wiped my cheeks with his fingers, so tenderly, that it succeeded in calming me. He really did regret what happened.

"I'm sorry," he said again. "It won't happen again."

Then he pressed my cheek once more against his shoulder. He picked me up in his arms, and carried me over to the Attendant.

"Can you clean off the equipment for me?" Drake said, his voice soft.

"Certainly, Master D. Do you need a private room?"

"Yes," Drake said. "Preferably one with a bathroom."

I kept my eyes closed, not wanting to see other people and how they responded to the little drama playing out before their eyes.

Soon, Drake carried me up the central staircase to a second-floor bedroom that looked like it belonged in some grand mansion in Florence instead of Yonkers, the carpets thick, the walls covered in rich brocade, the bed enormous. Drake carried me into a small bathroom and sat me on the vanity. I grimaced because my ass was tender but as he'd said to those watching the spanking, the small bit of discomfort would remind me that I'd been punished.

He ran some water and wet a washcloth with cold water, pressing it against my bottom lip for a moment.

"I'm fine," I said when he pulled the cloth away, a tiny bit of blood still on it. "Master."

"You're strong-willed," he said. "Stronger than I knew. I never wanted you to be scarred because of anything we did together, Kate. I never want to draw blood."

"Master, it's just a bit of skin I pulled off. It won't scar."

He pulled me into his arms and I slipped my arms around his neck, my tears stopped now, just a strange sense of calm descending over me.

He moved back and looked me in the eyes. "Do you want to go home now? Or do you want to stay? You've barely seen anything."

"Let's stay," I said, drawing in a deep breath. "If it pleases you, Master," I added quickly, making a face and tapping my head lightly with a fist. "I want to see the dungeon if you want to take me there."

"Are you sure?" he said, his expression now doubtful. "When we first met, I thought it would be good for your 'research' but now, I'm not so sure you'll enjoy it. Things can get pretty intense. There are people who *do* want to draw blood, Kate. Who do want to feel pain and administer pain. People will be fucking. It can be upsetting to you if you're not used to it."

"Whatever you think, Master. I trust you to know what I should do."

He nodded, just staring at me for a moment as if deciding.

"Maybe it would be good to go down there for a short while, just so you can satisfy your curiosity. But I may only go in a bit deep. Not to the really intense places."

"You're scaring me, Master."

"I don't intend to. Just want you to be prepared for what you'll see."

"I trust you, Master."

"I value your trust, Katherine. I take your trust in me very seriously."

Then he kissed me, softly, and stroked my cheek with the backs of his fingers, touched my bottom lip.

He pulled me off the vanity and we made our way back down to the main floor, walking through those assembled to watch various displays and demonstrations of technique. A few people nodded to Drake as we passed but didn't speak to him. It was all very respectful.

We descended a wide staircase to the basement and immediately the atmosphere changed. The basement was dark and made of old brick and had a cold-sweat feel to it like in a cave. Some heavy bass-filled electronic music played in the background, its beat insistent. Dubstep. I recognized it – *Trolley Snatcha* by The Future. It was probably the only Dubstep tune I knew. When I lived in residence at Columbia, one of my roommates played it endlessly.

The lighting was subdued and there were imitation torches on the walls, flickering with an eerie light that I knew was electric rather than a flame. But the effect was the same. A bit spooky and definitely darkly sexual.

The basement was divided into room-like spaces. Each room was open to a central aisle. Inside each room was some kind of apparatus and people inside using it to inflict various forms of pain or pleasure on each other. People down here were all dressed – or undressed – for the atmosphere. Leather, latex, rubber. They wore and used chains, masks, ball gags, spreader bars. There were whips and floggers of every design on boards, and over the sound of the music, I heard the crackle of electricity and turned, looking for the sound.

"Electricity, Master?"

"Yes," he said, his voice low. He squeezed my hand. "We won't go there."

We walked around a crowd watching a scene, threading through people who stood and watched, Doms with their subs on leashes, some kneeling at the Dom's feet, watching the events transpire inside the rooms.

In one room, a twenty-something male sub with short spiky white-blond hair was standing in the center of the room, his hands bound to hooks in the ceiling, his legs spread with a spreader bar. His testicles were imprisoned in some kind of cage-like structure and he was being struck on the ass and back with a flogger. His bald-headed older Dominant dressed all in black leather stood behind him, whispering something into the sub's ear every few strikes. The sub had a huge erection, obviously turned on by what was happening to him.

I was shocked by the explicitness of the scene, and everyone watched like we were children watching something we weren't supposed to.

"...not allowed to come until I give you permission..." I managed to hear the Dominant say.

Drake and I stopped for a moment and he stood behind me. "Cock and ball torture," he whispered in my ear. "I can feel myself shrink just watching it."

I smiled, thinking of him shrinking. It was clear that the sub enjoyed what was happening. He had a huge erection, and I suspected he was close to orgasm by how rigid he was, the way his face was red, his breathing fast.

Drake took me to a room where a Domme was busy flogging her male submissive, who was bent over, his hands and feet in manacles. It was then I realized she was Lara – Mistress Lara.

Sadist.

"Master, that's Lara."

"Shh," he whispered in my ear. "Remember your manners. She's in scene right now. Don't distract her. I said she might be here."

"Sorry, Master. That's Mistress Lara." I watched her, fascinated. Her blonde hair was pulled back into a high ponytail. Her submissive wore only a leather jock strap and leather boots, a ball gag in his mouth. She stood behind him and lazily slapped his bare ass with the flogger. It was as if she couldn't really be bothered to flog him with any focus.

"Why does she look so bored?"

Drake stood behind me, his arms around my waist. "He's likely into humiliation as well as pain and submission. She's humiliating him by appearing as if she doesn't really care. It's what he likes and needs."

The sub's ass was getting progressively redder as she flogged him with a bit more gusto.

"You. Are. A. *Worm*," she said, her voice derisive, punctuating each stroke with a word. "You should be wriggling on the ground at my feet, *slave*."

I turned to Drake. "He likes that, Master?"

"Oh, yes. He's actually a very hot-shot fund manager by day, but in private, he likes to submit."

"She did that to you, Master?"

He smiled. "Yes. I never intended to use these kinds of techniques, but she wanted to see if there was a sadist in me – or a masochist. There wasn't."

As we watched, Lara bent over her sub and spoke to him, whispering in his ear. His ass was thoroughly red. Then she went around beside him and picked up a cane. She ran the cane she held in her hand over his ass, trailing it between his ass cheeks before striking him several times, leaving long streaks across it.

We left Lara's scene and went to another room where a man dressed in leather chaps was busy fucking a woman suspended from a hook in the ceiling, her hands in cuffs above her head, her feet in straps also attached to the ceiling. She wore a blindfold and had a ball-gag in her mouth. I was fascinated with that scene for it was the least violent. It was pure sex, bondage and leather. *This* I could get into, but then I saw her ass, it was as streaked red. I saw several implements lying on the table next to the wall – floggers, riding crops, canes, tawses. The Dominant was ramming into her, hard, his hands on her hips, pulling her to him with each thrust.

Drake stood behind me, one hand on my belly, the other wrapped around me and resting on my neck as if measuring my pulse and respirations. I knew he was monitoring my response to what I saw, trying to understand what aroused me, what repelled me.

"You *like* this scene," he whispered in my ear. "Your pulse just increased, your breathing is more shallow. If I slipped my fingers between your lips, you'd be nice and wet. Do you want to try this one day?"

"Yes, Master," I said, butterflies in my stomach. "Except for the ball gag and the cane."

He squeezed me. I held his hands, which were now clasped around my waist.

"What do you think of all this, Katherine?"

"I think that these people need each other, Master," I said, somewhat saddened that they felt a need for pain, but whatever the reason they did, it pleased them. I liked watching. It aroused me, even when there was pain involved. Drake was one of these people. Maybe our kinks weren't so intense as theirs. Maybe neither of us liked pain or needed it, giving or receiving. But we needed submission and dominance. We needed what each other gave.

"I need *you*," I said quietly, realizing that I was one of *these people*, like Drake said. He kissed my neck.

"I think it's time to go back upstairs," he said, his voice a bit husky.

"Yes, Master."

He took me back up the stairs out of the darkness with its heavy scent of sweat and sex and other aromas I couldn't name, but would forever be associated in my mind with dungeons. We passed through the bright salon where couples stood and watched demonstrations of various techniques, and through the next room with darker lighting, where people danced to a VJ playing some Latin music, a video being projected on a wall, a mirror ball spinning, casting the room in thousands of sparkles.

We stopped at the edge of the dance floor and Drake took me in his arms and started to dance, placing one of my hands on his hip and the other on his shoulder while he held my hips. We swayed together for a few moments, him smiling down at me.

"Drake Morgan, MD," I said, smiling back at him. "I didn't know you could dance, Master."

"Oh, I have been known to cut a rug from time to time."

"Cut a rug?"

He laughed. "It's an old term for dance."

I realized as he led me around the dance floor for a few moments, smiling broadly, that I loved it when Drake smiled. His face lit up, and it seemed all the cares fell away and he was happy. It made me happy to see him so relaxed.

The next song was slow, something from the big band era I didn't recognize, and we just melted together, my arms around his neck, his around my waist, my head on his shoulder, his face in my neck. I loved the feel of his body against mine, how warm he was, his body so strong, reassuring. I felt totally safe here, at this high-roller BDSM party where people drew blood, electrocuted each other, and struck each other with whips and paddles. Drake made me feel safe. I felt as if I could do anything with him, give up total control to him, and he'd know what to do. Yes, he had gone a bit too far with the spanking, but it was my fault, trying to go beyond my own limits to please him, despite it upsetting me too much. It wasn't really his fault that I bled. I was determined to beat him in the game of how much could I take and how much was he willing to give.

"Ms. Bennet, I think I want to fuck you now," he whispered in my ear. His words sent a shock of lust through me, and I emerged from this sweet dreamlike state I'd been in from slow dancing with him.

"Yes, Master," I said, my voice breathless. He took my hand and led me out of the ballroom and to the staircase, back to the bedroom assigned to us. He pulled me over to the bed and practically threw me onto it, and I laughed as I bounced and he climbed on top of me, a smile on his face.

I waited to see what he'd do to me, my hands above my head, him between my spread thighs. He just rested on his hands above me and his gaze moved over me, from my face and lower. Then he bent down and kissed the tops of my breasts, which bulged out over the bodice.

"You look delectable."

He pulled the leather bodice down just a bit so that my nipples poked out over the edge and then he began to suck and nibble them, sending delicious chills through my body straight to my groin.

"Master," I said, my eyes closed as he sucked and licked my breasts. "Are you going to tie me up?"

"Shh," he said and sucked one nipple into his mouth, his tongue circling the areola. I groaned and arched my back, pressing my breast into him. "A slave doesn't ask what her Master has planned. She just waits. But I think I'm going to just fuck you missionary style tonight."

I frowned, wanting to see how being surrounded by all the kink would affect him. I thought it would make him more intense, maybe trying things with me that he hadn't yet. Instead, he wanted to fuck me vanilla? I bit my lip, holding back my protest.

"Don't do that," he said, touching my mouth. "Kate, you just have to let me decide how I want to fuck you. It shouldn't be your concern. You're going to come one way or the other, so leave this up to me. Do you understand?"

I nodded and let my mouth fall open slightly. "Yes, Master. I'm sorry. I just thought..."

"When we're in scene, don't think of anything but pleasing me. If it pleases me to fuck you missionary style, it should please you to comply."

I inhaled deeply and closed my eyes. "Yes, Master. I apologize but I just can't help but be curious why. I thought at a BDSM *party*..."

He didn't say anything for a while, and even though my eyes were closed, I could almost feel his eyes on my face, his expression so intense.

"I like contrasts and appreciate irony, Kate. Downstairs, everyone's busy getting their kink on, and here we are, fucking like a pair of ordinary lovers."

I opened my eyes and stared into his for a moment. Was he saying that's what he wanted? That's how he felt about me? Just ordinary lovers?

"So this is an ironic fuck, Master?" I said, unable to keep a grin from starting.

He grinned widely, his eyes crinkling, a mischievous look on his face. "*Very* ironic. How transgressive are we to fuck like this at this party? Now *shh* and spread your legs wide like a good vanilla girl."

Then, he very deliberately and very slowly began to seduce me with his touch and his mouth and his words, whispering in my ear how much he wanted me, what he would do to me. I didn't think it would be as intense as if I was bound and helpless, but it was in its own way. He undressed me slowly, removing the dress and the garter belt and hose, and I was surprised. I thought he'd want to keep them on, given he liked the look of them and how leather smelled when warm. But he seemed to want me completely naked instead.

Then he undressed as well and lay between my legs, fully naked, his thick erection pressed into my groin. He took his time, working me up with his fingers and his tongue, exploring every part of my body, so that I was aching with need. Then, he pulled me on top of him so that I lay with him between my thighs.

"Seduce *me* now," he said and closed his eyes. So I did, repeating exactly what he did to me, using my mouth and tongue and fingers, rubbing myself against him shamelessly, shoving my breasts in his face, my hair trailing down his body as I placed a trail of kisses down his belly and began teasing him, breathing on him, slowly licking him all over before sucking him into my mouth, my hands cupping his scrotum.

By the time it came to actual fucking, I was so ready, my face heated, my thighs quivering as he entered me, working me up in his way, stroking me with the head of his cock, and it didn't take long before I was ready.

"Master, I'm going to..."

But he didn't stop. He just kept on with what he was doing.

"Look in my eyes," he said, holding my face in his hands. I could barely keep them open, but did. "Say my name."

When my orgasm started, he just fucked me missionary style until I cried out, his name instead of *Master* on my lips.

He came as well in a few strokes, his face red with effort, then his jaw slack, his eyes half-lidded as his orgasm started, ramming himself into me with each spasm. He collapsed onto me and panted in my ear for a moment, then kissed my neck. I couldn't help but smile.

He pulled back and saw my smile and smiled himself, a trickle of sweat on his forehead.

"So?" he said, raising his eyebrows, grinning like a fool. "How was vanilla ice cream without any chocolate sauce and whipped cream tonight? Good enough?"

"More than good enough, in case you didn't notice, Master."

He bent down and kissed my throat.

Then he couldn't resist and sat up between my thighs and spread my legs wide so he could watch his come drip out of me.

I covered my face to stop my smile.

"What are you smiling about, Ms. Bennet?" he said and I could hear the amusement in his voice. "The fact I can't deny at least one of my kinks?"

I opened my hands and watched him as he cocked his head to the side, admiring his artwork.

He glanced back to my face, and smiled and his smile did something to me. I can't describe it, or explain it. Whatever it was we thought we'd be to each other, I felt as if that had been passed, surmounted, overcome. What we became I wasn't sure, but I knew the agreement was pretty much thrown out the window.

If Drake realized it, he didn't seem to care.

CHAPTER TWENTY-TWO

The Monday before Christmas Eve, on our night together because Dawn was working an extra shift, I was at 8th Avenue before Drake, which was very rare. I brought along a couple of strings of Christmas lights and some decorations, plus a sprig of real Mistletoe I picked up from a green grocer near my apartment. I was just wandering around his apartment, thinking of where I'd want to string up the lights when he arrived, wearing his camel colored overcoat and plaid scarf, his cheeks red from the chill.

"You're here," he said, smiling. "I was running a bit late in surgery."

"I'm here, breathlessly waiting for you."

"Just the way I like you."

I smiled and helped him with his coat and packages. Once he was out of the coat, I went to him with the sprig of Mistletoe behind my back.

"What have you got there, Ms. Bennet?"

I held it up, grinning. "Just this," I said. Try as I might, I couldn't hold it high enough over his head. "I need stilts to get it over you."

"No stilts for you," he said and grabbed me, his arms slipping around me. "Too dangerous. Don't you know you're supposed to hold it over your *own* head? Not that I need any excuse to kiss you..."

He kissed me and the mistletoe was all but forgotten. Once again, I was amazed at how quickly I responded to him, my body immediately wet and aching at the touch of his mouth on mine.

While he grabbed my ass with one hand, he slipped the other under my skirt to feel my garters and naked pussy.

"*Mmm*," he said against my throat. "Slave, you are nice and wet."

I smiled, gasping a bit when his fingers slipped inside of me.

"You've got me trained like Pavlov's little submissive, Master."

He laughed at that and then pulled away. "Speaking of Russians, do you have some Anisovaya?"

I nodded and went to the sideboard where the crystal glasses waited. We did a toast to each other.

While he nibbled my neck, I brought up something I had hoped to talk about.

"I wish we could go somewhere to celebrate New Year's, Master."

He didn't say anything for a moment.

"We'll meet here during your time off. I have no scheduled surgery for a week. I was thinking we could go to a special Fetish party for New Year's. Maybe you could pretend to get sick and we could sneak out and go. This time, we'd have to wear masks so no one would recognize us. The party I have in mind is in Brooklyn. There would be fewer people there that either of us would know compared to the one in Manhattan."

I liked that idea. It would be something special, and I was excited to see what an ordinary fetish club of ordinary Brooklynites would be like.

"What are you doing tomorrow, Master?" I asked, unable to keep from questioning him.

"I'll probably just stay around here. Play some music. You could sneak over if you can make an excuse to be alone for a couple of hours..."

I smiled. "I'll make sure. Will they dance at these Fetish parties?"

"You liked dancing with me the other night, did you, Ms. Bennet?"

"Yes," I said. "I did, Master."

I laughed when he picked me up and swung me around the way I'd seen my grandfather's generation do when dancing the Jitterbug. I giggled when he twirled me around, and then pulled me tightly against his body.

"I did learn in high school," he said. "Although I haven't had much time to practice. I know a few moves..."

Then he went to the sound system and sorted through some records until he found one. He pulled the album out of its sleeve and placed it on the turntable. When the song started, I heard some faint scratches.

"Rock Around The Clock," he said, smiling. "Bill Hailey and the Comets."

He started leading me around the room, showing me how to do the Jitterbug, tripping a bit over the loose Persian carpets on the smooth hardwoods. He picked me up, lifted me up high and then tried to swing me over his other hip, repeating the earlier move, but his foot caught on the carpet and he tripped just as I was coming down in a less-than-graceful arc. He fell backwards and we tumbled to the floor.

A little too close to the sideboard with it's sharp corner, which struck me on the side of my head, right above my eye. He was able to mostly save us, me falling on his body, his arm going back to stop the fall, but I still toppled against the sideboard. We came to rest on the floor, and immediately I knew something was wrong. Intense pain almost blinded me and I held my head. When the pain finally subsided a little, I was on my back on the floor, stars sparkling in my vision. Actual stars. Something like warm water flowed over my cheek.

"Oh, God, *Kate*," he said, his voice low, hushed. "You're hurt..."

He turned my face towards his using one hand, while he cradled the other against his body. I could barely see him through the swirling sparks of light. He left me lying on the floor, my hands touching the warmth on my cheek. My fingers came back bloody, and my whole brow hurt.

"How are you?" he asked when he ran back with some gauze and pressed the bandage against my brow. His face was pale as he examined me. "Did you black out at any time?"

"I don't think so. But I saw stars."

"Are you in pain? How many fingers can you see?" He held up a hand with three fingers out.

"Three," I said. "My head really hurt for a minute, but now it just stings."

"Look at me, in my eyes," he said, his expression so intense. I did and he examined the cut.

He exhaled. "*Goddammit*. I have to take you to the ER and get you stitched up. I don't have my bag here."

I smiled through the pain. "You have one of those little black doctor bags?"

"Something like that," he said, but he wasn't smiling. "Damn, Kate. You're going to have to just come with me. We'll have to risk it. That cut is too deep for butterfly sutures."

"You're the neurosurgeon."

After he bandaged me up enough, we took his Mercedes to St. Luke's ER. It wasn't the nearest hospital, but I didn't want to go to Harlem, because Dawn worked there. He didn't want to go to NY Presbyterian because he had too many colleagues and associates who might recognize us. The ER nurses at St. Luke's had me in an examining room within a very few minutes of registering.

I sat on the gurney in the tiny space and Drake stood between my knees, examining me, brushing my hair back, fussing over me like a mother hen. The young female physician entered and Drake stepped aside. She quizzed us about who Drake was and what happened. Drake related how we were dancing the Jitterbug, and he was clumsy and I fell and hit my head against a wooden table. She seemed upset that Drake spoke instead of me.

The physician looked at me carefully while I repeated the story. I watched Drake and smiled while I told it.

"He was a bit out of practice. Like twenty *years* out of practice."

"I'll be back in a bit to stitch that up," she said and left us alone.

Drake continued to examine me, his hand on my shoulder, smiling at me. He'd hurt his wrist trying to break the fall, and cradled it, a tensor bandage on it.

"I'm so *sorry*, he said. "I'm really not usually so clumsy." He grinned at me. "Kind of ruined the mood I was going for..."

I laughed and squeezed his good hand. "At least I was in the best hands. I mean, if you're going to fall and crack your head, who better than a neurosurgeon to look after you?"

The young doctor came back in.

"Can you excuse us, Dr. Morgan?" she said to Drake. "I'd like to speak with Kate alone for a moment."

Drake's mouth went hard at that. "Certainly." He leaned over to me and kissed me briefly where I sat on the examining table. "I'll be right back. You'll be fine."

I nodded. When we were alone, the physician turned to me.

"I just wanted to give you the opportunity to tell me if you're concerned at all about anything."

I frowned. "What do you mean?"

"If there's anything happening in your life that frightens you. If you've been harmed in any way that led to that injury. I'm obliged to ask about this any time a woman comes in with her partner, injured in a domestic accident."

"You think he did this on *purpose*?" I said, aghast. "*No*, it was just as we told you. He was showing me how to do the Jitterbug and tripped on a carpet on the floor. We fell and I hit my head on the sideboard. That's it. End of story. He hurt his wrist trying to stop the fall."

She looked down at my wrists, which were bare, my sweater rolled up. There were chafing marks where the leather edge of my restraints rubbed my skin from our last session. Just a slight red mark on the back of my hands. It didn't hurt, but I could see that she was worried.

"Just role playing," I said, smiling. My face turned bright red. "You know. We read those books, and like to try things out."

"As long as you're safe and this is your choice..."

"I'm *fine*," I said. "We're lovers. We got a little... enthusiastic the other night."

She nodded, a somewhat judgmental expression on her face. Then, she had me lie down and after preparing me, putting a sterile field over my eye and brow, she injected me with a local anesthetic and proceeded to stitch me up.

"Drake might want to be here for this," I said.

"Sorry about that," she said. "I can't stop now. Have to maintain sterile procedure."

Finally, Drake came back and pushed the door open to check on how I was. He stood watching the physician as she stitched me, examining each stitch carefully, holding my hand on the other side of the gurney.

When she was done, I sat back up and she gave me instructions about aftercare. Drake seemed a bit impatient with her, as if he didn't know proper procedure. Finally, we left the hospital and went back to the apartment.

"You're staying here tonight," he said when we were back inside. He brought me a glass of milk instead of Anisovaya and motioned to the couch.

"No bondage tonight?" I said, disappointed. "No Anisovaya?"

"No alcohol for you, just in case. No bondage because of my wrist," he said, holding it up. "I'm useless. Not in fighting form and neither are you."

I sighed and after he shot back his vodka and I my milk, we nestled on the couch.

He'd put on some music, something old, folksy.

"What's this?" I asked. It was a solo singer accompanied only by an acoustic guitar.

"A Canadian musician, Gordon Lightfoot. One of my dad's favorites. He had every single album. He was a big fan of Canada, raving about their health care system and welfare safety net. He almost wanted to move there after the war, but he was accepted to Columbia and wanted to go study medicine."

"If he was such a socialist, why did he go to war? Couldn't he get an exemption?"

"He volunteered. He said if the poor black kids had to fight, the middle-class white kids should as well."

"That's what my dad said. No wonder they were friends..."

Drake nodded. "He almost loved Canada as much as Mother Russia. We used to go to Northern Alberta every year on vacation and he'd do surgery up in the wilds. We'd fly in to these tiny communities and he'd donate his services. We'd always stop in Montréal and eat this absolutely horrible mess of French fries and gravy and cheese curds called Poutine."

I smiled and listened to the music. It was very haunting. "What is this piece?"

"It's very appropriate," he said and went over to a stack of old albums. "This song is called *Affair on 8th Avenue*." He brought some sheet music over and handed it to me.

He sat back down. I glanced over the words, which told the story of a pair of lovers at an apartment on 8th Avenue.

"It's beautiful. Can you play this?" I asked as I read it over.

"I can but not with this wrist. I guess my hopes of playing with the band over the weekend are out."

"It's that bad?"

"I think I tore something. My whole arm hurts."

Despite my injuries, I felt Drake's warmth through his clothing and it in turn warmed me up.

"So, what are we going to do?"

Drake shrugged, his good arm around me. "I don't know."

"I could *do* you," I said. "You don't want me to just, you know, crawl on top? You wouldn't have to do anything..."

He leaned his head back, eyeing me from the side. "You're going to try to top me, are you?"

"It's not topping and you wouldn't be bottoming. It's just having sex. I'm a little aroused. I was really looking forward to tonight."

"Ms. Bennet, you're a horny little thing but I just can't be safe with only one working hand and arm..."

"You don't have to restrain me."

I climbed onto his lap without him requesting it but he didn't fight me. I leaned down and kissed him, and he let me. Since that first night in my apartment, he always signaled when our scene would start by embracing me, then kissing me. I'd never made the first move.

At first, he didn't kiss me back. When I pulled away and looked in his eyes, searching for his permission, he said nothing.

"You don't want me to fuck you?" I said, a little hurt.

"Kate, I am never fucked. *I* fuck."

"But you're injured and can't manage. I could do all the work. If it would make you feel better, you could always *order* me to."

"*Katherine...*" He had this look in his eyes. A bit upset, but cautious. "Remember, we're always in scene at my place."

I sighed. He meant that even when we weren't having sex, I was still his submissive. Not his girlfriend.

"Drake, do I have to go home and resort to Big? I *need* you..." I kissed him again, angry now that he was so rigid that he couldn't stand to have me once make the first move or do the work.

"I don't want you going home by yourself," he said when I pulled away. "I want you to stay here tonight."

"I want to lick you, and suck you, then I want to get on top and ride you. That wouldn't please you?"

"I thought you were uncomfortable taking the lead in sex, Kate. That's why submission appeals to you."

I looked in his eyes. "I feel like I could do *anything* with you."

He ran one hand up my back, his gaze moving over my body, then back into my eyes.

"Convince me," he said, his voice a bit husky.

"I *need* you," I said, thinking of reasons. "I may see you only two or three times over a week but I want you *every* day and—"

He placed a finger over my lips. "I didn't mean with *words*..."

I smiled. He was giving in. I crawled up a little bit closer to him, my arms around his neck, my groin pressed against his. I kissed him, starting off softly and then deepening the kiss, my tongue finding his. He was totally passive. I ground myself against him, pressing my breasts against his chest. Then, I pulled my sweater up and off my body so that I was in my bra, my skirt and of course, my garter belt and nylons. I rose up onto my knees and embraced his head, my breasts against his face. I pulled the fabric of my bra down to expose my breasts the way he always did, then I squeezed them, tweaking my own nipples until they were hard. I closed my eyes, wanting him to suck them, but not feeling right demanding it from him, so I just imagined it while I touched myself.

Finally, he reached behind me with his good hand.

"Let me help you with that." Then, he pulled me closer, his mouth covering one nipple. After that, he pretty much kept one step ahead of me, always turning whatever I did into something he ultimately controlled. When I climbed on top of him as he lay naked on the bed, he subtly directed me, telling me where to put my hands, how fast to move, when to kiss him. But I had my way with him. He didn't tie me up, he didn't blindfold me, he didn't make me come four times before *he* did.

I came once and then he did, fucking me from behind doggie style, which didn't rely on his hand for anything.

I didn't call him *Master* once.

Afterwards, as we lay there with our limbs entwined, the sheets wrapped up around us, I turned to him.

"You survived vanilla sex yet again."

He grinned. "It's all I ever used to do."

I said nothing for a moment, wondering about his introduction to the lifestyle. "How did you start doing BDSM?"

He rubbed my back with his good hand, not saying anything.

"You don't want to talk about it?"

"Not really. Let's just say I recognized my Dominant side, got some instruction—"

"From Lara," I offered.

"From Lara," he said.

"This was after your divorce?"

"Kate," he said, exhaling. "I'm tired. I have to sleep..."

"I'm sorry," I said, a stab of hurt in my chest. "This is hard for you. We're mixing up the food on your plate too much, right?"

"Shh," he said and shut the light off. Then he pulled closer, spooning against me the way he always did when it was time to sleep.

In the middle of the night, I got up and went to the bathroom. I closed the door and turned on the light to check my wound and my eye was already bruising. I was going to have a black eye.

I turned off the bathroom light and went back to the bedroom. Drake was asleep, his breathing slow and deep. Seeing him lying there, knowing that he was so uncomfortable with a normal romantic relationship, I felt a sense of grief somewhere in a dark corner.

I wanted more from him, but I had the sense that it was impossible. I'd have to settle for what he could give me. I'd have to accept only seeing him in secret several times a week, when we were lucky. It made me sad, but it was just the way things had to be.

I didn't want to stay there feeling the way I felt, so I dressed quickly and snuck out of the apartment. I hailed a cab and went back to my own apartment. I couldn't pretend to be 'in scene' with him after that. It felt too much like 'pretending'.

So, at just after three o'clock in the morning on Christmas Eve Day, I was getting out of a taxi outside my apartment building when who should get out of a parked car but Dawn.

"There you are," she said, rushing across the street to me as I had the key in the lock to the building. When I realized it was her, shock went through me.

"*Dawn*," I said, acutely aware of my bandaged head and now-bruising black eye. "What are you doing here?"

"Your father was trying to get a hold of you but you weren't answering your phone. He was worried about you and called me at work. I was so *worried* about you."

I pulled out my cell, curious as to why I never got any calls. Then I saw that my cell had shut off, the battery dead. "Oh crap," I said showing her. "The battery died." I shrugged.

Then she saw my injury.

"Kate, what *happened?*"

"I fell," I said, stumbling to come up with an explanation on the fly. "I had to go to the hospital and get stitches."

"Oh you poor kid. How did you fall?"

"I slipped on the way to the bathroom in the dark."

She saw my wristband from the hospital ER and took my wrist in her hand. "St. Luke's? Why didn't you *call* me? You should have come to Harlem and I would have stayed with you."

"We're not really on friendly terms..." I said and sighed. "Listen, I'm really tired. I'm going to bed."

I opened the door and before it closed, I turned. I didn't want to antagonize her.

"I'm sorry I didn't answer your calls. I didn't even *know* you had called. Why are you even here? You've just been sitting in your car?"

"I got off my shift at 3:00 and thought I'd come by and see if you were at home. I was almost ready to call the police. Kate, how are you doing?"

"I'm fine," I said. "I'm over it. Look," I said, wanting to leave. "I have to go to bed. Thanks for being concerned about me but I'm fine. I'll charge my phone and send my dad a text."

I forced a smile and went inside, leaving her on the sidewalk. I just couldn't lie to her any longer.

Crap. Almost caught.

I didn't sleep the rest of the night, wondering if Dawn would accept my explanation and what Drake would say when he learned I was almost caught. Instead of sleep, I looked over an article I was writing for *Geist* but in truth, my heart just wasn't into it. That black hole of sadness threatened at the thought that Drake and I wouldn't be able to spend time together during Christmas, except for a few hours where we might be able to fuck. I enjoyed my time with him – more than I thought I ever could, but I felt as if something was missing. Tonight, Drake's reluctance to just be with me as an ordinary couple having vanilla sex made me sad in a way I didn't think I'd feel so soon.

I had to face it. He was the hottest man I had ever met or could imagine. I never thought I'd have as many orgasms as I'd had with him. I never thought I could get so deeply into bondage and D/s. But if he'd hoped to keep our personal lives separate from the kinky sex, he'd failed miserably.

I knew too much about him. He was too human to me and not just a mysterious and very hot Dominant. He was someone I really liked.

Regardless, I couldn't have him that way. With another man, I might be able to have those things – going out for Sunday brunch, going to movies, spending time together with family and friends. Living a vanilla lifestyle. I knew I'd never feel with another man in a vanilla relationship what I felt with Drake.

Given a choice, at that point, I chose Drake. There was no hesitation. But I still felt this mote of sadness somewhere deep in my chest. A sense of loss.

I sighed and pushed it back into its dark dusty corner, ignoring it for as long as possible.

CHAPTER TWENTY-THREE

Once my phone charged, it blinked on and showed that I had ten text messages and five voice mail messages. I yawned and picked it up, checking to see what my father and Dawn had sent. I just finished taking a shower, a towel wrapped around my body and my head.

My father had texted me first, wanting to know how I was doing. When I didn't answer as I usually did, he called and left a message.

Katie, is everything OK? Call me. I know you're still upset about Drake. If you need to talk...

He called me *Katie*. He must really be worried about me. Once again, it struck me how strange that my father, *the Drill Sergeant*, wanted to talk to me about a breakup.

Then Dawn called and asked where I was.

Your father's worried about you. I'm worried about you. Why aren't you answering?

She texted me three times, each one more frantic. At 3:05 a.m., just before I arrived, she sent a final text.

Do I have to call the police to come break down your door? Where are you?

Crap. I was that close to her doing so. Luckily, she only came to my apartment, waiting outside.

I sent a text to my father, hoping he got it first thing and wasn't worried. He seemed to calm down long before Dawn did. His last voice mail at midnight was far less anxious.

Just give me a call, dear, when you get this message.

That was it. Drake and I would have to be more careful. Dawn was suspicious. She was willing to wait outside my apartment... Was she hoping to catch me with Drake?

At about 5:30, while I was sitting on the couch, watching CNN, my phone dinged, indicating a new text.

Drake.

Why did you leave?

I looked at the message for a few moments, trying to compose a response in my mind.

I couldn't sleep. You were sleeping like a baby. I didn't want to wake you up so I just left.

In a few moments, he replied.

> *You can always wake me up. I wanted you to stay with me so I could watch over you, make sure you're all right. Kate, I'm a neurosurgeon. We get concerned with any kind of head injury. You should have stayed until I said you were OK to go home. Do you have a headache? Nausea?*

Poor Drake. He really was worried. He must be angry with himself over the fall and my injury.

I'm fine. My mind just won't slow down. I have a deadline and am working on my article.

In a few seconds, he responded.

> *You think too much. When you're with me, you don't have to think. That's what I'm for. But I suspect something's bothering you for you to leave without saying anything. Tell me what's the matter...*

I sighed. Of course, something was bothering me. This *keep everything separate on the plate* requirement of his. I felt like he was leaking into my life, into my thoughts, and I wanted him in it. He didn't want me to mix in the separate compartments he kept for things. Kinky sex. Neurosurgery. The Foundation. The Band.

Drake, I still have to think, even when I'm with you. I still have to think when I'm not with you.

You want the truth?

He didn't respond for some time, as if deciding if he wanted it. Finally, he called. When I saw his name on the caller ID, my throat choked up. I ignored his call and texted him instead.

Drake, I don't like being shoved into a small box in the corner of your life.

He called again, but I ignored his call once more, my emotions too close to the surface. He replied to my text.

You're not in a small box in the corner. In case you didn't realize it, you're in a very big and very central box in the middle of my life.

That made my heart melt a bit, but still, it wasn't what I really wanted. If I was honest with myself, if I let my self really feel what I was feeling, I knew being in that box would never satisfy me.

I don't know if that's enough.

I bit my nail and waited for what he said to that, afraid that he'd break it off with me if I pushed things, but wanting to be completely truthful. He said that a Dom had to trust that his sub was being completely truthful and not just trying to please him by lying.

I'm coming over.

Oh, God. He *couldn't* come over.

Don't. It's too much of a risk.

When he didn't reply right away, I knew he was coming anyway. How many times would I have to run away from him for his own good?

I had to leave the apartment. I couldn't be here when he arrived. I dressed quickly, grabbed my bag and left through the rear of the building, taking the back alley, intending to walk to my one place of refuge when I'd been a student. The library at Columbia.

I walked down the street, wanting the air to try to calm myself. If he did come by my apartment and Dawn was there or had someone watching me, at least I wouldn't be there. I could write it off as Drake being unreasonable.

I texted him once more.

> *I'm not at my apartment any longer so don't come by. Don't risk it. We'll talk later. I just need to be alone for a while.*

He wouldn't give in.

> *Being alone is the last thing you need, Kate. Meet me at 8th this morning. My surgical slate is empty the rest of the week because of the holidays.*

I was just about to reconsider when Dawn texted me again.

> *I called my friend at St. Luke's. I know everything. The ER doc you met with thought you had been abused, Kate. WHAT IS WRONG WITH YOU? I'm calling your father.*

Oh, God...

I texted her back right away, my hands shaking. I had to stop this. I had to end this now.

Besides the fact that you and whoever gave you access to my personal records could get in big trouble, you should know that I'm ending it with Drake. I realized that I can never be anything to him besides a kinky sex partner. He's not into having a real relationship with a woman – no girlfriend, no dating, no romance, no marriage. I realize this now. That's why I was coming home so late, Dawn. He can't give me what I need. He's not what you think – he's a good man. He never hurt me <u>ever</u>. What happened was an accident when he was showing me how to Jitterbug. But he can't love me and I know that now. It's not enough for me.

So please, don't make this worse for me than it already is.

She phoned. I answered.

"Kate, what happened? Come and stay with me. I don't want you to be alone now."

"I can't," I said, in tears. "I'm as mad at you as I am sad about him. You shouldn't be interfering, Dawn. I know your heart is in the right place, but this is *my* life and my decision."

"I'm your best friend."

"You *were*. Best friends don't threaten. Now, please, *please* just let things die naturally. It's going to be hard enough for me without you threatening me."

I ended the call.

Drake had to know. I had to text him in case she didn't hold off.

Drake, this person knows that I was with you last night and thinks you've abused me. This person may tell my father no matter what I do. I just want to warn you. I told her we broke up. We <u>have</u> to just say

*goodbye for real, Drake. I can't take this any longer –
this compartmentalization of my life. This pretending
that we're not seeing each other, worrying that
someone will find out and hurt you. I don't do
compartmentalization, Drake. My life is a stew. I
don't know anything different. I've tried it your way,
but being just one part of your life isn't enough. The
truth is that I could love you if I let myself. I can't do
that because you don't do love. Lara told me that
before we met and you made that abundantly clear to
me.*

*You'll have no trouble finding another sub who wants
to be a compartment in your life but that's not me. I'd
only always want more and we'd have to end it,
eventually. The longer we wait, the harder it will be.
That night, you said that someone would love me one
day, and the truth is, despite how amazing the sex is
with you, I realize I'd rather wait to find him than
accept anything less. If you thought you could stop me
from falling in love with you, you failed miserably. I
can't accept what you can give. I deserve more.*

*Goodbye, Drake. I'm sorry, but this is the way it has to
be for both our sake's.*

I read it over and hesitated. I could see no other way out of
this. There was no way Dawn would accept that we'd broken
up without proof – not after the injury. She wouldn't believe
me no matter what and I feared that she was going to hurt
Drake for real.

I sent the text, my heart heavy, tears blurring my eyes. I
walked for blocks, wiping my face with my gloved hands,
unable to imagine not seeing Drake again.

Then, my phone dinged. Drake responded.

You do deserve more.

That was it. He didn't say I deserved more from him. He didn't say he could give me more. Just that simple statement, as if he recognized it, too. Finally, I sat on a bench that faced the park and cried.

My phone dinged, indicating an incoming text and it was my father.

> *Katie, come by and stay with me and Elaine for a while. You shouldn't be alone on Christmas Eve. Dawn just called and said she was worried about you and that I shouldn't allow you to stay by yourself. Let me send a car to pick you up. Come and stay with me until this thing with Drake blows over.*

I knew it was no use trying to go to the library when I was like this. My eyes were red and swollen from crying and in truth, I didn't feel at all like going there.

I'll come by later, Daddy. I prefer to walk.

The truth was, I couldn't face going to my apartment alone. I couldn't go to the library. I couldn't face work. Dawn's place was out of the question.

I called Lara.

"What's the matter now, Kate?" she said, her voice a bit impatient.

"Something happened. I just broke up with Drake but I'm afraid this person is going to hurt him no matter what I do."

She exhaled heavily on the phone.

"Meet me at the coffee shop. We'll talk."

By the time I arrived, my eyes were less red and she was waiting in the back for me. Her face betrayed her frustration or anger, I couldn't tell which.

I sat down, ordering some tea, and clasped my hands in front of me.

"My God, Kate," she said when she saw my injury. "What happened? Drake didn't do that, did he?"

"Lara, you won't believe it."

"Tell me what happened. I texted Drake but he didn't respond."

I sighed and recounted how we fell and I hurt myself. How he took me to the ER and how Dawn found me, and discovered that I went to the ER with Drake.

How I had to break it off with Drake because Dawn was hell-bent on telling my father.

"What is it with this person? Why do they want to hurt Drake?"

I shook my head. "She saw her own sister abused." I told her about Dawn's family and how dysfunctional it was when she was growing up. "I think she judges everyone really harshly because she was judged harshly. She has no tolerance."

Then Lara's phone dinged and she picked it up, read something.

"Just a minute," she said, typing away on her keyboard. Finally, she put the phone on the table between us.

"You were saying? You broke up with Drake? Why? I thought you said things were good."

I shook my head. "The sex part was great. Better than anything I could ever imagine, Lara. This is just too much risk for Drake. I could never stand to live with myself if he was hurt because of me, because of my greed for him. But even more, I just can't do only sex. I'm not cut out for it. He doesn't want more. Considering all the shit he could get into because of me, I had to just make a clean break."

"It's probably for the best."

"You understand," I said, but my chest hurt. I covered my eyes, biting back a sob.

"I *do* understand," she said and took my hand. "This is my fault. The reason I chose Drake for you was precisely because he *wasn't* interested in anything long-term. I thought that was what you wanted as well. You know, just doing interviews, learning about the lifestyle. That's what you said to me..."

"I *know* I did," I said, feeling incredibly guilty. "I *did* say that. I meant it at the time. But Drake is so much *more*..." I closed my eyes, exhaling heavily. "I think I could fall in love with him. All I know is that it isn't enough anymore."

She nodded. "Nothing like a new Dom to wash away the taste of the old one. Listen, I can hook you up with a Dom who's looking for a life partner, if you'd like. Not every Dom is like Drake. Some *want* a relationship. Why don't you come to a fetish night with me? You could come under my protection and I could introduce you to a few Doms I know. Only the ones who are looking for a relationship beyond play. I already have someone in mind. His name is Steve. He's closer to your age. He's even in the arts – he does copy editing for a publisher. He's kinkier than Drake, but not a sadist. I know you're not into pain."

"I can't meet with anyone else, Lara. I can't even *think* of it."

"You were alone for what – a *year* before Drake? Don't you want someone else?"

I shook my head. "I want *Drake*. I can't have him. Not the way I really want him."

"Well, I offered. I still think you should come to a fetish night with me. There are lifestyle partners and there are lifetime partners. It is possible to meet someone who wants D/s and a real relationship. You won't find another man who will satisfy your submissive side outside of the lifestyle, Kate."

I forced a smile, wiping my eyes, acutely aware of other patrons watching me. "Maybe I'll just go with my friend to India and become a nun, working at Mother Theresa's hospice."

"Yeah, *sure* Kate," Lara said, smiling back at me, shaking her head. "If you liked Drake as much as you claim, you'll never be able to go back to normal again."

"That's hopeful."

"Look, it's hard enough to find compatible lifestyle partners, let alone someone who you could be with in a permanent relationship. If that's what you really want, you have to get out there and meet people."

I shook my head. "It's too soon. I can't imagine it. I only want Drake."

"When you're ready, just let me know."

We finished our drinks and parted ways.

I walked the rest of the way to my father's. When I got there, I ran up the stairs to his apartment instead of taking the elevator. He must have heard me close the front door because he emerged from the hallway to his study, his half-eye glasses on the end of his nose, a paper in his hand.

"Katie, what on earth happened to you? My God – your eye..."

"I fell in the bathroom, Daddy. I'm fine."

"Come here. Give your old man a hug. You look like you need one."

I threw my bag and coat on the floor and went to him, hugging him, my tears starting fresh.

"There, *there*," he said, his gravelly voice soft, squeezing me in a bear hug. "You'll stay with us over Christmas and New Year's. You shouldn't be alone now."

I didn't argue.

CHAPTER TWENTY-FOUR

I didn't even go back to my apartment.

My father sent the driver over with Elaine and they went in and retrieved my things from my apartment, my laptop and a few items from my closet plus the presents I'd bought but hadn't wrapped. I'd wrap them later.

We went to Midnight Mass, and I managed to have a shower and look somewhat presentable, although the choir singing "*O Magnum Mysterium*" by Morten Lauridsen made me cry, of course, and my tears at the beautiful music morphed into tears for myself and for the loss I felt for Drake.

On Christmas morning, I realized that breaking it off with Drake was the right thing to do. We *should* have been together on Christmas morning, exchanging gifts, spending the day together, having Christmas dinner together. I should have been with him the entire time. He had no surgeries. His band played a few gigs over the holidays but he'd hurt his hand and wasn't playing. He had the rest of the vacation to spend as he chose. Instead, we couldn't be together except for a few hours here and there when I could find an excuse to sneak away. And then, it would be just to fuck.

That was no life. That was no relationship.

Still, I cried myself to sleep each night and each day, I forced myself to get up and go through the motions. I wore Elaine's slippers, an old pair of pajamas, and my hair in a messy ponytail, doing little else than mope around, watching old movies, and eating ice cream directly from the container.

My father let me mope, but he was there as company when I felt like it, and when I didn't, he left me to my own devices. As New Years approached, I dreaded the day. My father was having a dinner party with his 'people' and I would be expected to dress up and greet them, sit with him and Elaine. Then, he and Elaine had tickets to a fancy party to ring in the New Year. Heath and Christie would join them, but I bowed out.

On New Year's Eve Day, I checked the guest list. As I stood in the kitchen, my father came up behind me and glanced over my shoulder.

"Drake isn't on the list," he said. "I didn't think you'd want to see him, but I felt incredibly bad. He's like a son to me and I would have invited him if it wasn't for your breakup."

"I'm sorry Dad. I could always just spend the evening at my apartment if you want to invite him."

"Too late," he said. "Besides, you belong with me. Did you know he's leaving NY Presbyterian for a year? Can you believe it?"

"What?" A shock of adrenaline went through me, making my knees weak.

"Yes, I called over to speak with him, see how he was doing, and he said he'd cleared his slate and had a definite leave of absence. He's spending four months in Africa, teaching and doing Foundation work in Kenya. Going to see where his dad died, helping fix up a few hospitals in the area. Then he's coming back to focus on the Foundation. His band."

"How did he seem?" I asked, my throat choked with emotion.

"Who can say? He seemed to be busy making plans." My father looked at his watch. "Well, I've got a conference call. Seems as though this campaign stuff goes on no matter that it's New Year's Eve."

He kissed my cheek and left me alone in the kitchen.

I went to my room and laid on my bed, devastated that Drake felt he had to leave NY Presbyterian over this. It was *my* fault. I *never* should have agreed to see him again. That day when I sat in the storefront window and he texted me from across the street, I should have just let him go.

Elaine popped her head in the doorway.

"Katie? Are you OK?"

I rolled over away from the door. "No, I'm not."

She came in, closing the door behind her. She sat on the bed beside me and took my hand.

"What's the matter, Kate. Tell me. Is it Drake? Your father told me that he was leaving for Africa in a few days."

I nodded and then covered my face with my hands, unable to stop my tears.

She bent down and put her arms around my shoulders. "There, there... I thought you would be sad. You two seemed to be really good together. His eyes seemed so bright when he was with you in the Bahamas. I just can't believe you two broke up. What happened?"

"I had to break up with him," I said to her. "He isn't interested in anything long term, just casual. I knew that when we started out, but I fell in love with him, Elaine. There's just so much more to him than I ever thought was possible. He loves music, he is so good hearted, he's so strong and warm and smart. But I need more than he can give."

"Aw, sweetheart," she said and pulled me into her arms. "It's OK. These things have a way of working out for the best." She hugged me and just let me cry. How I wished my mother was here to comfort me, but she wasn't. I hugged Elaine tighter.

We sat like that for a while and she stroked my hair, murmured in my ear and soon, I regained control over myself.

"Have a bath and put a cold compress on your eyes. We'll have a nice dinner. I wish you would come with us to the dance, but I understand if you decide to stay here."

She left me on the bed and I lay there, deciding what I should do.

I didn't have Drake any more. I didn't have Dawn. I didn't have my own mother. I felt incredibly sorry for myself.

I slept the afternoon away, hiding from the world under the covers of my childhood bed.

Later, before dinner, I did what Elaine suggested. There was no good reason to make my father upset so I had a bath, put a cold washcloth over my eyes, and did the best I could to look presentable, wearing that dress I wore the night I attended my father's first campaign dinner. No amount of makeup could disguise my bloodshot black eye so I decided to carry a tissue around and plead allergies if anyone asked me. I prepared a story about falling in the bathtub for when people asked about my stitches.

Finally, the time came for guests to start arriving. I went to the bar and looked for something to drink, needing alcohol to take away my sadness. The bartender was gone to the kitchen for ice, and so I bent down and checked the bar. There was every kind of scotch, some bourbon, gin, but my dad kept the vodka cold. I opened the small bar fridge under the counter for some vodka and cold soda. In the back of the fridge was a bottle with a label I recognized from Drake's apartment. *Anisovaya.* On a small label attached to the bottle was a note in Drake's handwriting:

"To my second father, Happy New Year, my best regards, Drake"

I picked it up and when I stood, I glanced up, thinking the bartender was back only to be looking into the clear blue eyes of Drake Morgan.

Devastatingly handsome Drake Morgan, MD. Neurosurgeon on leave from NY Presbyterian, bass player, philanthropist, Dominant. Wearing a beautiful dark grey suit with a white shirt and black tie, hands behind his back, a half-smile on his face.

He brought his hands forward and in them were the two crystal shot glasses that were rumored to have once belonged to Yelena Kuznetzova, Stalin's housekeeper at his dacha in Soviet Georgia.

"I brought these along just in case you didn't have anything quite so special."

He placed them on the bar and smiled at me.

I put the bottle on the counter and stepped back, leaning against the wall, a bit dizzy as the blood drained from my face. I closed my eyes, taking in a deep breath. He came behind the bar and took me in his arms, practically holding me up because my knees went wobbly.

He took my chin in his hand and I opened my eyes, barely able to see him through my tears.

"Drake, you can't *do* this to me," I said, biting back a sob. "This is cruel."

"You're the one who left. You can't do this to *me*." Then he kissed me, his arms squeezing me against him and I could do nothing to stop him, he was so strong and determined. When he pulled away, he held my face in his hands, wiping my tears away with his fingers.

"Why are you here?" I said, my voice a whisper, barely able to speak. "You're leaving. I don't want to see you..."

"Your father called me and told me you'd be here tonight. That if I was going away, I should come over and say goodbye."

"This is torture."

He smiled as if nothing was wrong. "Kate, your father knows. He gave me a dressing down, telling me that he already knew about the restraining order. About my 'proclivities' as he called them. He's known all along."

"He *knows?*"

Drake nodded. "He's been watching me for years, monitoring me for my father. He knew about the restraining order. He knew about the BDSM through Nigel."

He led me to the couch in the living room and sat with his arm around me, touching my bottom lip, brushing a strand of hair off my cheek.

"He and Nigel go back a long way. I guess Nigel faced some blackmail over his sexuality years ago when your dad was still a defense lawyer and your dad advised him. Nigel told him about me after he saw me at a Fetish night."

"That's why Nigel was looking at you that way the night of my father's campaign fundraiser..."

"Yeah, he told me that I had better not ever hurt you or he'd have my balls. I had no idea he'd told your father."

"My father *knows* you're a Dom?"

Drake laughed ruefully. "Who would ever have believed it? He knows even more about me than my own dad did."

"And he *approved* of you as my boyfriend..." I shook my head. "I don't understand. I thought he'd be horrified."

"So did I but I guess not. He said," and Drake put on a mock voice that sounded gravelly like my father, "*For some reason I can't think of off the top of my head, Kate seems to have a preference for a dominant man and you're a helluva lot better than some jackass who doesn't know what the Sam hell he's doing, like that flyboy she had the sense to get rid of.*"

I covered my mouth to stifle a sob, tears filling my eyes.

"He said *that?*"

"His *exact* words."

I closed my eyes and leaned against him, but even though I was relieved that my father was so accepting of this, Drake was *leaving.*

"But you left NY Presbyterian. You're going to Africa..."

He pulled back and looked in my eyes. "I figured that if I did, I could lay low for a year and return when all this blows

S. E. Lund

over. I talked to the head of the College and we agreed that I'd take a year leave of absence. I've been meaning to go to Africa and do a longer stint. Teach a class at the College in Nairobi."

I shook my head, a feeling building in me that I couldn't identify.

"So you came to say goodbye."

He took my face in his hands again. "I *came*," he said, taking in a deep breath, "to say that I've developed a taste for potatoes and gravy and meat all on the same fork." He stared into my eyes, his expression so earnest, his brow furrowed. "Lara played a recording of you telling her you thought you could love me. She even tried to entice you to meet another Dom and you refused, saying you wanted me. That *almost* made me reconsider leaving, but *could* isn't *does*." He moved closer, his eyes so intense. "When Elaine called me this afternoon and told me that you said you *had* fallen in love with me, I realized that I would never meet anyone like you again in my life. So perfect for me in every way. And I think I'm good for you, too. I think I could make you happy."

He leaned down and kissed me tenderly.

"I couldn't stand it. I couldn't lose you. So I came over and spoke with your father while you were sleeping, perfectly willing to accept what ever he said I should do. He admitted to knowing about me all this time and said that if I had feelings for you, I shouldn't leave without telling you. Then, he sent me home to change and I came back as quickly as I could so we could talk and I could confess my feelings for you."

I bit my lip to control my emotions.

"Ms. Bennet," he said and shook his head, his eyes searching mine. "Kate, I *love* you. I never, *ever* want to be separated from you again."

Emotion built in me, my vision blurring. I couldn't speak.

"Kate," he said, his smile indulgent. "Your face is getting red. You should *breathe* now."

I burst out crying at that, covering my face with my hands, and he just wrapped his arms around me, cradling me, my face in the crook of his neck. He pulled a handkerchief out of a pocket and gave it to me so I could mop up my eyes, rocking me back and forth. Then he tilted my head up and kissed me.

"But you're leaving..." I said when he pulled away.

"I want you to come with me."

I shook my head. "Africa was so hard for me."

He brushed hair off my cheek. "Not where we'll be. Kenya is so beautiful, Kate. Where I'll work, it's so full of hope and promise. You'll love it. The wildlife is spectacular. You could work on your art, your photography, write..."

"I haven't finished my MA."

"You can take a leave of absence. When we come back, you could finish it."

"What would I go as? Your submissive?"

"As my *love*. As the woman I can't live without. And, when we wanted it, and needed it, as my submissive."

I sighed, my eyes still brimming, and leaned against him, my face in the crook of his neck, his cologne filling my nose, his warmth, his strength, soothing me.

When a guest arrived at the front door, Drake took my hand and led me to the bathroom, closing the door behind us. He made me sit on the vanity while he rifled through the drawers in search of a washcloth, which he ran under cold water. Then, he held it to my eyes and leaned against me, his gaze so comforting – his eyes so tender. Only less than two months ago, I could barely bring myself to look in his eyes, but now, I wanted to look in them.

I was surprised at what a caregiver he was, thinking that surgeons were usually a bit distant but that was the story of our relationship – from that first night at the bar when he saved me from a fall, to the fundraiser when he tended my wounds, to the concert when he wiped my tears, to the Bahamas when he cut me out of the wetsuit and applied aloe vera to my burns, to the ER when he bandaged me up.

I just let him look after me, my happiness almost too much to bear, bringing more tears to my eyes. I had to breathe in deeply to calm myself.

Finally, I was able to regain control and let him wipe my face. I reapplied some makeup while he watched.

"You don't have to stay with me for this," I said and I applied foundation to cover up my red nose.

"I forgot how much I love watching a woman dress and put on her face. It's so intimate."

"You used to like it?"

He smiled, his smile a bit wistful. "When I was married."

I said nothing, even though I wanted to hear more about his marriage. I didn't want to push him to talk about what was such a painful memory.

But he seemed to want to tell me. While I applied my mascara, he sat on the edge of the bathtub and watched me in the mirror.

"I used to watch her in the morning before she went to work."

"What did she do?"

"A nurse – of course. Who else do doctors spend so much time with? We worked together at NYP. If the nurses have a bad opinion of me, it's because of the divorce. It split them into two camps – those who still liked me and those who hated me because of the split."

"Sorry to hear that. It's hard to stay neutral in a divorce."

I applied a bit of lip gloss and then I turned around, leaning against the vanity and watched him. He seemed to want to keep talking.

"I thought I'd never make the same mistake as my father, but I made every single one. He neglected my mother, he was so busy with his business and with his charity and his music, she finally gave up and left him."

"She didn't keep in contact with you?"

He shook his head. "My dad won custody. He had a really great *lawyer*..."

"Who?" I said, my eyes widening. "My father?"

He nodded. "Yep. Your father was working in Family Court then and advised my dad. My dad was just really starting to make money and was able to hire nannies and housekeepers to look after me. The judge thought I'd have a better life with my dad even if it meant I was kept away from my mother. She left and went back to California where her family was, remarried and that was it. My father never remarried."

"I'm so sorry, Drake. To grow up without a mother..."

He shrugged. "It explains a lot, really."

I nodded, not saying anything else.

Then he stood up and came to me, putting his arms around me. "But I've learned the hard way. Now, enough reminiscing. I want to have a nice evening with you now that we can. Your father wants us to come out with him to dance, but I pointed to my arm and used it as an excuse. I said I wanted to bring in the New Year with you alone. He thought that was probably a better idea, considering..."

"I can't believe he accepted that you're into BDSM..."

Drake shook his head, smiling. "He said *I don't care what bedroom games people play in the privacy of their own homes for God's sake. I've played a few of my own. You have to in order to keep a marriage alive and I was married to the same woman for twenty one years...*"

"Bedroom games," I said, smiling. I closed my eyes and leaned against Drake, my arms slipping around his waist. "Do you suppose he's a bit of a Dom himself?"

"I wonder..." Drake said. "Sly old bastard if so. Still, it must be hard for a father to think of his beloved daughter being sexual."

"And vice versa. But, as long as he thinks of it as bedroom games, that's OK by me."

"Seriously, Kate, I'm pretty tame when it comes to Doms. A lightweight. He said he did his research."

"You're just right for me."

He smiled at that. "I think so."

"I *know* so."

He kissed me and all the tender emotions quickly turned to ones more passionate, his hands slipping down to the hem of my dress to search for garters, which I hadn't worn.

"No garters?"

"I was too sad to wear them."

"Do you have them here?"

I nodded, a smile starting on my face.

"Go put them on with nothing on underneath."

"Are you serious? At my parent's New Year's Eve dinner?"

"*Please*," he said, grinning. "I didn't get a present from you and I'm feeling all deprived. Consider it your present to me."

I left the bathroom and went to my bedroom where my bag was on the dresser. Inside were the garter belt and nylons I'd worn the last time I saw him. While he waited in the living room, I slipped off my undies and pantyhose and put on the garter belt and nylons. I took in a deep breath, knowing that just wearing them alone would make me aroused.

I went out to the living room where he stood by the bar talking to the bartender, who was pouring some Anisovaya into Yelena Kuznetsova's shot glasses. Drake took them and turned to me, and when he saw me, his face just brightened, then a leer started on his face, his mouth turning up into a half-grin.

He came to me where I stood by the fireplace and handed me one of the glasses, with the delicate filigree pattern etched onto the crystal.

"Za vas, *moya lyubov*," he said. "To you, *my love*."

I couldn't repeat it because of emotion, covering my mouth with my hand, smiling through tears.

We shot the Anisovaya back and I grimaced, although I had come to associate the taste with pleasure.

He leaned in and kissed me immediately, and I could taste the anise on his lips and tongue.

"With you looking like that," he said, stepping back to examine me up and down. "Knowing what's underneath that dress? I don't know if I can wait until later. We may have to sneak off in between courses for a quickie."

Heat rose in my cheeks at that, warmth between my thighs.

"You haven't given me a present yet either," I said a grin spreading on my own face. "Maybe you could use me the way I've always wanted — a fast fuck in the broom closet that leaves me panting, in need of you. Later, you could take your time and satisfy me... Maybe pour some of that Anisovaya over me and lick it off..."

He pulled me against him. "You *are* a kinky little thing, Ms. Bennet. You're going to make me very uncomfortable if you keep up with that teasing mind of yours and I'll be embarrassed in front of your father's guests because of the tent in my pants. But maybe later, after dessert when there's a lull in things before we get into liqueurs, I'll tug at my ear and you'll go into the bathroom off your bedroom and wait for me. I may just have a nice *big* present for you..."

I closed my eyes, a thrill going through my body thinking of it.

Somehow, we made it through the cocktails and chat before dinner, my father's huge smile and boisterous gravelly voice clearly indicating he was happy to see us standing together, one of Drake's hands on the small of my back. Drake never left my side, and together, we talked to whoever came by to greet us.

Nigel arrived and I was surprised to see him with his partner, Brian. Short, well-dressed with impeccable taste, Brian was barely up to Nigel's shoulder. I turned to see my father and wondered how he'd respond. He smiled and shook Brian's hand and that was it. He was accepted into the inner circle. Nigel spied us and came right over, introducing Brian to Drake and me. After we said our hellos, Elaine came by and pulled Brian away for a moment to show him some artwork.

Nigel leaned in to me.

"So I see your father's matchmaking succeeded."

I smiled. "I tried to fight it, Nigel, but you know my father. He has to have his way."

Nigel laughed. "Yes. That he does." Nigel laid a hand on Drake's shoulder. "I already had my little talk with Drake about you so I won't say anything more."

Drake smiled, but I could tell there was still something between them.

"Quit being my big brother, Nigel," I said, pointing a finger at him.

"Someone has to be. Heath seems too busy with his own children."

Then Nigel leaned down and kissed me on the cheek. "Happy New Year, Kate."

I squeezed his hand and watched him walk over to where Brian and Elaine stood, admiring a piece of art.

I sighed and turned to Drake, who put his arm around my shoulder.

"What did he say to you that night?"

"He just told me if I ever hurt a hair on your head, he'd have me thrashed soundly."

I laughed at that and Drake grinned.

Mostly, we spoke to each other, him leaning down to whisper in my ear, telling me what he wanted to do to me if we did get a chance to go to the bathroom later.

"Ms. Bennet, I want to slip my hand down under your dress and feel you. Are you already wet for me? I bet you are, you *vixen...*"

"Shh, *Drake*," I said, my cheeks heating, unable to keep a smile off my face.

At dinner, we sat in the same places as before, but this time, I kept slightly turned to Drake, barely able to keep my eyes off him or a smile off my face. My stomach was all butterflies as we ate our meal, and I wondered if he would do it – tug his ear and signal that I was to go to my bathroom and wait for him.

Finally, once dinner was over and the servers took away our dessert plates, my father announced that we'd take our after dinner drinks in the living room. As my father spoke to Drake about something to do with the dance afterwards, Drake tugged his ear. I glanced away quickly, my body responding.

He was going to go through with it.

I stood up. "Please excuse me."

I left the dining room just as people started to filter out and make their way to the living room. I slipped to my bedroom and into the bathroom, breathing deeply, wondering how long it would take for him to escape. In a couple of minutes, he opened the door and came inside, closing the door and leaning against it.

"I have something for you, Ms. *Bennet*."

"You do?" My face was hot, butterflies in my stomach.

"In my pants. Come and see for yourself. I need you to take it out. It's very uncomfortable."

I went to him and opened his suit jacket, then ran my fingers over his groin. Something hard protruded from it but it didn't seem the right shape. I opened his fly and reached in only to find a long black velvet case.

A jewelry case.

"*Drake...*"

I opened it to find a velvet choker with a pendant attached. A single teardrop diamond in a white-gold setting. It must have been several carats in weight.

"I had it made specially for you back before all this happened. I thought a black velvet choker would substitute pretty well for your leather collar and would be more appropriate to wear at special events like tonight." He went behind me and slipped the choker around my neck, fastening it, his eyes meeting mine in the mirror.

I covered my mouth, tears once more springing to my eyes.

He remained behind me, adjusted the choker so that the diamond fell in the hollow at the base of my throat, watching in the mirror.

"*Beautiful...*" he whispered in my ear, his breath warm on my skin. Then, he pushed me forward so that I leaned over the vanity facing the mirror. He lifted up my dress, groaning when his hands slid over the garters, and he gave me my Christmas present.

He *tried* to give it to me just the way I asked.

He really tried but he couldn't stand not seeing me fulfilled as well.

CHAPTER TWENTY-FIVE

Packing up my apartment was harder than I thought. I'd been there since I left the dormitory in my senior year and although it was tiny and had little closet space, I had amassed a lot of stuff. It took a week just to go through everything and sort it into send, store, donate or junk. Most of it was in the store category. I wasn't going to take very much with me. Having lived in Africa briefly, I knew a lot of extra baggage was a burden rather than of benefit.

Besides, when you lived in an impoverished land where people survived on very little, having a lot of superfluous stuff was disrespectful.

The very last things to go through were my pieces of art, the ones I did and those of friends and fellow art students.

I held up a framed photograph of Dawn taken when she was in India at the hospice run by Mother Theresa's nuns. She wore traditional dress of the region, a shawl over her head, and a Sari. She stood with a nun and smiled at the camera. I would keep this, despite the fact that the two of us had not mended our fences. I tried, explaining how I felt, that my father already knew, and how Drake was leaving NYP for a year and that his boss knew about the restraining order.

"You can't hurt him," I said. "All you can do is hurt our friendship. Is that what you want?"

She hung up on me. I called back, wanting to force her to listen, but she wouldn't answer. Finally, I phoned her sister, Brenda, whose number I had on my contact list from when

Dawn had stayed with her for a while after her wedding. We spoke about our friendship breaking up, about Dawn's fears for me. Brenda explained how her first relationship had been abusive and how the much younger Dawn had witnessed the abuse.

"I can understand her being worried about you, Kate. She's very stubborn and fixed in her thinking. She hasn't really forgiven me yet for putting her through that."

"She never said anything," I said, trying to think back to our conversations from right after we first met in college. "I knew she didn't like your boyfriend."

"She went pretty religious afterwards," Brenda said. "Well, as religious as she felt was necessary. Give her time."

We said our goodbyes after I asked her to try to explain things to Dawn. She thought it was highly unlikely to work.

Everything seemed to find its place in my life except for Dawn, and that left a hole in my heart that I knew time would never heal.

I sorted through my artwork, taking down the framed pictures and stacking them against the wall. Drake stood at the sound system, hooking his iPhone into it, selecting a song to play.

Something soft came on, and it wasn't his usual sixties music.

"What's this?" I said, liking its somber tone.

"*Please Don't Go* by Barcelona."

I listened for a moment. "Sounds awfully sad for you."

"I listened to this a lot during those days between Christmas and New Years."

I smiled, amazed that he admitted that. I turned back to the pictures and started to sort through them. He came and stood beside me.

"I want to keep all of these, but none of them have to come with us."

"I want this one to come," Drake said. He stood and examined my pencil drawing of the knight and his lady.

"You like that one?"

He nodded. "That was me when you met me."

"Really?" I remembered that first time he was in my apartment. "I thought you said it was about me and how I couldn't have sex without intimacy because I wanted to feel like a good girl."

He shook his head and pulled me against him, his arms slipping around my waist.

"I can rationalize anything," he said and kissed my neck. "I was trying so hard to keep everything separated, my emotions under control."

I took his hands in mine. "Why? I don't understand. I *want* to fall in love. It's a loveless relationship I couldn't imagine."

"When my marriage failed and I was given that restraining order, it was as if I had failed as a man." He was silent for a moment as if considering. "Kate, I was like Flyboy. I was the asshole who didn't know what I was doing. I had to face up to who and what I was. I had to keep myself under complete control. Whatever the reason, I tried to keep you under control, confined to one spot, my emotions restrained. Luckily, I failed miserably."

"I thought you had me quite well under control. I submitted completely and willingly. If it hadn't been for Dawn, you might have had your wish. She kind of forced things."

"Like I said, luckily."

"Do you really feel that way? If she hadn't, we might have been happy in a simple D/s relationship and none of this would have happened."

"I was already in love with you. Just in denial."

"Already?"

He kissed my neck, his hands moving up under my left breast, as if to feel my apical pulse.

"I think I fell in love with you at the concert. No, I *know* I fell in love with you then."

I turned around in his arms, my hands on his chest. I wanted to look in his eyes.

"Why the concert? That was so soon after we met. You hardly knew me."

He shook his head slowly. "You don't understand. I'd heard your father speak about you for years. Katherine the beautiful, the brilliant, the humanitarian, the sweetheart who cried when she listened to music."

"He told you that? You knew that when we went to the concert?"

He nodded, a sheepish grin on his face. "That's why I had to be there with you."

"But you left when I asked you to."

"Yes, but I hid and watched you. I had to see you, see if what he said was true."

I turned back around, still in his arms, and stared at the drawing. It was as if Drake *wanted* to fall in love with me.

"I asked someone who met you what you looked like," Drake said as we examined the drawing. "He was sniffing around you, another hungry dog like me, and he said you had these huge green eyes and long dark hair. Fair skin like your late mother. How petite you were but with lush breasts and curvy hips. I think I was a bit in love with you before I even met you. I kept hoping your father would bring you to a function, but he never did, as if he was protecting you. I should have known it was you when I saw you in the hallway at your father's apartment, and then I was so close to you in the bedroom, but I was distracted by your garters."

I smiled. "Those garters were my undoing."

"No, it was the heels. The heels did it. They're responsible for everything, so as much as I hated Dawn, she made you wear them and I could kiss her for it. You bumped into me and practically fell into my arms at the bar because of them, and you did fall in the alley because of them, and then you were in my arms when I carried you to the bed. You were so lovely and desirable with your cut knees and ripped nylons, your scraped hands and those damn garters. It brought out the doctor in me and the Dom all at the same time. Even before I knew you were her, I was a goner. Not a chance in hell."

He nuzzled the back of my neck.

"Her?"

"The beloved *Katherine*. The daughter of my second father. He was so proud of you. But he would never bring you anywhere as if you were this princess who was too good for the rest of us. He was the kind of father I felt would never let a man anywhere near you unless he was top notch. I was so damn curious about you but you were like this mythic creature."

I inhaled, so amazed at how wrong I was about my father all those years. "I feel like such an idiot. I thought my father disapproved of me. That he thought I was a lightweight compared to Heath and that's why he never invited me to join him."

"He didn't invite you to join him because he was sensitive about your problems after Africa. He wanted to give you time. My father died soon after your return and that's when your father and I really started to be friends. When I asked about you, he said to me that a daughter embodied a father's hopes and dreams. He said he wished for you the kind of man he wanted to be to his own wife – someone who would love you forever, deeply, passionately, and be devoted to you, would allow you to be who you were, and respect you for it, but who would help bring out the best in you."

"That's so sweet," I said, my throat choking up.

"That's why I didn't ask you out after we met, despite wanting to. I didn't think I'd be able to be that man."

I turned around again and hugged him, my arms slipping around his waist.

He ran his hands over my hair. "He talked about your trip to Africa. He talked about your thesis. About your position at the school newspaper. I knew you'd be amazing before I ever met you. Like I said, a goner. And then I met you at the fundraiser and you were the girl with the luscious tits and garters and you were Katherine. I wanted to know you so badly. I wanted so badly to be with you despite knowing it was probably impossible for us to be together, given what I was. I thought your father would hate me if he knew..."

I smiled and ran my fingers through his hair. "He loves you like another son."

"And then," he said, pulling me closer. "Then a miracle happened and you were this little subbie, pretending to be a researcher who wanted to meet a Dom and learn about BDSM. You were this sweet little thing Lara wanted me to mentor because she thought you wanted this for real and I was the best teacher she knew. *God*, Kate... You can't understand how I felt when I saw you at the café and realized it was you."

"I was so mortified."

"I was *ecstatic*. There you were, this woman I'd always wondered about, this delicious little morsel of womanflesh I couldn't wait to eat, and you wanted a Dom. It was like I'd won the lottery. Found the pot of gold at the end of the rainbow."

My heart did a flip at that. "I felt like a silly girl in above her head, mortified that you knew I was interested in kink."

"I felt like the luckiest man alive. I knew I'd have the battle of my life with you, keeping things under control, but it was a battle I just couldn't turn away from, no matter what."

I just stared at him, amazed. "My dad talked about you, too. He used to talk about your father. Liam the crazy man, his best friend from 'Nam. A wild sonofabitch. A crazy idealistic socialist. He talked about Liam's son – this brilliant young neurosurgeon who spent time in Africa doing delicate surgeries for free. Donating hospital equipment. A man's man. Solid. Strong. Intelligent. Professional. In control. You sounded like a dream, a fantasy. If it wasn't for the fact you were a Republican, I would have wanted to meet you."

"I told you none of that matters when we fuck." He grinned. "Do you suppose he was matchmaking even then? Before we ever met?"

"He was! I realized it the night of his first campaign fundraiser." I shook my head in amazement. "He knew you were a Dom and yet he was pushing us together. He thought I needed someone like you."

"He did."

"I do." I pulled him down and kissed him.

"My father would love you, too," he said when he pulled away. "I think he'd especially love the thought that you're Ethan's daughter."

"I remember the moment I fell in love with you," I said, cupping his cheek. "It was that night on 8th Avenue when you played that song for me. Hearing you play and sing that song, knowing it was from my father to yours and that it meant so much to you, it was as if you were letting me in. Letting go of all the control and dominance and confidence to see right into your heart and I just *fell*."

We embraced, our arms around each other, the bright sun of the clear January day streaming in from the bare windows.

"You know," he said, looking around the apartment. "I always felt deprived after that first night..."

"What do you mean?"

"I never *did* get to fuck you here. If I recall correctly, I walked out of here that night with a boner."

"That was entirely your choice," I said, unable to keep a huge grin off my face. "You could have done me. Why didn't you?"

"I didn't want you to think that I would use you like that."

"You still won't even though it's a fantasy of mine. Even on New Year's Eve, you made me come."

"No, that was just you being far too hot," he said, grinning now, too.

"One of these days, I want you to just fuck me until you come, leaving me panting and desperate for you."

"Why on *earth* would I want you not to come? I said that for psychological purposes because I knew it turned you on. But I wouldn't enjoy myself unless you did."

"Chivalry is not dead with you, Drake Morgan."

"I don't want to leave this apartment without at least christening it," he said, pressing his hips against me. I could feel his erection through my clothes. "I want my last memory of this place to be a good one."

Then he kissed me, his mouth finding mine, pulling me up and into his embrace so that my feet lifted off the floor. As usual, my body responded to him immediately, my heart racing, a thrill going through me.

"Let's fuck missionary-style on the bed. It's still here."

"Missionary style?" I said, running my hands up under his shirt. "Again? Where's your imagination?"

"It's the middle of the day. I want to see you naked beneath me in the full light so I can watch you come."

My body trembled as he bent down and ran his tongue over the tops of my breasts. He took my hand, dragging me into the bedroom, throwing me across the bed. Then, he lay on top of me, his hands on either side of my face. He had that look in his eyes – I could see the Dom take over in that way that thrilled me so much because I knew underneath the kink was a man who could love, *deeply*.

"We're having a lot more plain old vanilla sex since New Year's Eve," I said. "I hope you're not losing your taste for D/s and bondage."

"No fear of that," he said, one hand slipping beneath my sweater. "I love that you're such an eager student. I want to see how far I can take you. I'm always going to be a Dom, Kate. I'm always going to want to have control, but I don't need to use it any longer as a shield to keep things in their proper place."

"Meat, potatoes and gravy touching each other?"

"My plate is thoroughly mixed up now," he said, smiling, his gaze moving over my face. "There's no chance of keeping things compartmentalized any longer. You're in each part of my life and I'm in yours. "

My breath hitched at that, and I pulled him down in a kiss that moved quickly from tenderness to passion.

He *was* deep in every part of my life.

That was exactly where I wanted him to stay.

THE END

About the Author

S. E. Lund is a writer who lives with her family of humans and pets in a century-old house on a quiet tree-lined street in a small city in Western Canada. She writes erotic and contemporary romance and paranormal romance. You can find her on Twitter @selundwriter , on Facebook as well as on Goodreads.

Series by S. E. Lund

The Unrestrained Series of Contemporary Erotic Romance

Book One: The Agreement

Book Two: The Commitment

Book Three: Unrestrained

Prequel to The Agreement: Drake Restrained (From Drake's Point of View)

The Dominion Series of Paranormal Romance

Book One: Dominion

Book Two: Ascension

Book Three: Retribution

Book Four: Redemption (Available May 2014)

Look for details and updates on current and new releases at www.Selund.com

Made in the USA
Middletown, DE
04 August 2015